Refresh Refresh

First Second

NEW YORK & LONDON

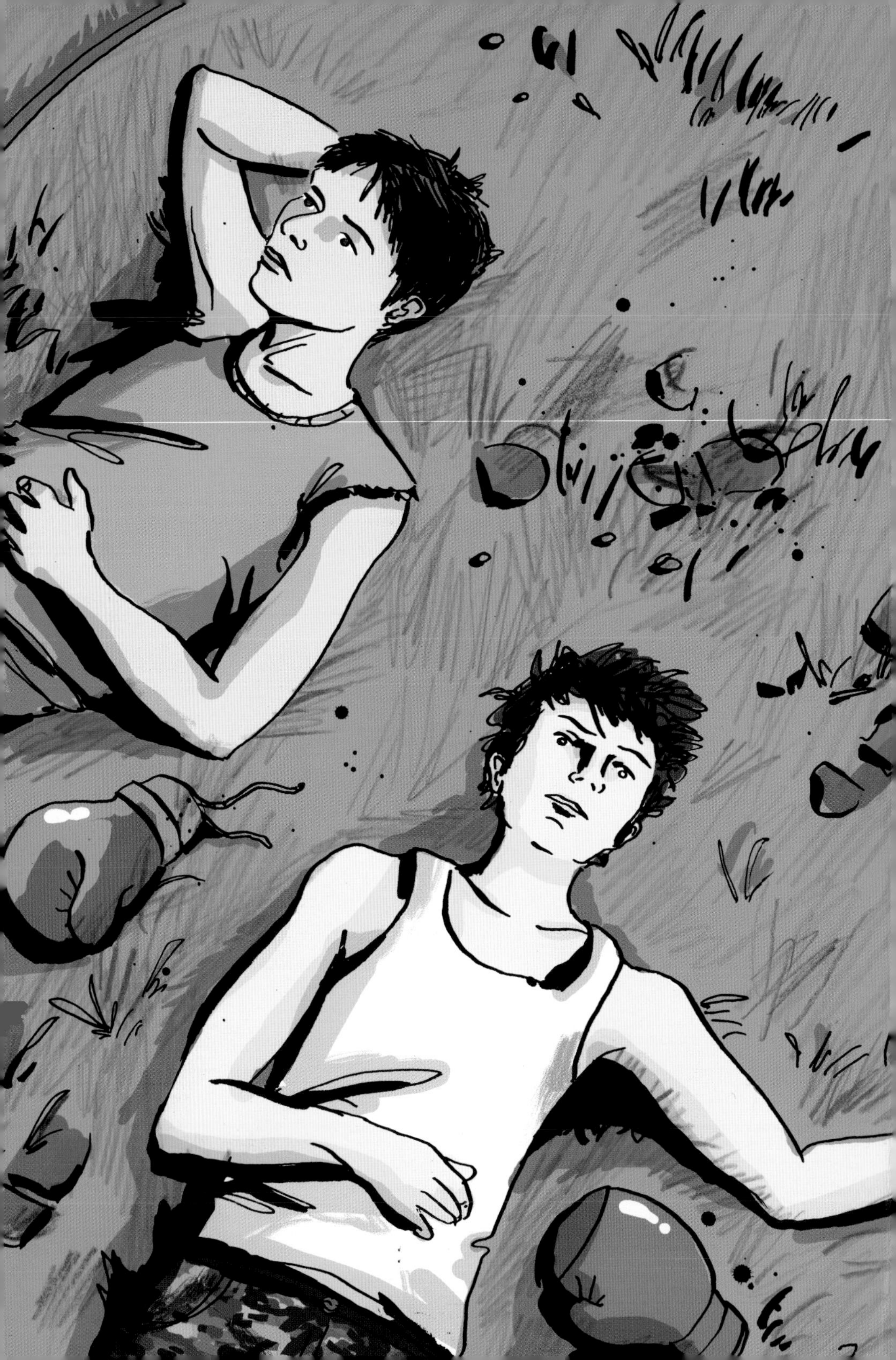

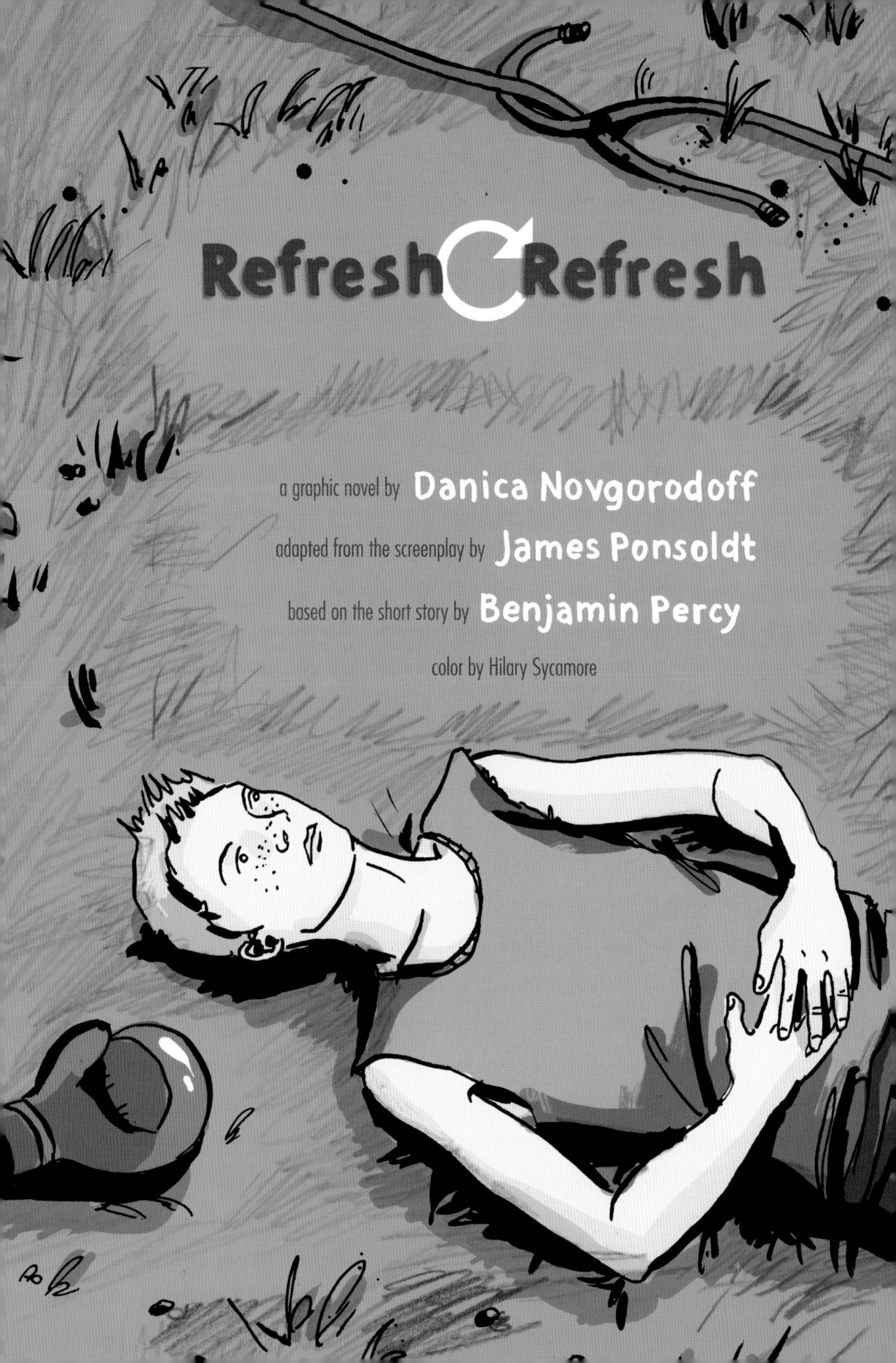

Refresh Refresh

a graphic novel by **Danica Novgorodoff**

adapted from the screenplay by **James Ponsoldt**

based on the short story by **Benjamin Percy**

color by Hilary Sycamore

Hit him in the face!

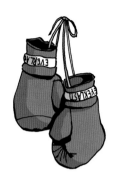

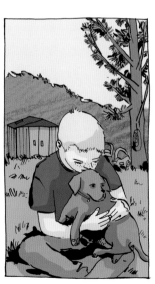

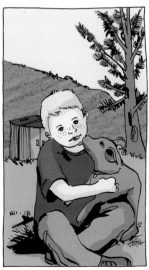

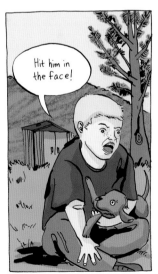

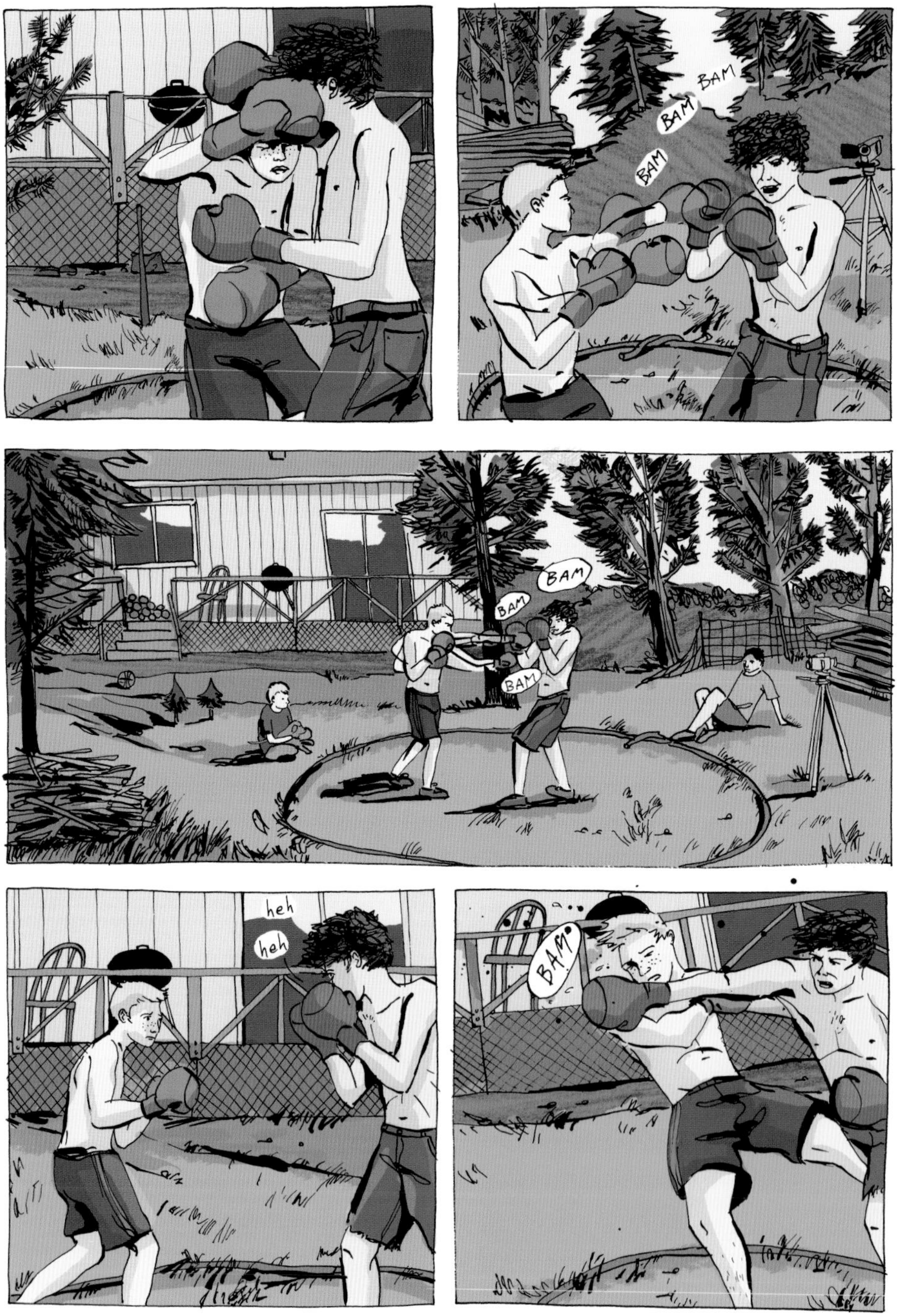
BAM
BAM
BAM
BAM
BAM
BAM
heh
heh
BAM

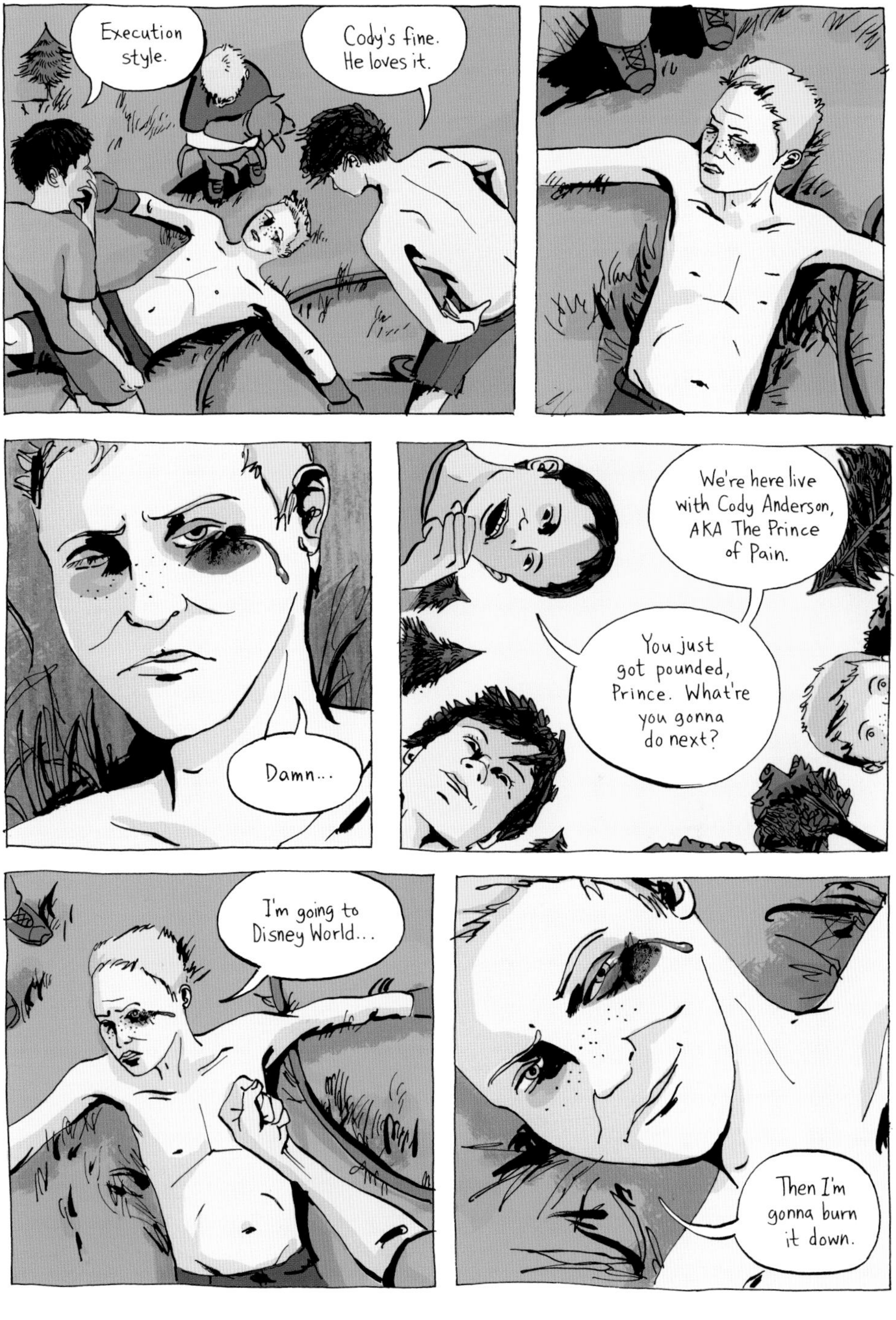
Execution style.
Cody's fine. He loves it.
Damn...
We're here live with Cody Anderson, AKA The Prince of Pain.
You just got pounded, Prince. What're you gonna do next?
I'm going to Disney World...
Then I'm gonna burn it down.

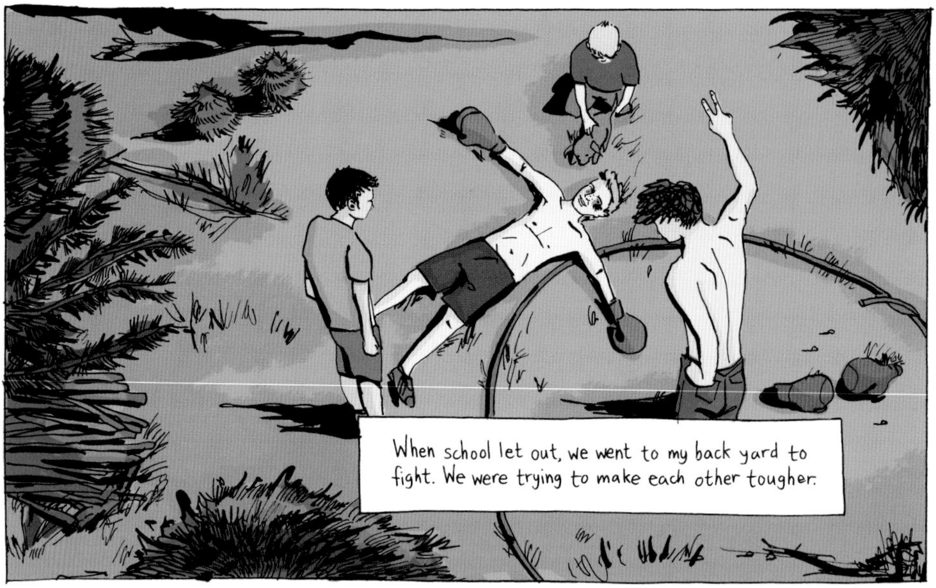
When school let out, we went to my back yard to fight. We were trying to make each other tougher.

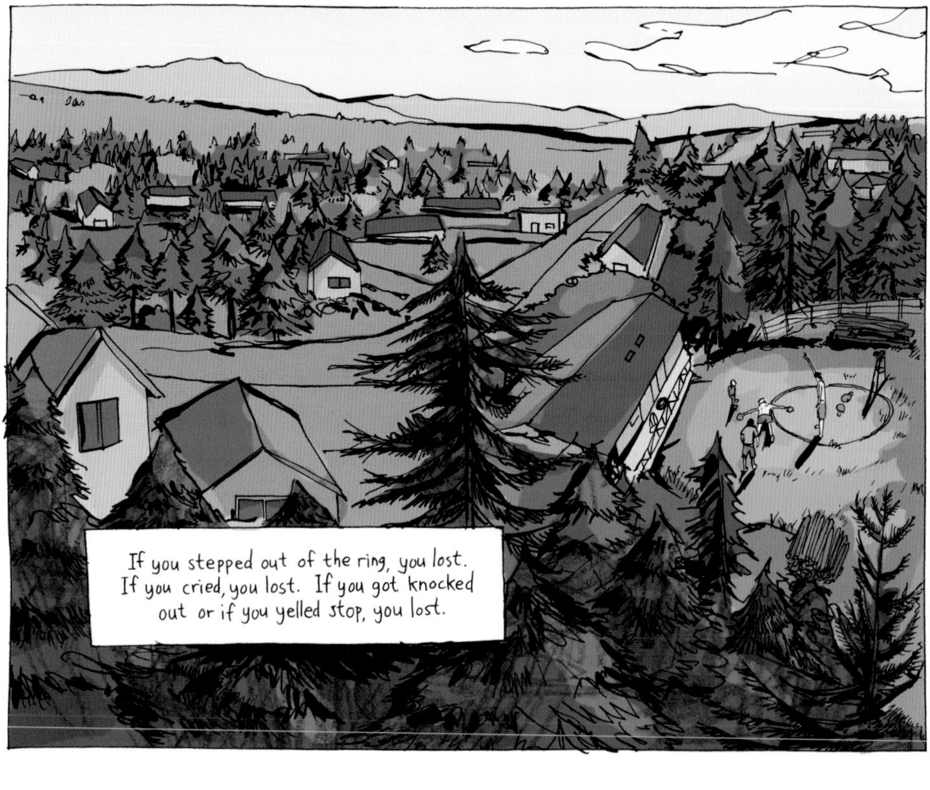
If you stepped out of the ring, you lost. If you cried, you lost. If you got knocked out or if you yelled stop, you lost.

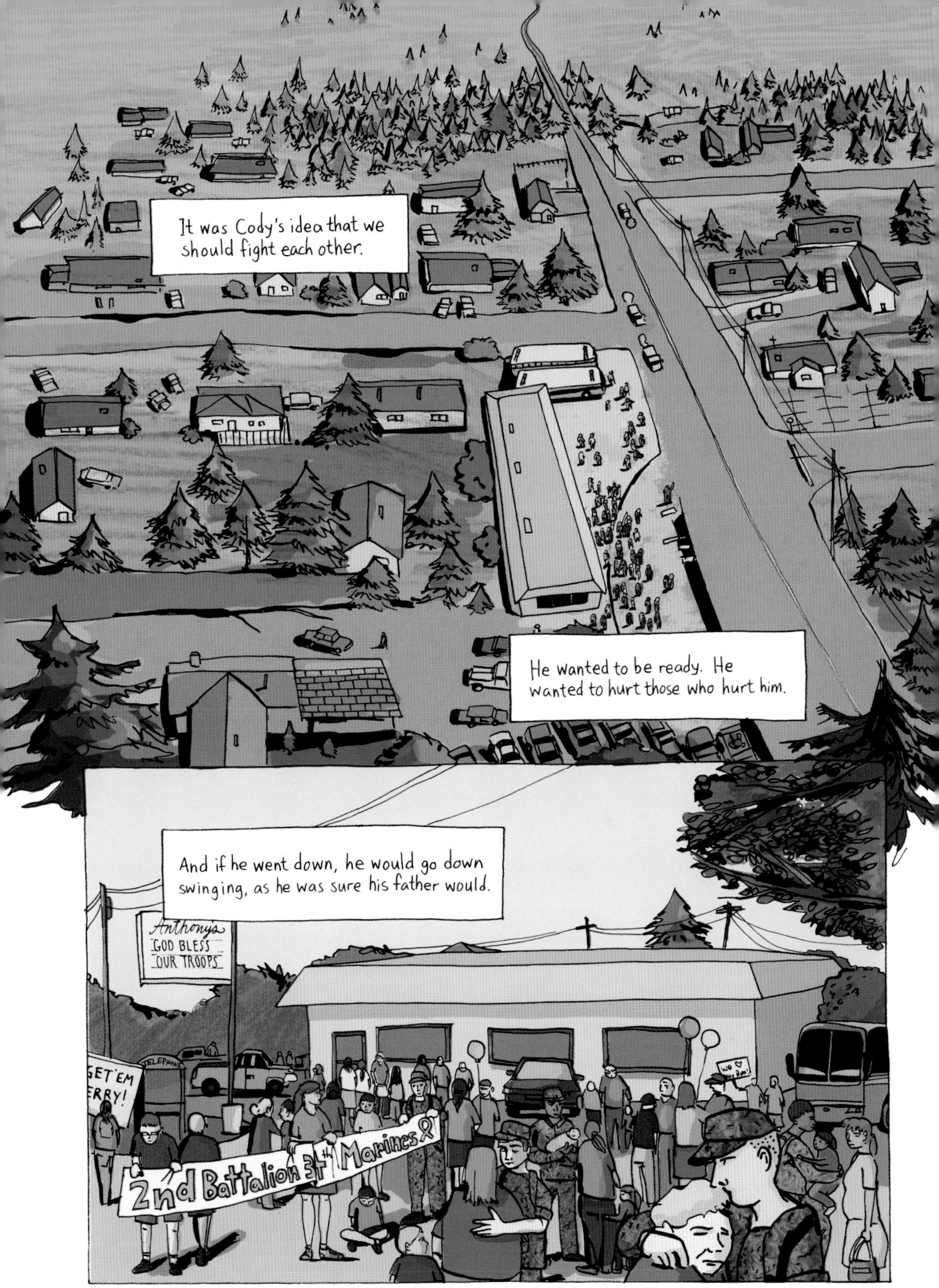
It was Cody's idea that we should fight each other.
He wanted to be ready. He wanted to hurt those who hurt him.
And if he went down, he would go down swinging, as he was sure his father would.
Anthony's
GOD BLESS OUR TROOPS
TELEPHONE
2nd Battalion
Marines

We'll
miss
642
U.S. MARINE

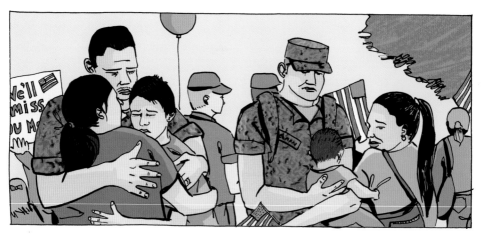

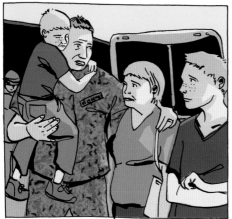

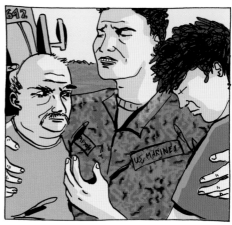

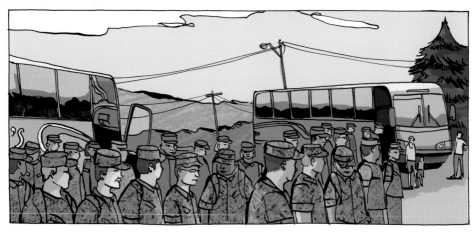

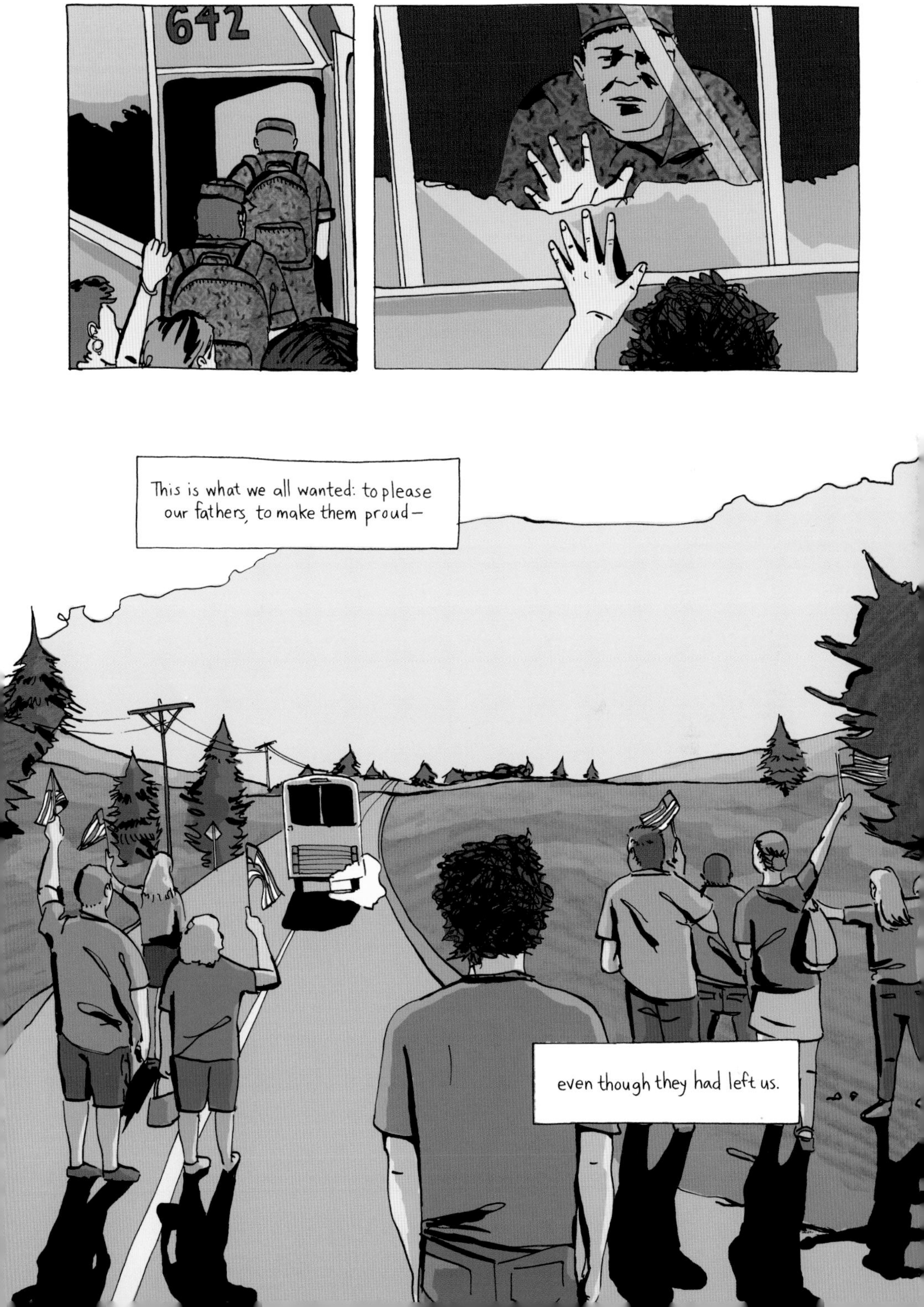
642
This is what we all wanted: to please our fathers, to make them proud—
even though they had left us.

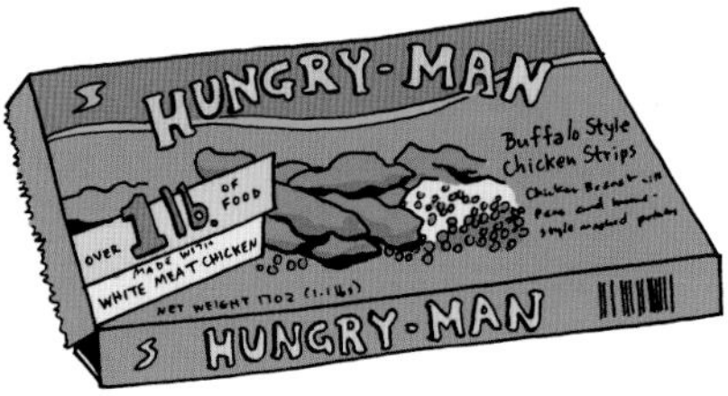
HUNGRY-MAN
Buffalo Style Chicken Strips
OVER 1lb. OF FOOD
MADE WITH WHITE MEAT CHICKEN
HUNGRY-MAN

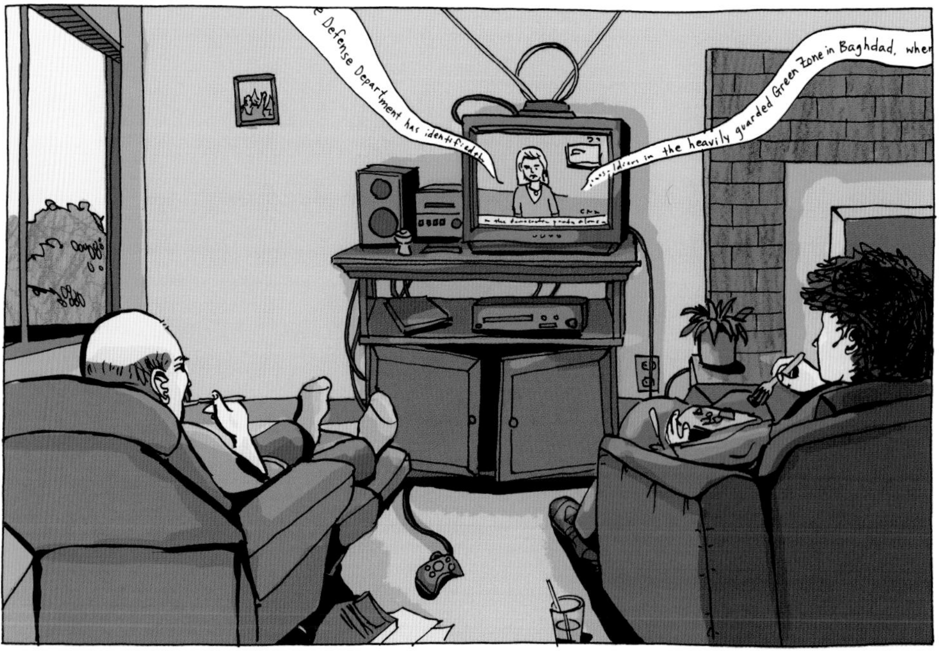
e Defense Department has identified
the heavily guarded Green Zone in Baghdad, wher

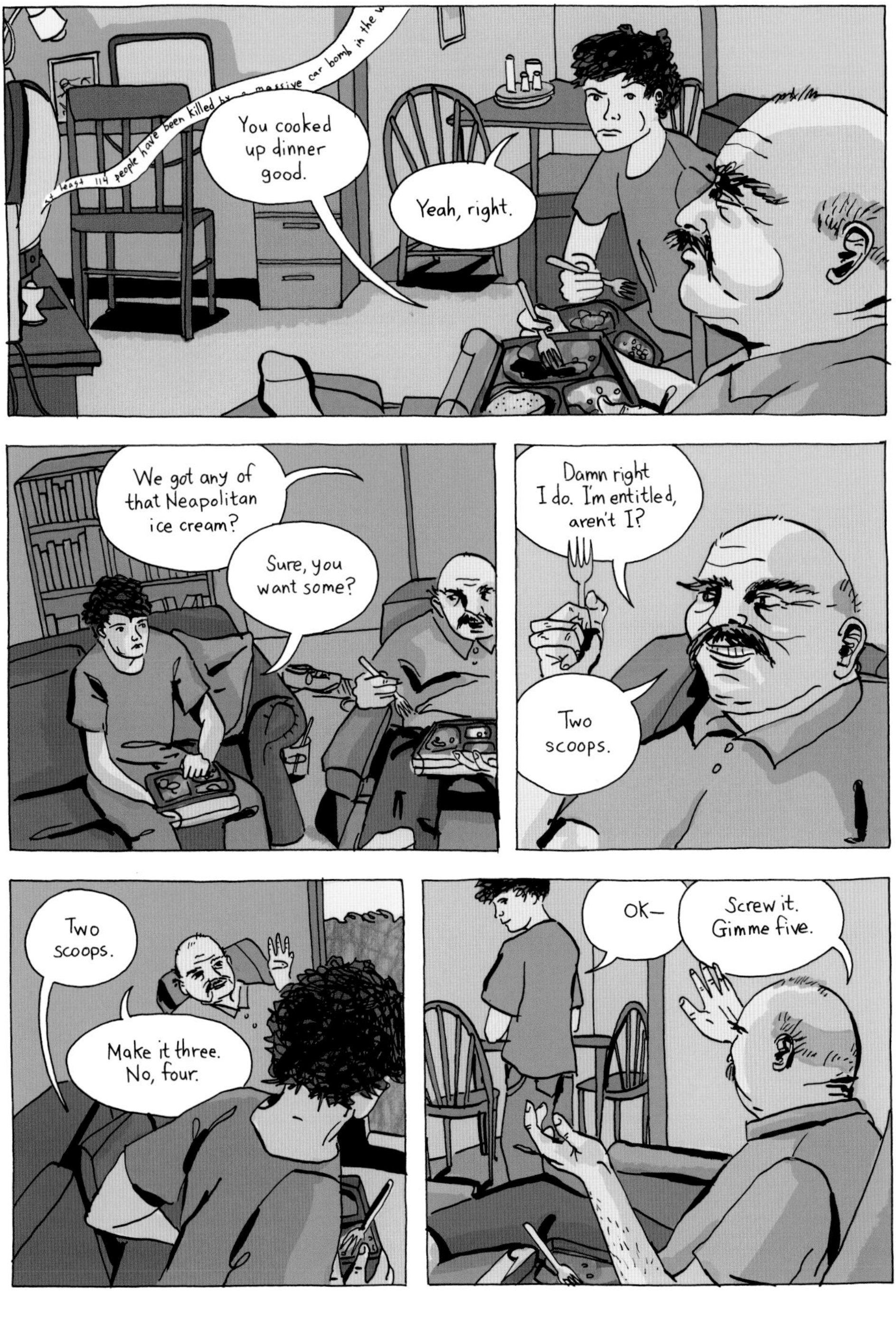

at least 114 people have been killed by
massive car bomb in the
You cooked up dinner good.
Yeah, right.
We got any of that Neapolitan ice cream?
Sure, you want some?
Damn right I do. I'm entitled, aren't I?
Two scoops.
Two scoops.
Make it three. No, four.
OK–
Screw it. Gimme five.

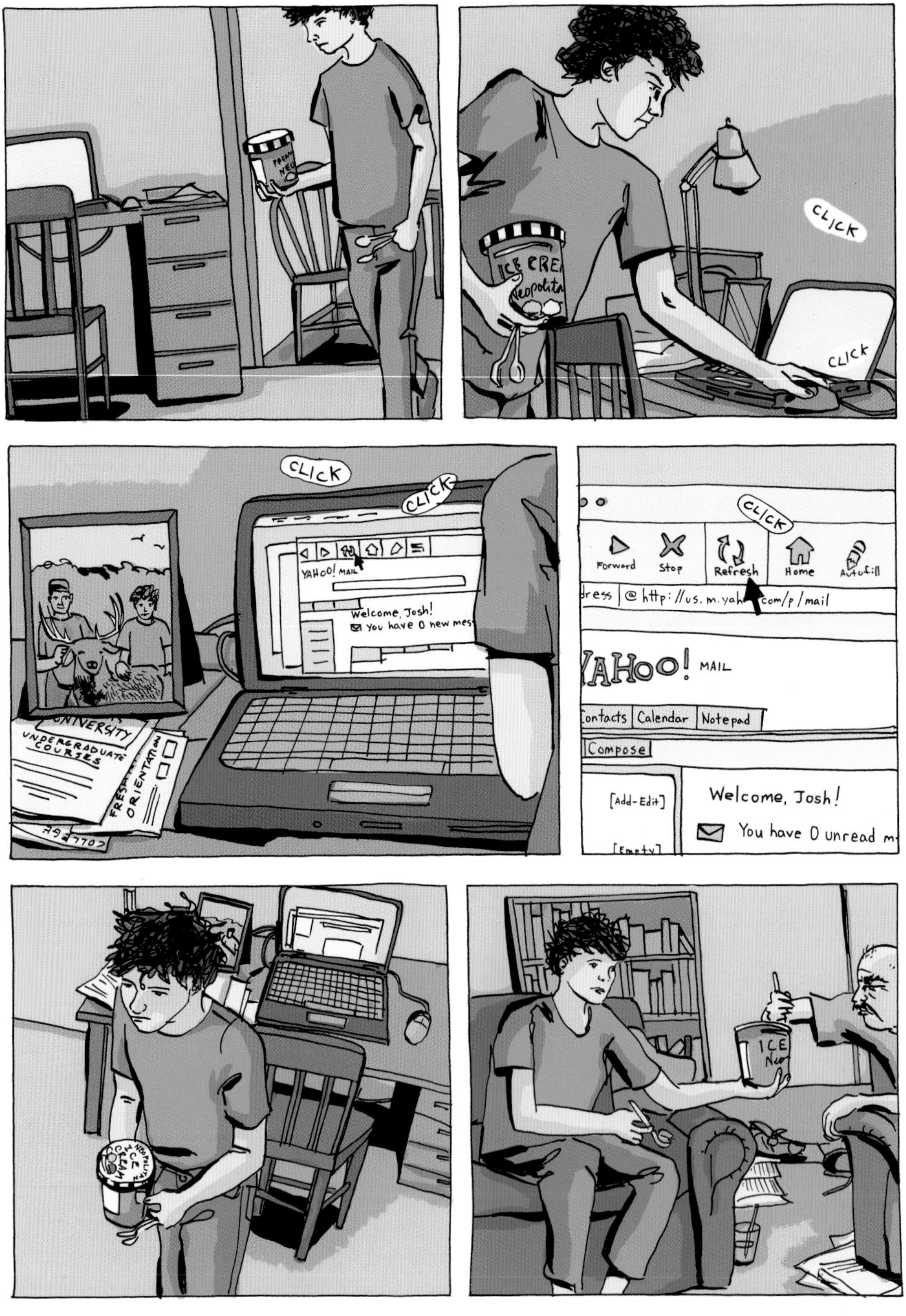
CLICK
CLICK
CLICK
CLICK
YAHOO! MAIL
Welcome, Josh!
You have 0 new mes
UNIVERSITY
UNDERGRADUATE COURSES
ORIENTATION
CLICK
Forward
Stop
Refresh
Home
Autofill
@ http://us.m.yah com/p/mail
YAHOO! MAIL
Contacts
Calendar
Notepad
Compose
[Add-Edit]
Welcome, Josh!
You have 0 unread m
ICE CREAM
ICE

officials said seven of the dead and ten of the wounded were Iraqi police offic

CLICK

Make Y! your home page

MAIL
classic

Calendar | Notepad

Welcome, Josh!

You have 1 unread message:
Inbox (1)

In the News

Spam

Shut out unwanted images
Don't let images fr

Calendar | Notepad

se

Previous | Next | Back to Message

Delete | Reply ▽ | Forward | Spam | Move ▽

Edit]

Re: Hi Dad
From: "Mitch Simpson" <msimpson_jr_45109@yaho
To: "Josh Simpson" <buckhunter_js1990@ya

Hi Josh,
I'm ok. Don't worry. Do your homework.
Love, Dad.

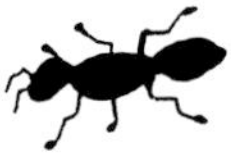

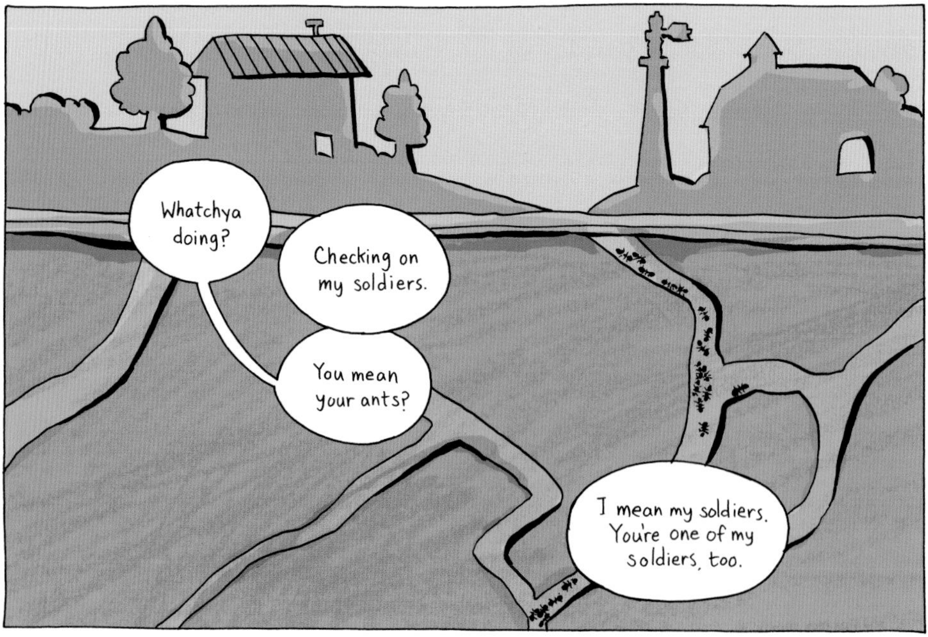
Whatchya doing?
Checking on my soldiers.
You mean your ants?
I mean my soldiers. You're one of my soldiers, too.

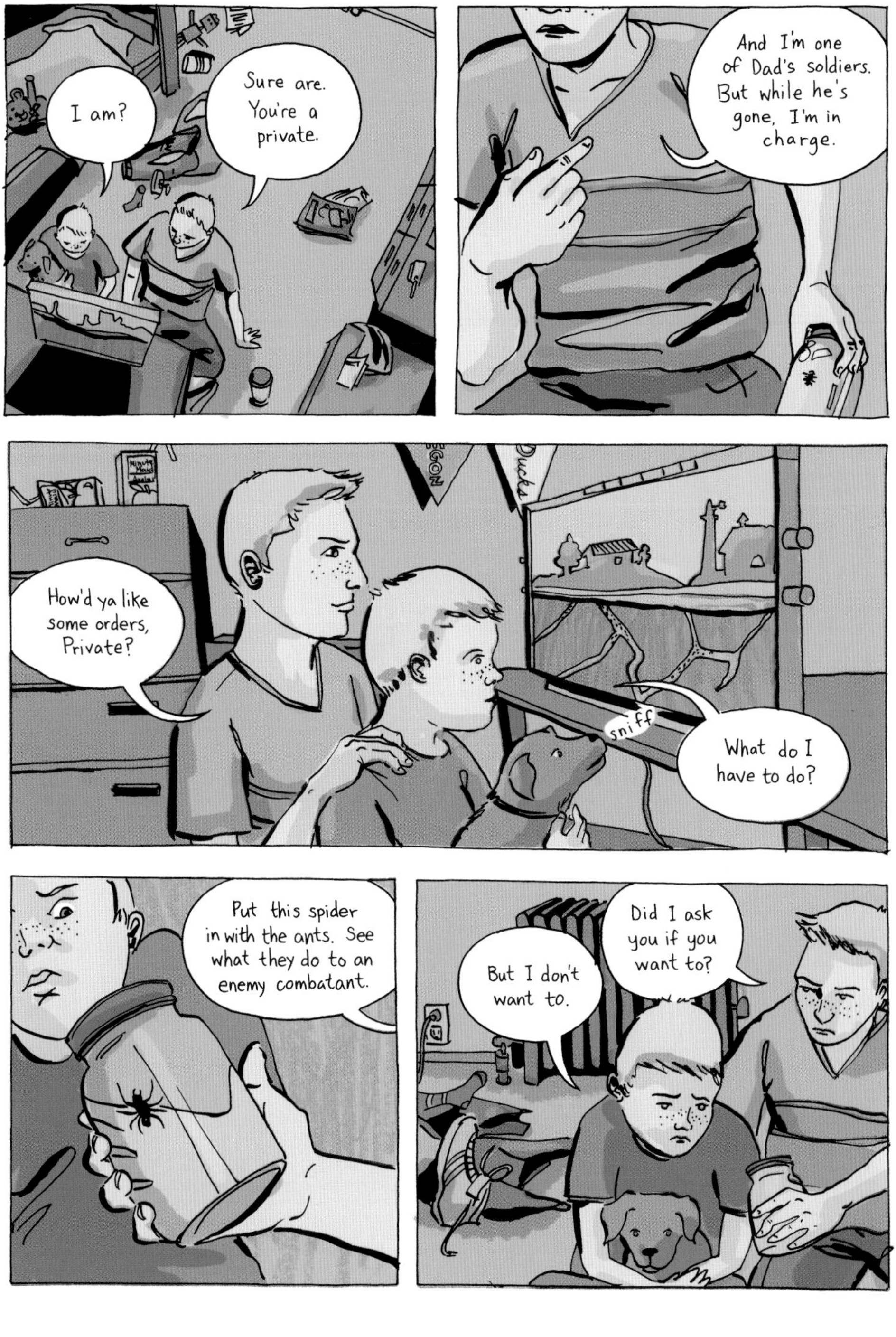
I am?
Sure are. You're a private.
And I'm one of Dad's soldiers. But while he's gone, I'm in charge.
How'd ya like some orders, Private?
sniff
What do I have to do?
Put this spider in with the ants. See what they do to an enemy combatant.
But I don't want to.
Did I ask you if you want to?

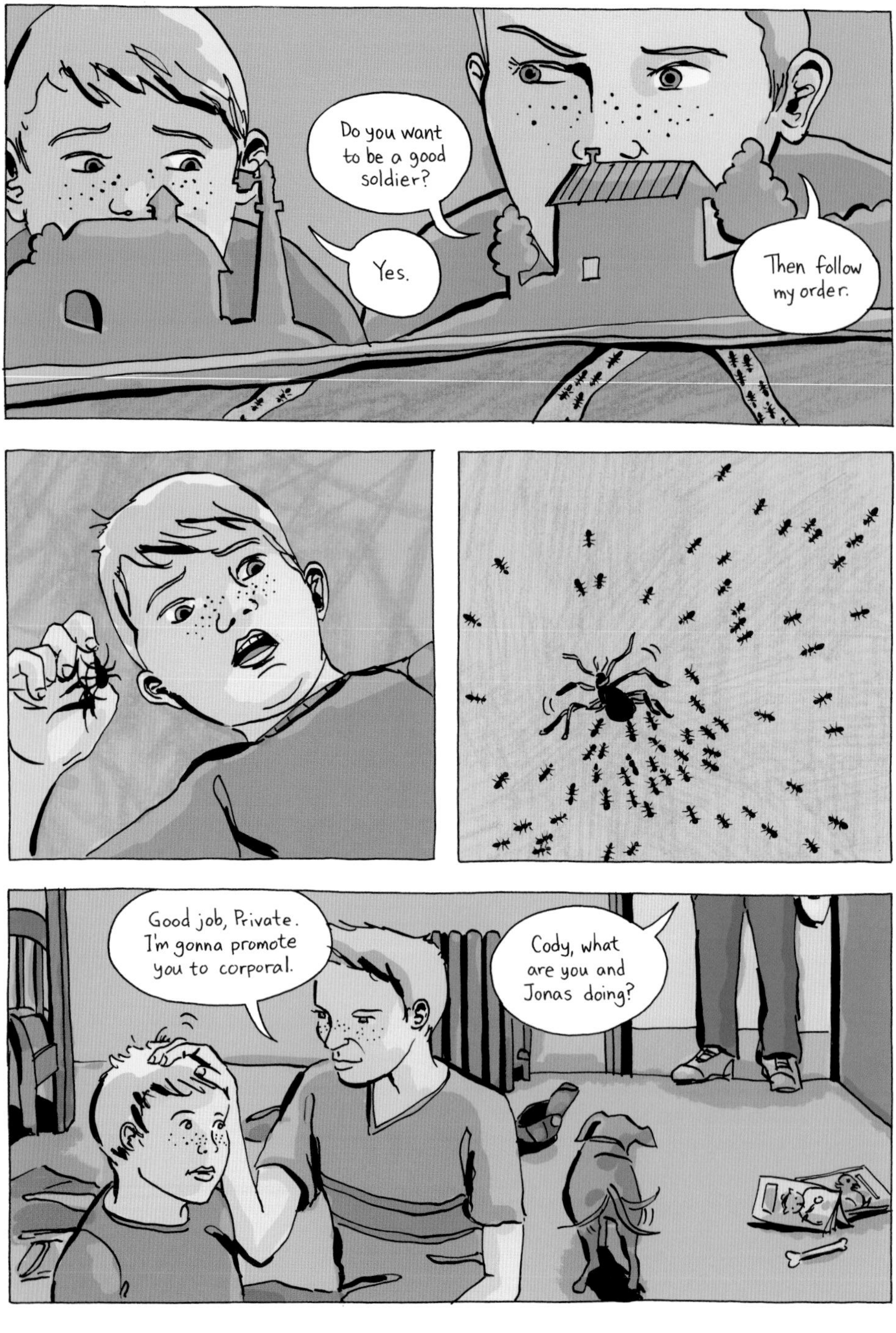
Do you want to be a good soldier?
Yes.
Then follow my order.
Good job, Private. I'm gonna promote you to corporal.
Cody, what are you and Jonas doing?

Just playing.

Well, I'm off—

Jack Townley's letting me take some of your father's shifts at the plant.

Dang... another job?

You're never gonna be home to make us food.

Your father's gone and so is his over-time pay.

You want to pay the mortgage?

scritch

Be good, boys.

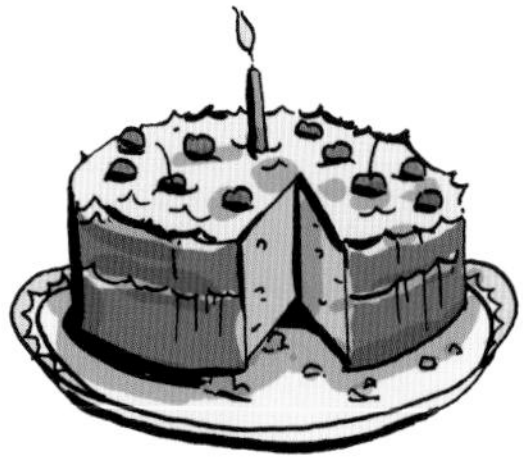

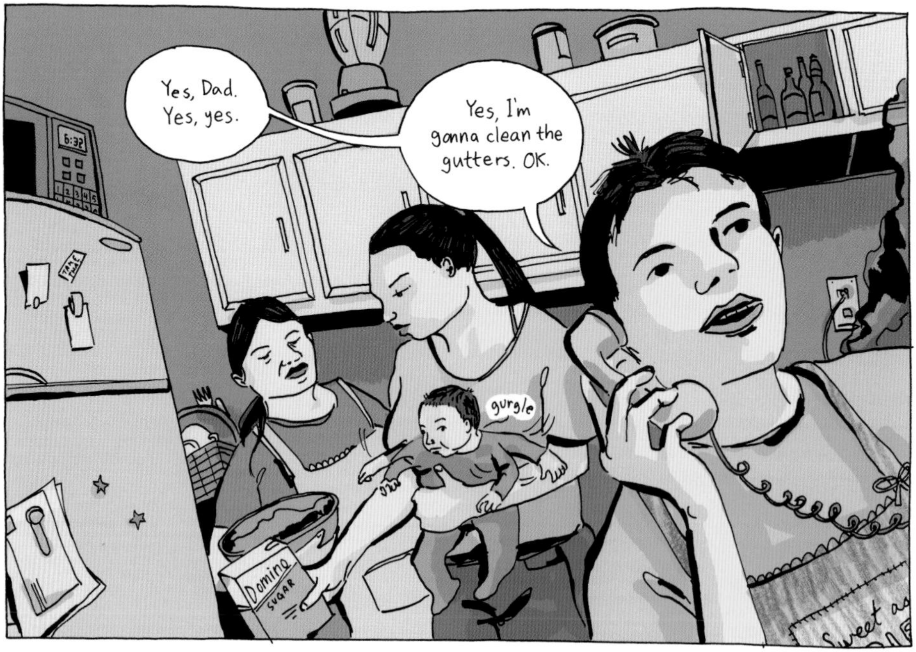
Yes, Dad.
Yes, yes.
Yes, I'm gonna clean the gutters. OK.
gurgle
Domino SUGAR

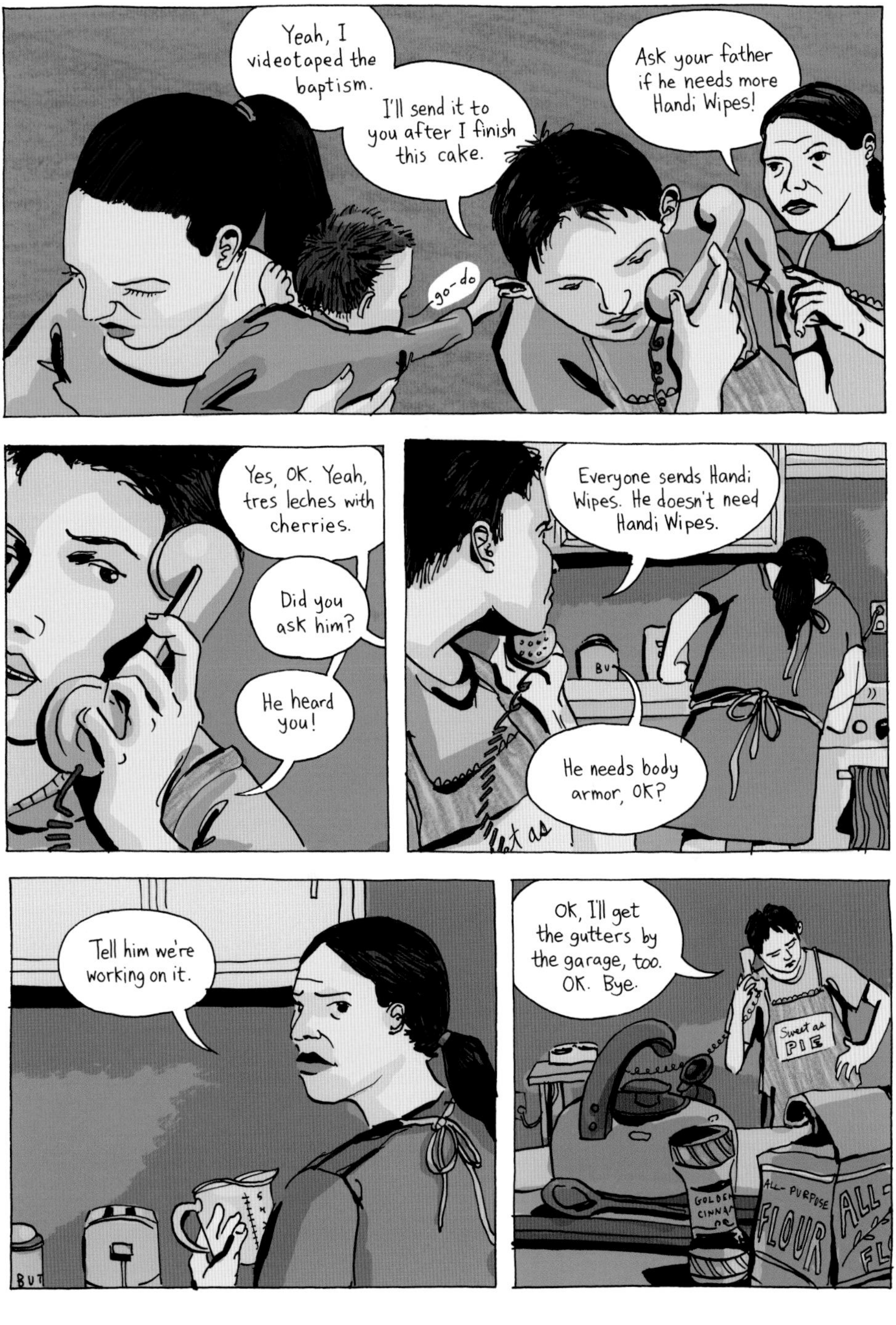
Yeah, I videotaped the baptism.
I'll send it to you after I finish this cake.
go-do
Ask your father if he needs more Handi Wipes!
Yes, OK. Yeah, tres leches with cherries.
Did you ask him?
He heard you!
Everyone sends Handi Wipes. He doesn't need Handi Wipes.
He needs body armor, OK?
Tell him we're working on it.
OK, I'll get the gutters by the garage, too. OK. Bye.
Sweet as PIE
ALL-PURPOSE FLOUR

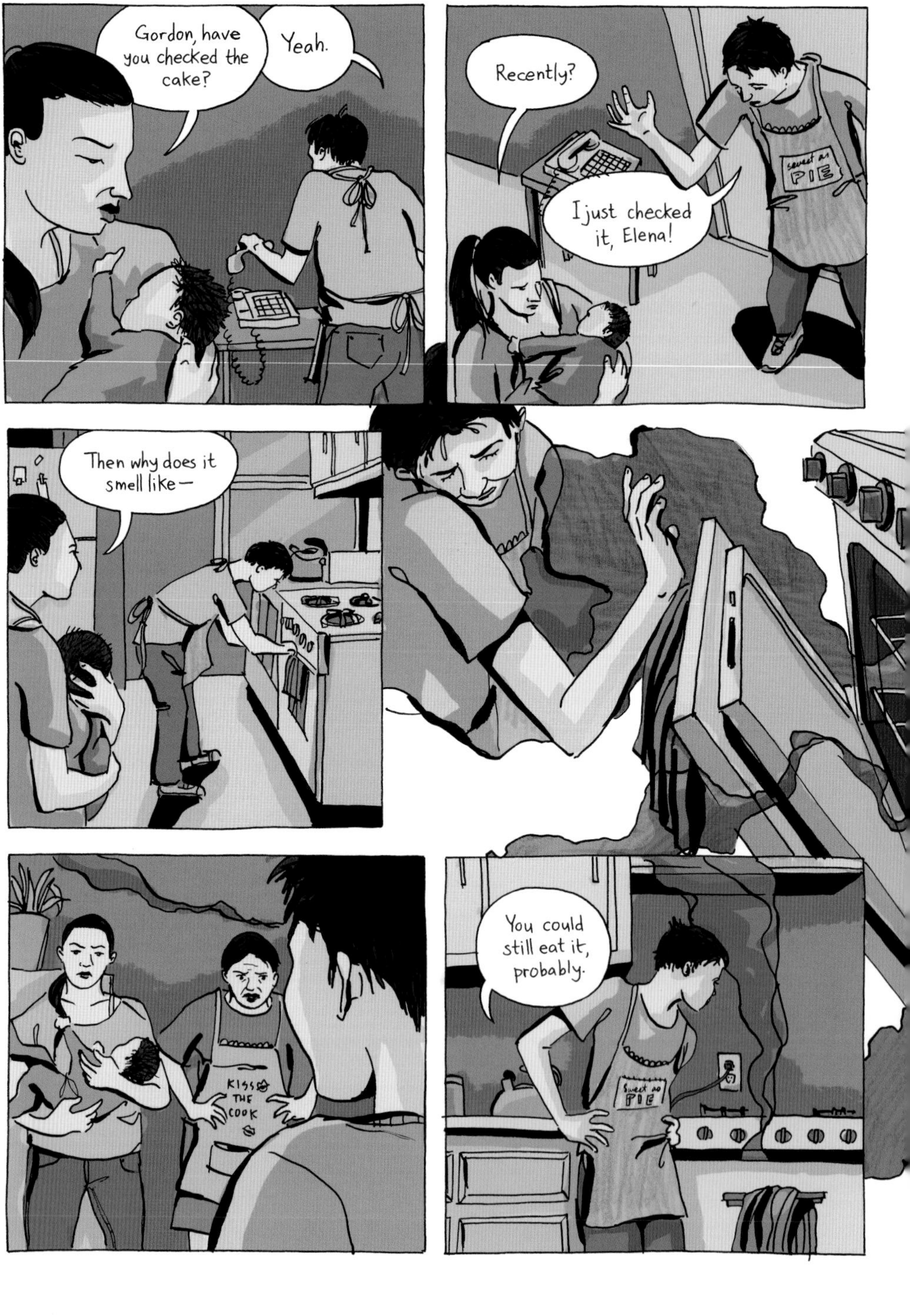
Gordon, have you checked the cake?
Yeah.
Recently?
I just checked it, Elena!
Then why does it smell like—
You could still eat it, probably.

You should have a license for these guns, son!
CENTENNIAL BANK
Ha Ha

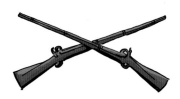

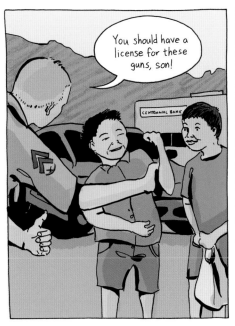

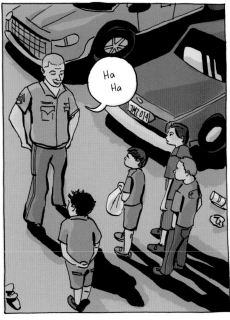

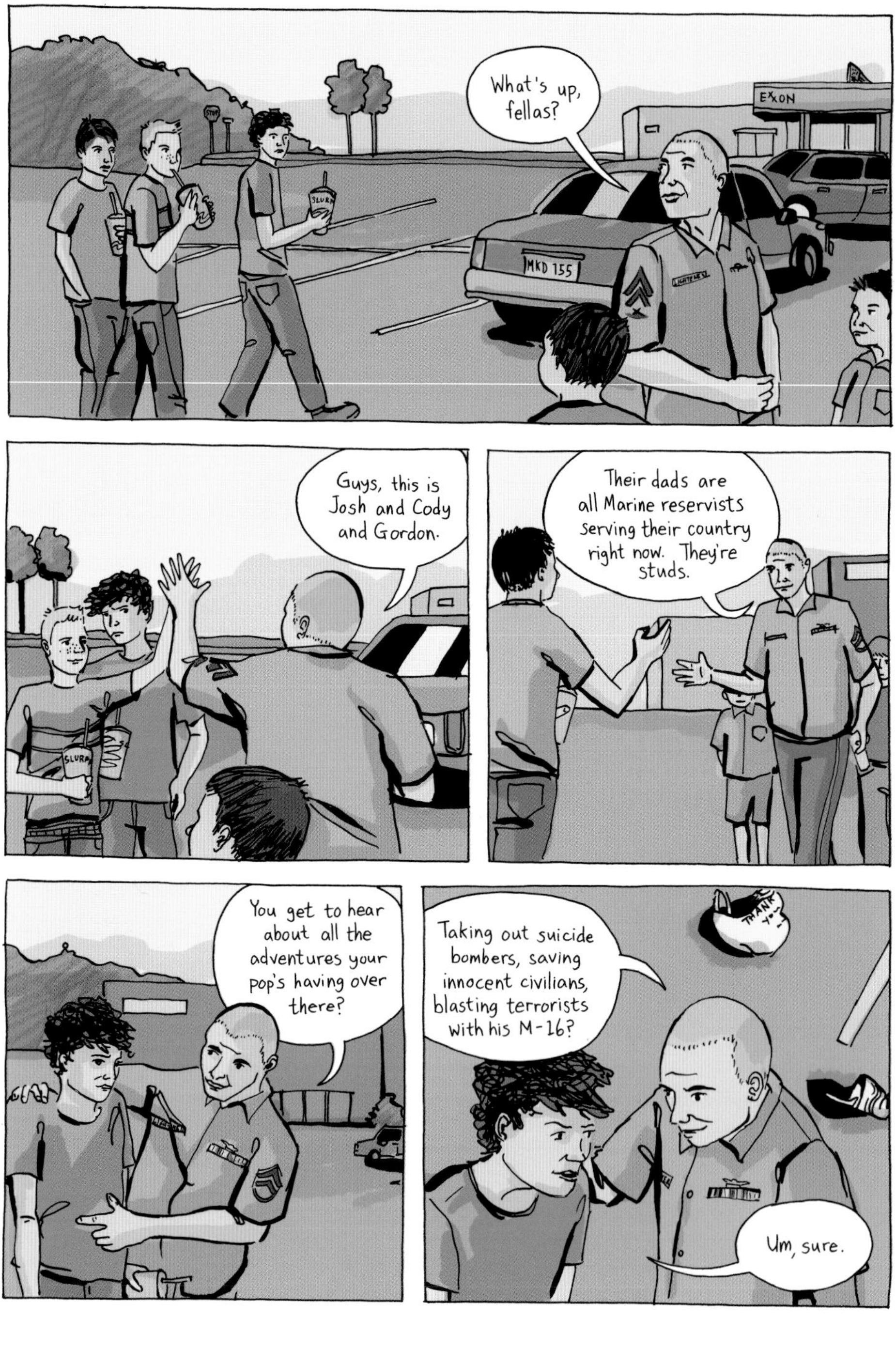
What's up, fellas?
Guys, this is Josh and Cody and Gordon.
Their dads are all Marine reservists serving their country right now. They're studs.
You get to hear about all the adventures your pop's having over there?
Taking out suicide bombers, saving innocent civilians, blasting terrorists with his M-16?
Um, sure.

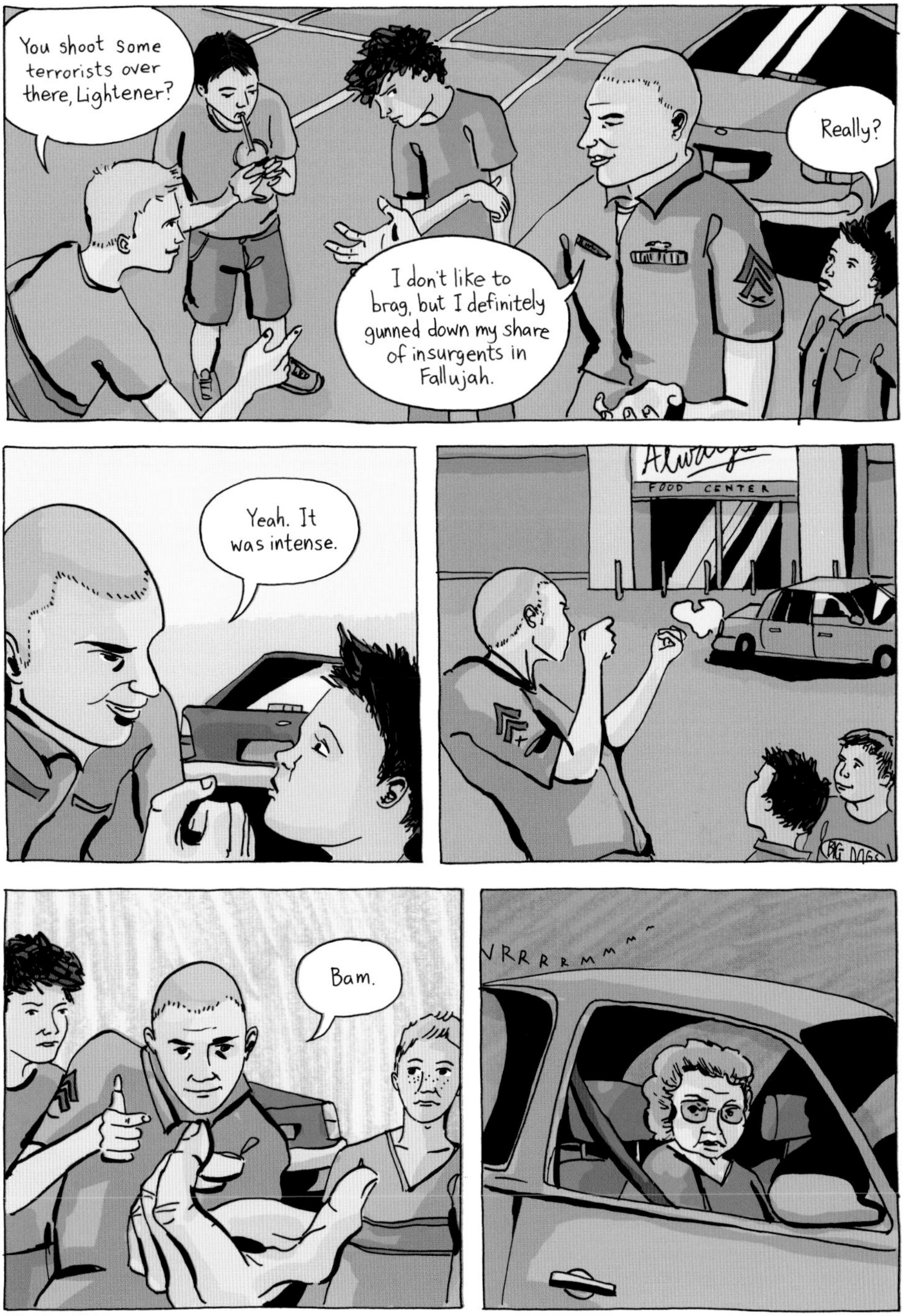
You shoot some terrorists over there, Lightener?
I don't like to brag, but I definitely gunned down my share of insurgents in Fallujah.
Really?
Yeah. It was intense.
FOOD CENTER
Bam.
VRRRRMMMM

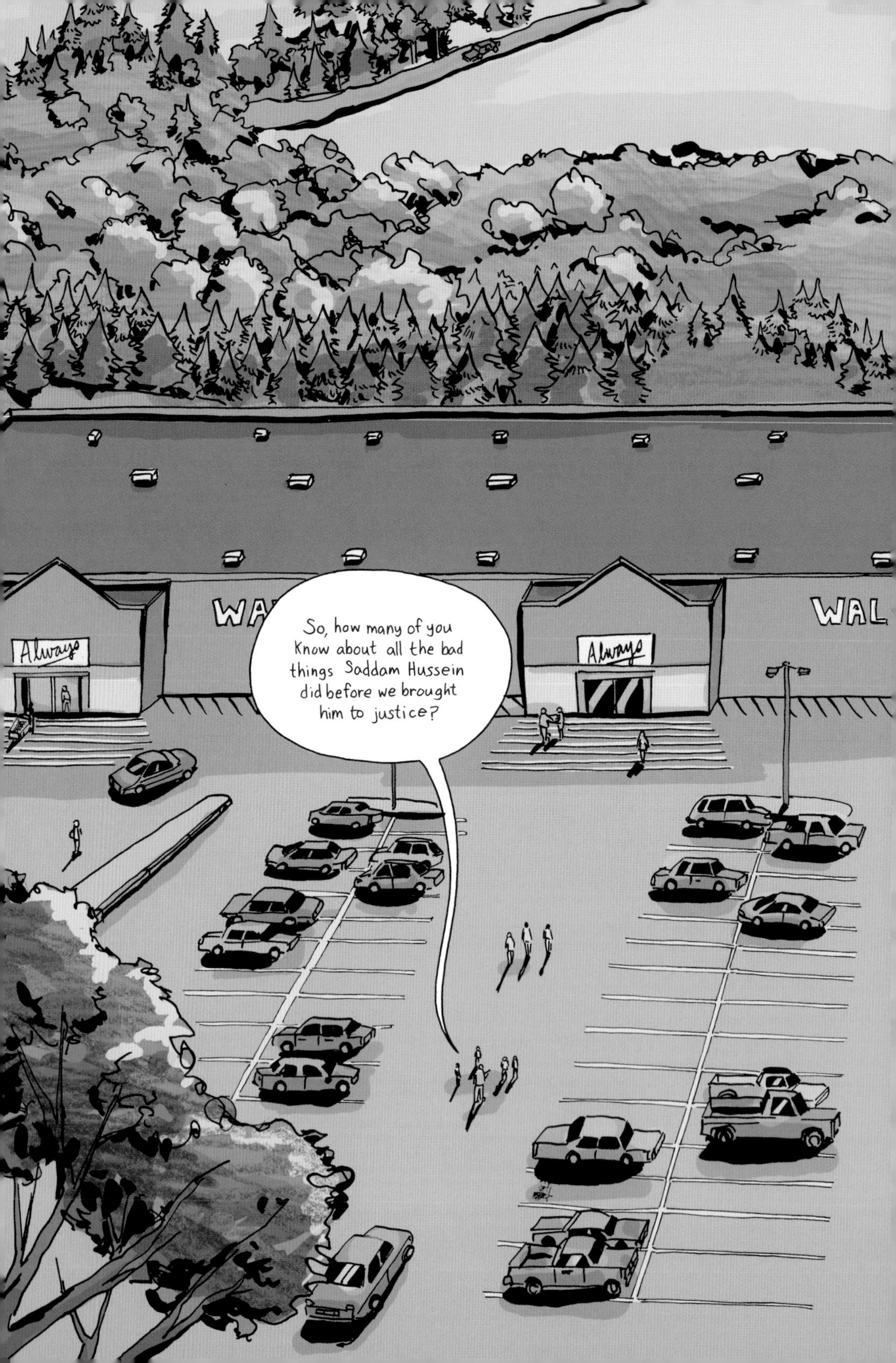
WA
WAL
Always
Always
So, how many of you Know about all the bad things Saddam Hussein did before we brought him to justice?

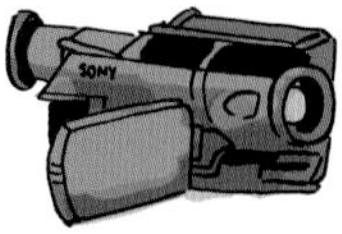
SONY

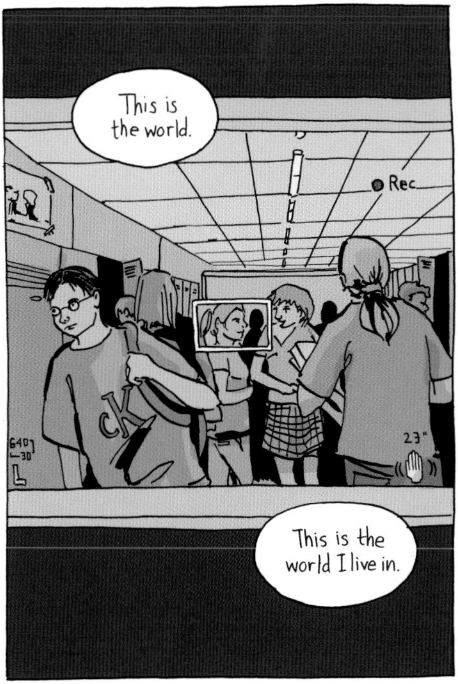
This is the world.
Rec
This is the world I live in.

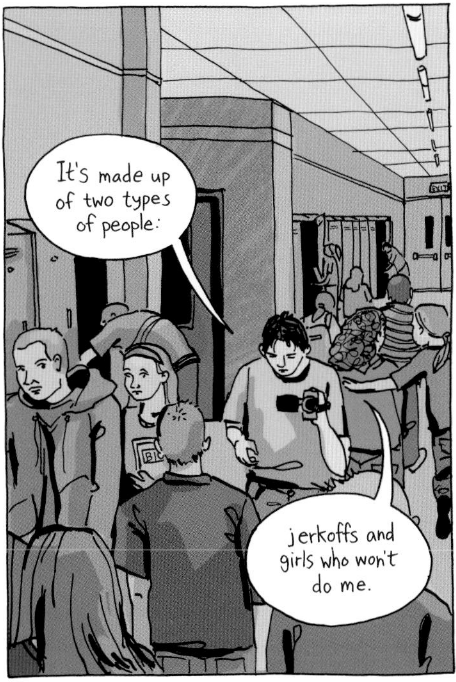
It's made up of two types of people:
jerkoffs and girls who won't do me.

The hell do you want?

That's my bike.

R

4:03"

It's dirty.

I take it off-roading.

ha ha

That's no excuse. You guys wanna clean it for him?

ha
ha ha
ZZZZIPP
ZZZIIPP
ha
ha
ha
Psssssss
HONDA
Rec
We won't even charge you for the wash.
5:16"
Retard.
Rec
SF
49ER
5:20"

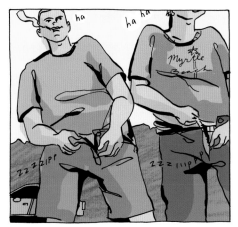

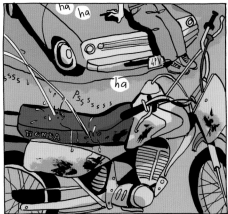

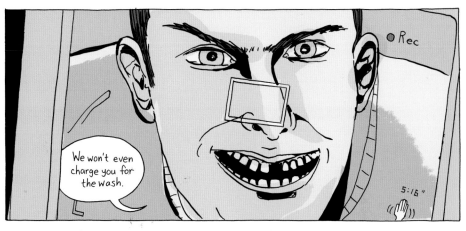

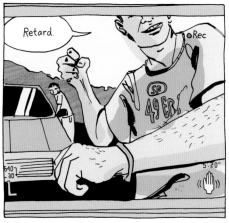

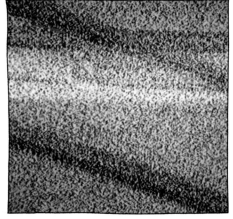

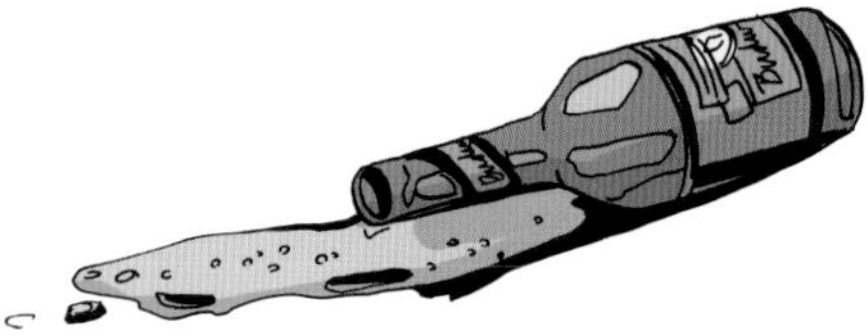

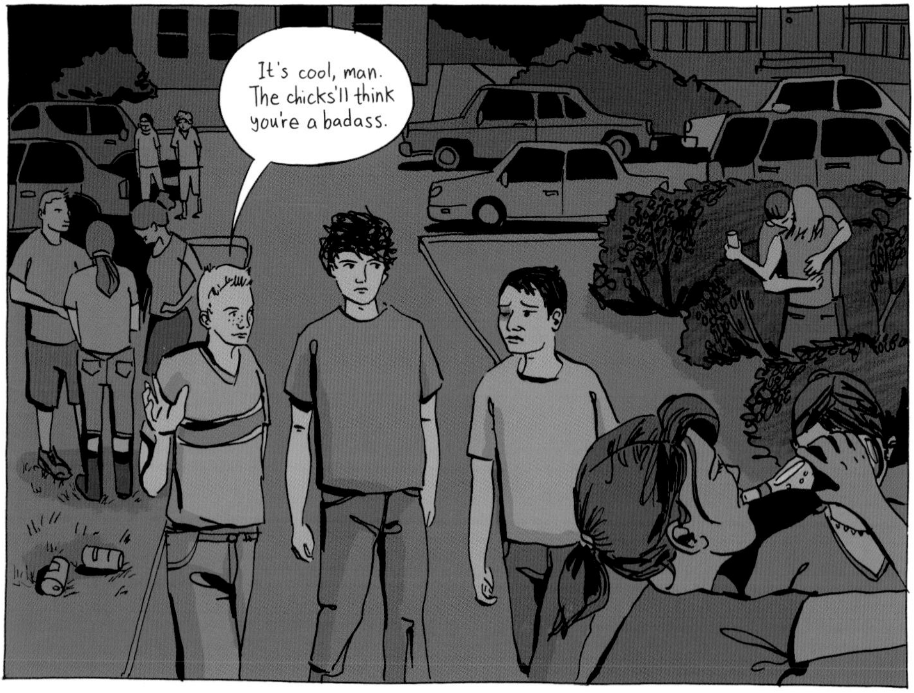
It's cool, man. The chicks'll think you're a badass.

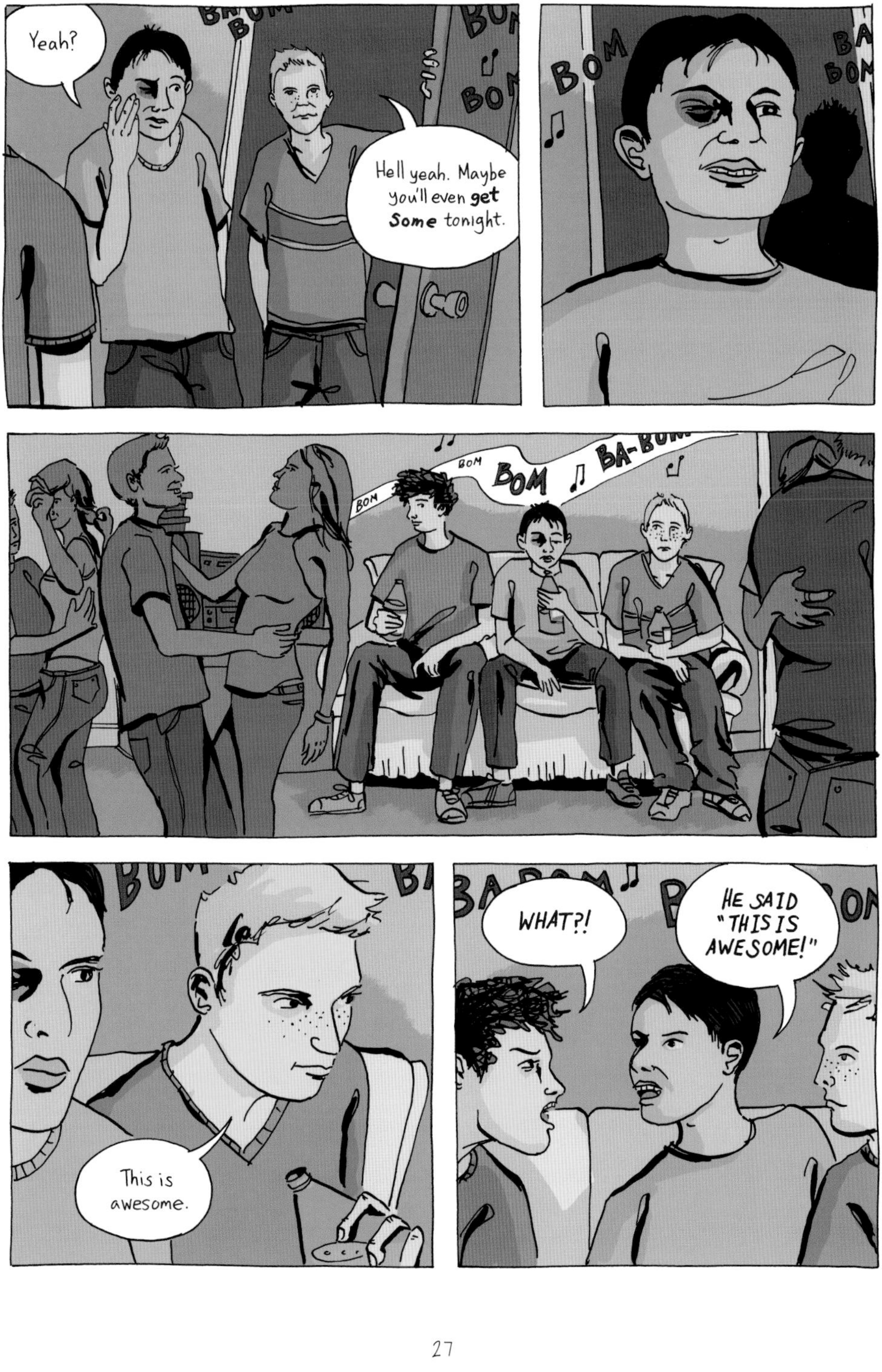
Yeah?
Hell yeah. Maybe you'll even **get** **some** tonight.
BOM
BA BOM
BOM
BOM
BOM
BA-BUM
This is awesome.
WHAT?!
HE SAID "THIS IS AWESOME!"

BOM
BOM
Oh. Yeah.
BOM
BOM
ha
ha
BOM BOM BOM
Totally.
BOM BOM BA-BOM
GLUG
I'M GONNA GET LAID!!

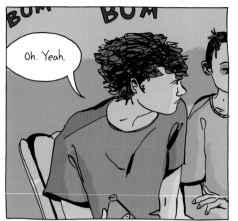

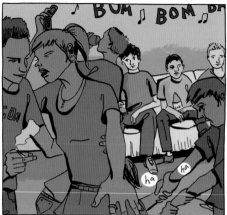

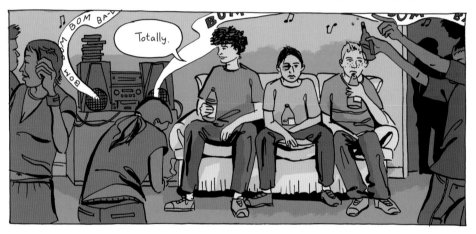

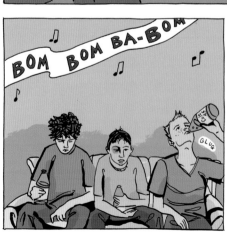

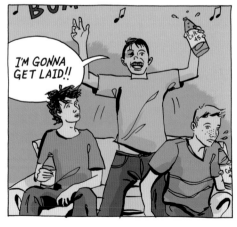

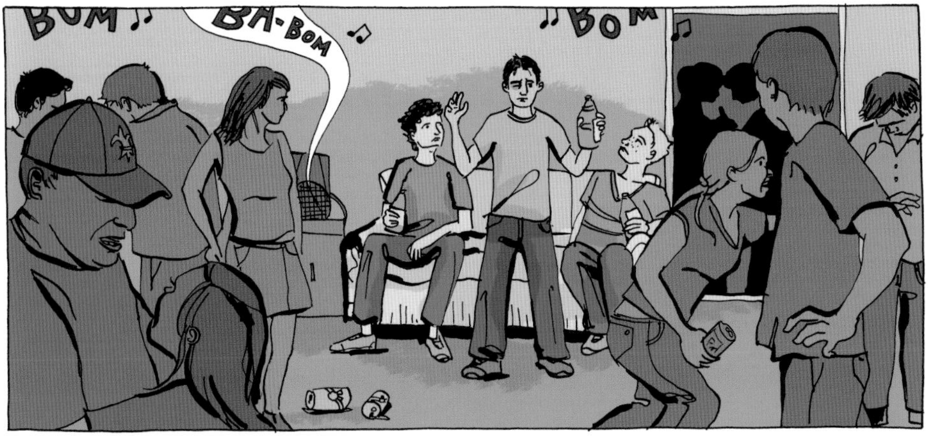
BOM
BA-BOM
BOM

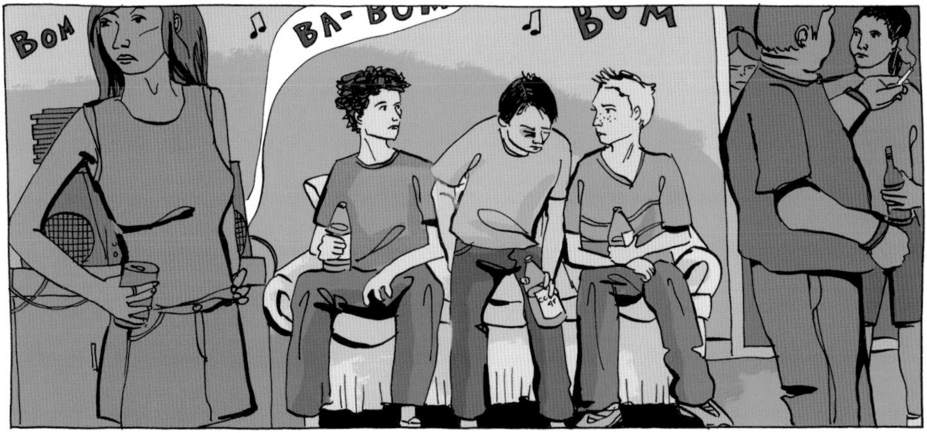
BOM
BA-BOM
BOM

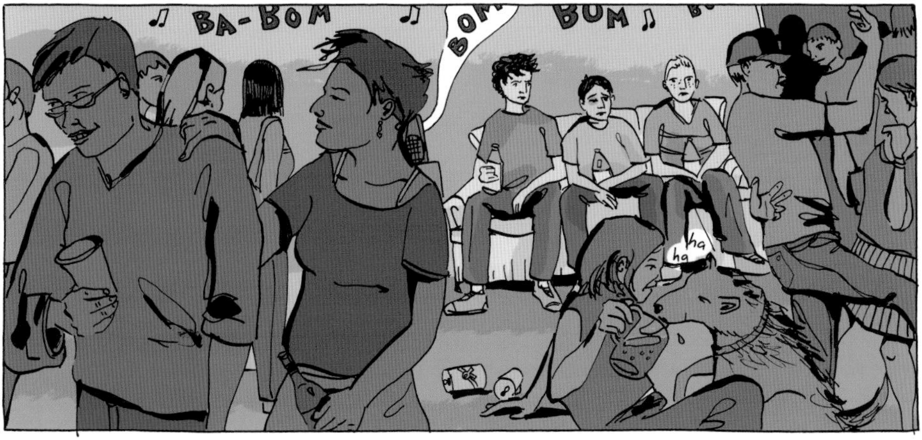
BA-BOM
BOM
BOM
ha
ha

UNIVERSITAS OREGONENSIS
MDCCCLXXVI
MENS AGITAT MOLEM

CLACK
CLICK
CLACK
OPEN HOUSE
CLICK
CLICK

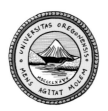

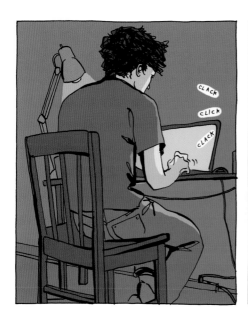

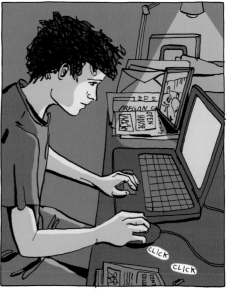

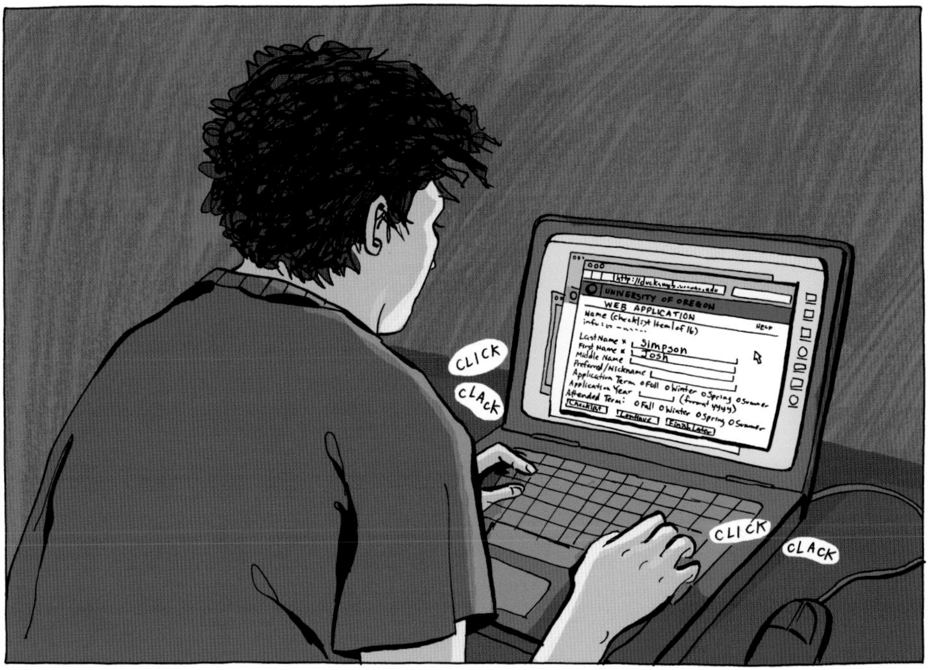
UNIVERSITY OF OREGON
WEB APPLICATION
Simpson
Josh
CLICK
CLACK
CLICK
CLACK

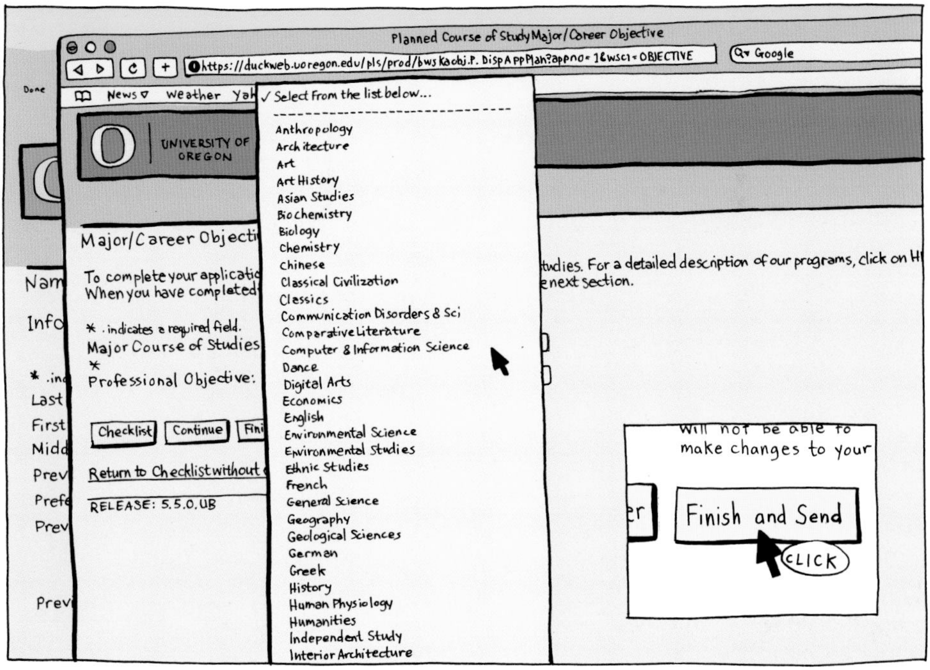
Planned Course of Study Major/Career Objective
https://duckweb.uoregon.edu/pls/prod/bwskaobj.P_DispAppPlan?appno=1&wsct=OBJECTIVE
Google
Done
News Weather Yah
UNIVERSITY OF OREGON
Major/Career Objecti
To complete your applicati
When you have completed
* . indicates a required field.
Major Course of Studies
*
Professional Objective:
Checklist
Continue
Fini
Return to Checklist without
RELEASE: 5.5.0.UB
✓ Select From the list below...
Anthropology
Architecture
Art
Art History
Asian Studies
Biochemistry
Biology
Chemistry
Chinese
Classical Civilization
Classics
Communication Disorders & Sci
Comparative Literature
Computer & Information Science
Dance
Digital Arts
Economics
English
Environmental Science
Environmental Studies
Ethnic Studies
French
General Science
Geography
Geological Sciences
German
Greek
History
Human Physiology
Humanities
Independent Study
Interior Architecture
tudies. For a detailed description of our programs, click on H
e next section.
Nam
Info
* .in
Last
First
Midd
Prev
Pref
Prev
Prev
will not be able to
make changes to your
Finish and Send
CLICK

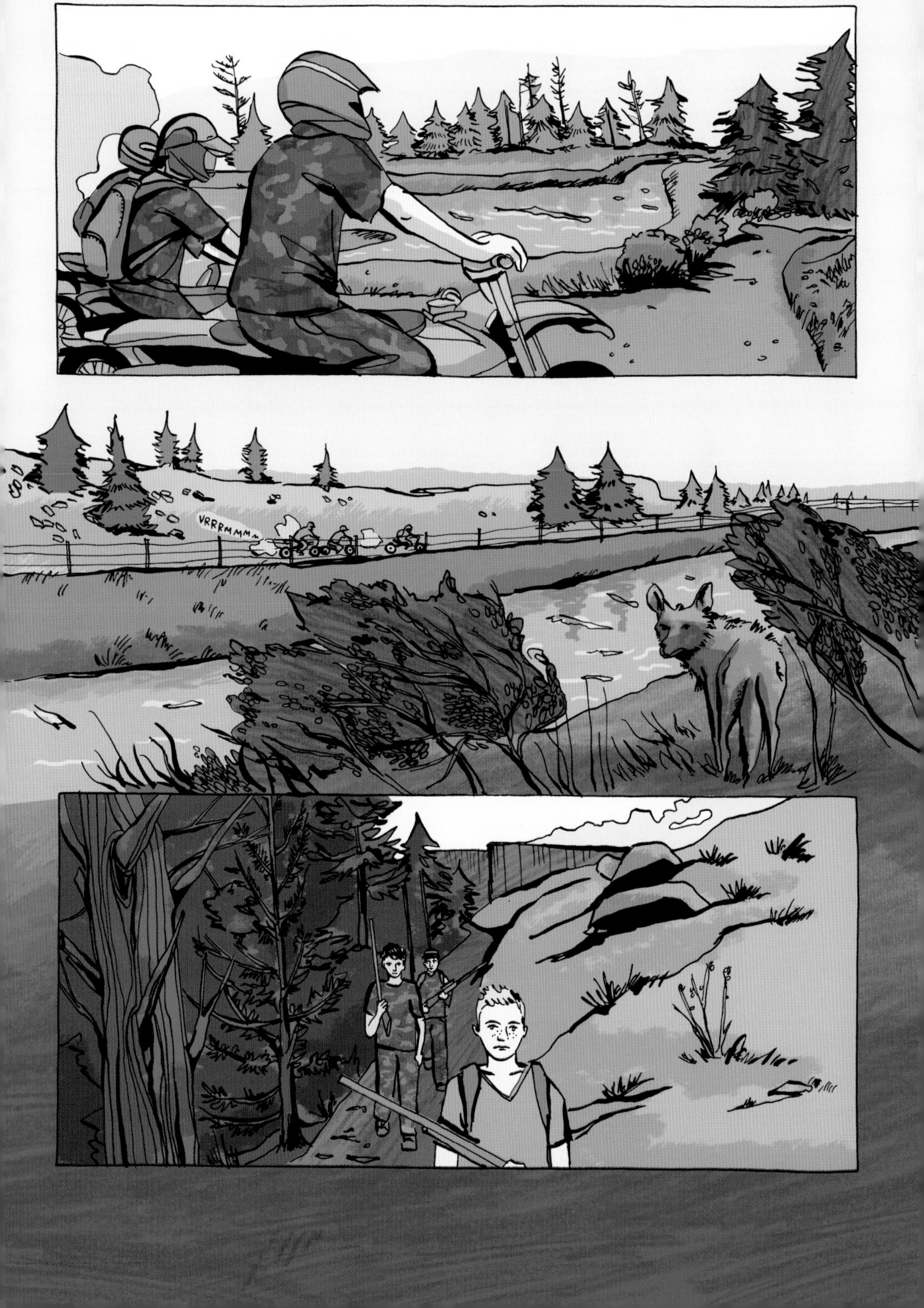
VRRRMMMM

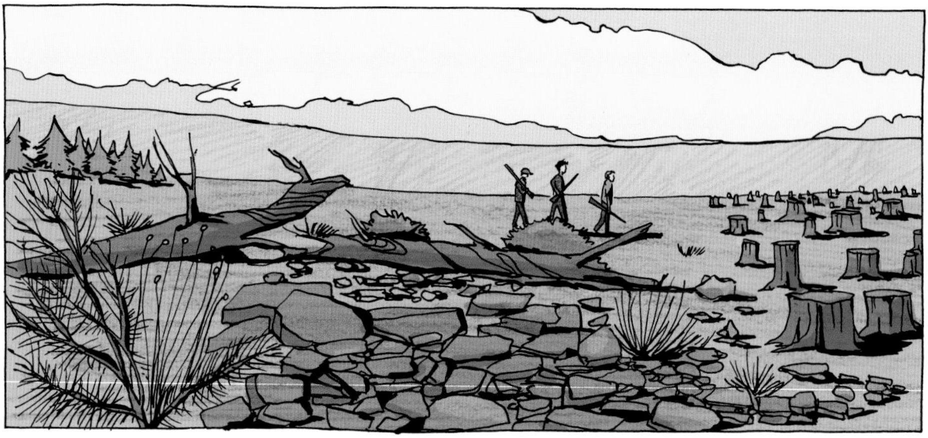

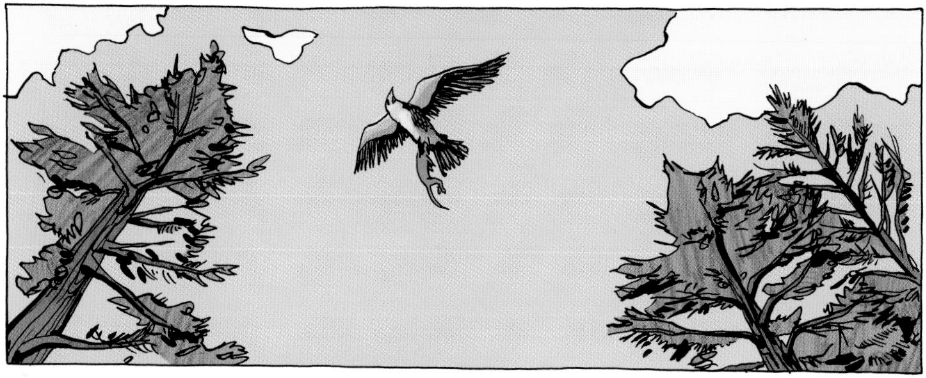

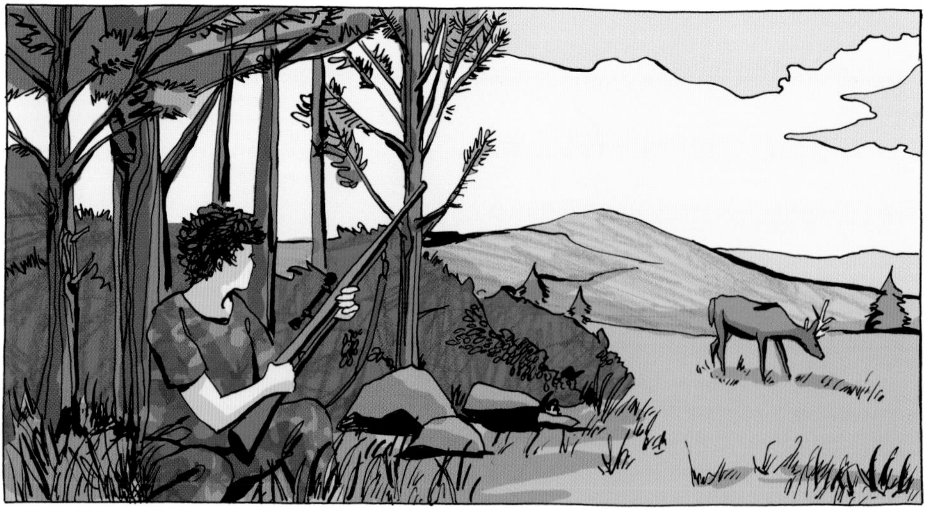

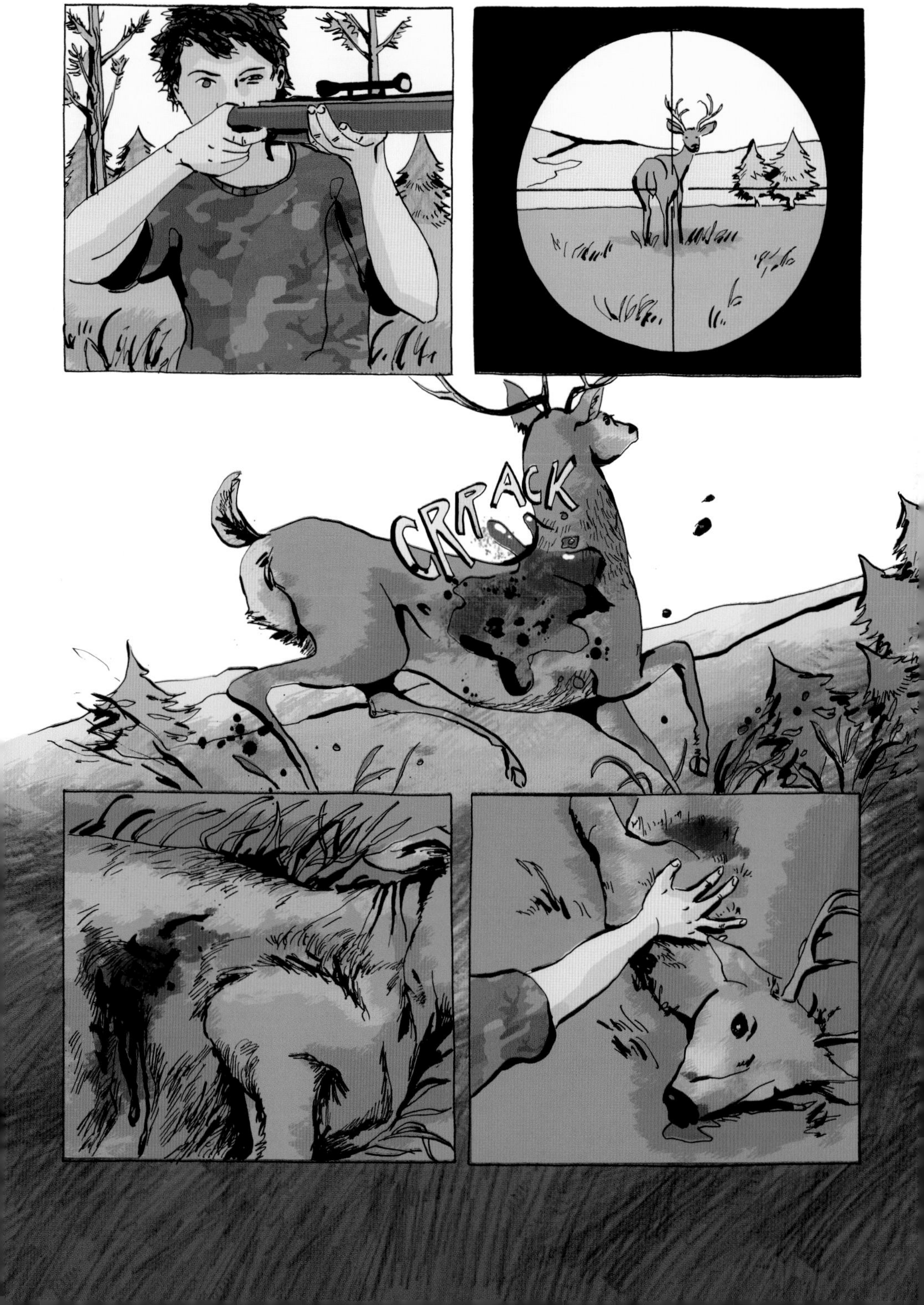
CRRACK

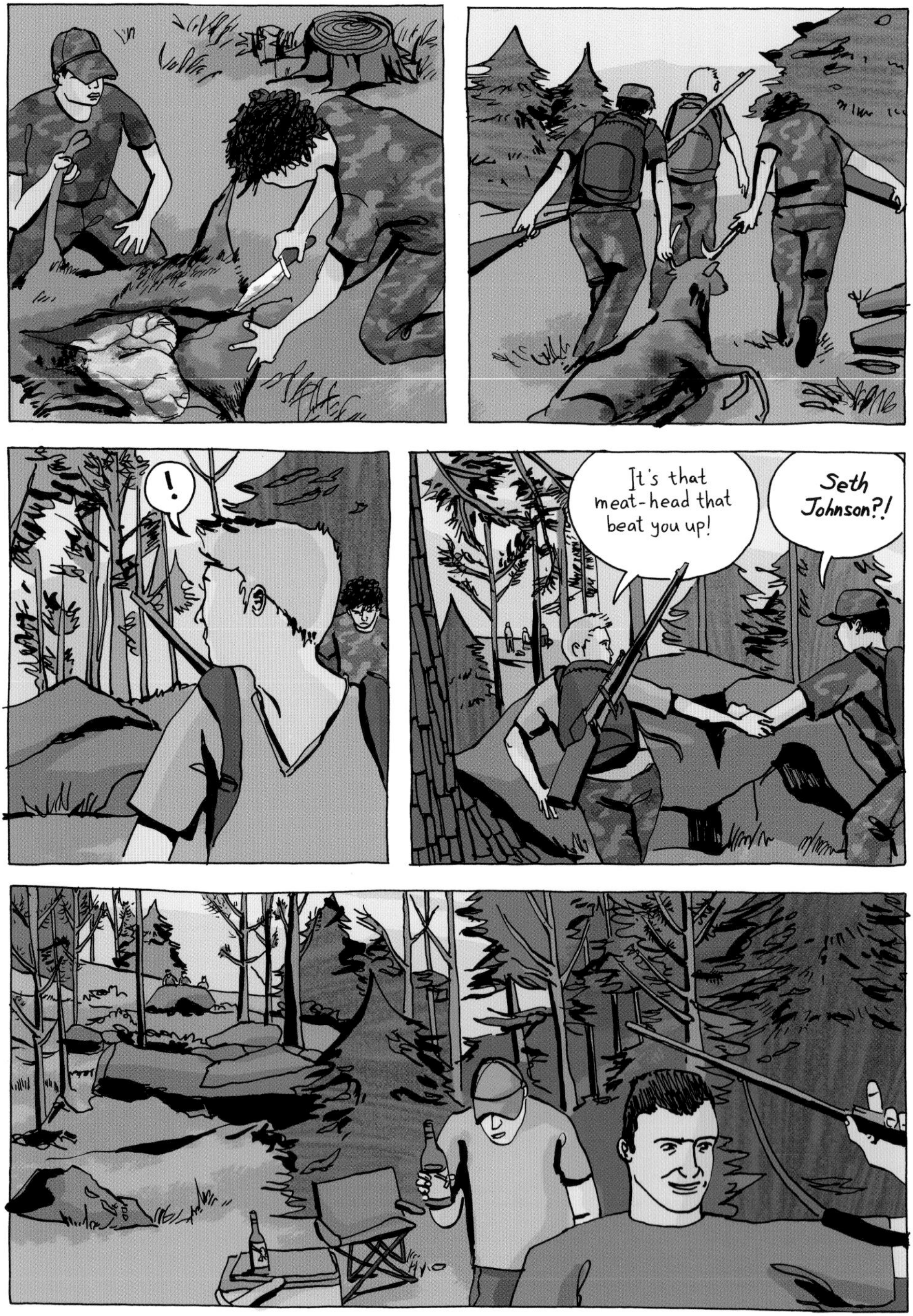
!
It's that meat-head that beat you up!
Seth Johnson?!

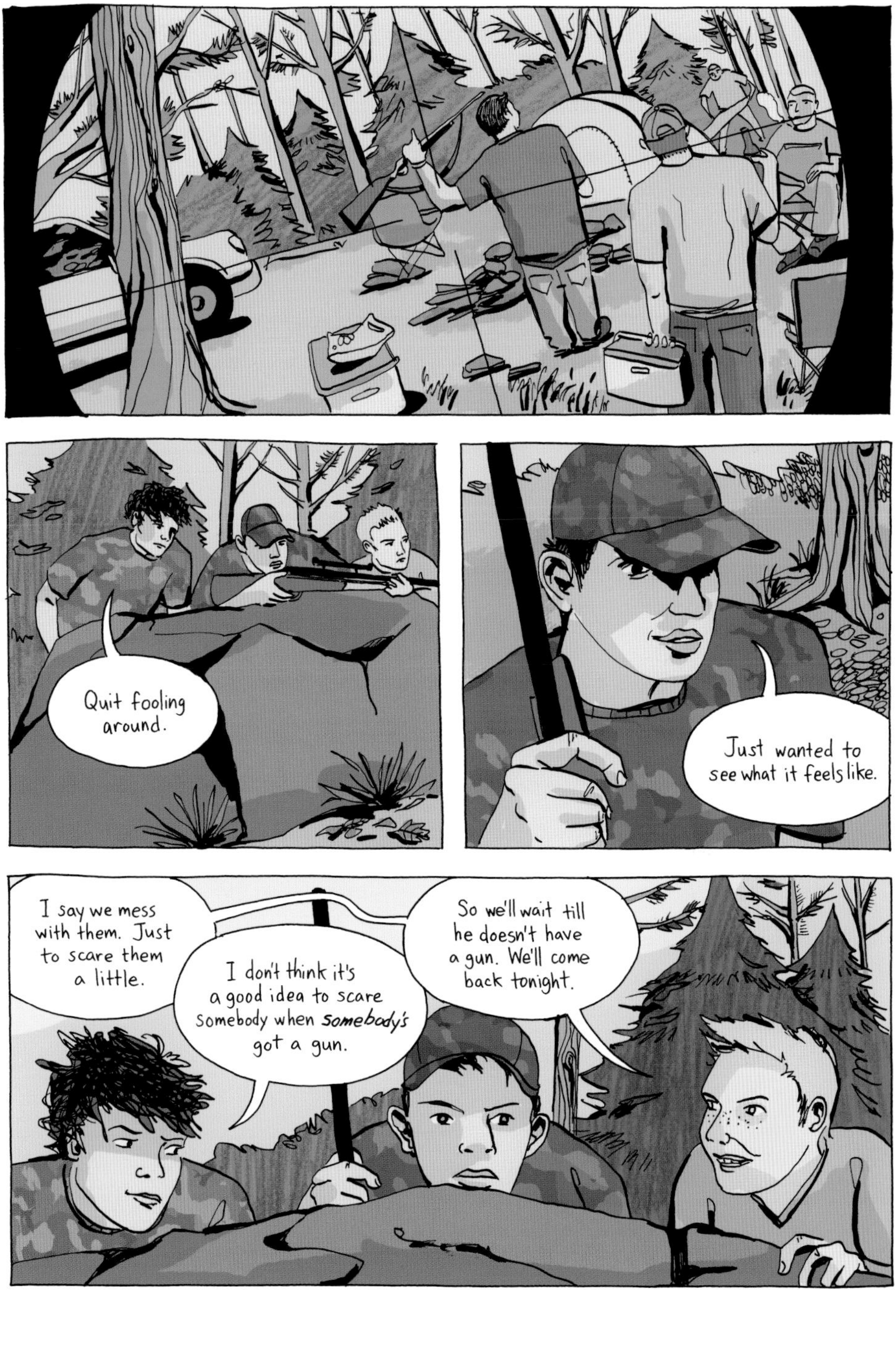

Quit fooling around.
Just wanted to see what it feels like.
I say we mess with them. Just to scare them a little.
I don't think it's a good idea to scare somebody when *somebody's* got a gun.
So we'll wait till he doesn't have a gun. We'll come back tonight.

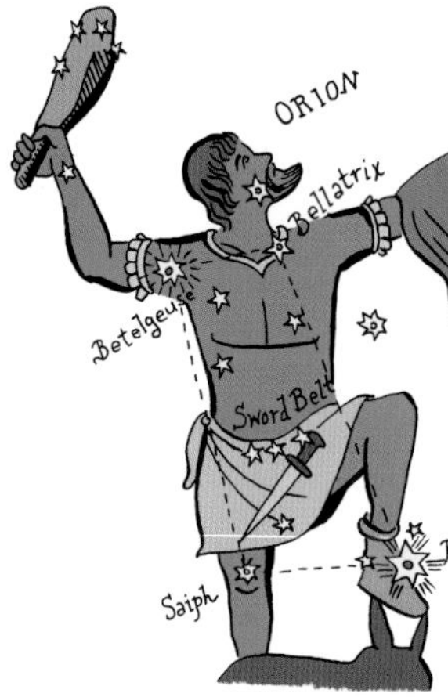
ORION
Bellatrix
Betelgeuse
Sword Belt
Rigel
Saiph

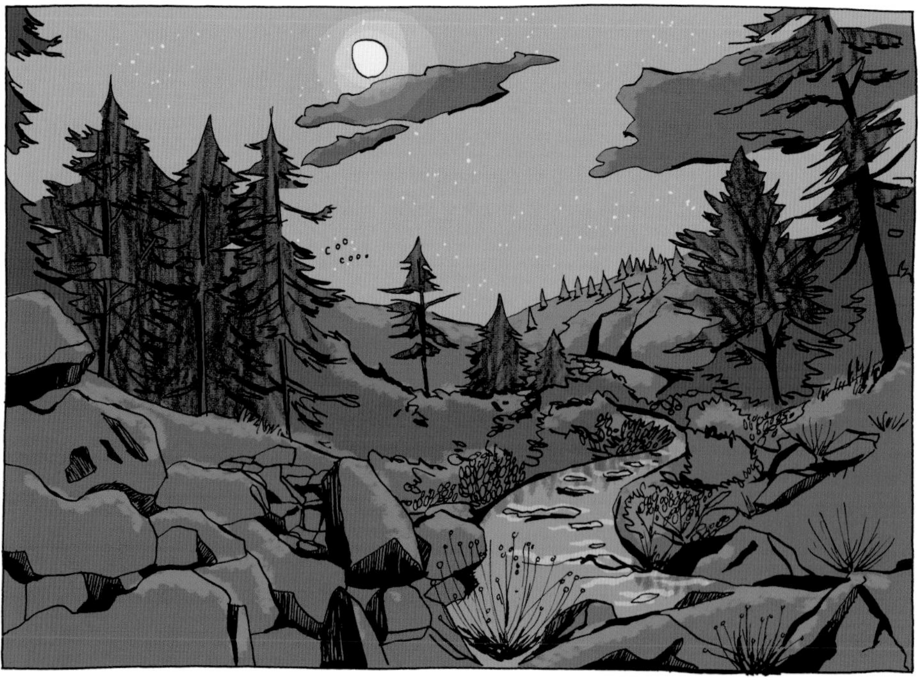
coo
coo.

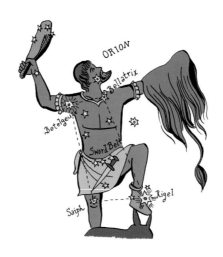

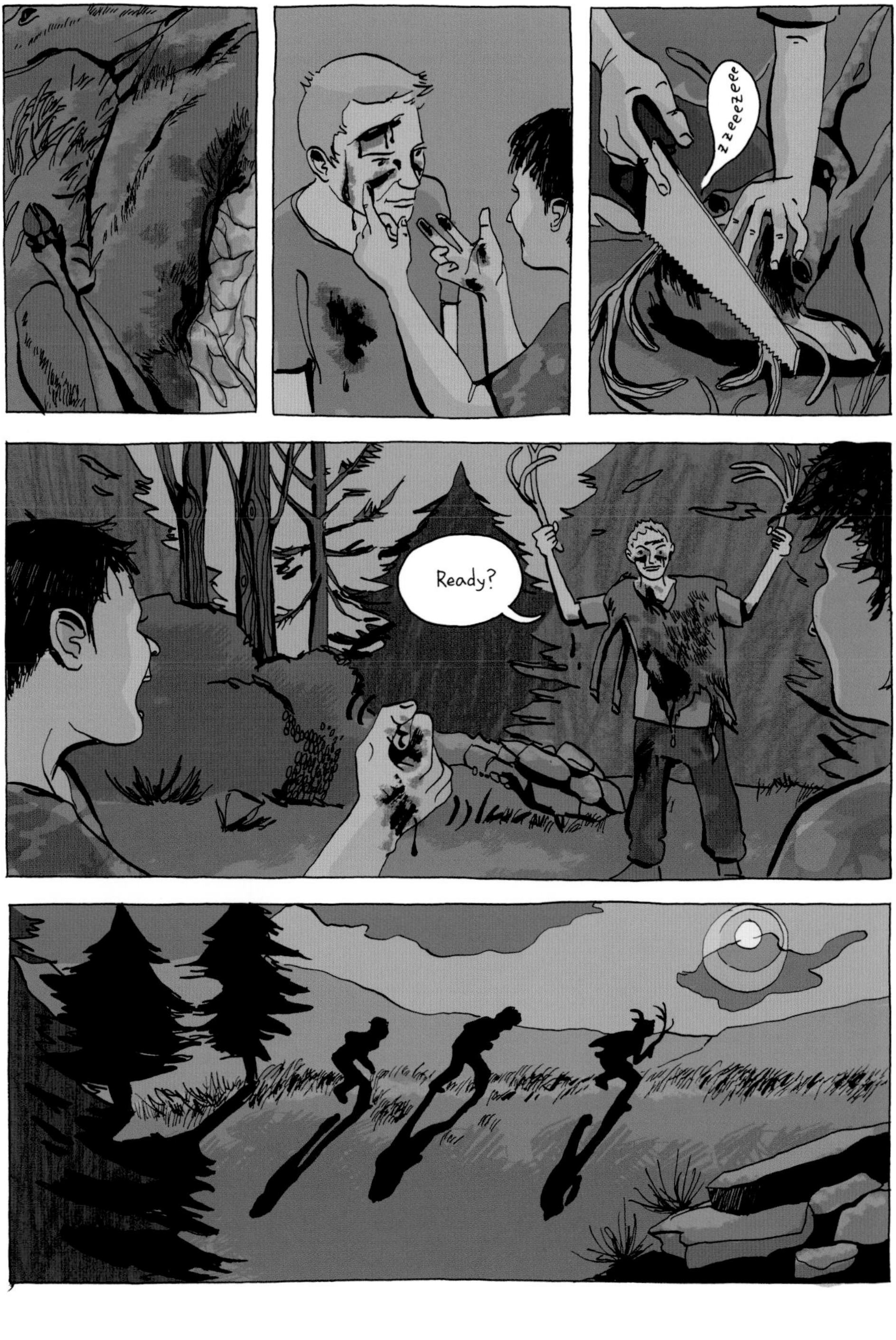
zzeeezeee
Ready?

How many of you have felt up Jessica Robertson?

ha ha ha ha ha

That girl's a dollar-store slut!

hic

thunk

zzziiP

psssi

Budweis

40

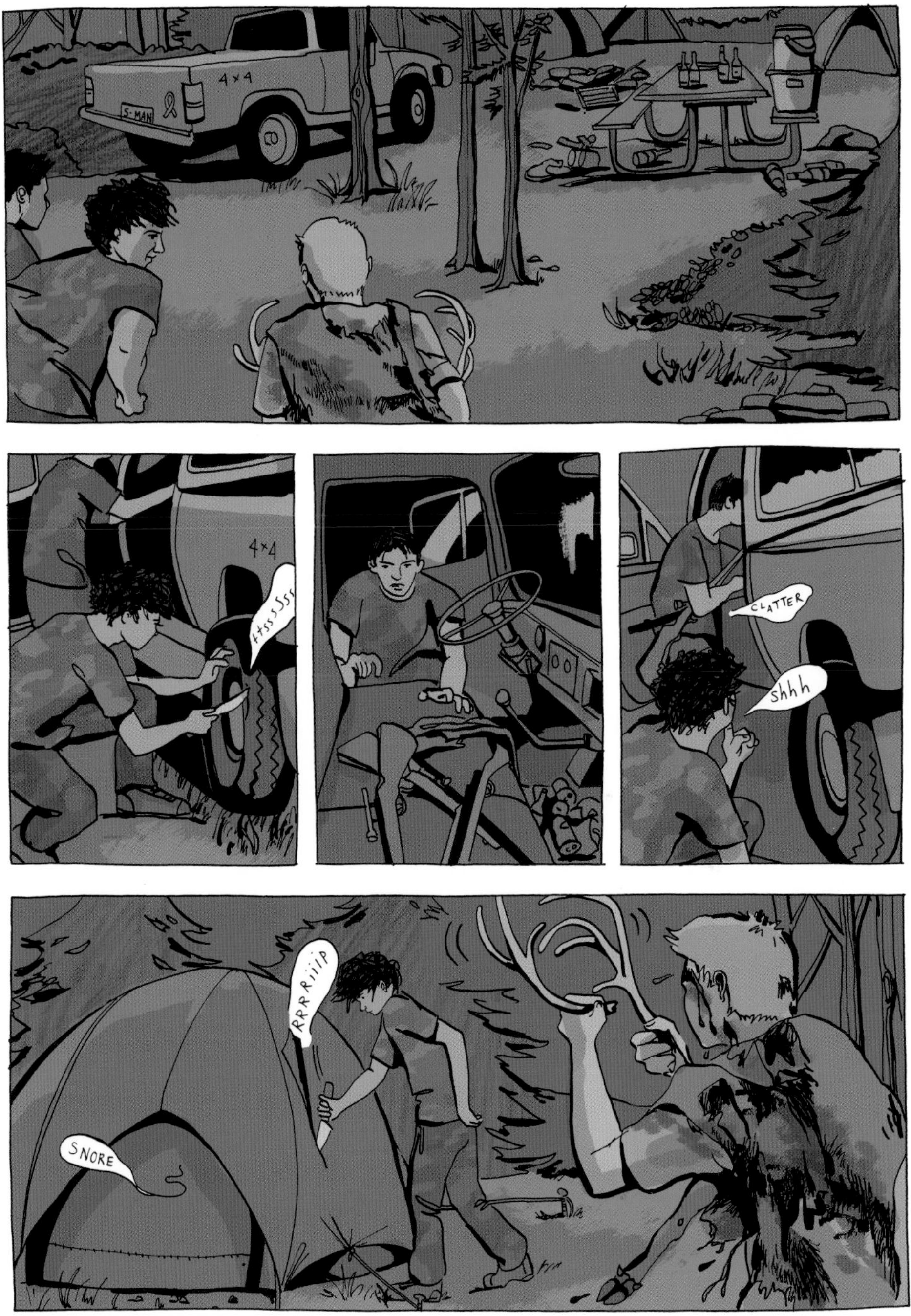
4×4
S-MAN
4×4
ttssSSss
CLATTER
shhh
RRRRiiiip
SNORE

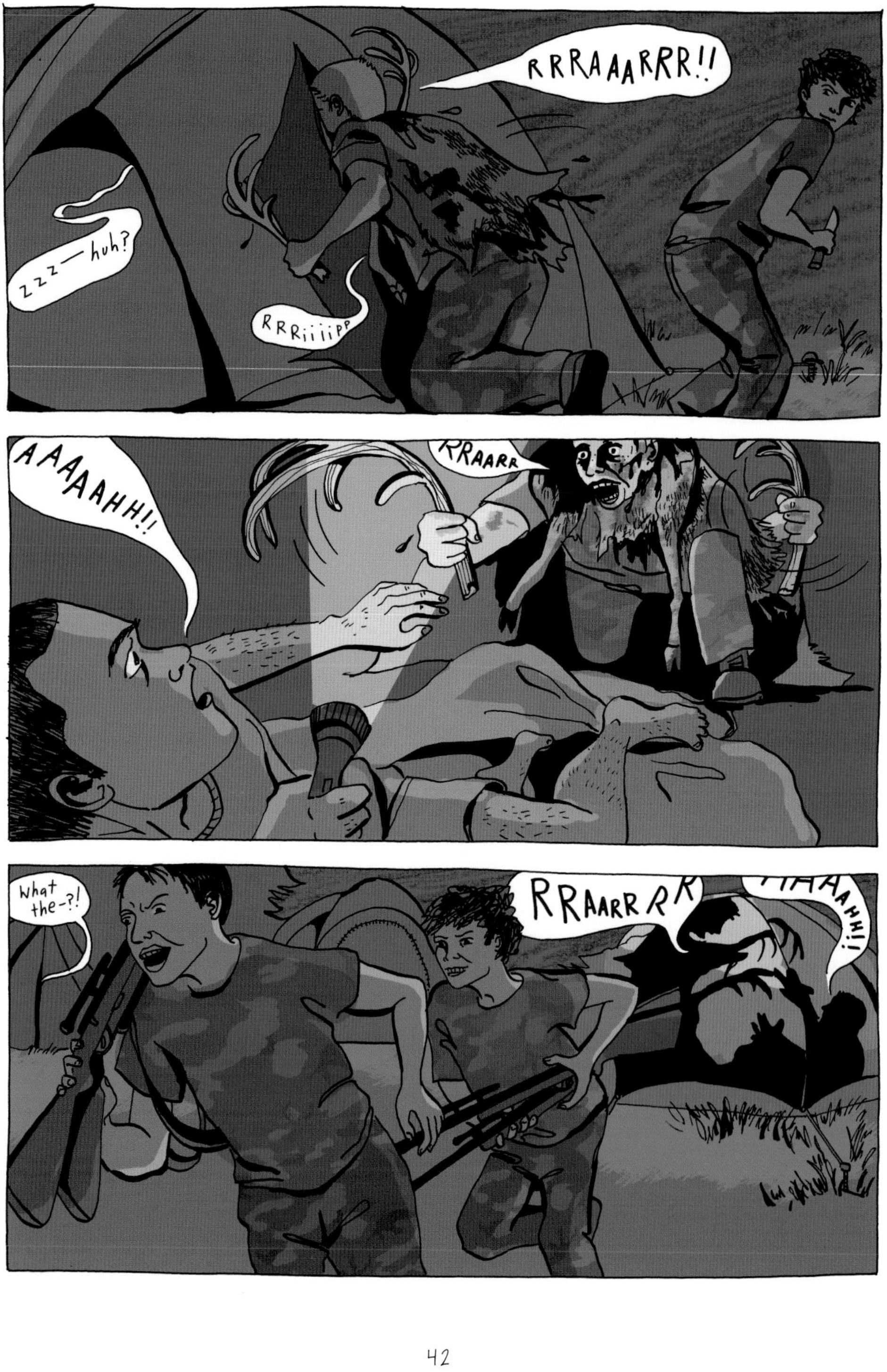
RRRAAARRR!!
zzz—huh?
RRRiiiipp
AAAAAHH!!
RRAARR
What the-?!
RRAARRRR

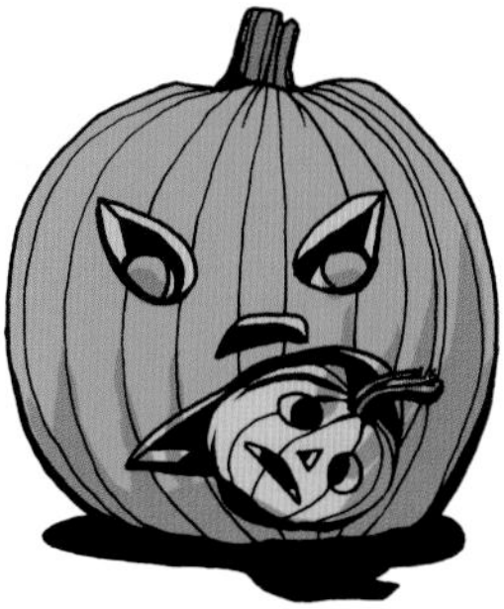

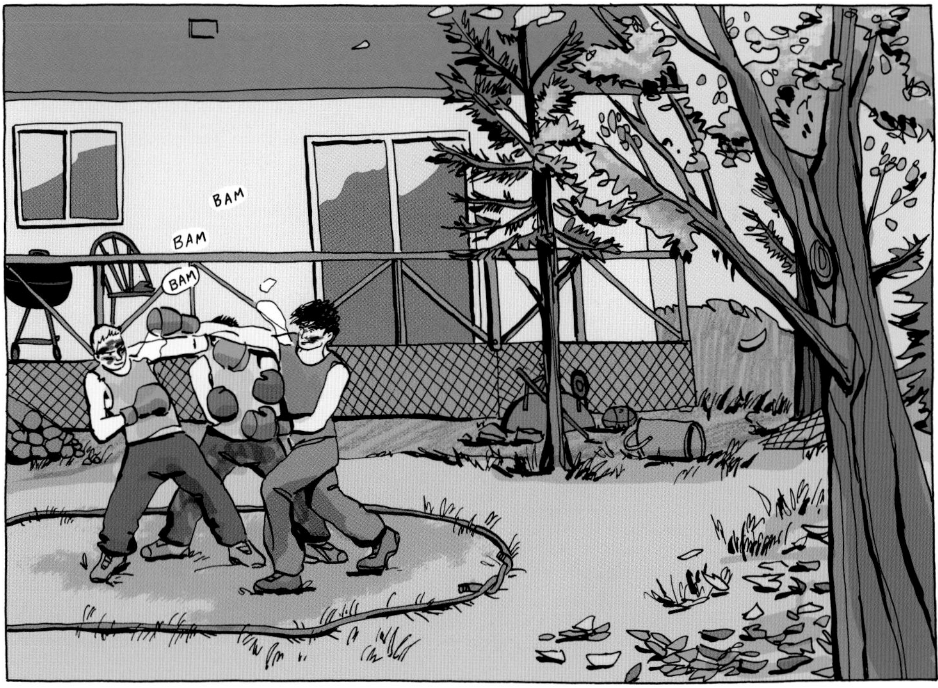
BAM
BAM
BAM

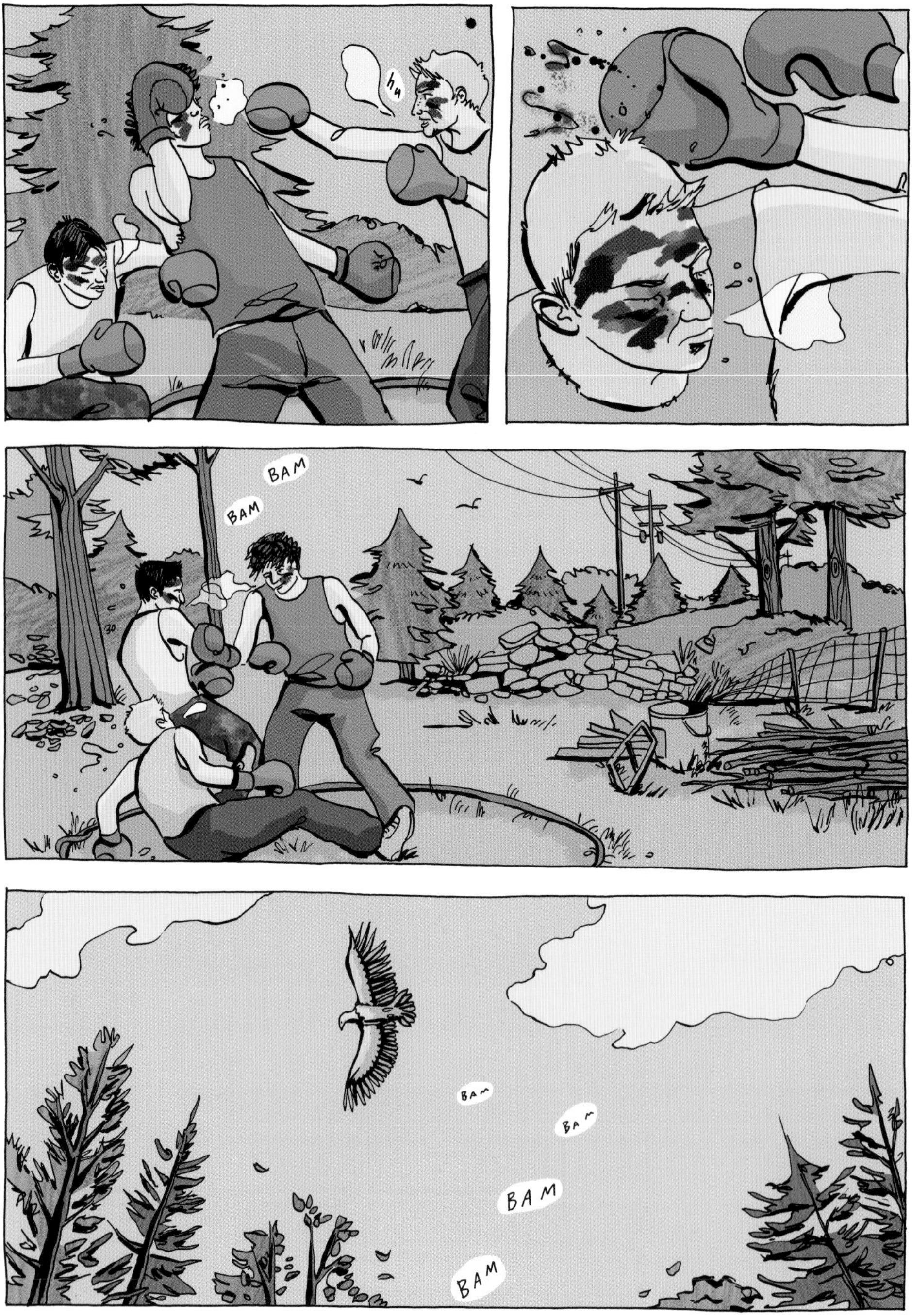
hu
BAM
BAM
BAM
BAM
BAM
BAM

Contacts
Calendar
Notepad
Compose
k Tickets Save Big
offers for You
ext Theme Park
[Add-Edit]
(1)
Welcome, Josh!
You have 0 unread messages.
Top Stories
World
Explorer File Edit View Go Favor
Back
Forward
Stop
Refresh
Home
Autofill
Address:
CLICK
YAHOO
ave Big
our
Park
- Edit]
Welcome, Jos
You have 0 unrea

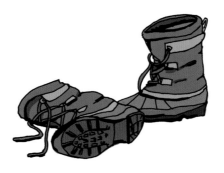

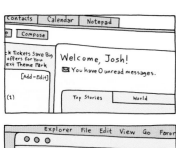

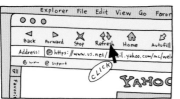

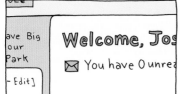

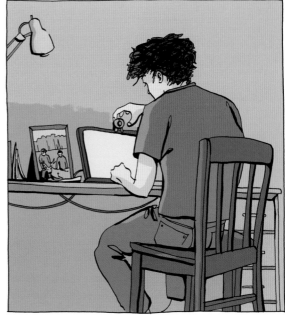

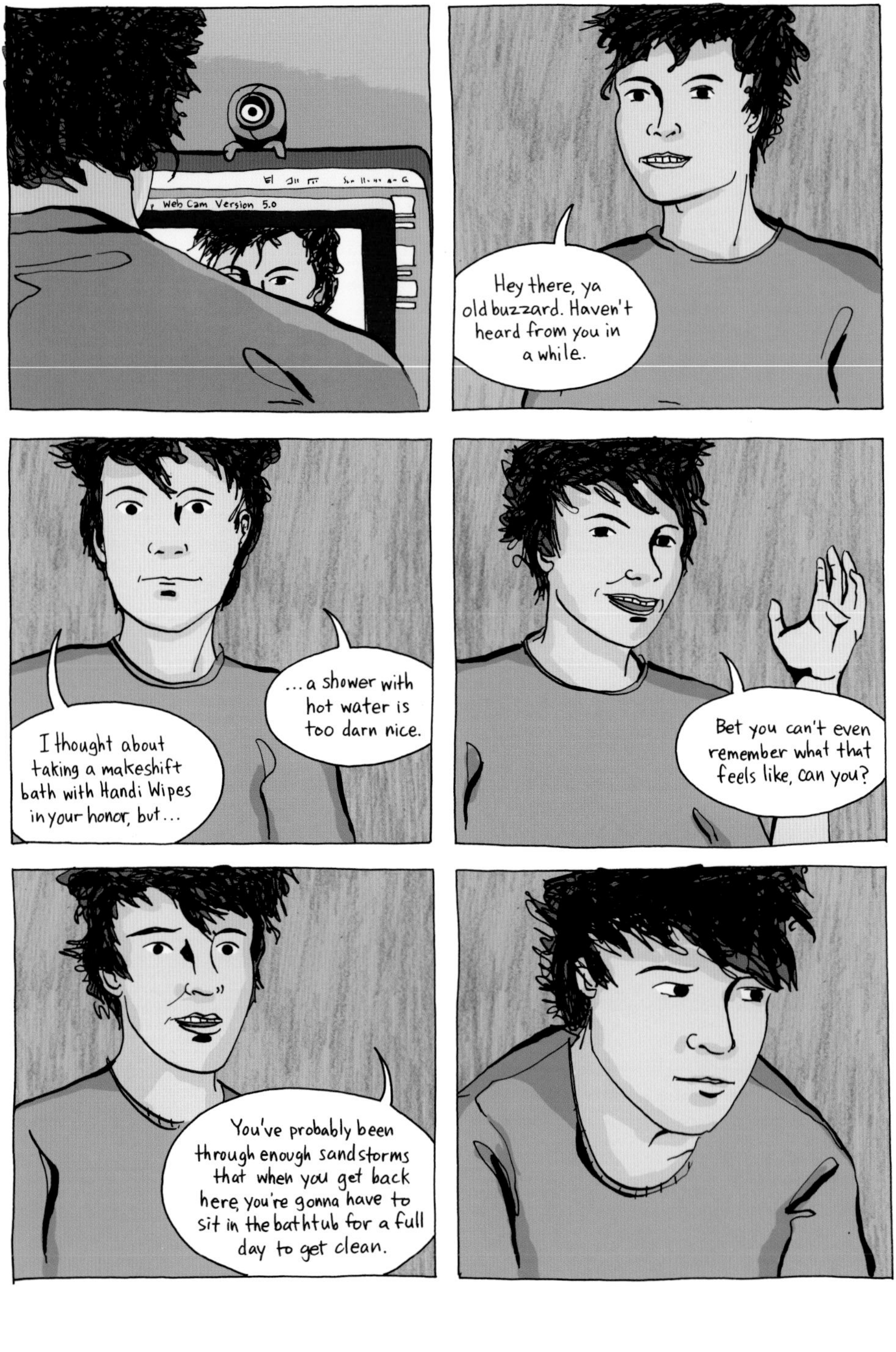
Web Cam Version 5.0
Hey there, ya old buzzard. Haven't heard from you in a while.
I thought about taking a makeshift bath with Handi Wipes in your honor, but...
...a shower with hot water is too darn nice.
Bet you can't even remember what that feels like, can you?
You've probably been through enough sandstorms that when you get back here, you're gonna have to sit in the bathtub for a full day to get clean.

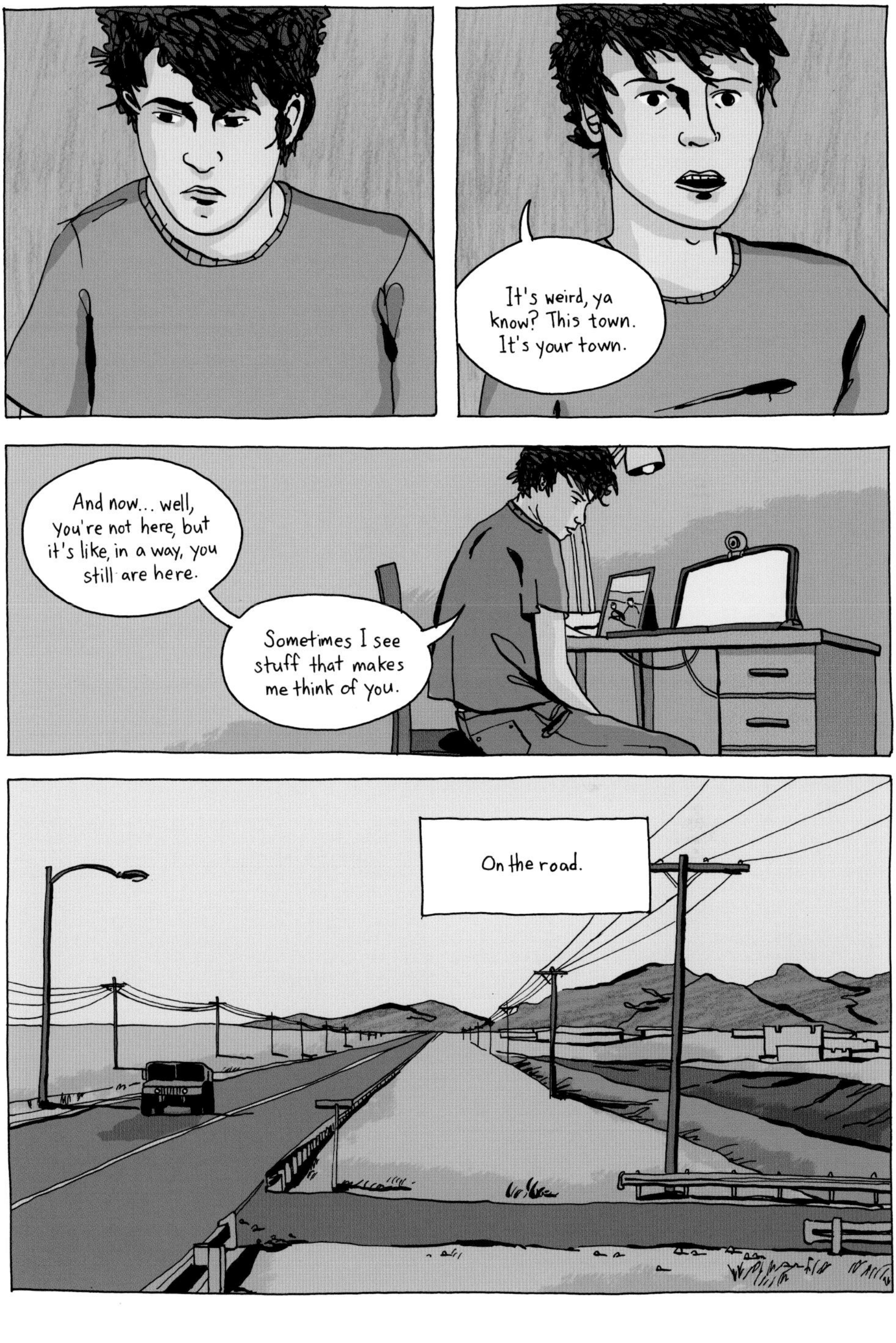

It's weird, ya know? This town. It's your town.
And now... well, you're not here, but it's like, in a way, you still are here.
Sometimes I see stuff that makes me think of you.
On the road.

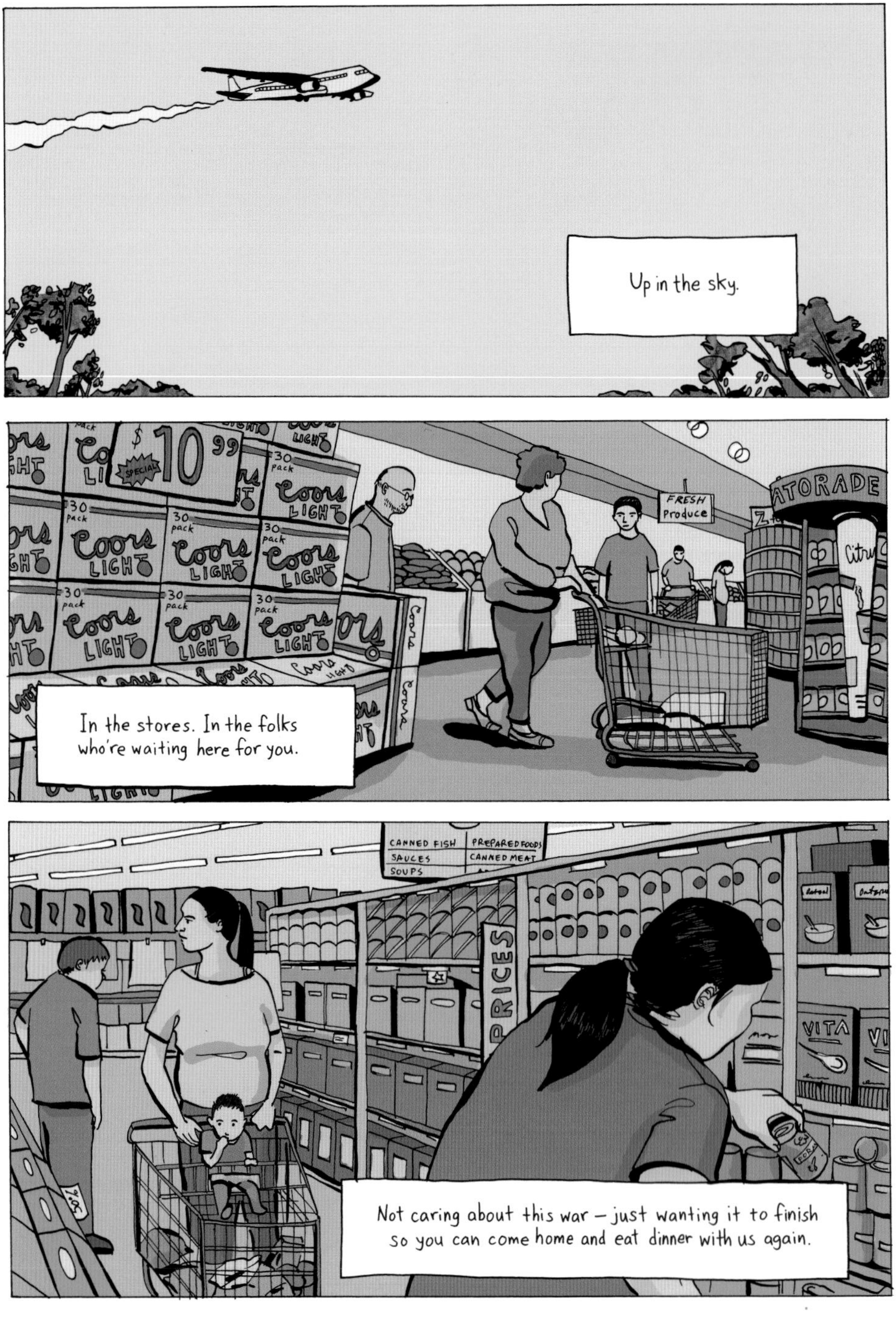
Up in the sky.
In the stores. In the folks who're waiting here for you.
FRESH Produce
CANNED FISH
SAUCES
SOUPS
PREPARED FOODS
CANNED MEAT
PRICES
Not caring about this war – just wanting it to finish so you can come home and eat dinner with us again.

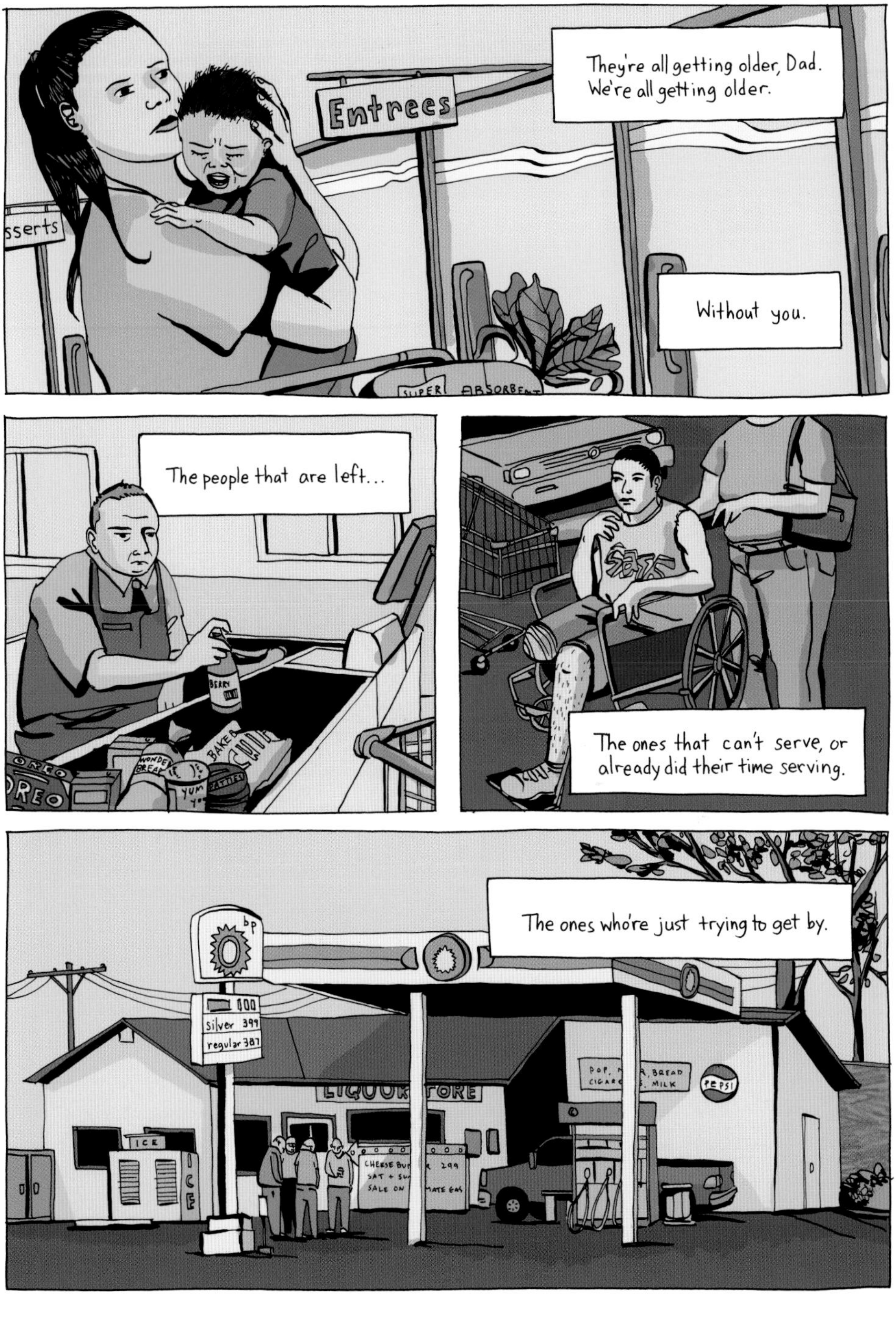
They're all getting older, Dad. We're all getting older.
Entrees
sserts
Without you.
SUPER ABSORBENT
The people that are left...
BERRY
OREO
The ones that can't serve, or already did their time serving.
The ones who're just trying to get by.
bp
silver 399
regular 387
PEPSI
ICE
ICE

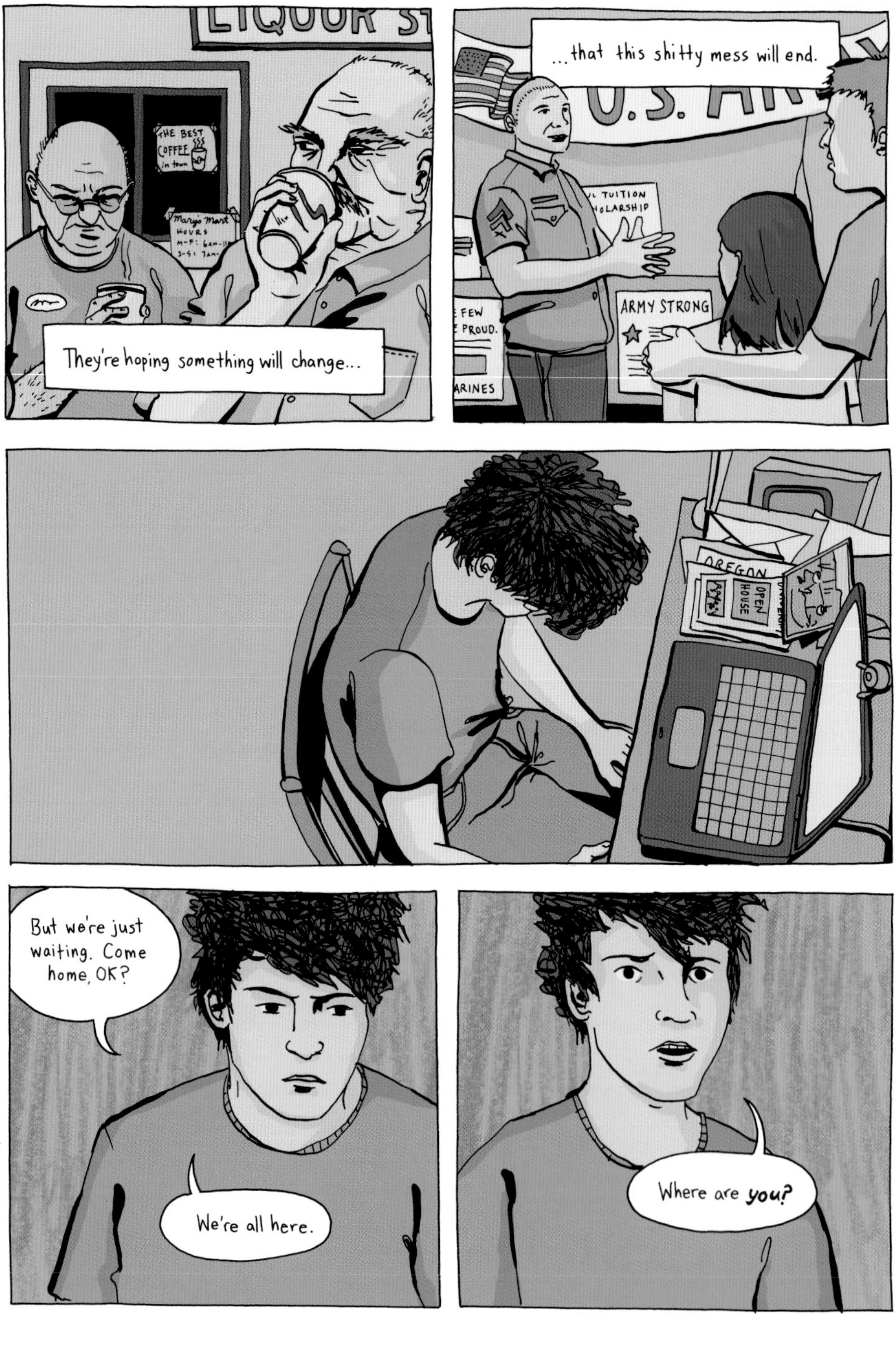
THE BEST COFFEE in town
They're hoping something will change...
...that this shitty mess will end.
ARMY STRONG
OREGON
OPEN HOUSE
But we're just waiting. Come home, OK?
We're all here.
Where are **you?**

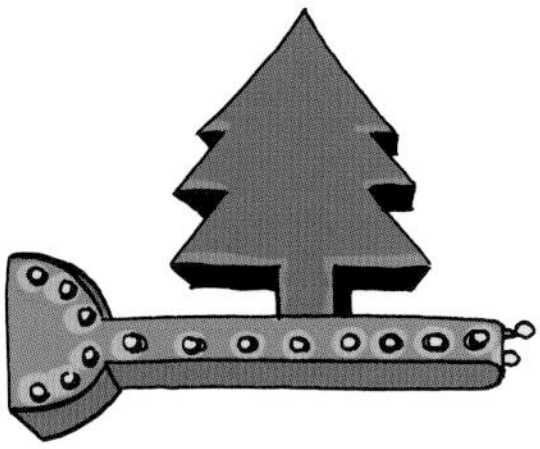

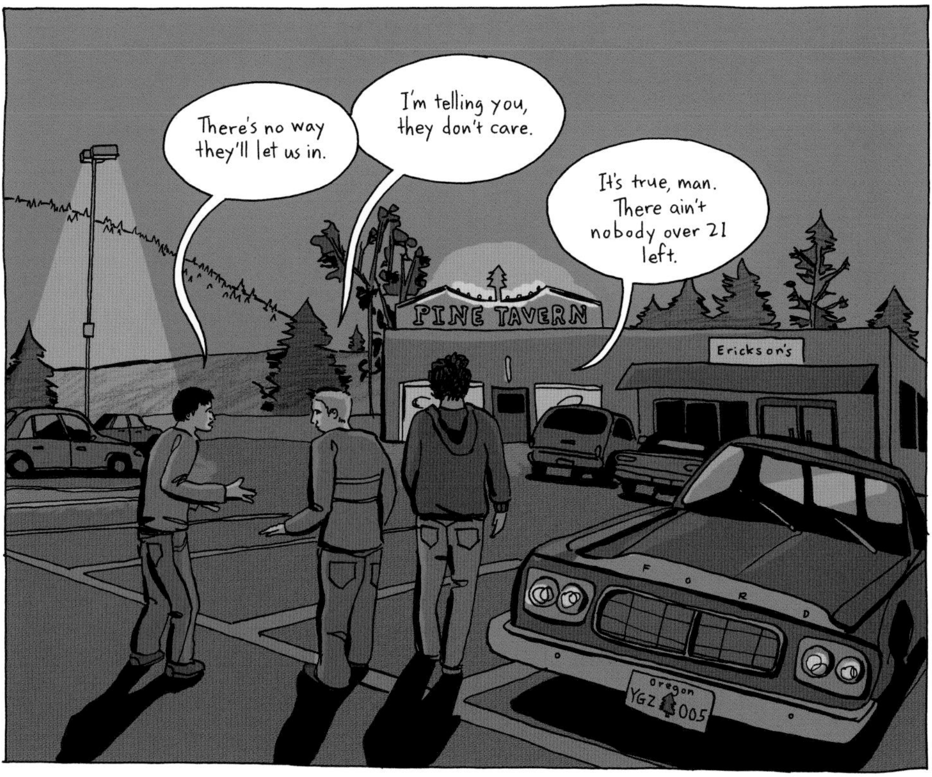

There's no way they'll let us in.
I'm telling you, they don't care.
It's true, man. There ain't nobody over 21 left.
PINE TAVERN
Erickson's
FORD
oregon
YGZ 005

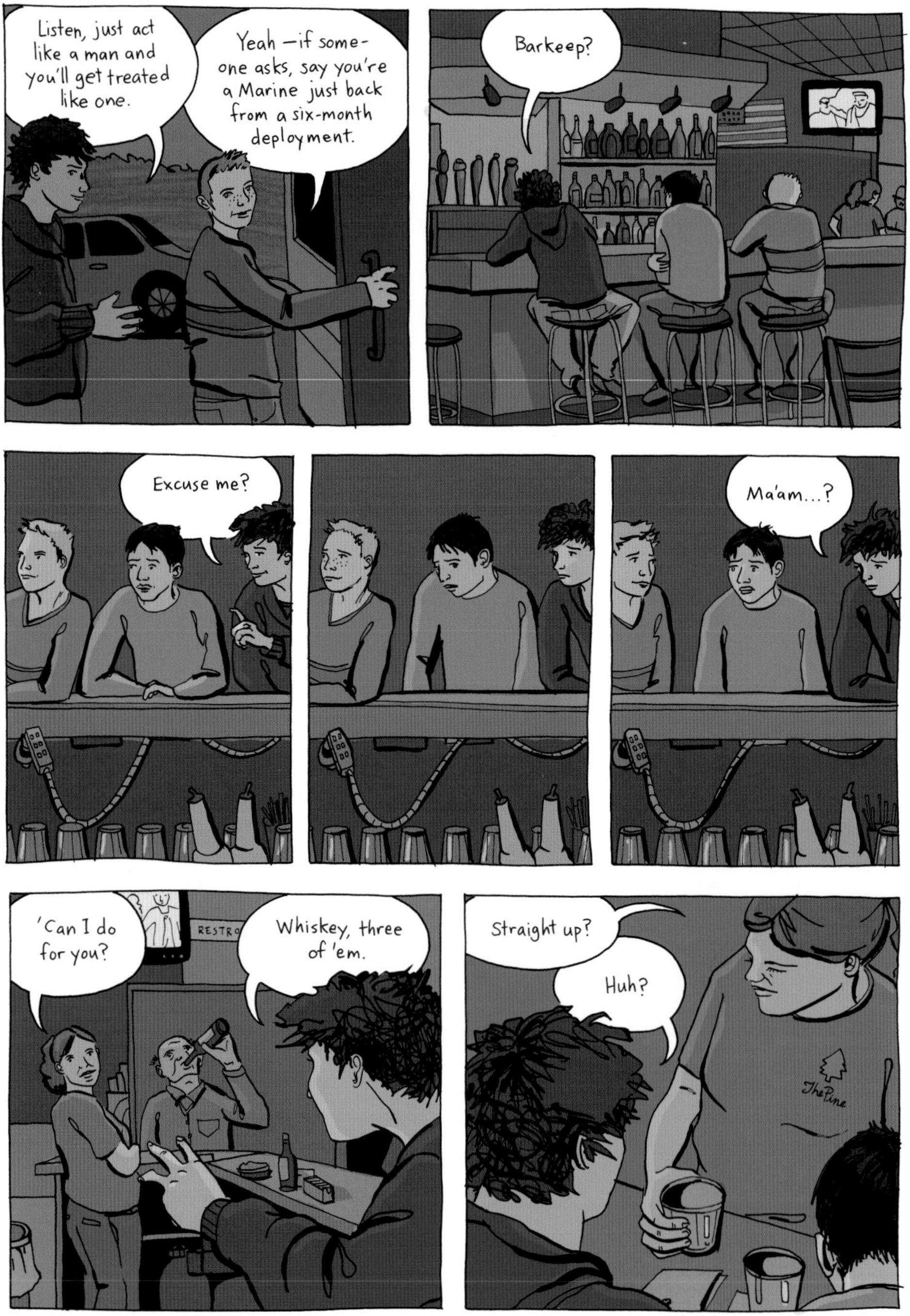
Listen, just act like a man and you'll get treated like one.
Yeah —if some-one asks, say you're a Marine just back from a six-month deployment.
Barkeep?
Excuse me?
Ma'am...?
'Can I do for you?
RESTRO
Whiskey, three of 'em.
Straight up?
Huh?
The Pine

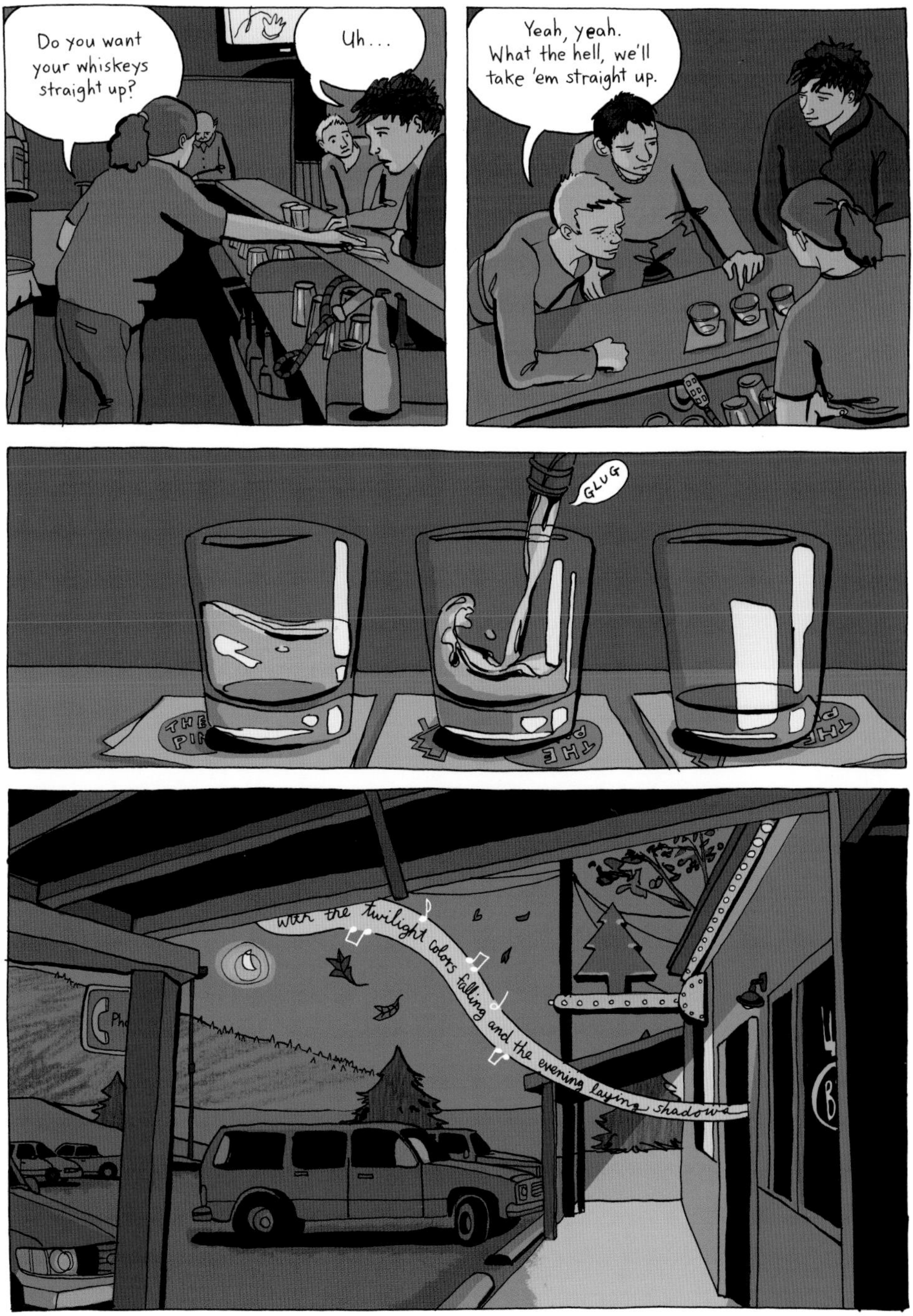
Do you want your whiskeys straight up?
Uh...
Yeah, yeah. What the hell, we'll take 'em straight up.
GLUG
the twilight colors falling and the evening laying shadows

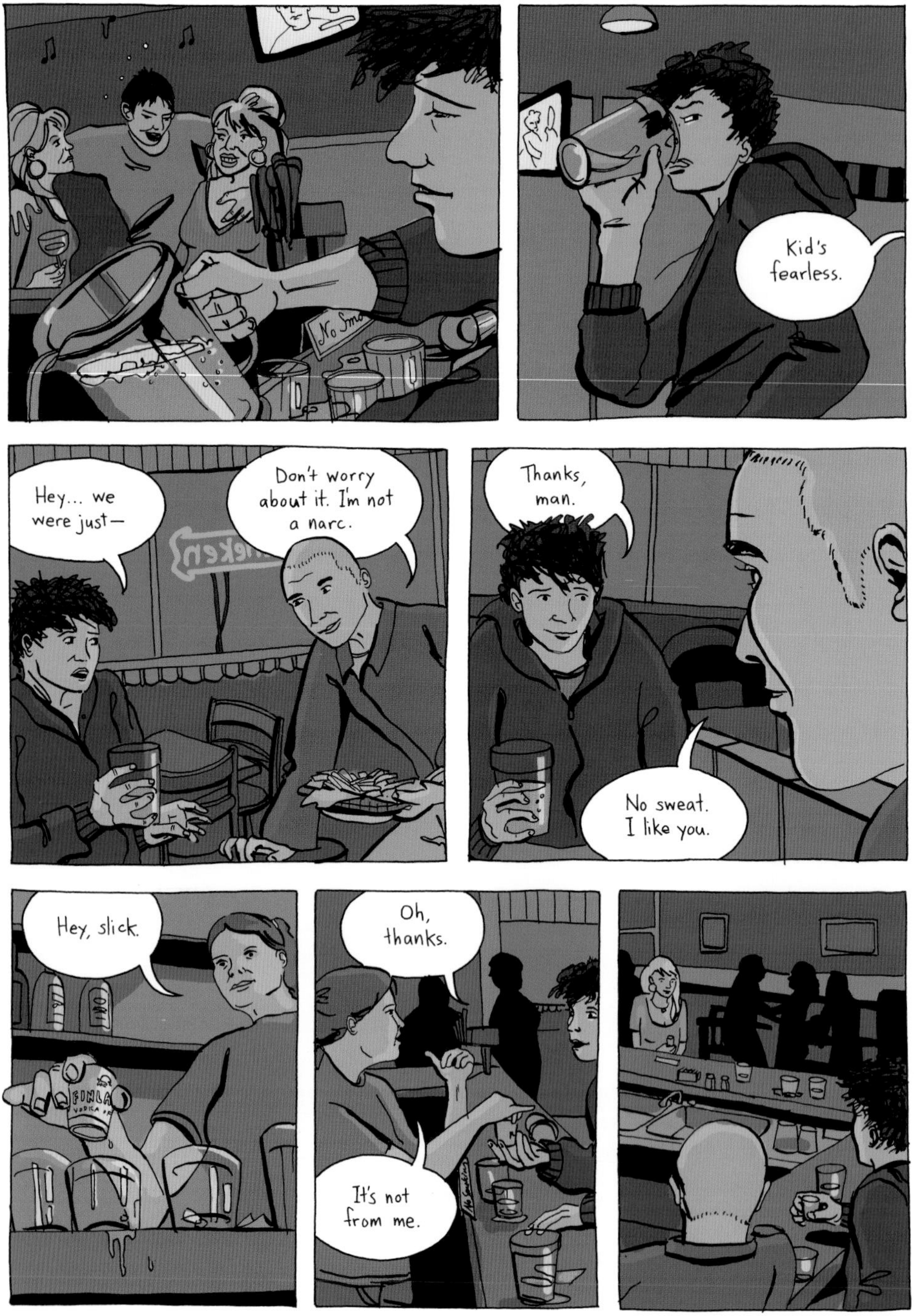
Kid's fearless.
Hey... we were just—
Don't worry about it. I'm not a narc.
Thanks, man.
No sweat. I like you.
Hey, slick.
Oh, thanks.
It's not from me.

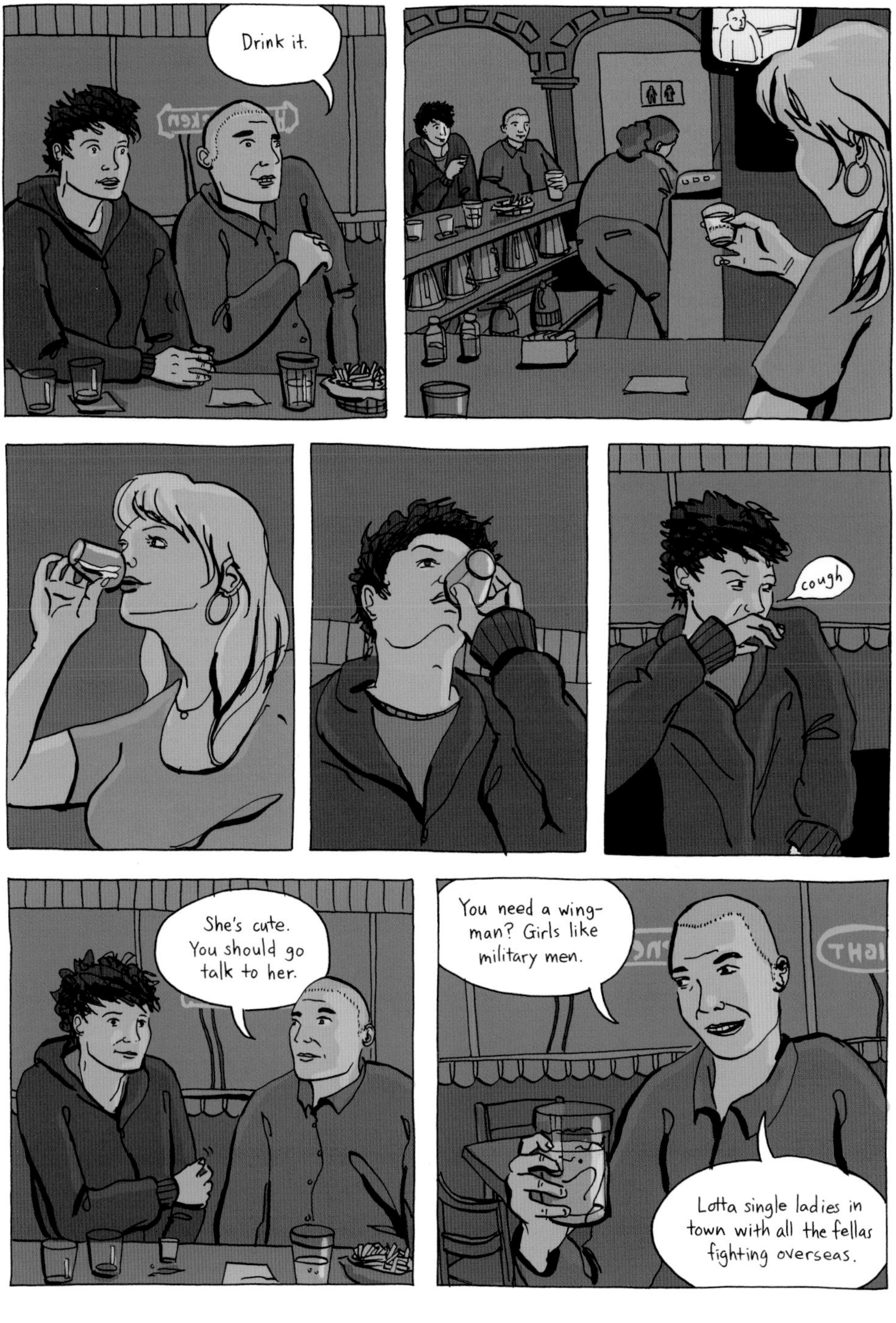
Drink it.
cough
She's cute. You should go talk to her.
You need a wing-man? Girls like military men.
Lotta single ladies in town with all the fellas fighting overseas.

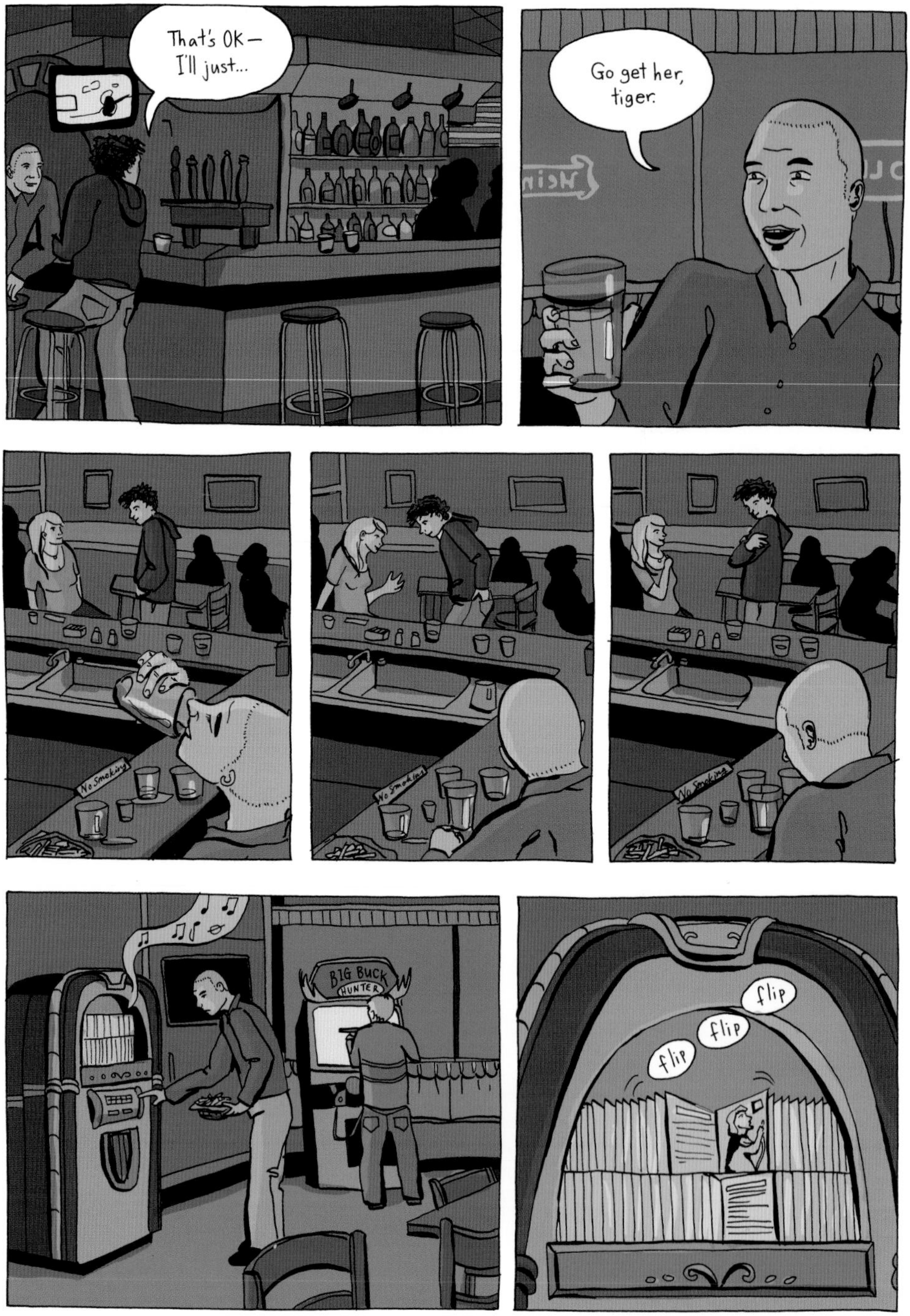
That's OK—
I'll just...
Go get her,
tiger.
No Smoking
No Smoking
No Smoking
BIG BUCK
HUNTER
flip
flip
flip

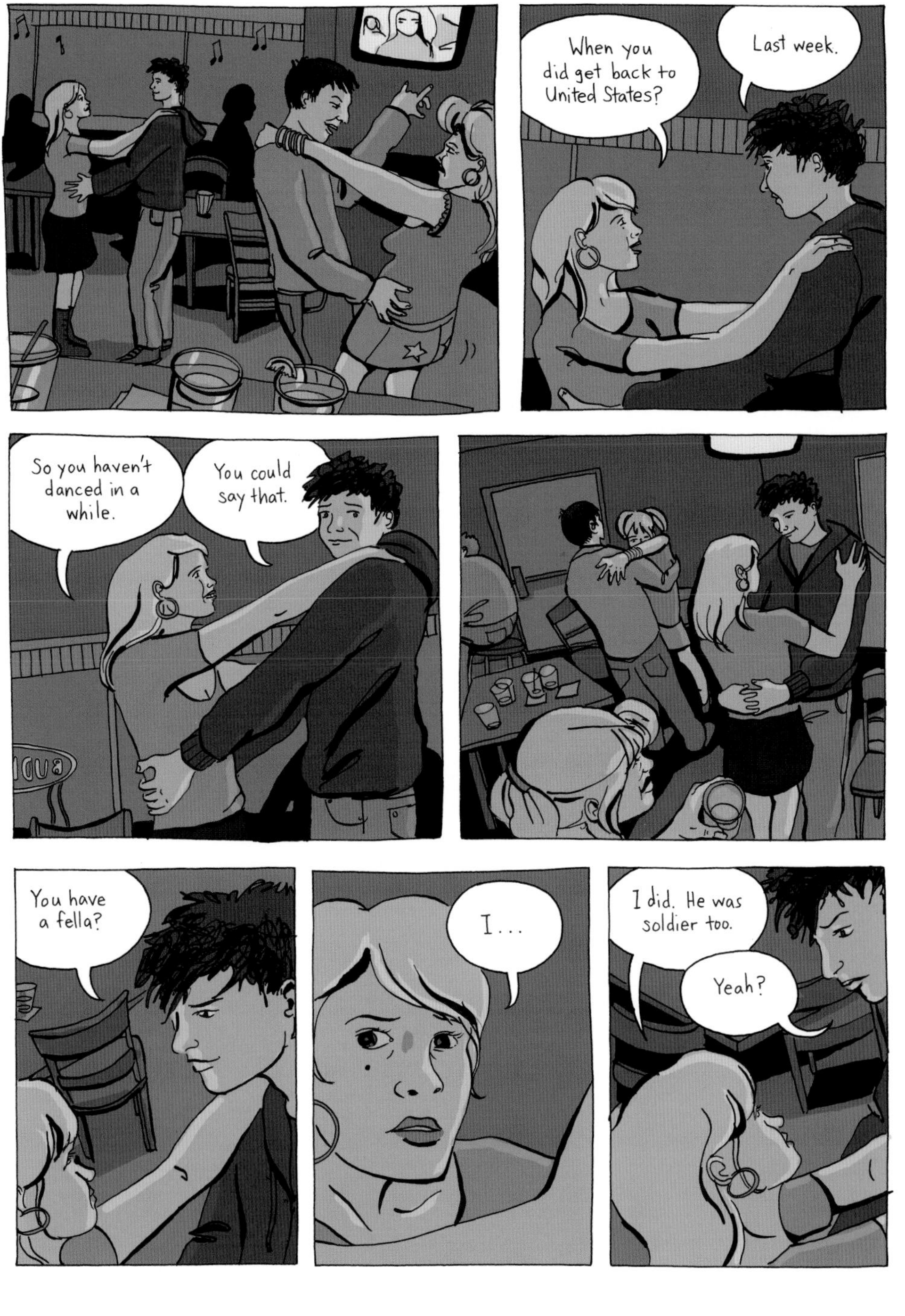
When you did get back to United States?
Last week.
So you haven't danced in a while.
You could say that.
You have a fella?
I...
I did. He was soldier too.
Yeah?

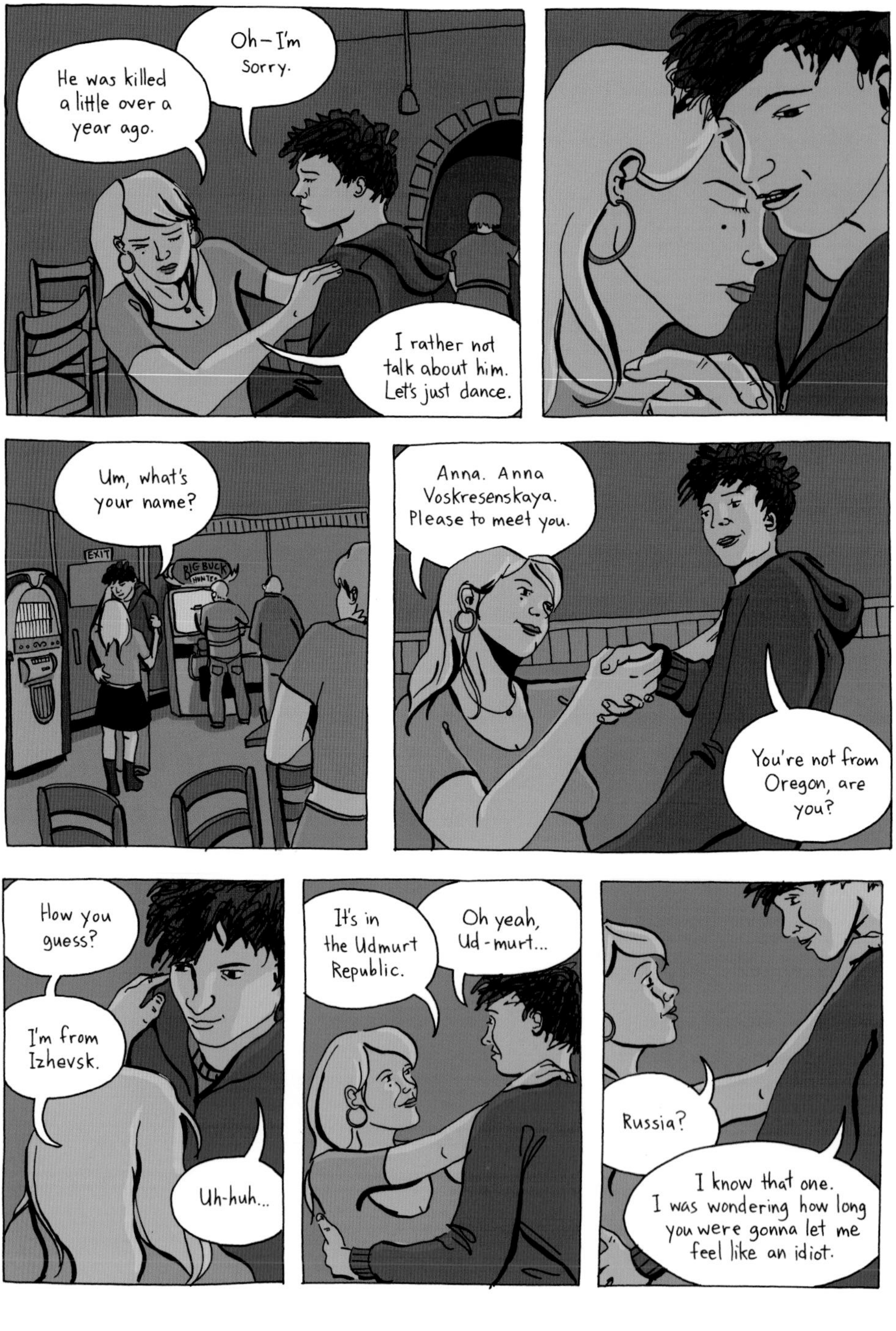
He was killed a little over a year ago.
Oh—I'm sorry.
I rather not talk about him. Let's just dance.
Um, what's your name?
EXIT
BIG BUCK HUNTER
Anna. Anna Voskresenskaya. Please to meet you.
You're not from Oregon, are you?
How you guess?
I'm from Izhevsk.
Uh-huh...
It's in the Udmurt Republic.
Oh yeah, Ud-murt...
Russia?
I know that one. I was wondering how long you were gonna let me feel like an idiot.

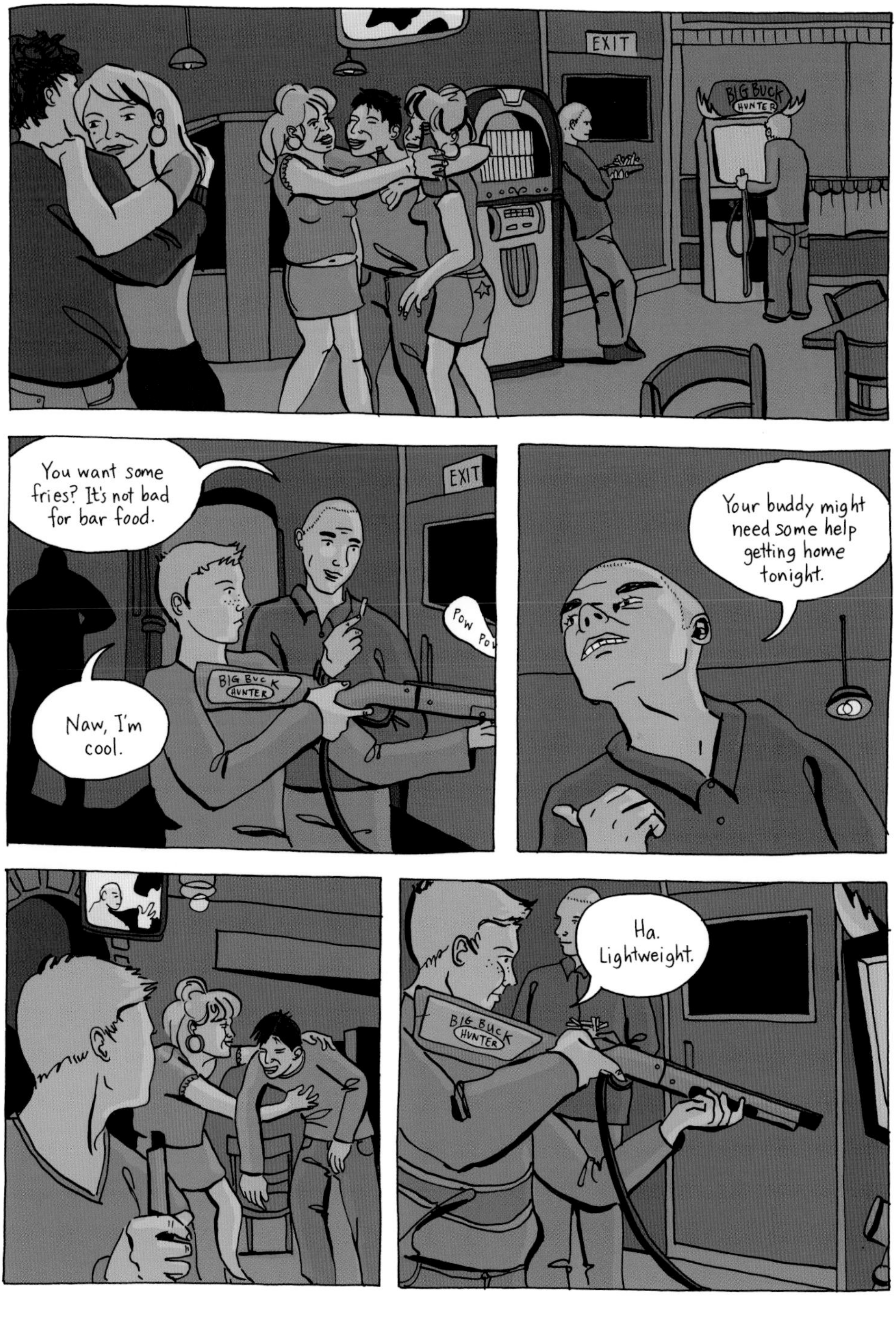
EXIT
BIG BUCK HUNTER
You want some fries? It's not bad for bar food.
EXIT
POW POW
BIG BUCK HUNTER
Naw, I'm cool.
Your buddy might need some help getting home tonight.
Ha. Lightweight.
BIG BUCK HUNTER

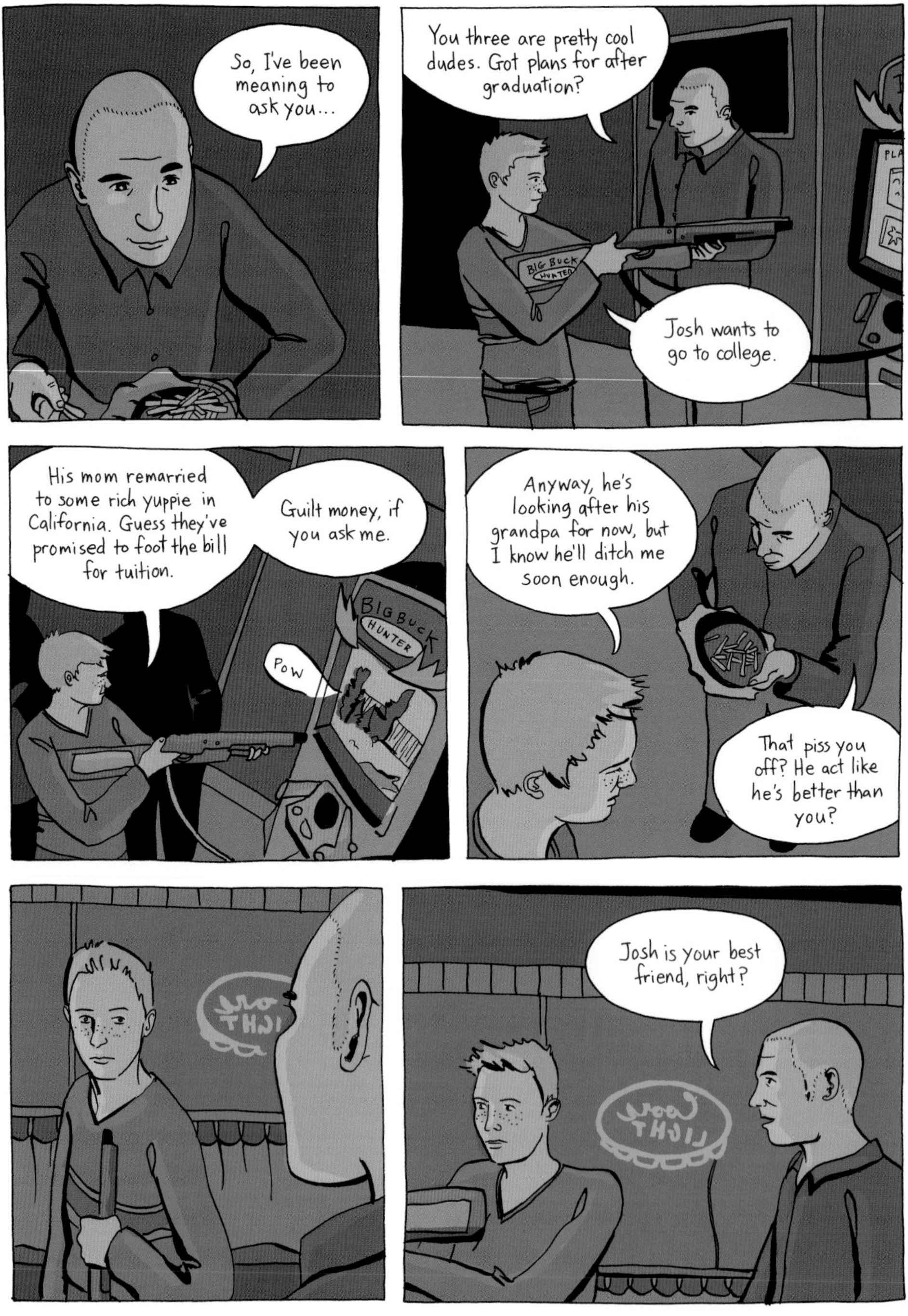
So, I've been meaning to ask you...
You three are pretty cool dudes. Got plans for after graduation?
BIG BUCK HUNTER
Josh wants to go to college.
His mom remarried to some rich yuppie in California. Guess they've promised to foot the bill for tuition.
Guilt money, if you ask me.
BIG BUCK HUNTER
POW
Anyway, he's looking after his grandpa for now, but I know he'll ditch me soon enough.
That piss you off? He act like he's better than you?
Josh is your best friend, right?

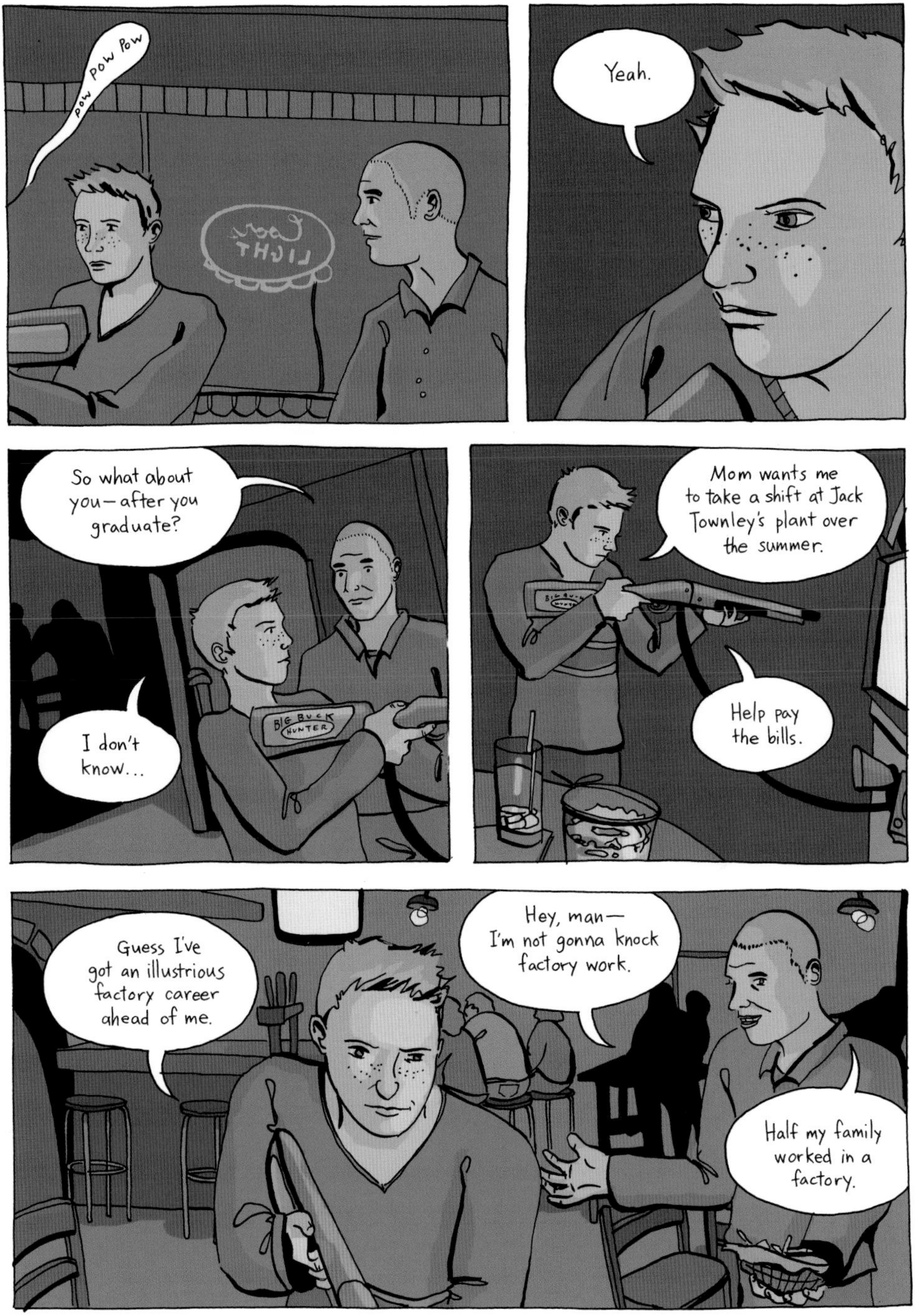
pow pow pow pow
Coors LIGHT
Yeah.
So what about you—after you graduate?
I don't know...
BIG BUCK HUNTER
Mom wants me to take a shift at Jack Townley's plant over the summer.
Help pay the bills.
Guess I've got an illustrious factory career ahead of me.
Hey, man— I'm not gonna knock factory work.
Half my family worked in a factory.

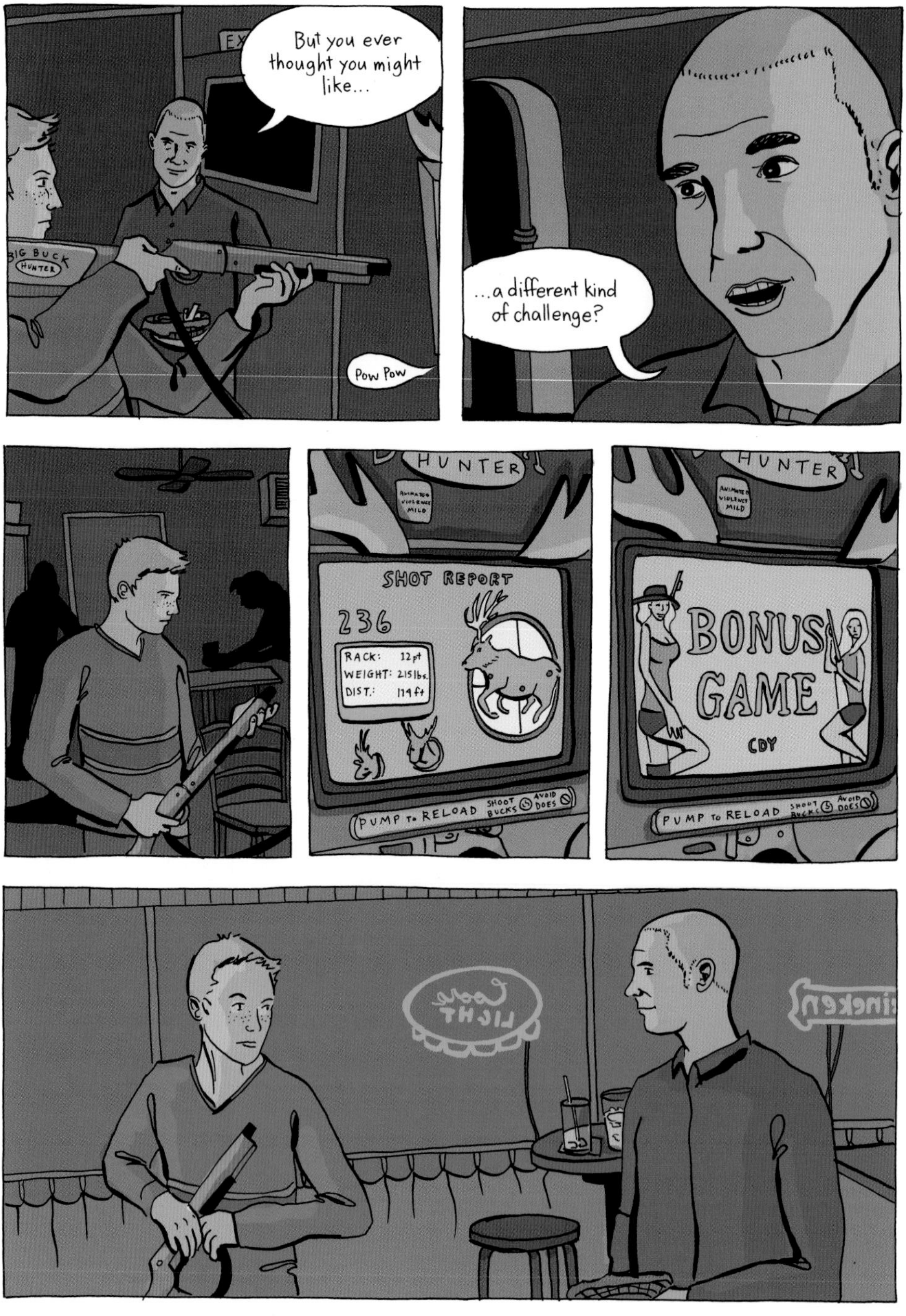
But you ever thought you might like...
Pow Pow
...a different kind of challenge?
BIG BUCK HUNTER
HUNTER
ANIMATED VIOLENCE MILD
SHOT REPORT
236
RACK: 12 pt
WEIGHT: 215 lbs.
DIST.: 174 ft
PUMP TO RELOAD
SHOOT BUCKS
AVOID DOES
BONUS GAME
CDY

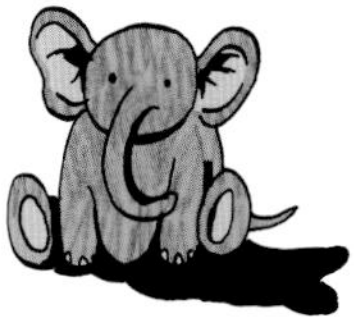

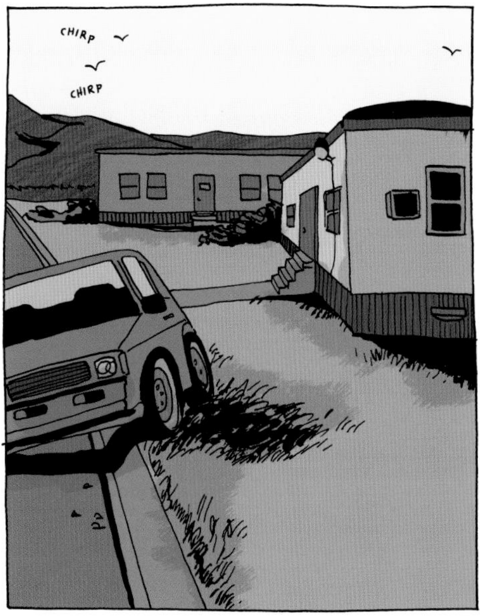
CHIRP
CHIRP

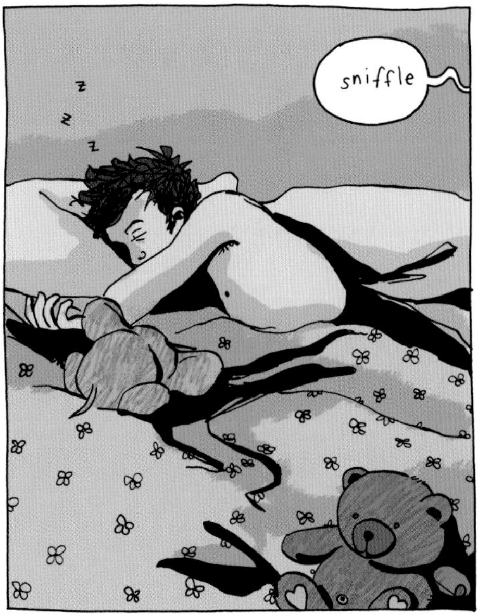
Z
Z
Z
sniffle

sob

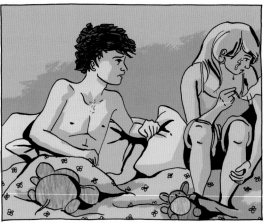

Was I that bad?

sniff

What's wrong?

Nothing, go back to sleep.

Hey, don't cry... Were you thinking about him?

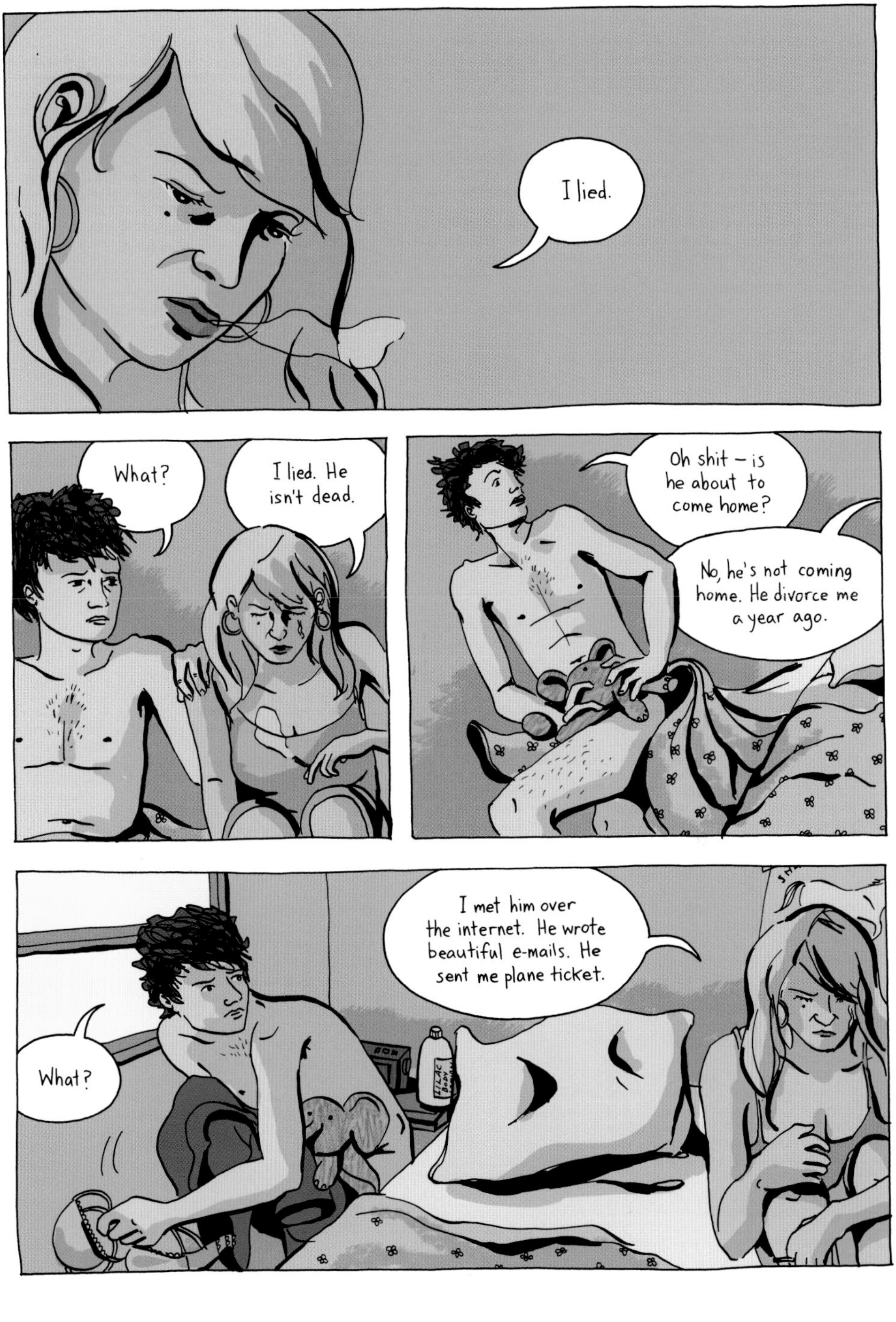
I lied.
What?
I lied. He isn't dead.
Oh shit – is he about to come home?
No, he's not coming home. He divorce me a year ago.
What?
I met him over the internet. He wrote beautiful e-mails. He sent me plane ticket.

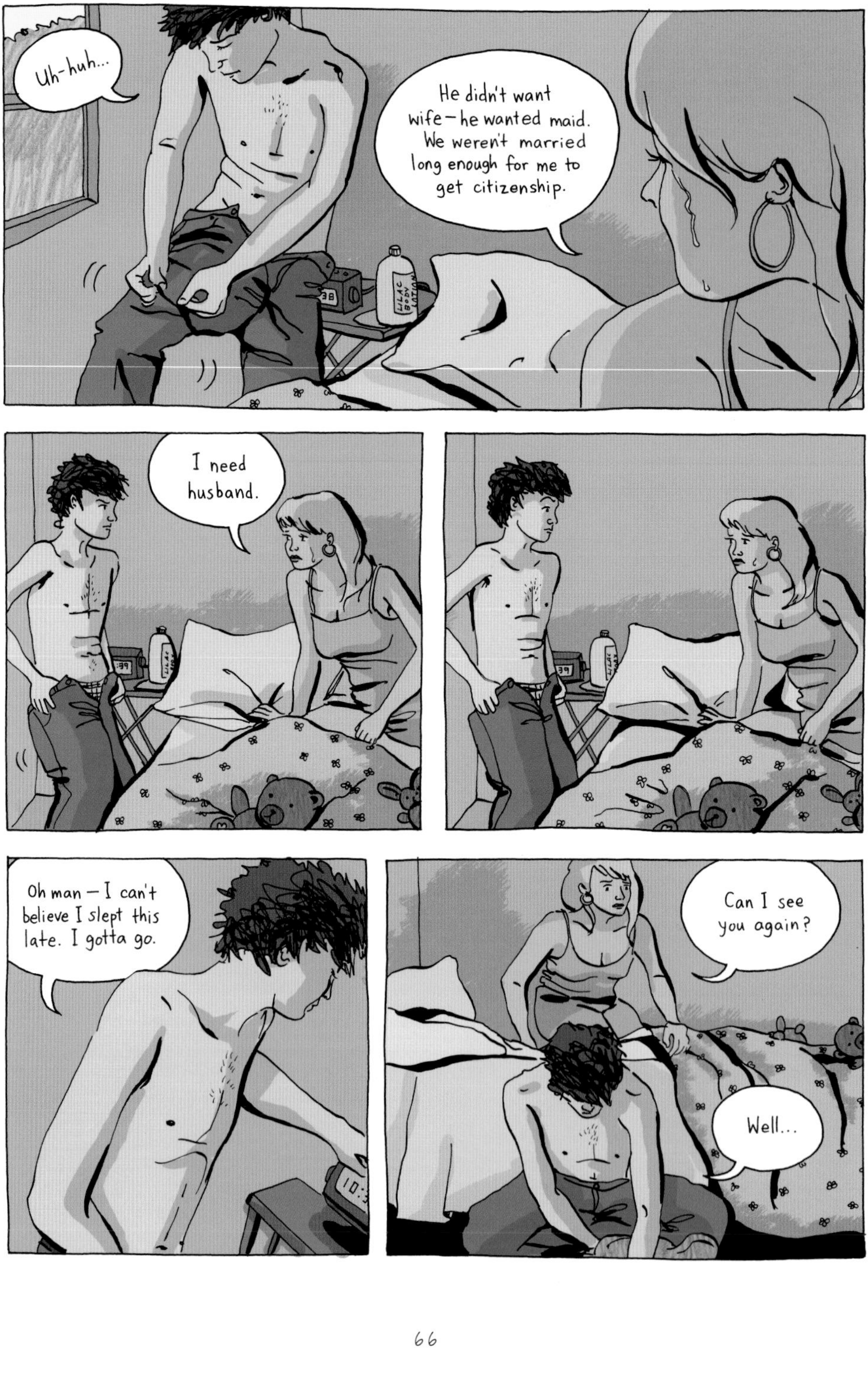
Uh-huh...
He didn't want wife—he wanted maid. We weren't married long enough for me to get citizenship.
I need husband.
Oh man—I can't believe I slept this late. I gotta go.
Can I see you again?
Well...

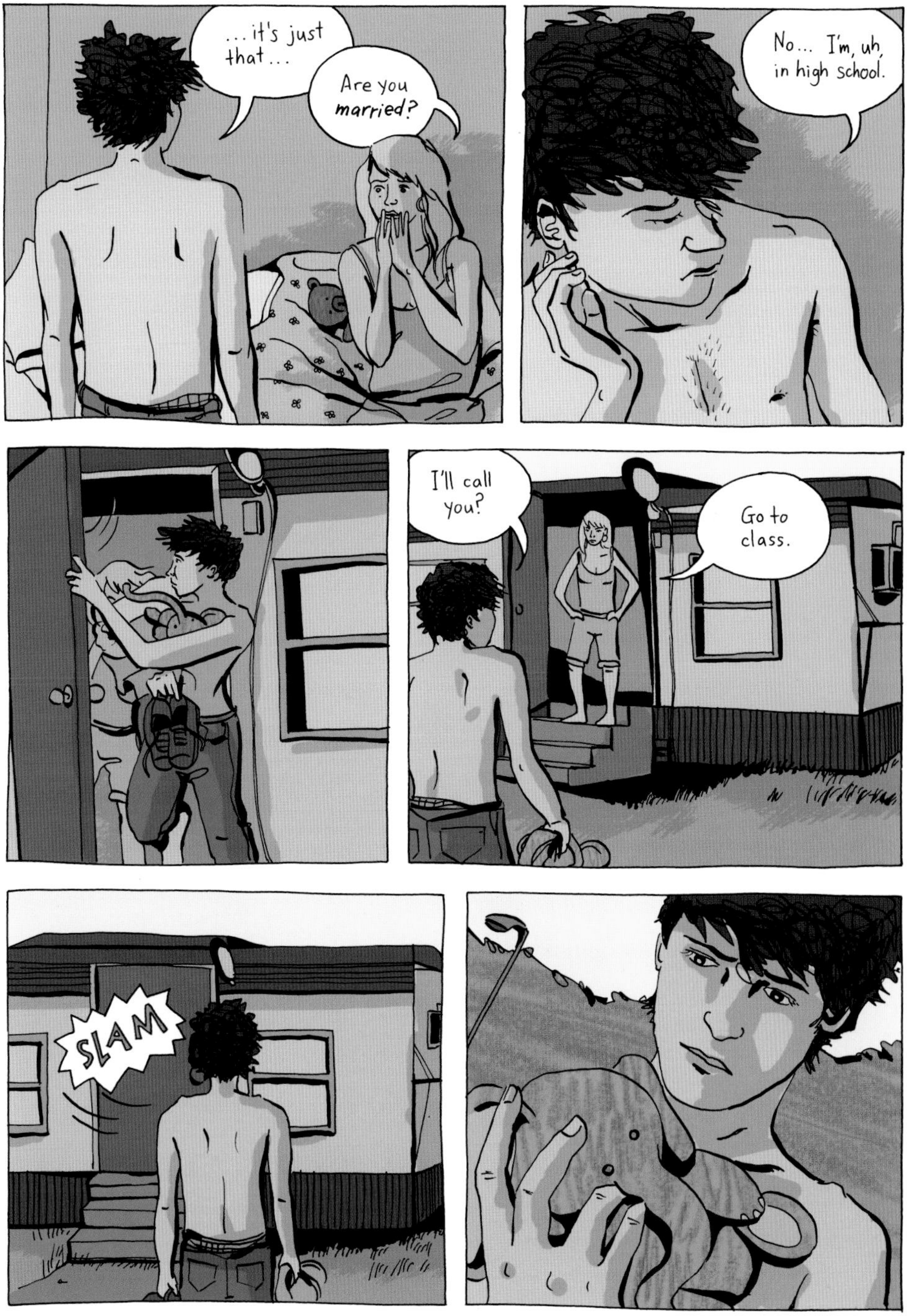

... it's just that ...
Are you married?
No... I'm, uh, in high school.
I'll call you?
Go to class.
SLAM

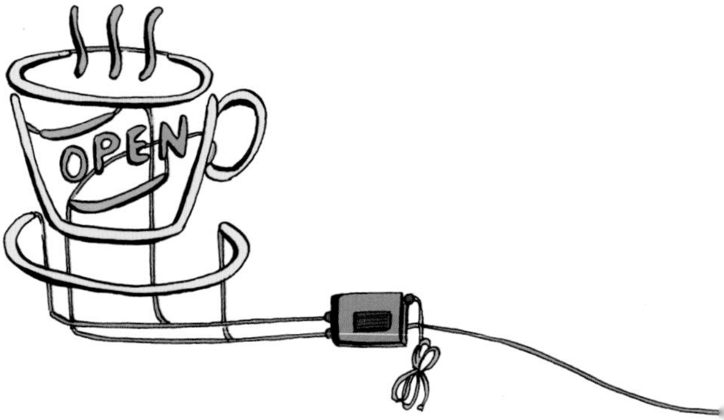
OPEN

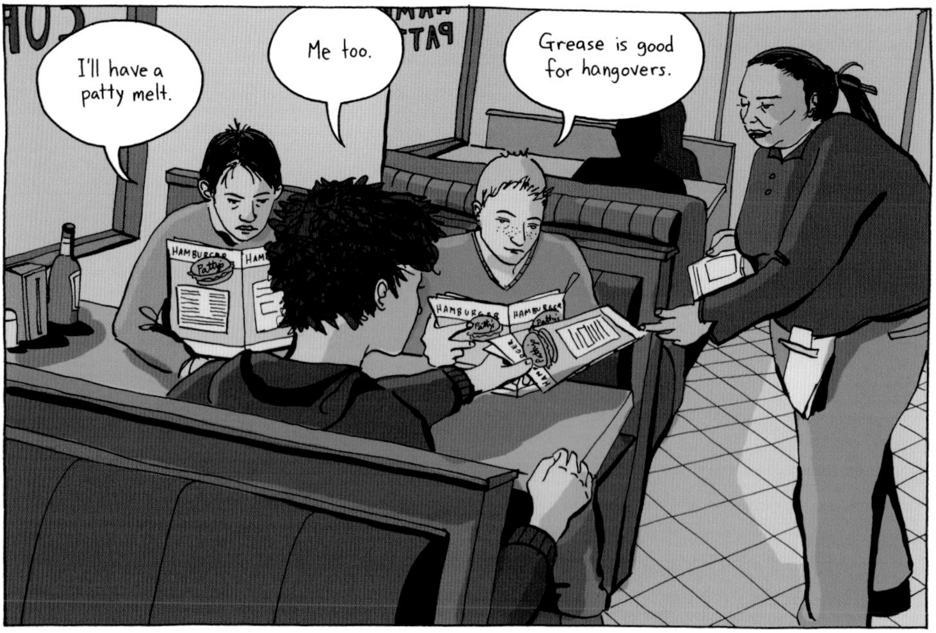
I'll have a patty melt.
Me too.
Grease is good for hangovers.

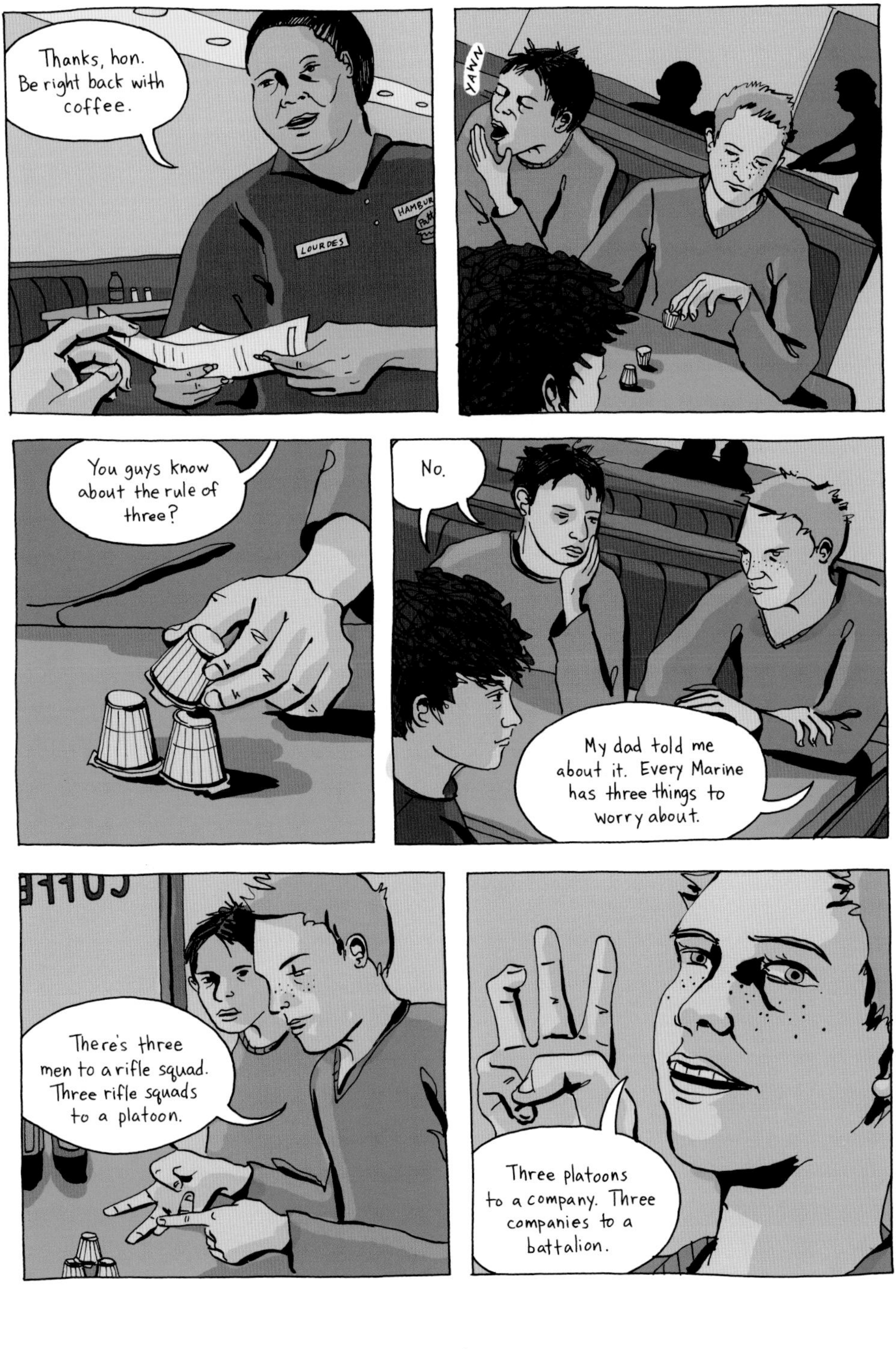
Thanks, hon. Be right back with coffee.
LOURDES
YAWN
You guys know about the rule of three?
No.
My dad told me about it. Every Marine has three things to worry about.
There's three men to a rifle squad. Three rifle squads to a platoon.
Three platoons to a company. Three companies to a battalion.

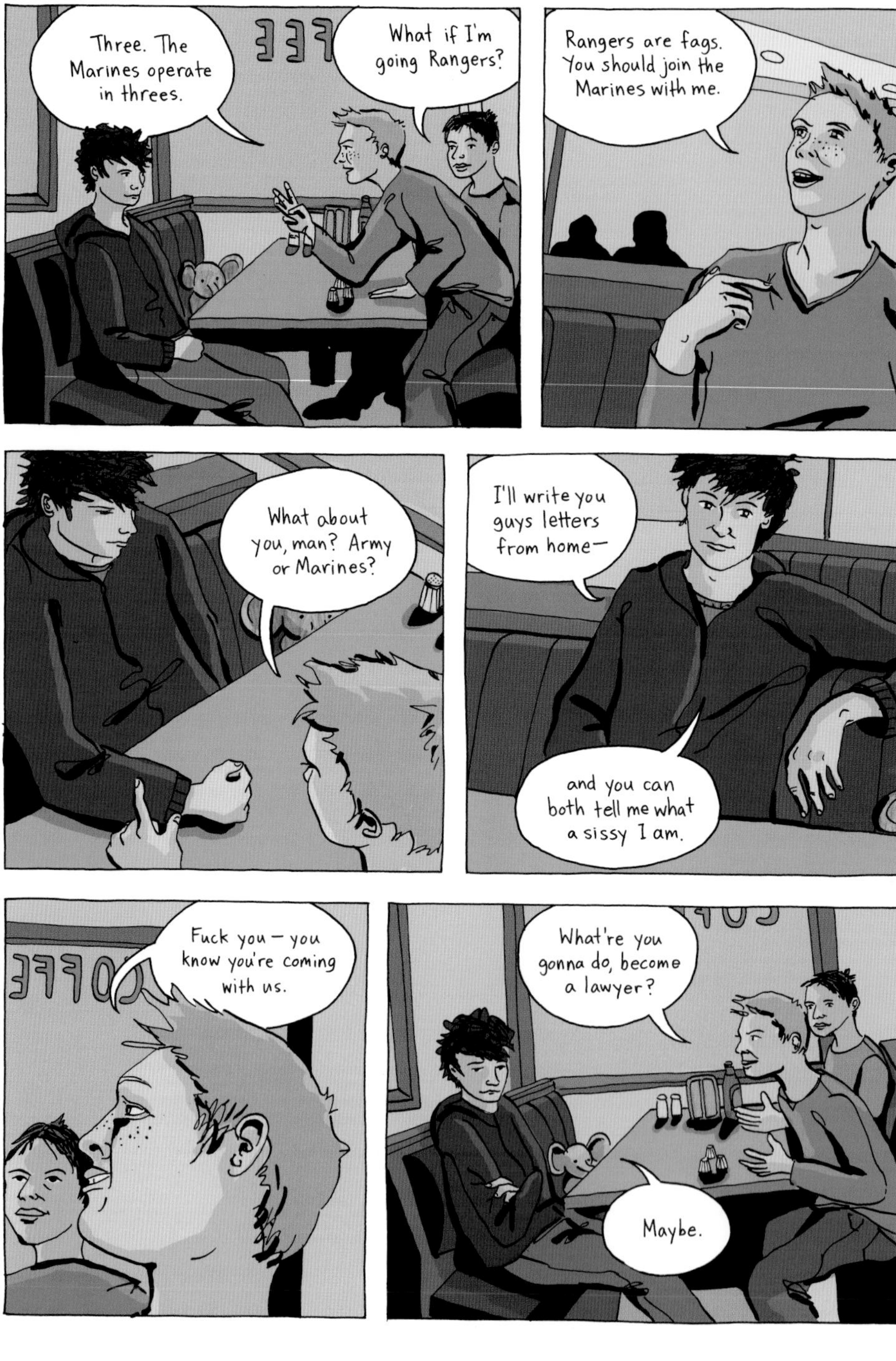
Three. The Marines operate in threes.
What if I'm going Rangers?
Rangers are fags. You should join the Marines with me.
What about you, man? Army or Marines?
I'll write you guys letters from home—
and you can both tell me what a sissy I am.
Fuck you — you know you're coming with us.
What're you gonna do, become a lawyer?
Maybe.

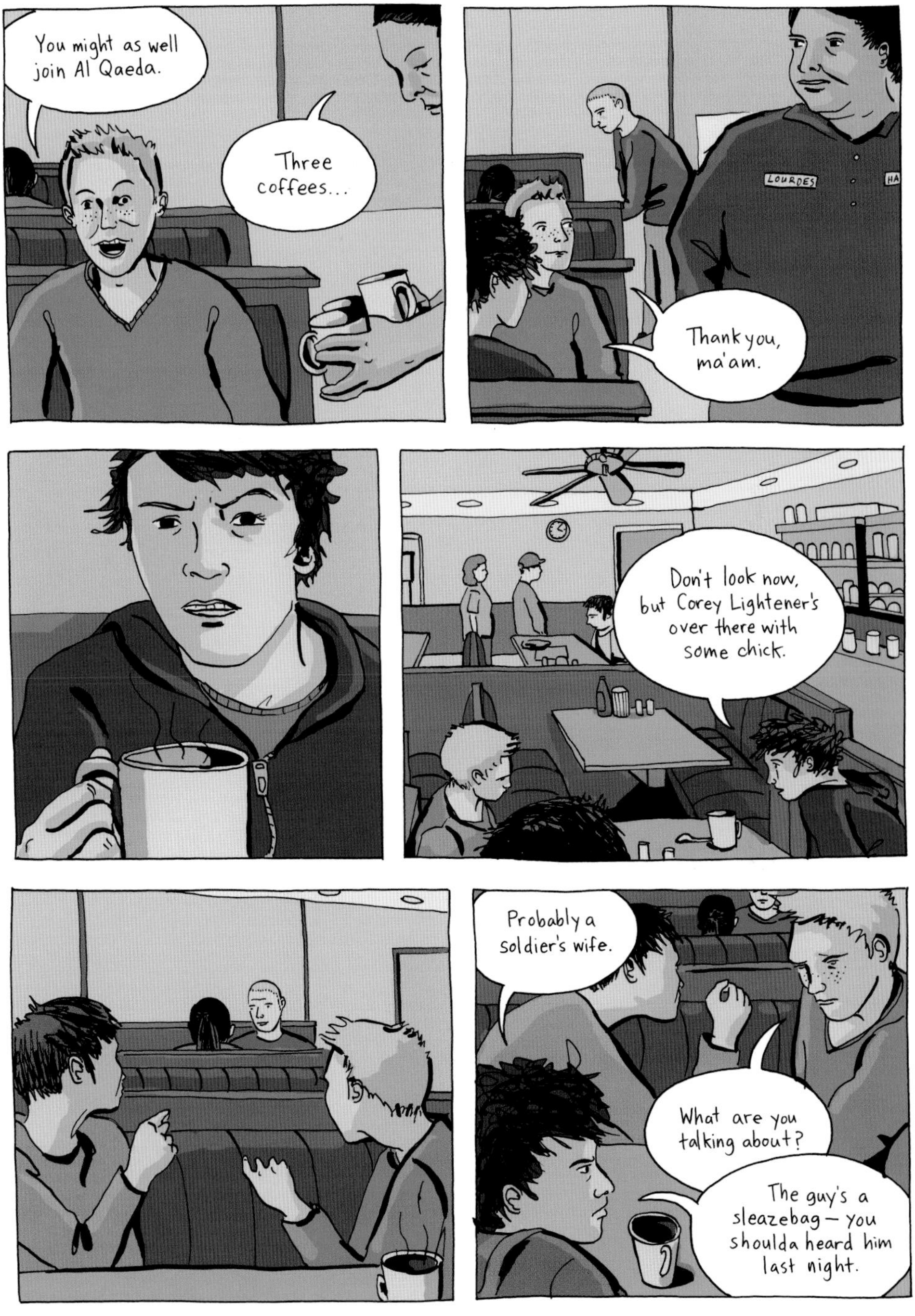
You might as well join Al Qaeda.
Three coffees...
LOURDES
HA
Thank you, ma'am.
Don't look now, but Corey Lightener's over there with some chick.
Probably a soldier's wife.
What are you talking about?
The guy's a sleazebag — you shoulda heard him last night.

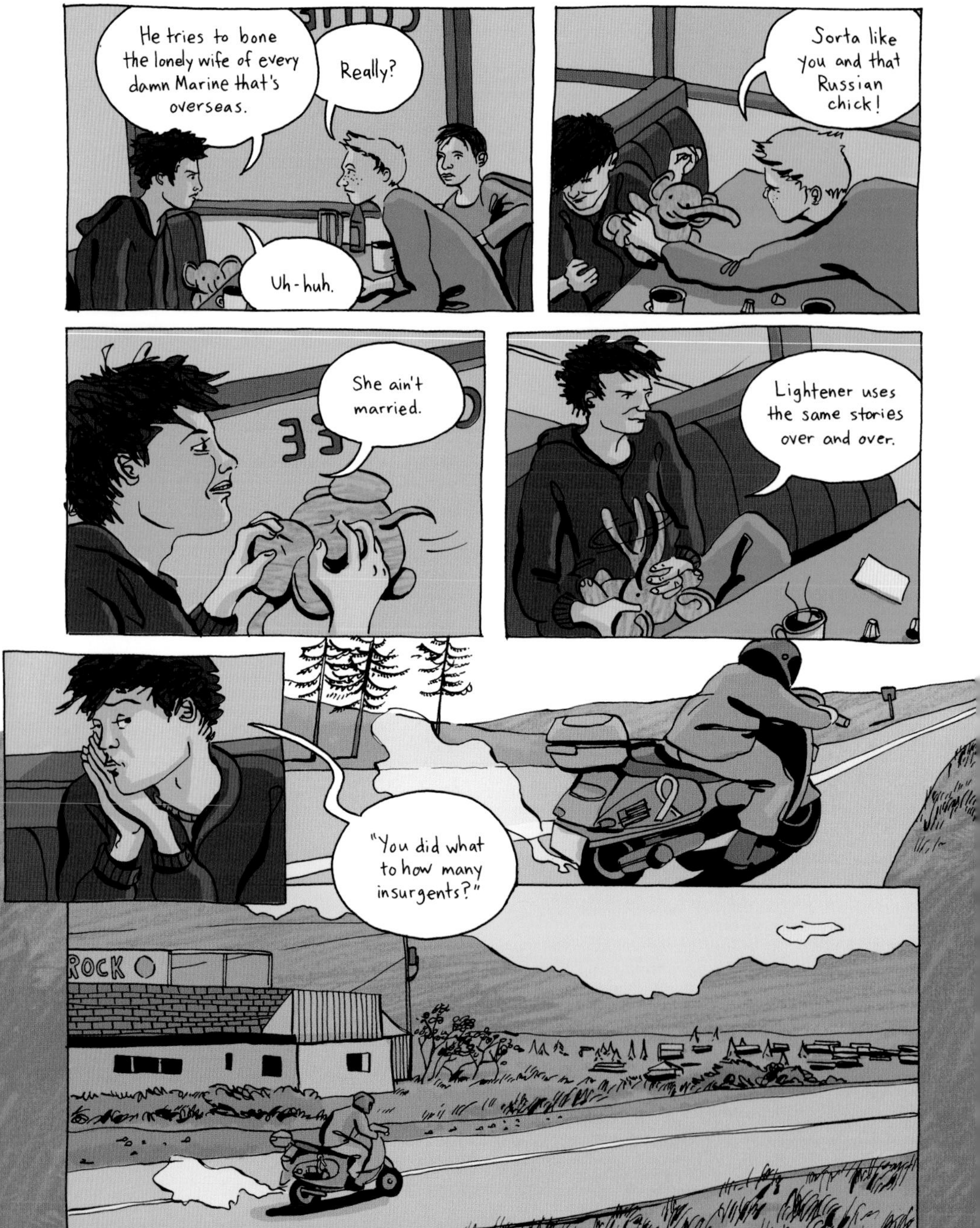
He tries to bone the lonely wife of every damn Marine that's overseas.
Really?
Uh-huh.
Sorta like you and that Russian chick!
She ain't married.
Lightener uses the same stories over and over.
"You did what to how many insurgents?"
ROCK

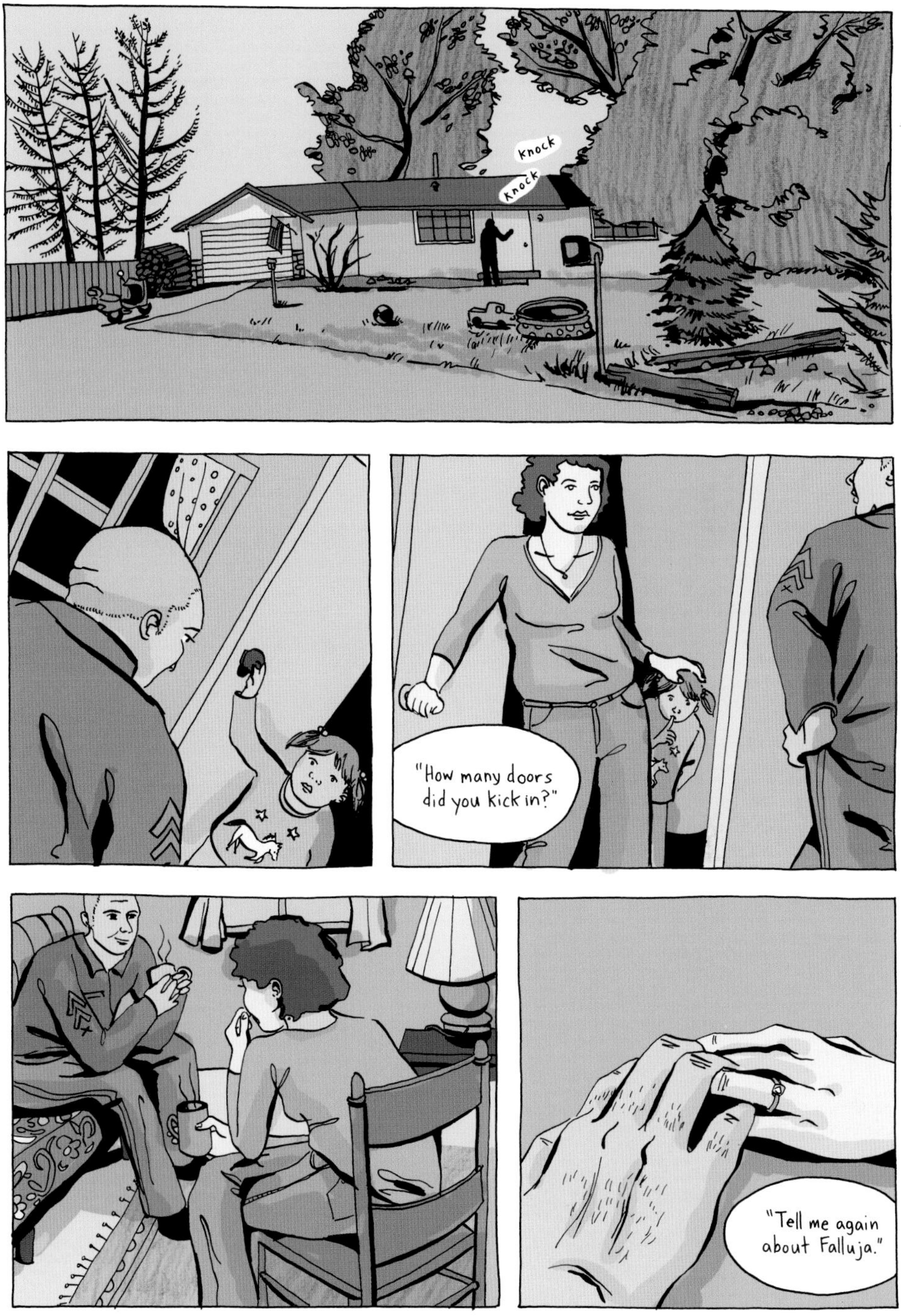
knock
knock
"How many doors did you kick in?"
"Tell me again about Falluja."

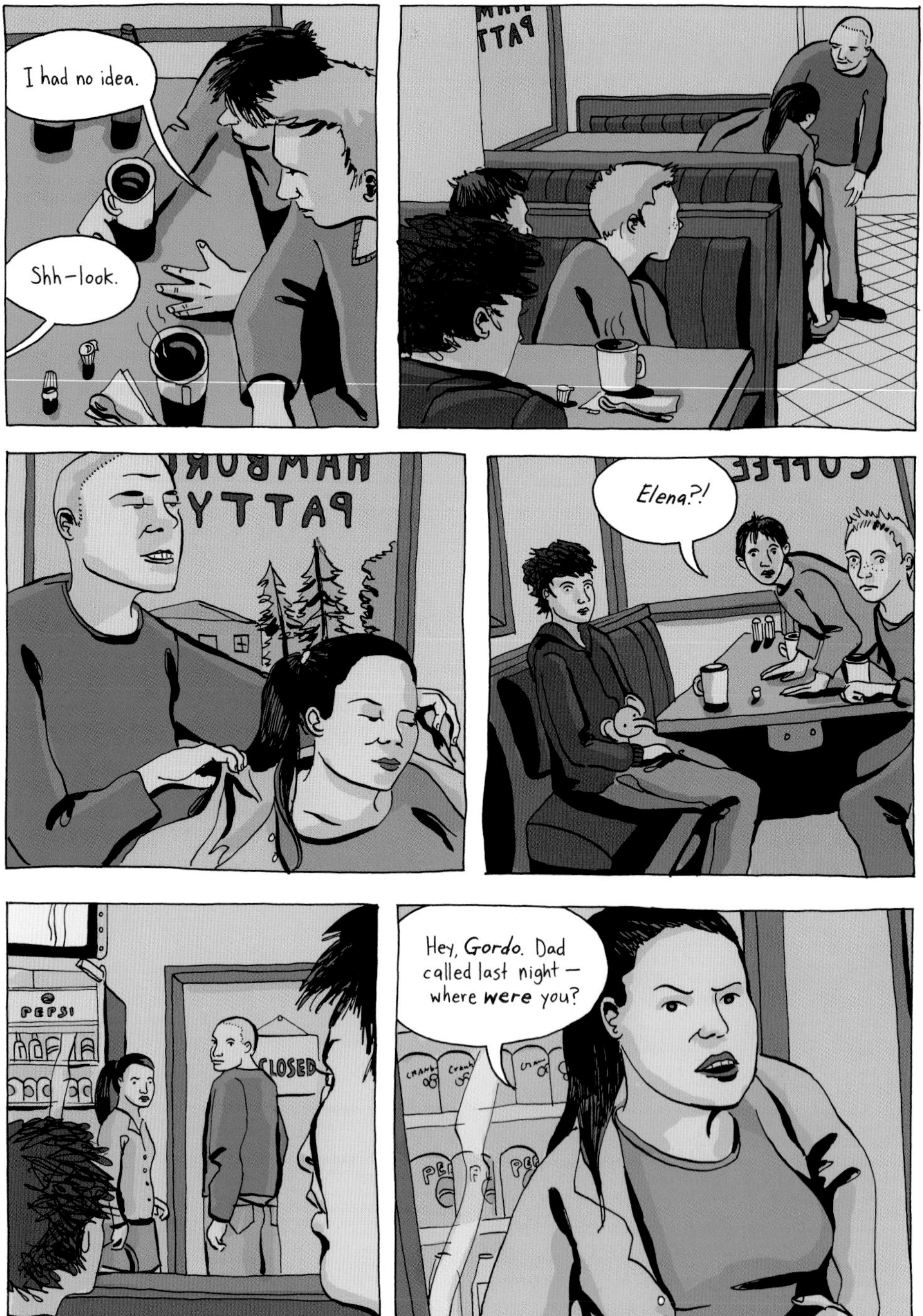
I had no idea.
Shh—look.
Elena?!
PEPSI
CLOSED
Hey, Gordo. Dad called last night— where were you?

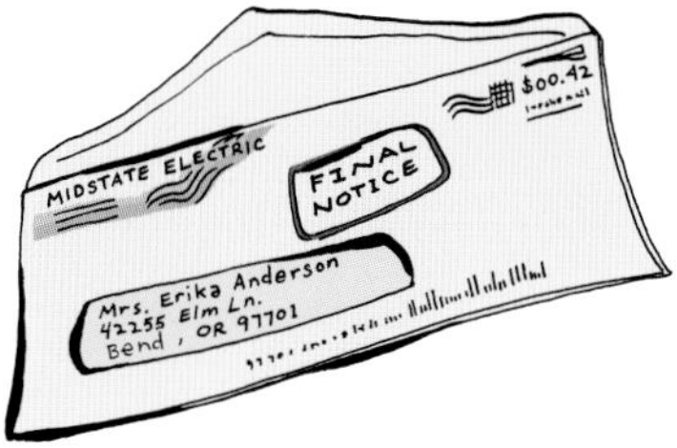
MIDSTATE ELECTRIC
FINAL NOTICE
$00.42
Mrs. Erika Anderson
42255 Elm Ln.
Bend , OR 97701

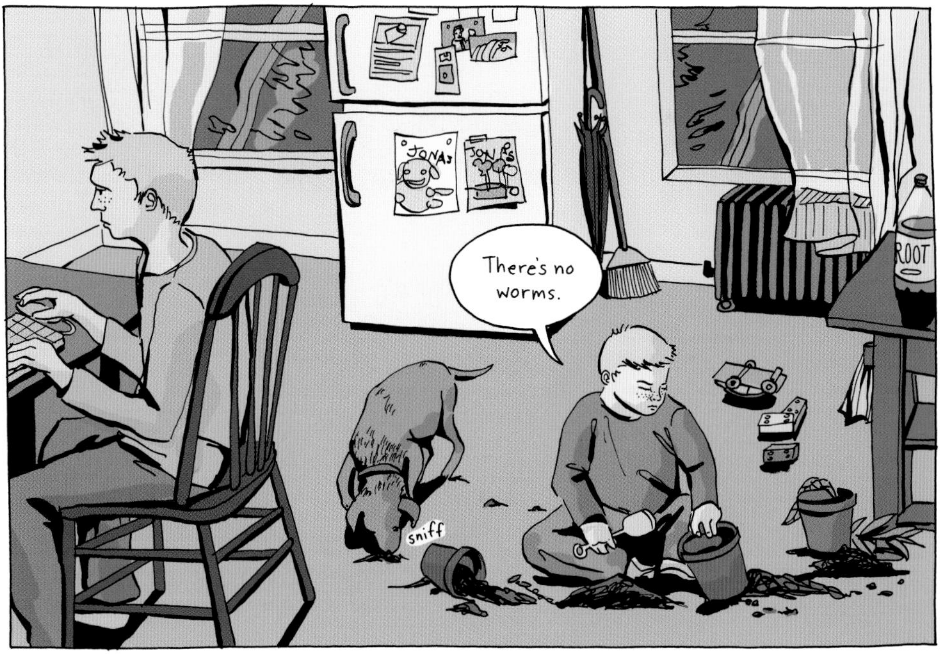
There's no worms.
sniff
ROOT

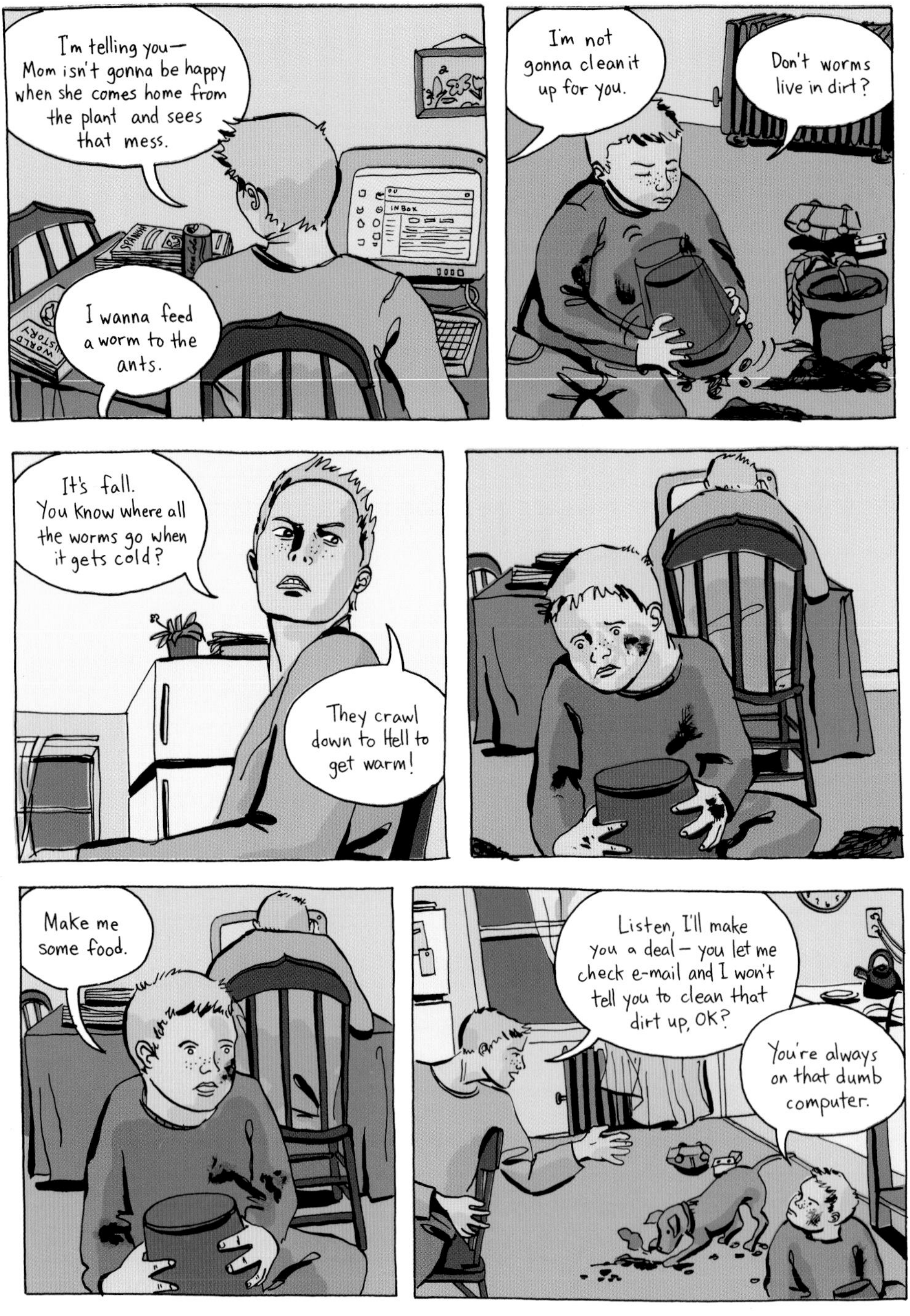
I'm telling you— Mom isn't gonna be happy when she comes home from the plant and sees that mess.
I wanna feed a worm to the ants.
I'm not gonna clean it up for you.
Don't worms live in dirt?
It's fall. You know where all the worms go when it gets cold?
They crawl down to Hell to get warm!
Make me some food.
Listen, I'll make you a deal — you let me check e-mail and I won't tell you to clean that dirt up, OK?
You're always on that dumb computer.

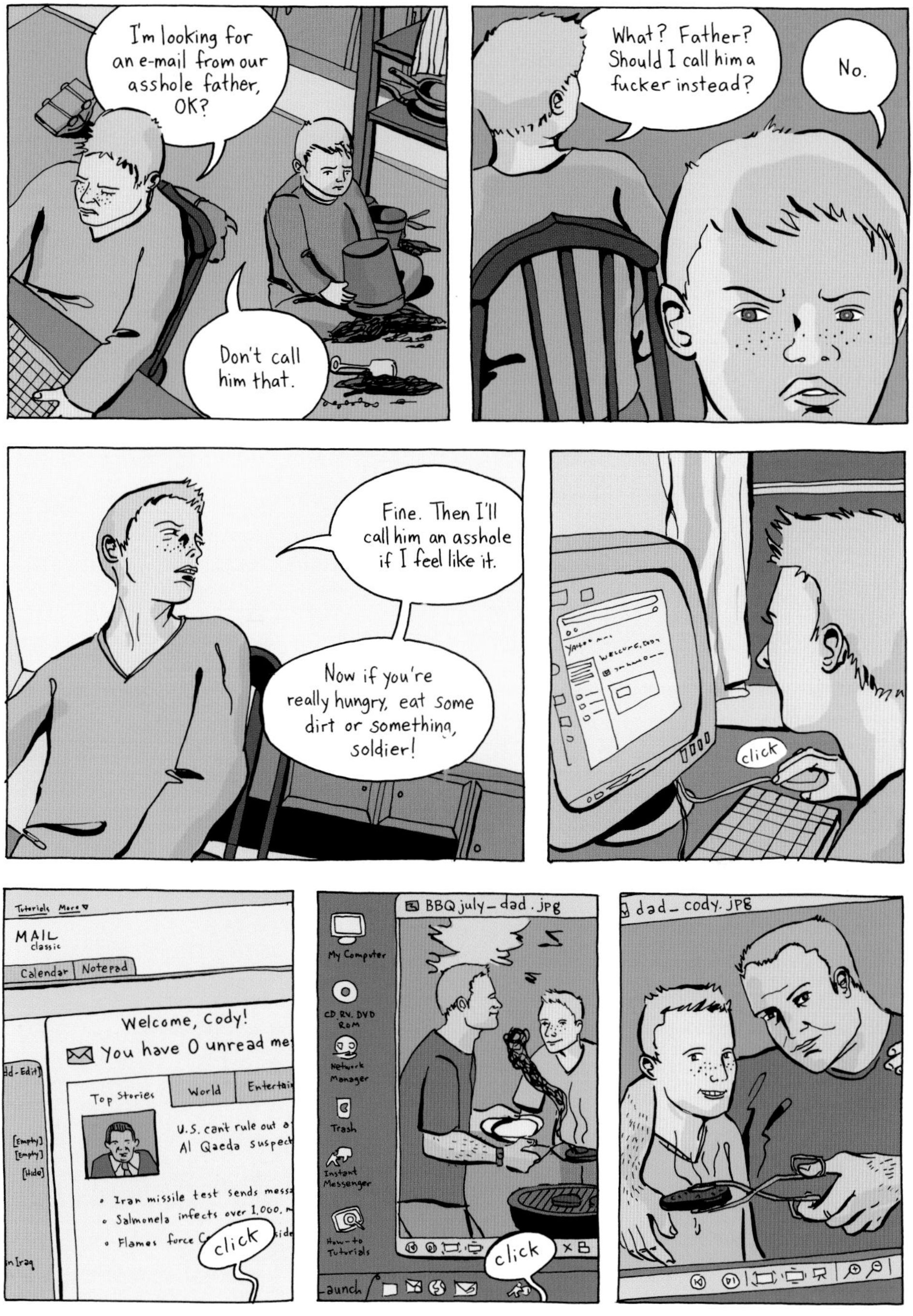
I'm looking for an e-mail from our asshole father, OK?
Don't call him that.
What? Father? Should I call him a fucker instead?
No.
Fine. Then I'll call him an asshole if I feel like it.
Now if you're really hungry, eat some dirt or something, soldier!
click
Tutorials More
MAIL classic
Calendar
Notepad
Welcome, Cody!
You have 0 unread me
Top Stories
World
Entertai
U.S. can't rule out a
Al Qaeda suspect
[Empty]
[Empty]
[Hide]
Iran missile test sends mess
Salmonela infects over 1,000,
Flames force C
in Iraq
click
BBQ july_dad.jpg
My Computer
CD.RV.DVD ROM
Network Manager
Trash
Instant Messenger
How-to Tutorials
aunch
click
dad_cody.JPG

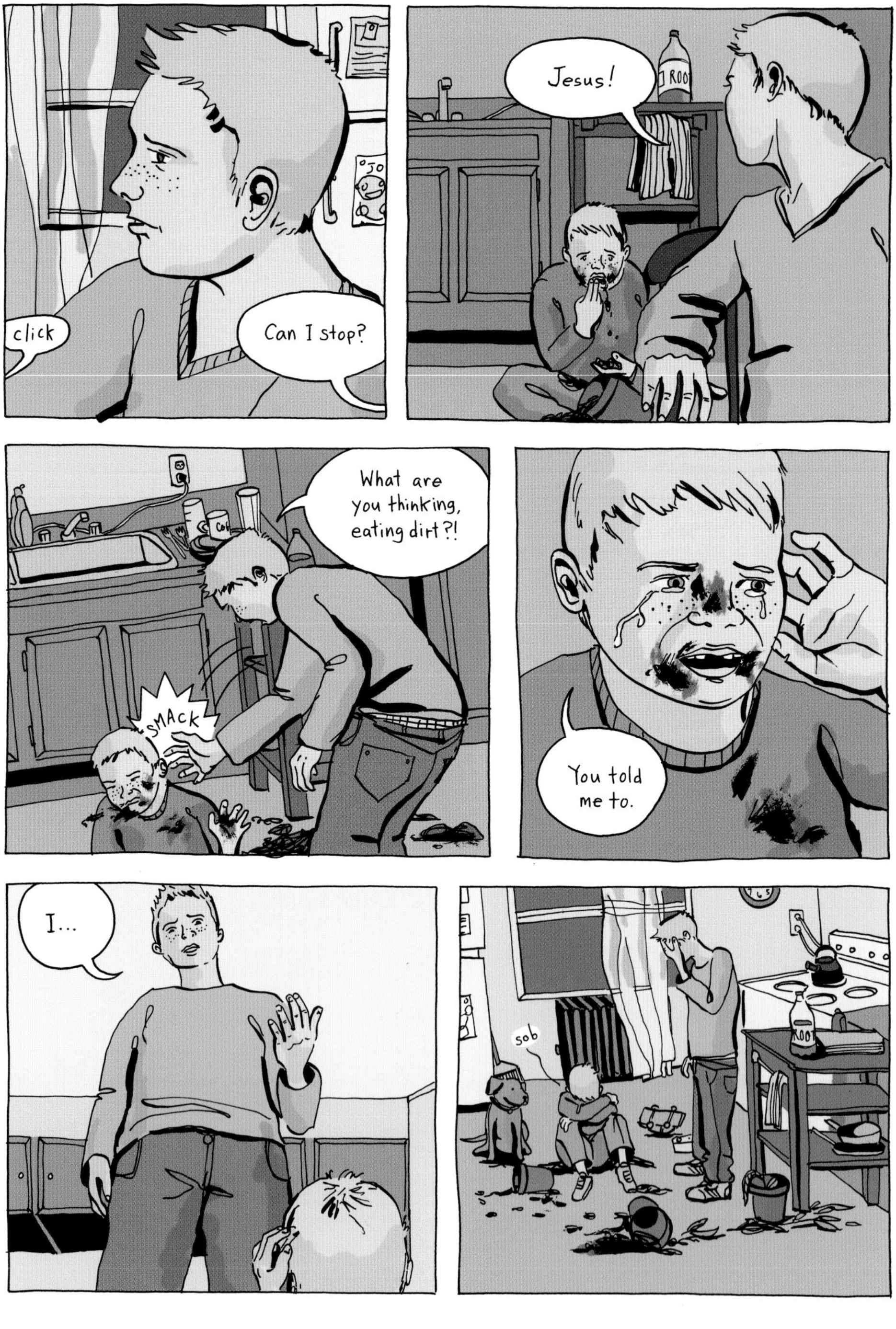
click
Can I stop?
Jesus!
ROOT
What are you thinking, eating dirt?!
SMACK
You told me to.
I...
sob
ROOT

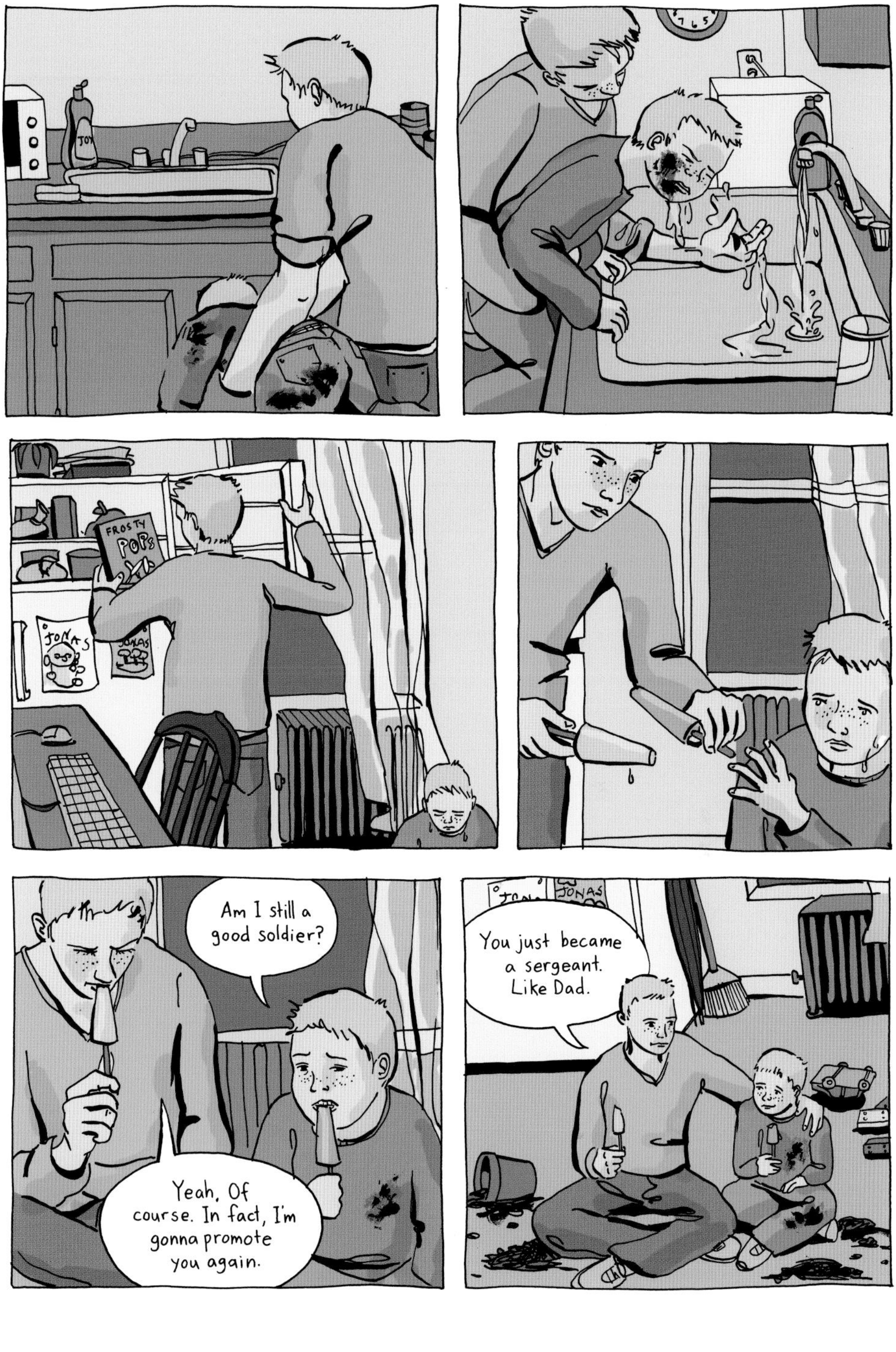
FROSTY POPS
JONAS
JONAS
Am I still a good soldier?
Yeah, Of course. In fact, I'm gonna promote you again.
JONAS
JONAS
You just became a sergeant. Like Dad.

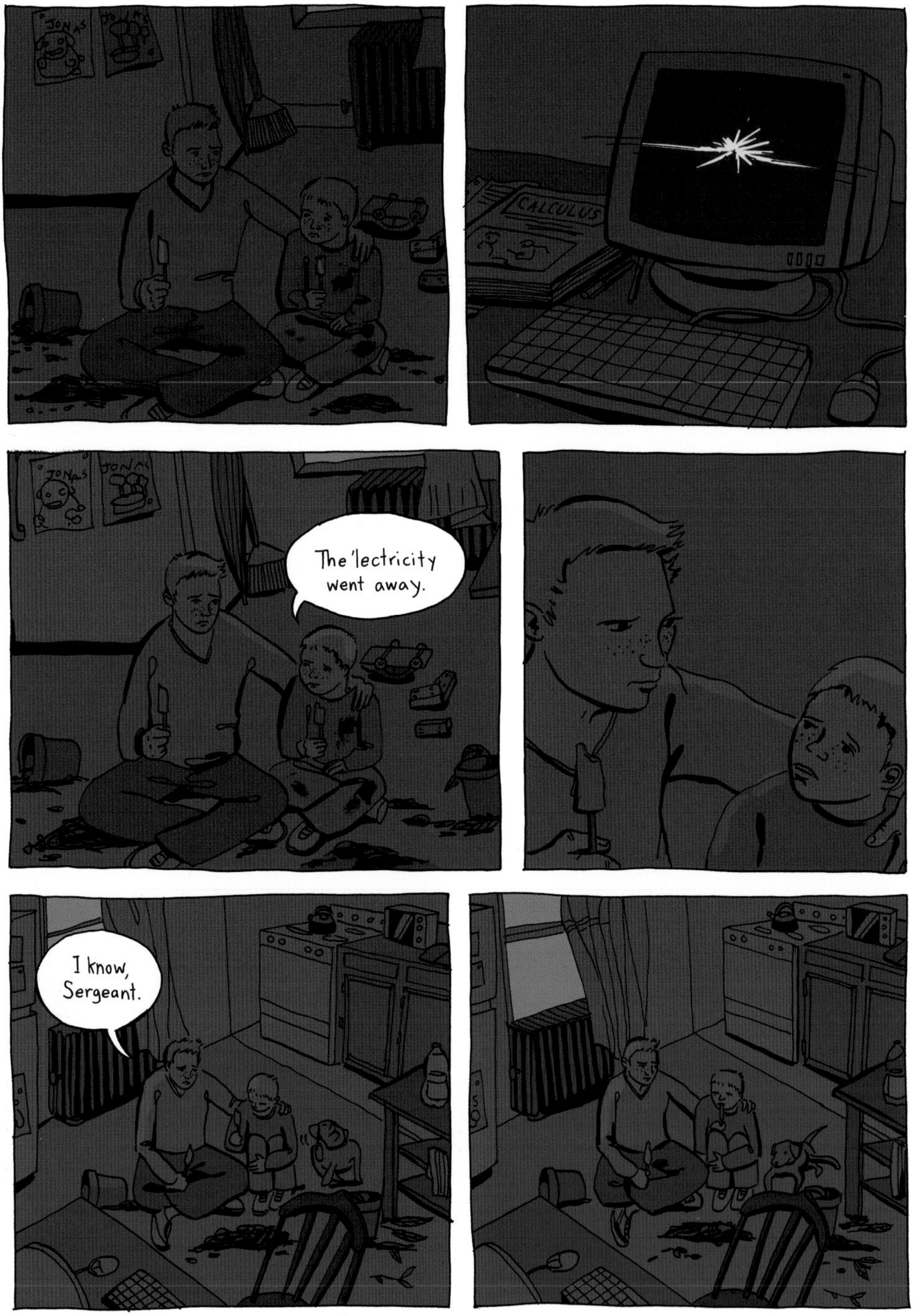
The 'lectricity went away.
I know, Sergeant.

SEMPER
FIDELIS

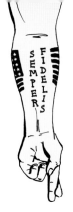

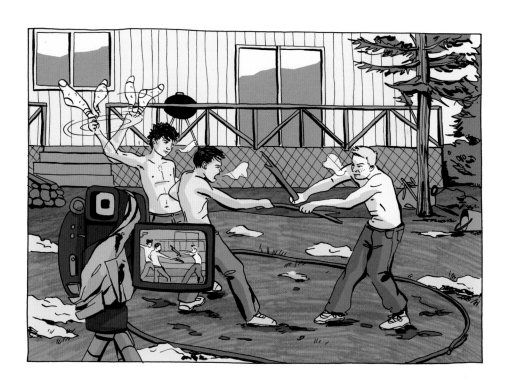

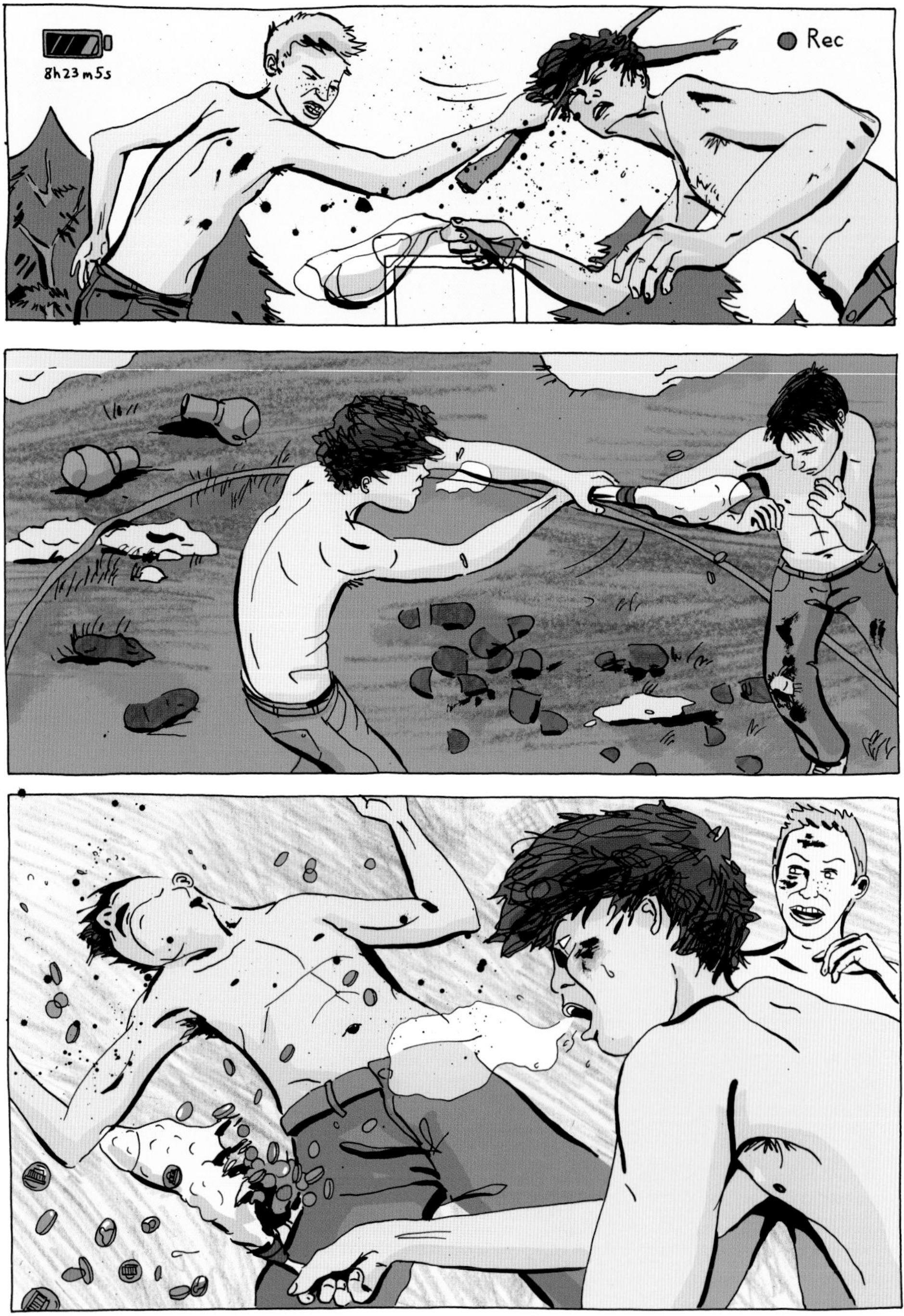
8h23m5s
Rec

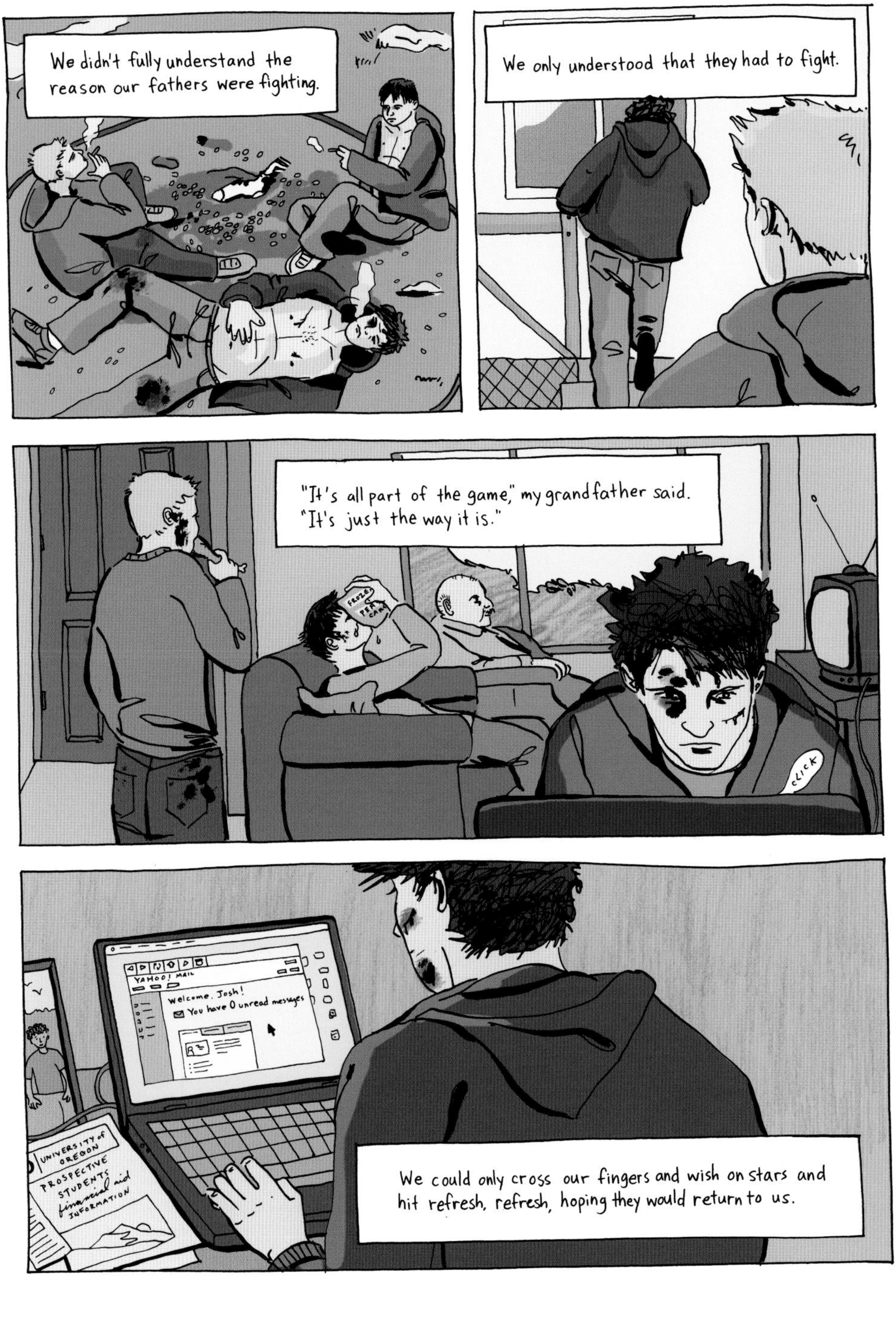
We didn't fully understand the reason our fathers were fighting.
We only understood that they had to fight.
"It's all part of the game," my grandfather said. "It's just the way it is."
CLICK
YAHOO! MAIL
Welcome, Josh!
You have 0 unread messages
UNIVERSITY of OREGON
PROSPECTIVE STUDENTS
financial aid INFORMATION
We could only cross our fingers and wish on stars and hit refresh, refresh, hoping they would return to us.

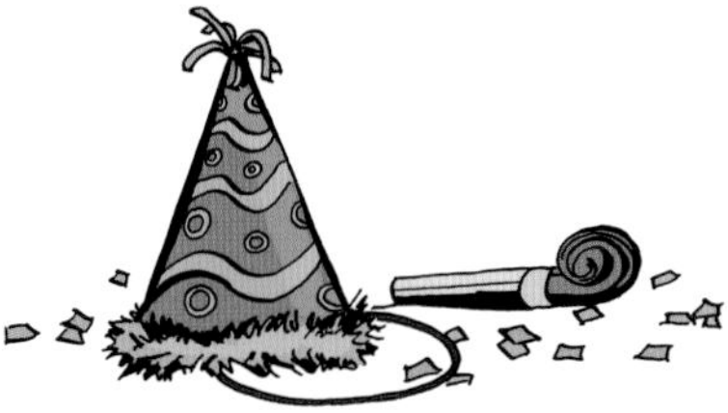

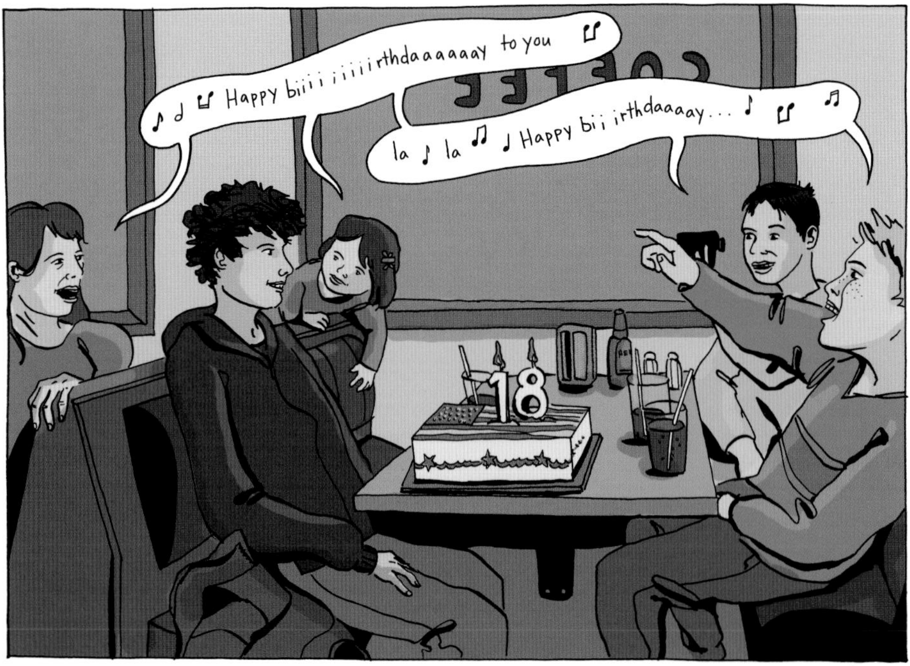
Happy biiii iiiiirthdaaaaaay to you
la la Happy bii irthdaaaay...

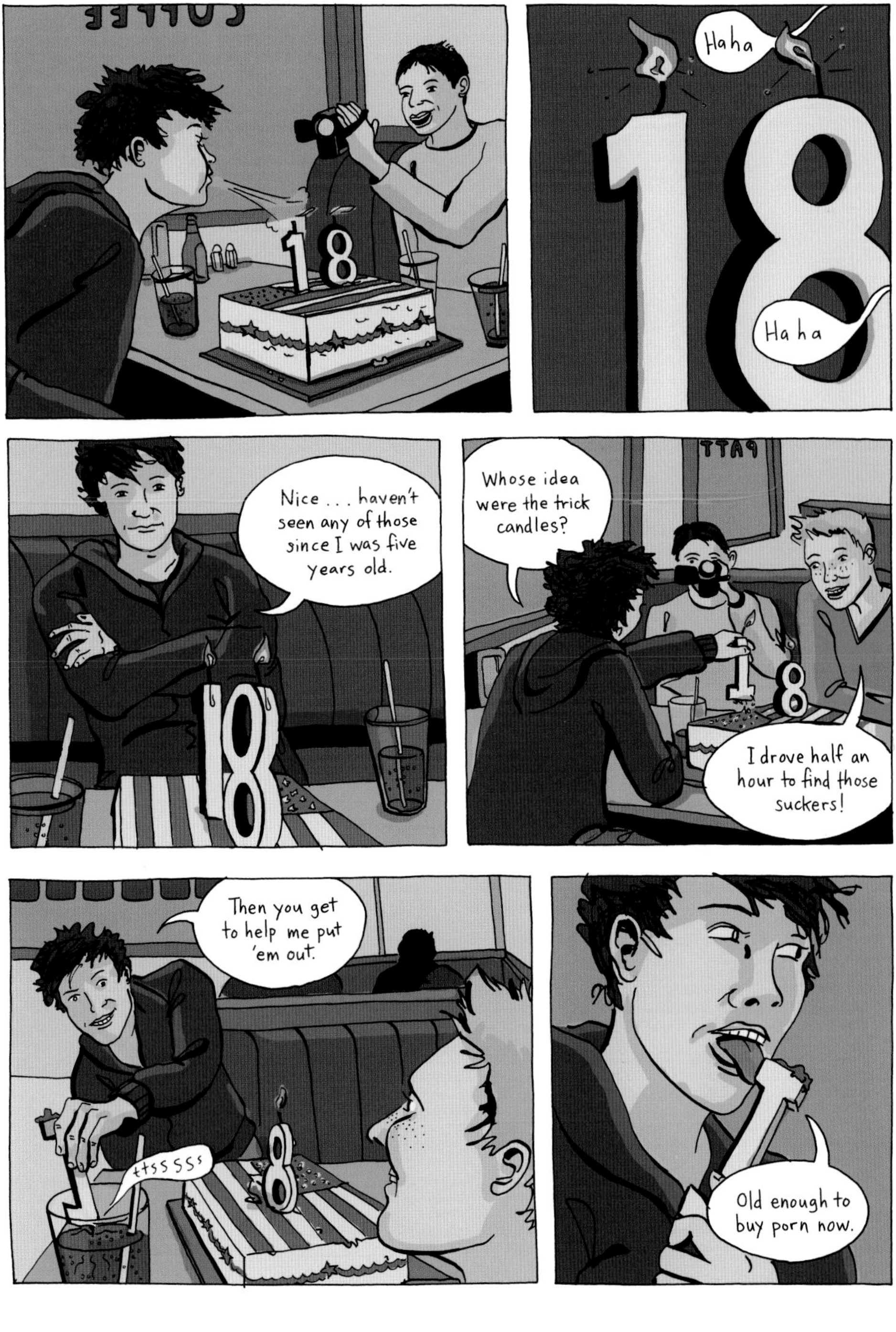

Haha
Ha ha
Nice . . . haven't seen any of those since I was five years old.
Whose idea were the trick candles?
I drove half an hour to find those suckers!
Then you get to help me put 'em out.
ttsssss
Old enough to buy porn now.

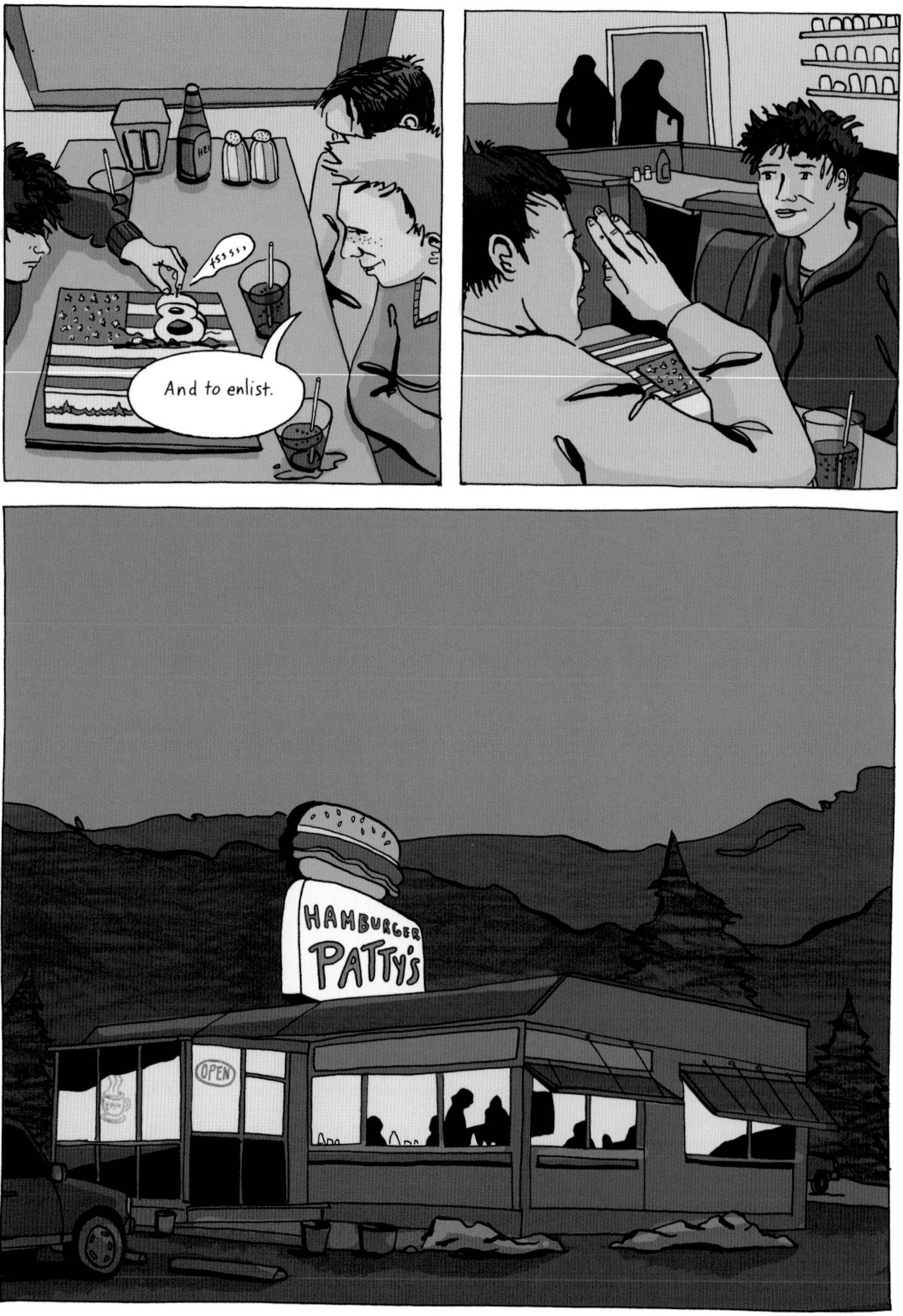
tsssss
And to enlist.
HAMBURGER
PATTY'S
OPEN

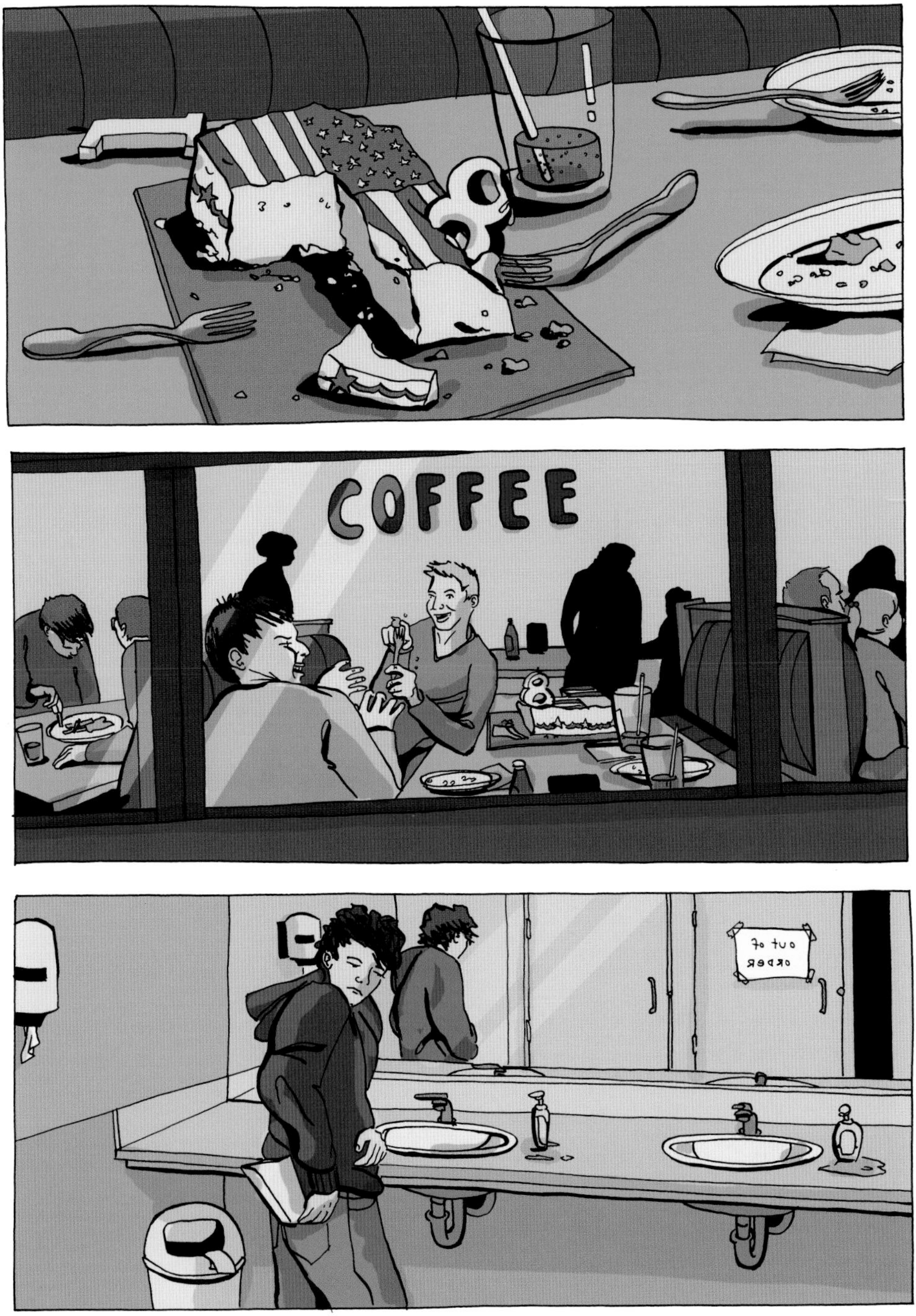
COFFEE
out of
ORDER

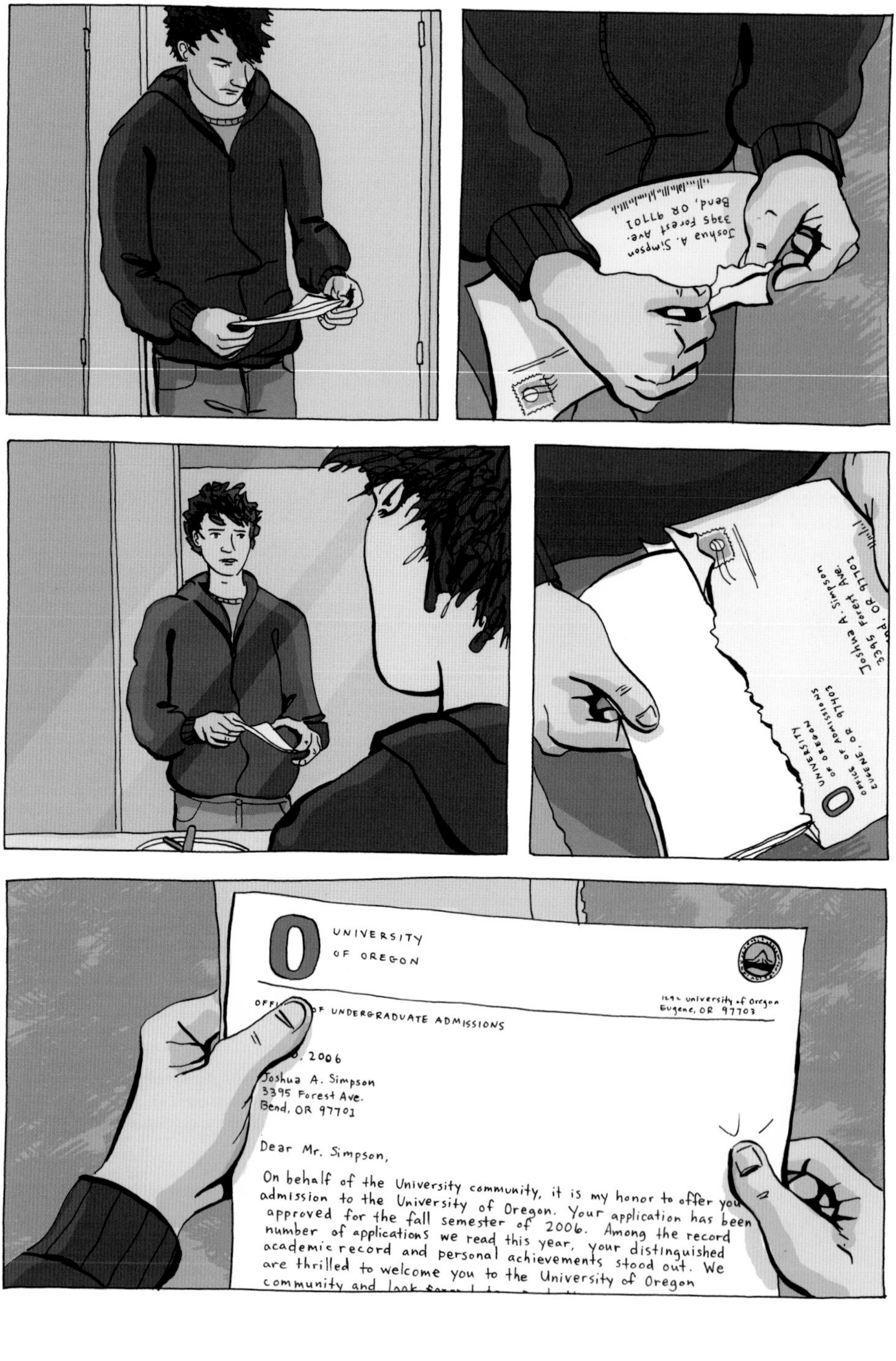
Joshua A. Simpson
3395 Forest Ave.
Bend, OR 97701
UNIVERSITY
OF OREGON
OFFICE OF ADMISSIONS
EUGENE, OR 97403
Joshua A. Simpson
3395 Forest Ave.
OR 97701
UNIVERSITY
OF OREGON
1292 University of Oregon
Eugene, OR 97703
F UNDERGRADUATE ADMISSIONS
. 2006
Joshua A. Simpson
3395 Forest Ave.
Bend, OR 97701
Dear Mr. Simpson,
On behalf of the University community, it is my honor to offer you admission to the University of Oregon. Your application has been approved for the fall semester of 2006. Among the record number of applications we read this year, your distinguished academic record and personal achievements stood out. We are thrilled to welcome you to the University of Oregon community and look

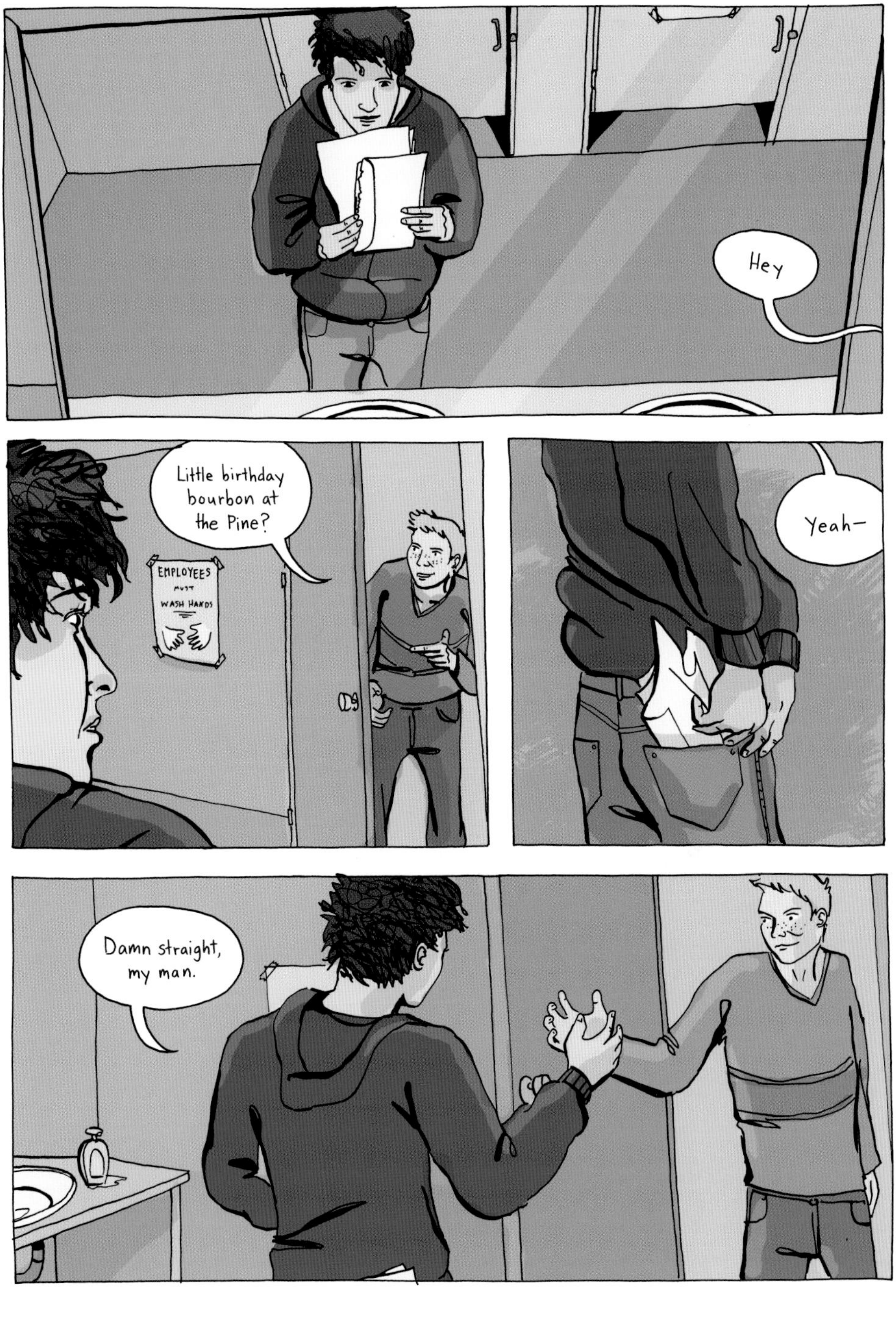
Hey
Little birthday bourbon at the Pine?
EMPLOYEES MUST WASH HANDS
Yeah–
Damn straight, my man.

Everyone has enemies. That's the way of the world.

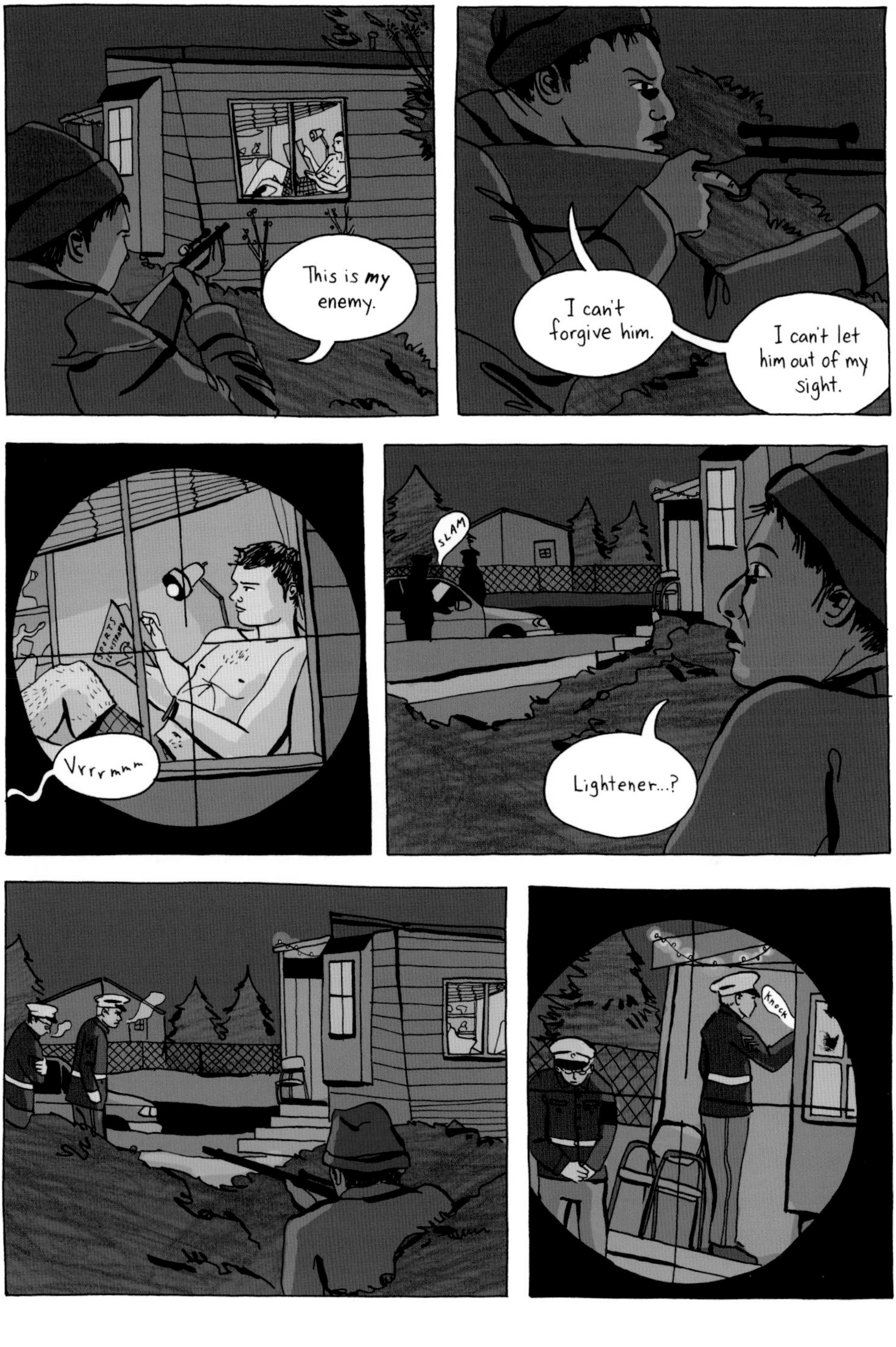
This is **my** enemy.
I can't forgive him.
I can't let him out of my sight.
Vrrrmmm
SLAM
Lightener...?
Knock

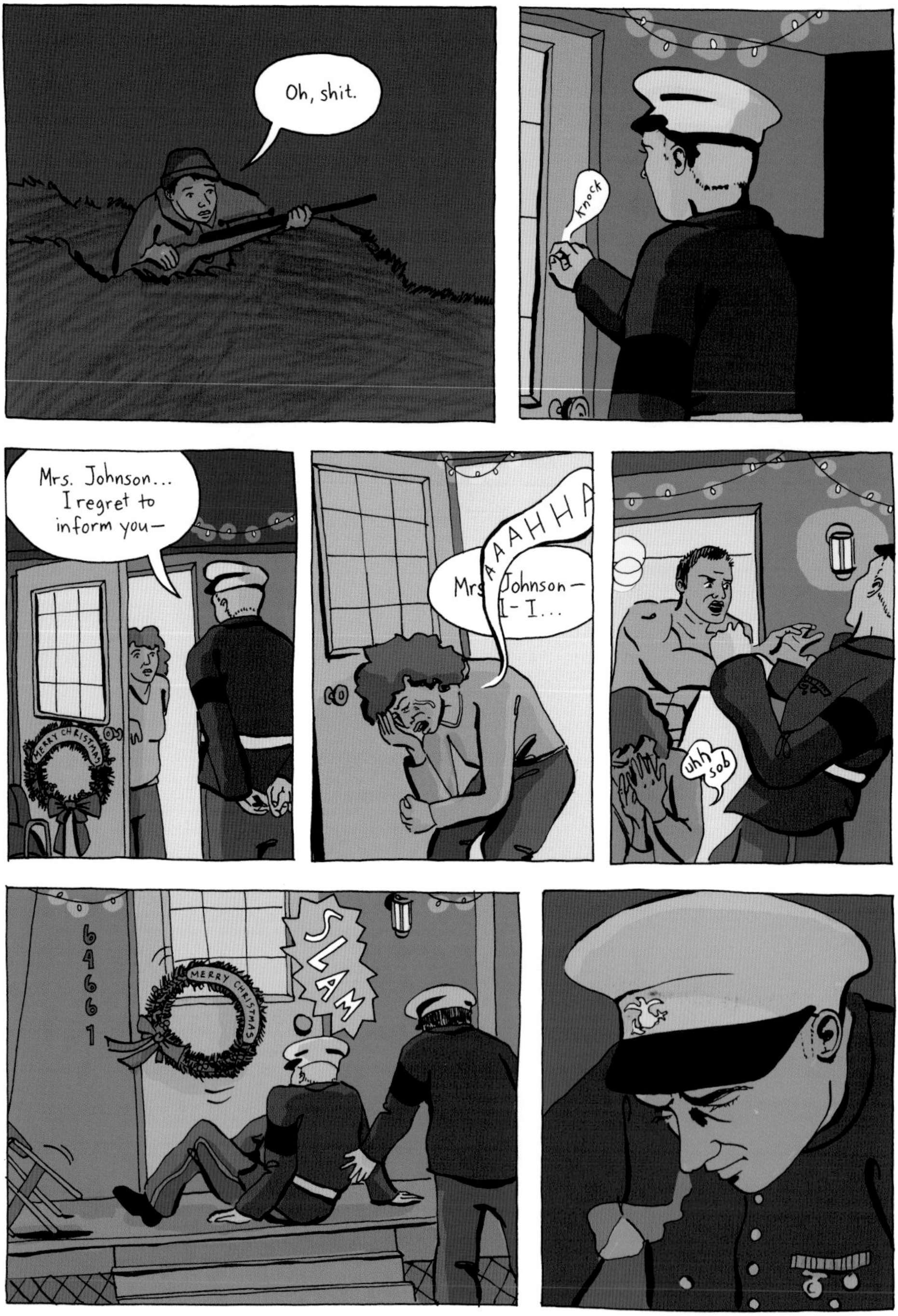
Oh, shit.
knock
Mrs. Johnson...
I regret to
inform you—
AAAHHHA
Mrs. Johnson—
I- I...
uhh
sob
MERRY CHRISTMAS
64661
SLAM

64661
knock
Knock
knock
knock
VRRRMM

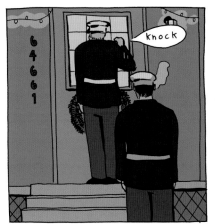

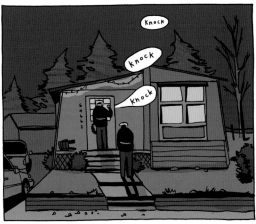

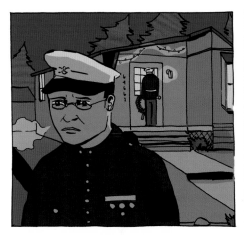

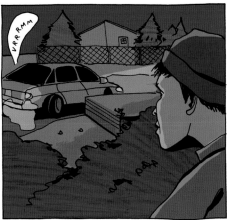

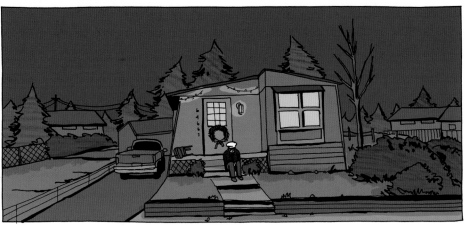

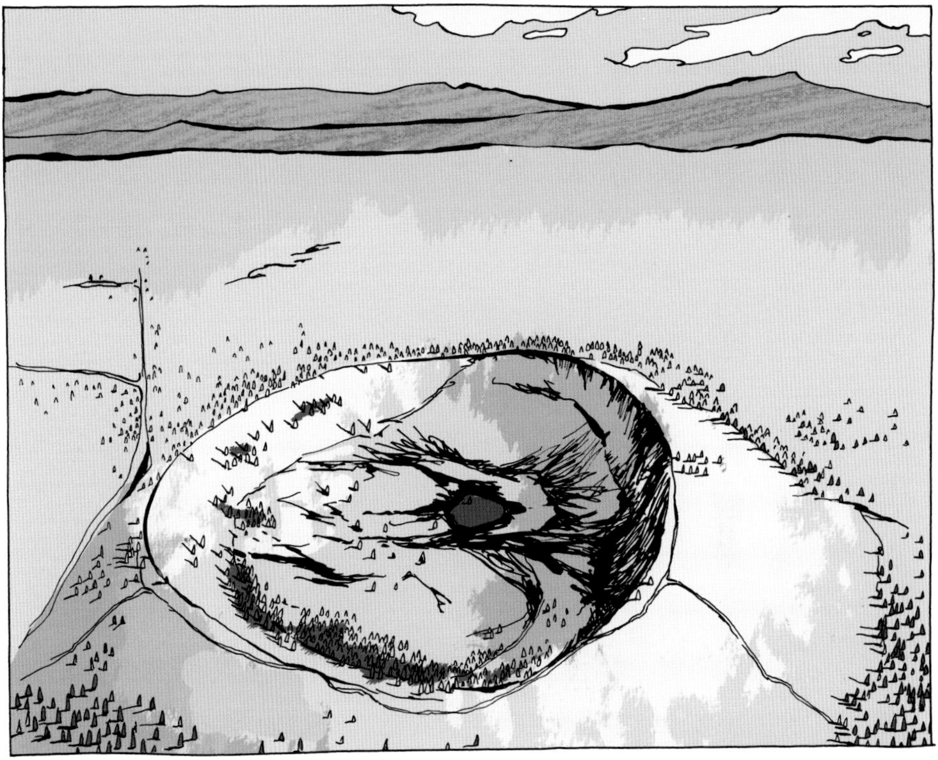

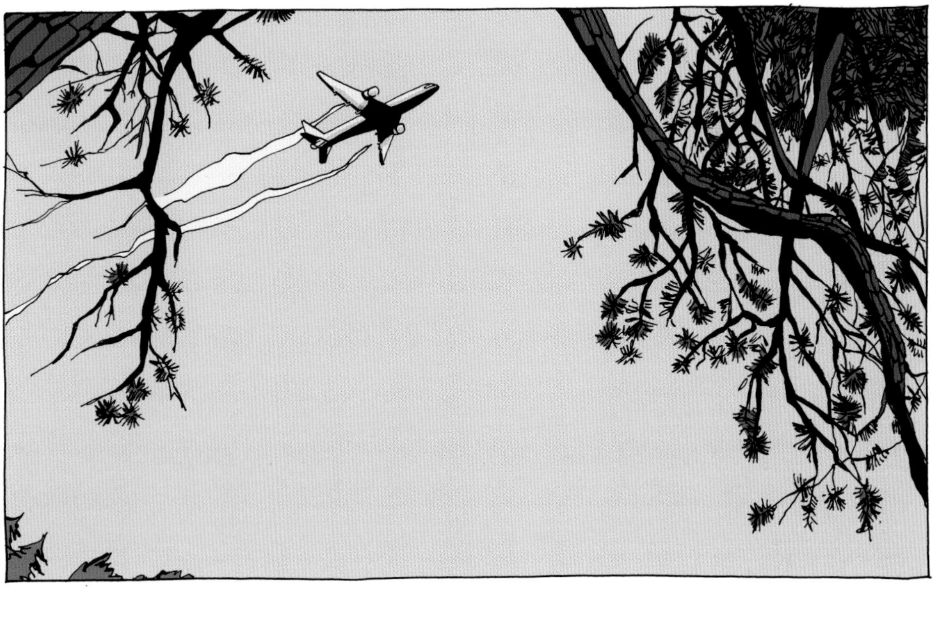

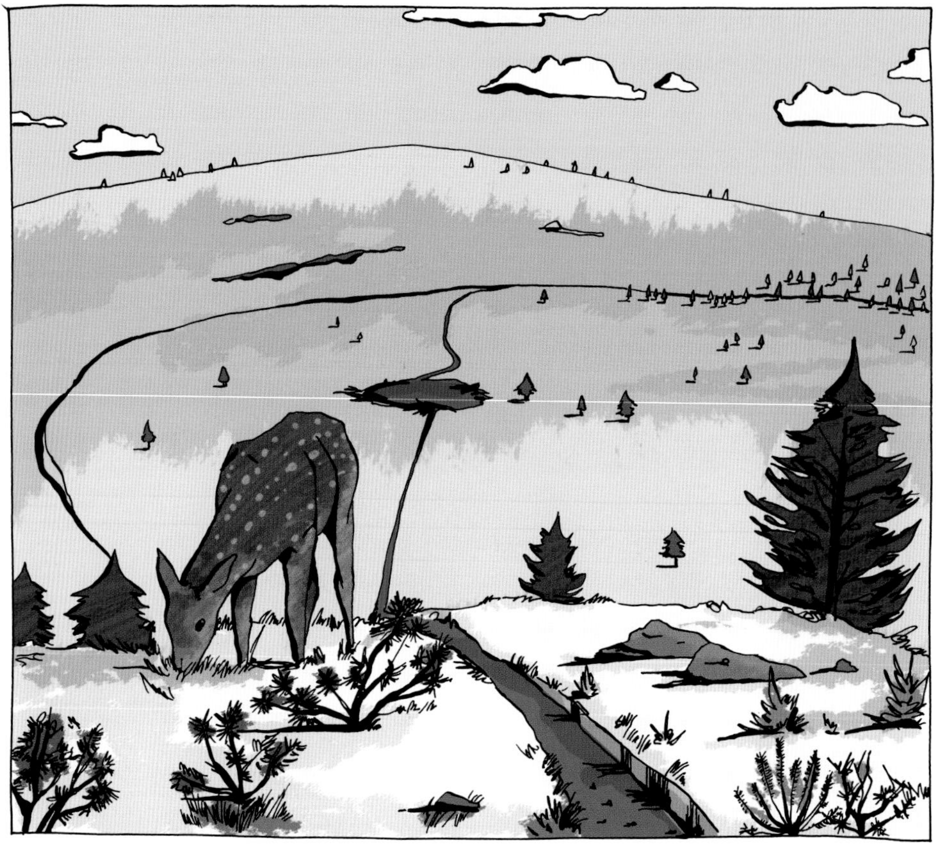

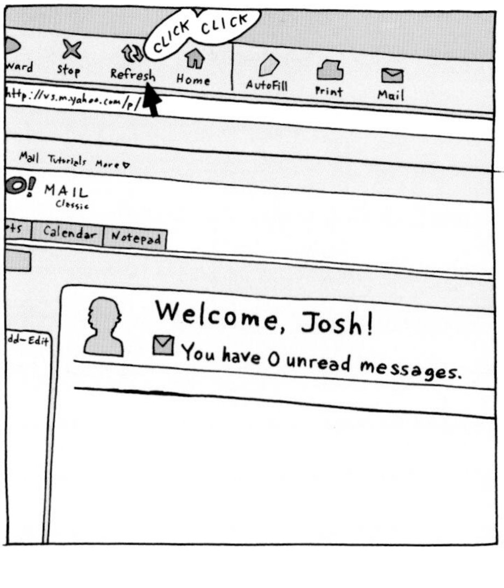
CLICK CLICK
ward
Stop
Refresh
Home
AutoFill
Print
Mail
http://us.m.yahoo.com/p/
Mail Tutorials More
MAIL
Classic
Calendar
Notepad
dd-Edit
Welcome, Josh!
You have 0 unread messages.

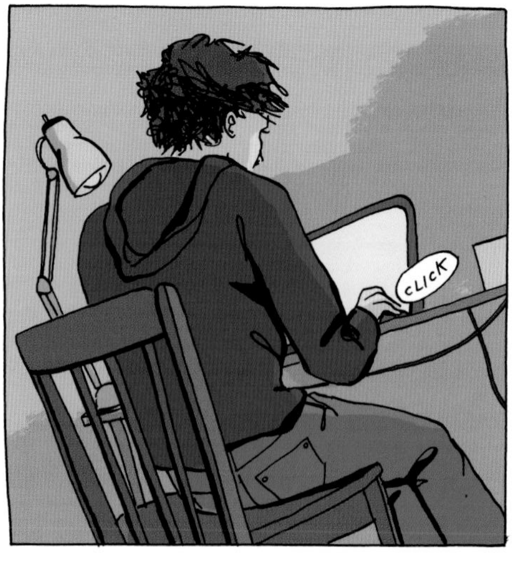
CLICK

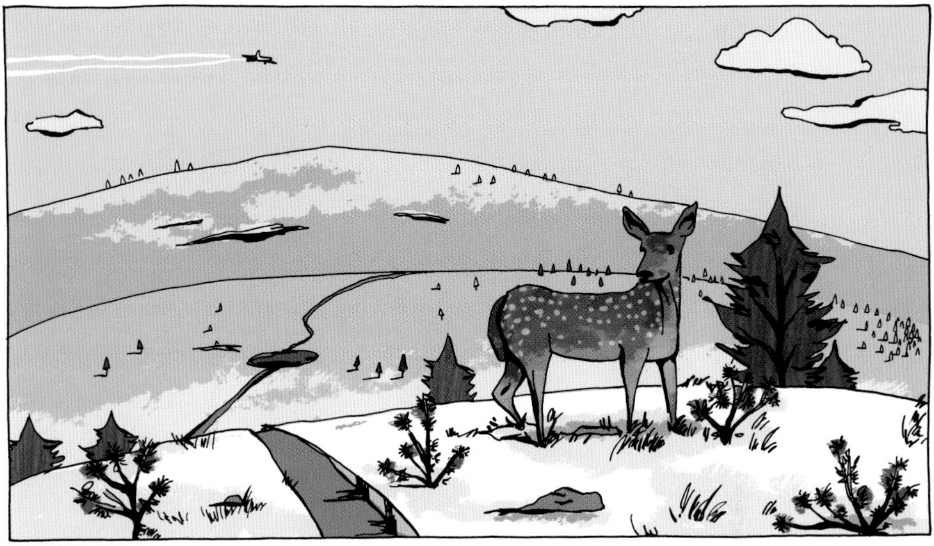
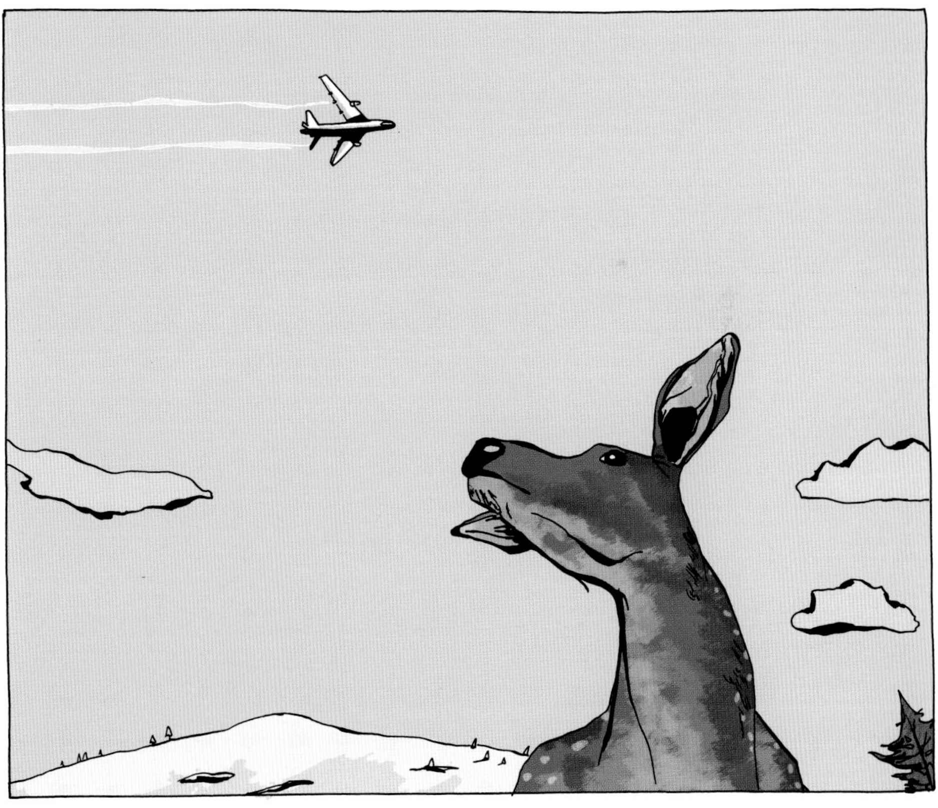

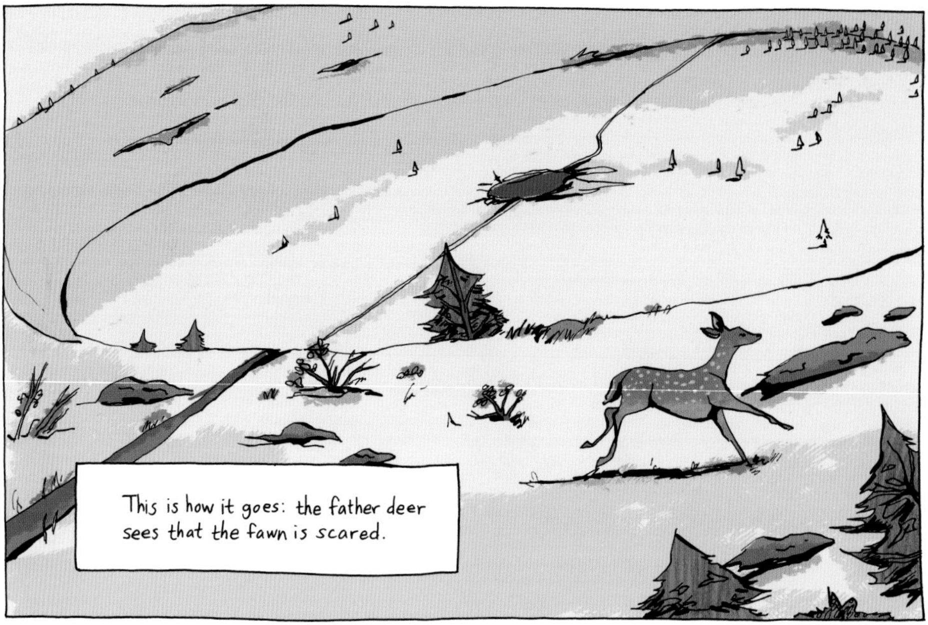
This is how it goes: the father deer sees that the fawn is scared.

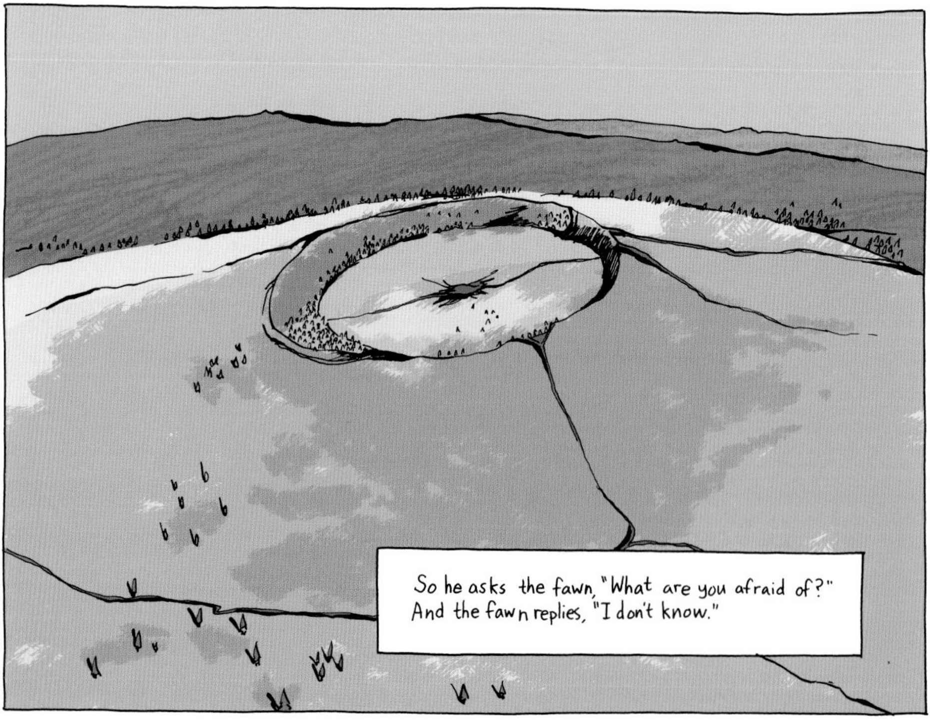
So he asks the fawn, "What are you afraid of?" And the fawn replies, "I don't know."

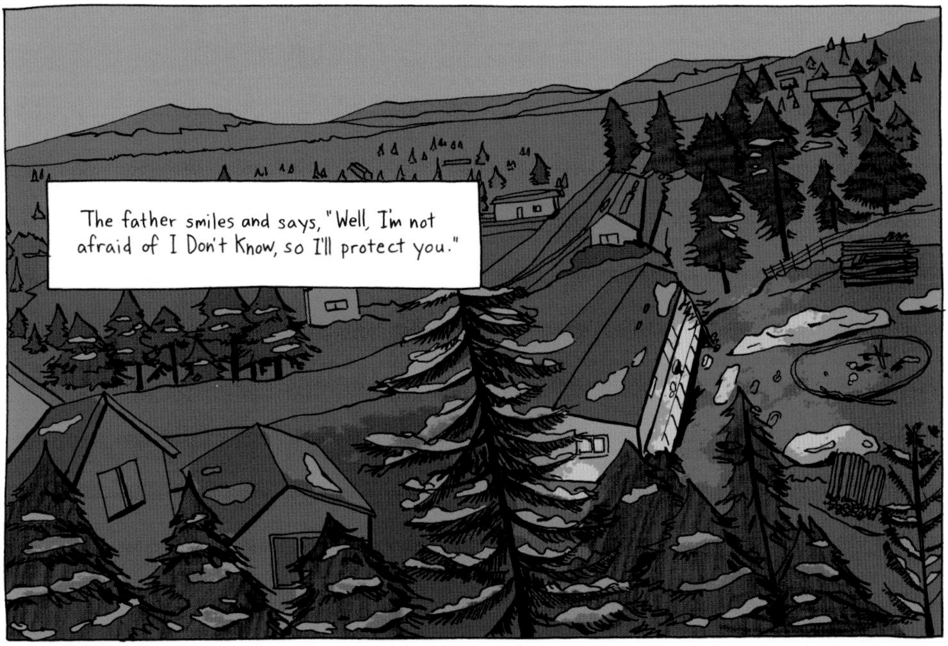
The father smiles and says, "Well, I'm not afraid of I Don't Know, so I'll protect you."

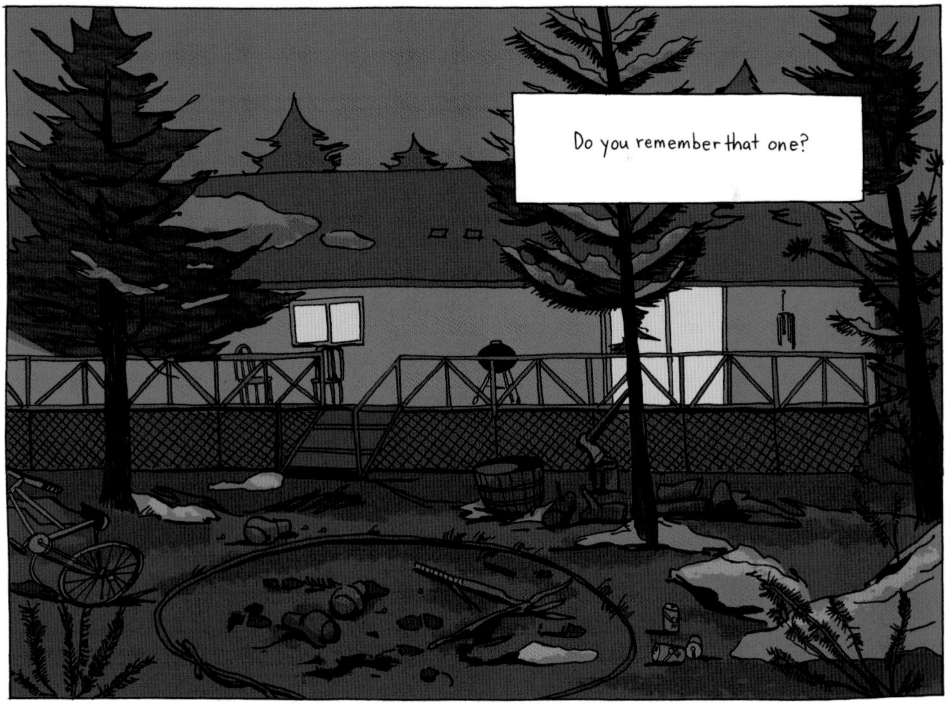
Do you remember that one?

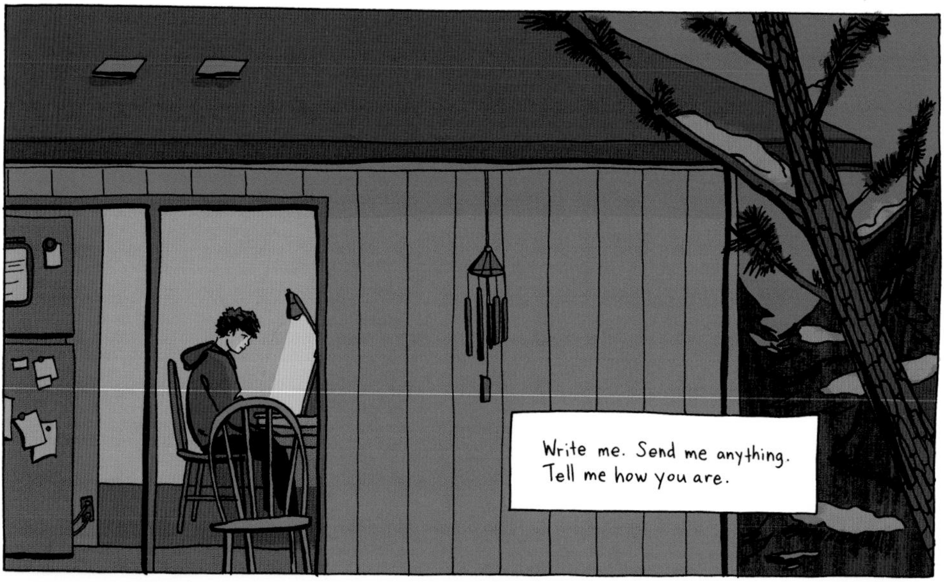
Write me. Send me anything.
Tell me how you are.

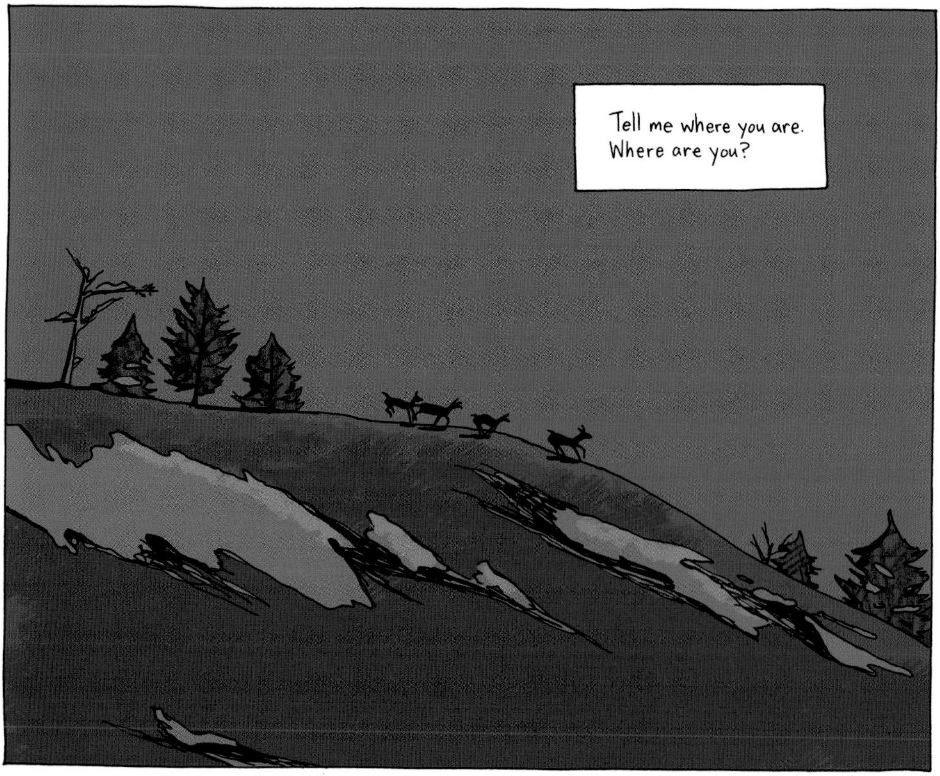
Tell me where you are.
Where are you?

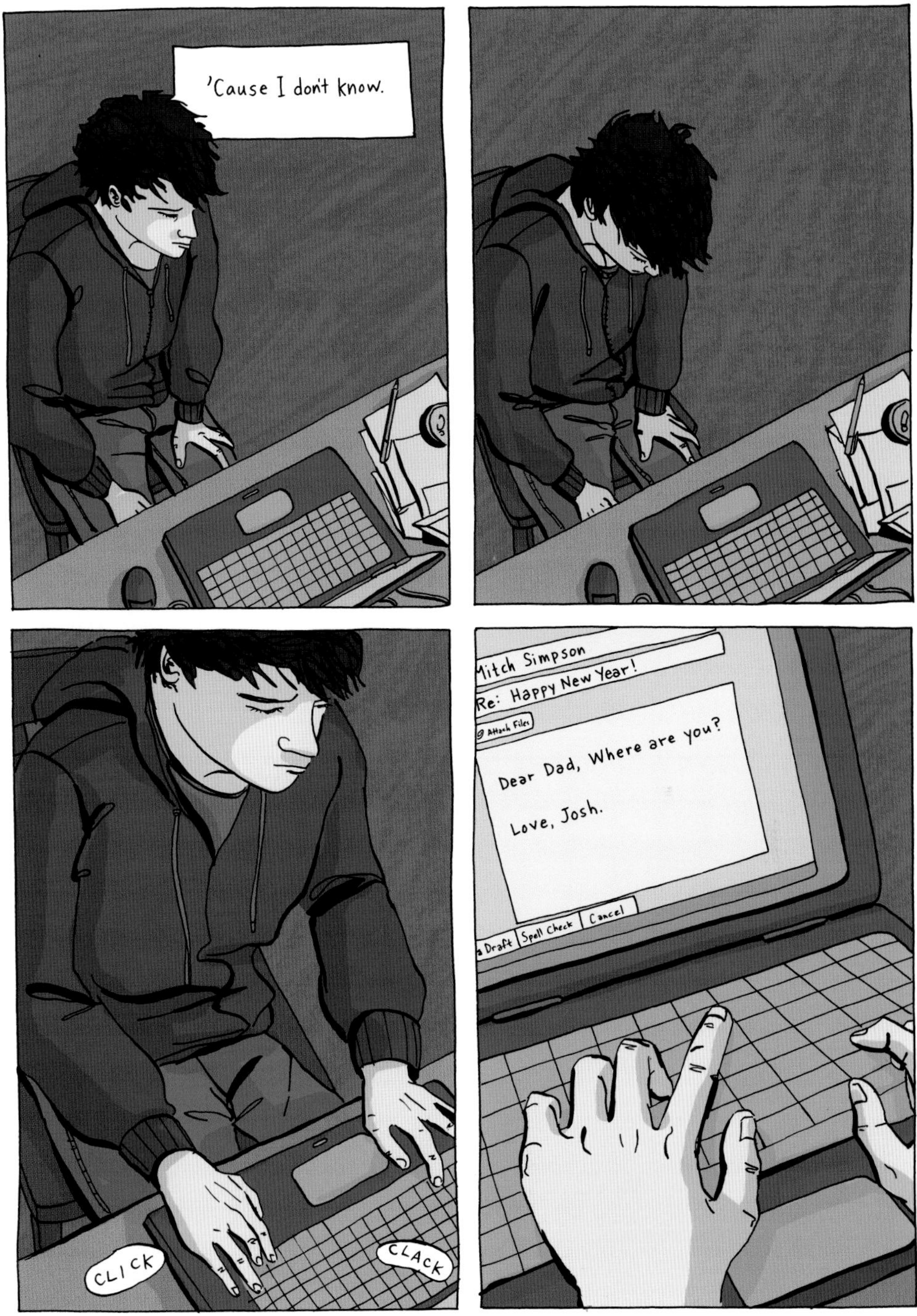

'Cause I don't know.
CLICK
CLACK
Mitch Simpson
Re: Happy New Year!
Attach Files
Dear Dad, Where are you?
Love, Josh.
s Draft
Spell Check
Cancel

64661
MERRY CHRISTMAS

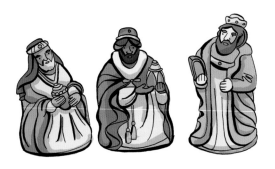

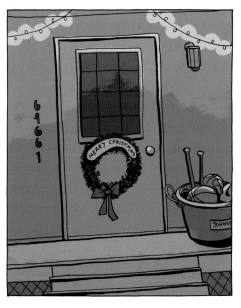

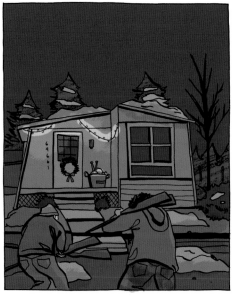

Coors
MERRY CHRIST
JOHN

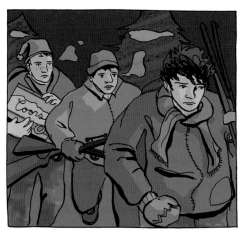

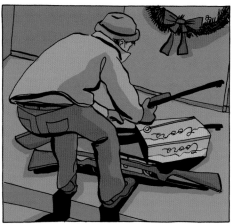

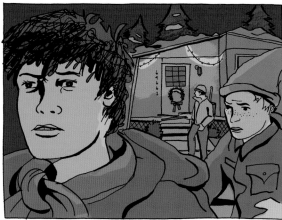

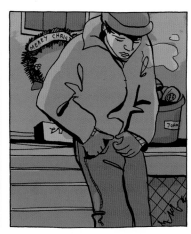

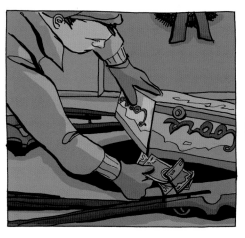

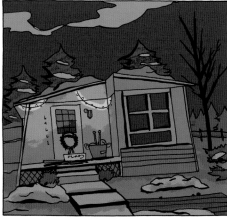

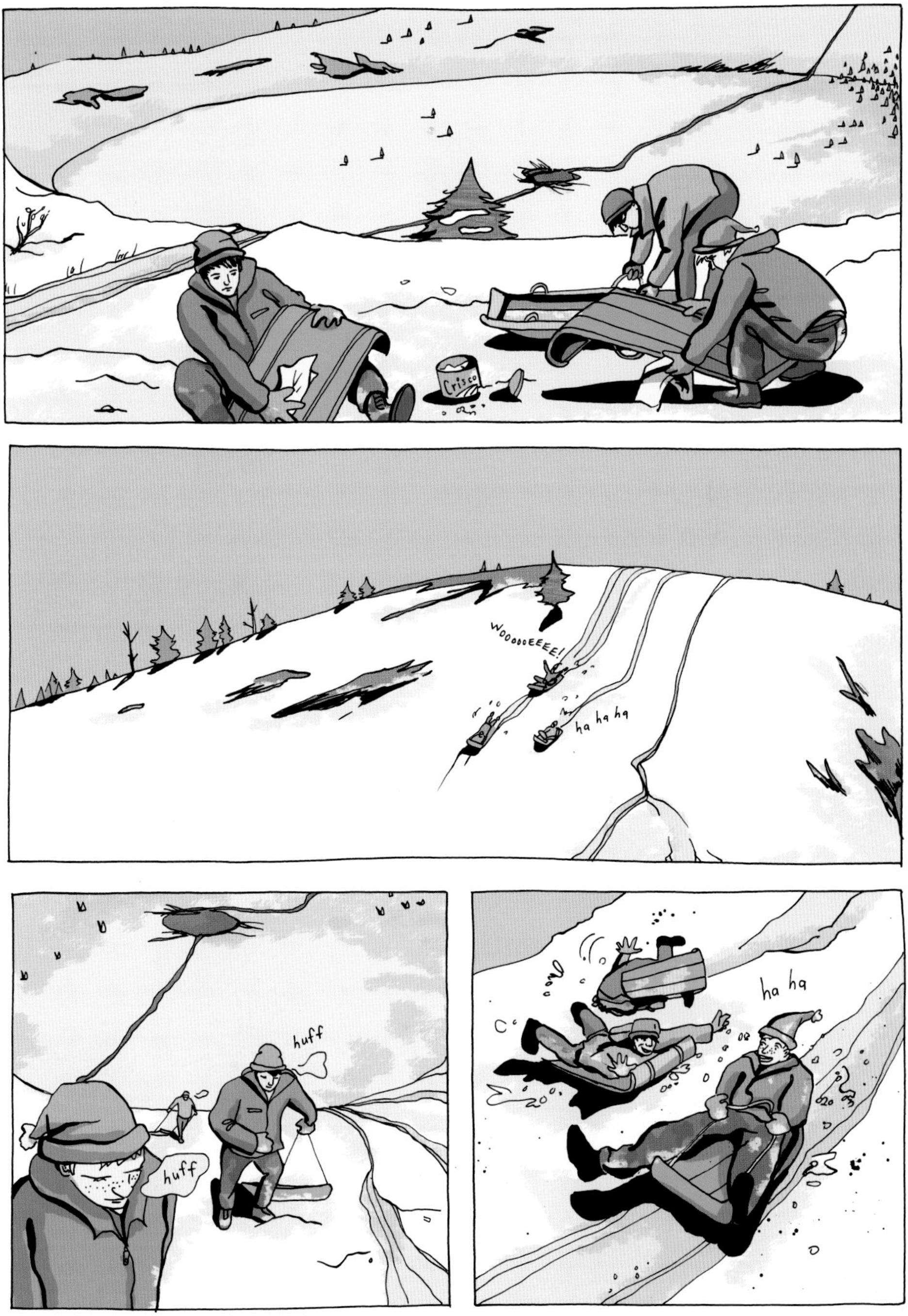
Crisco
WOOOOOOEEEE!
ha ha ha
huff
huff
ha ha

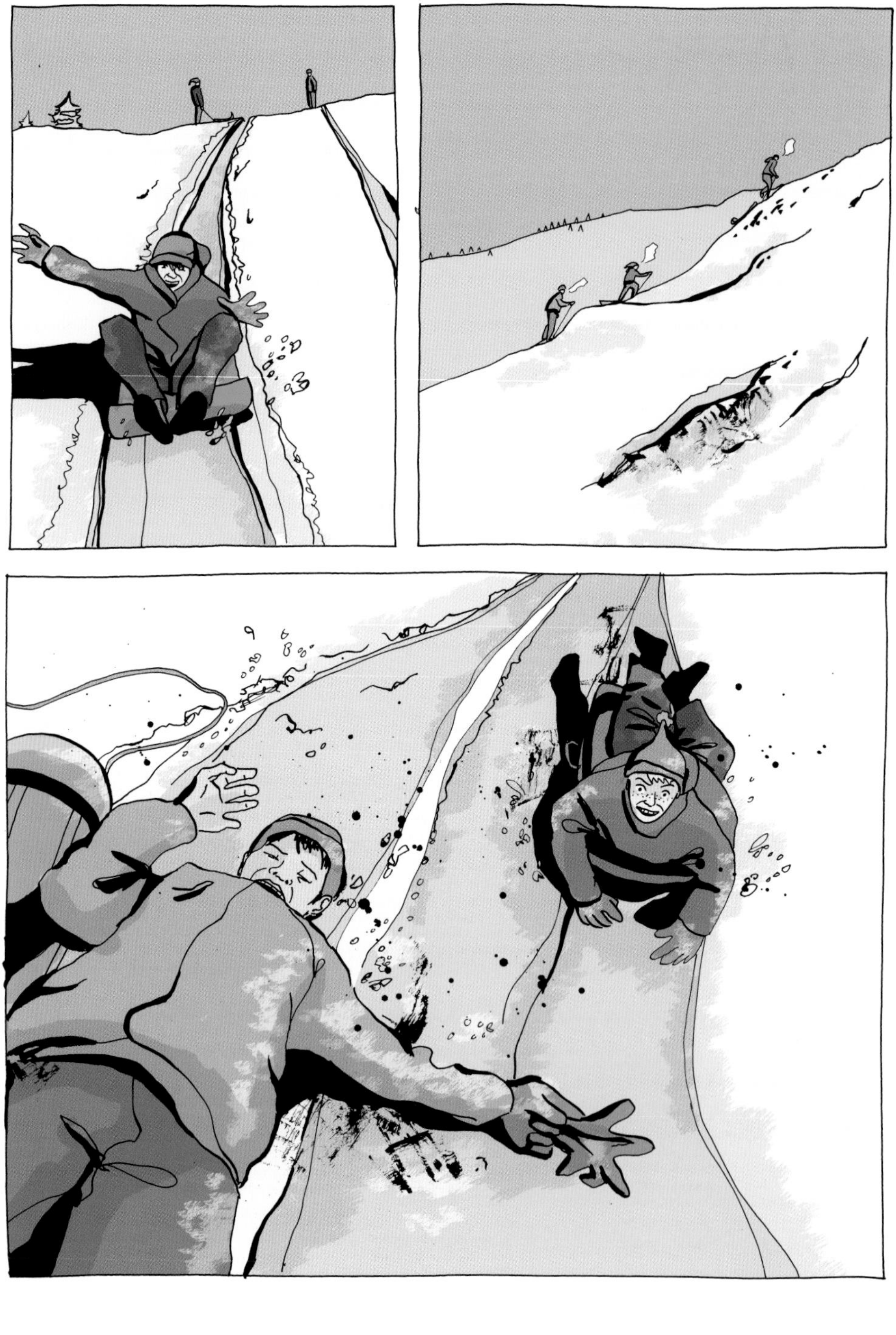

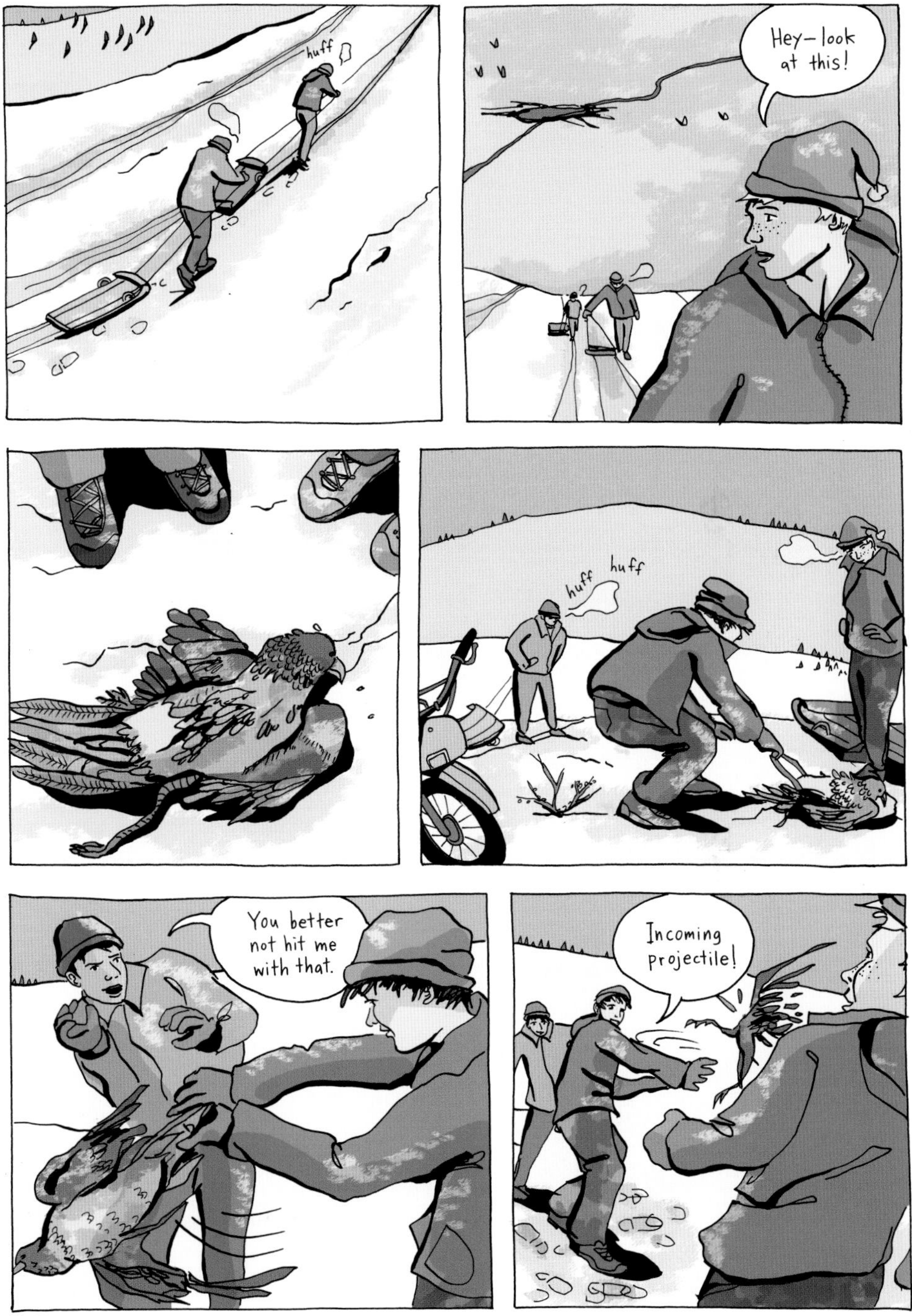
huff
Hey—look at this!
huff huff
You better not hit me with that.
Incoming projectile!

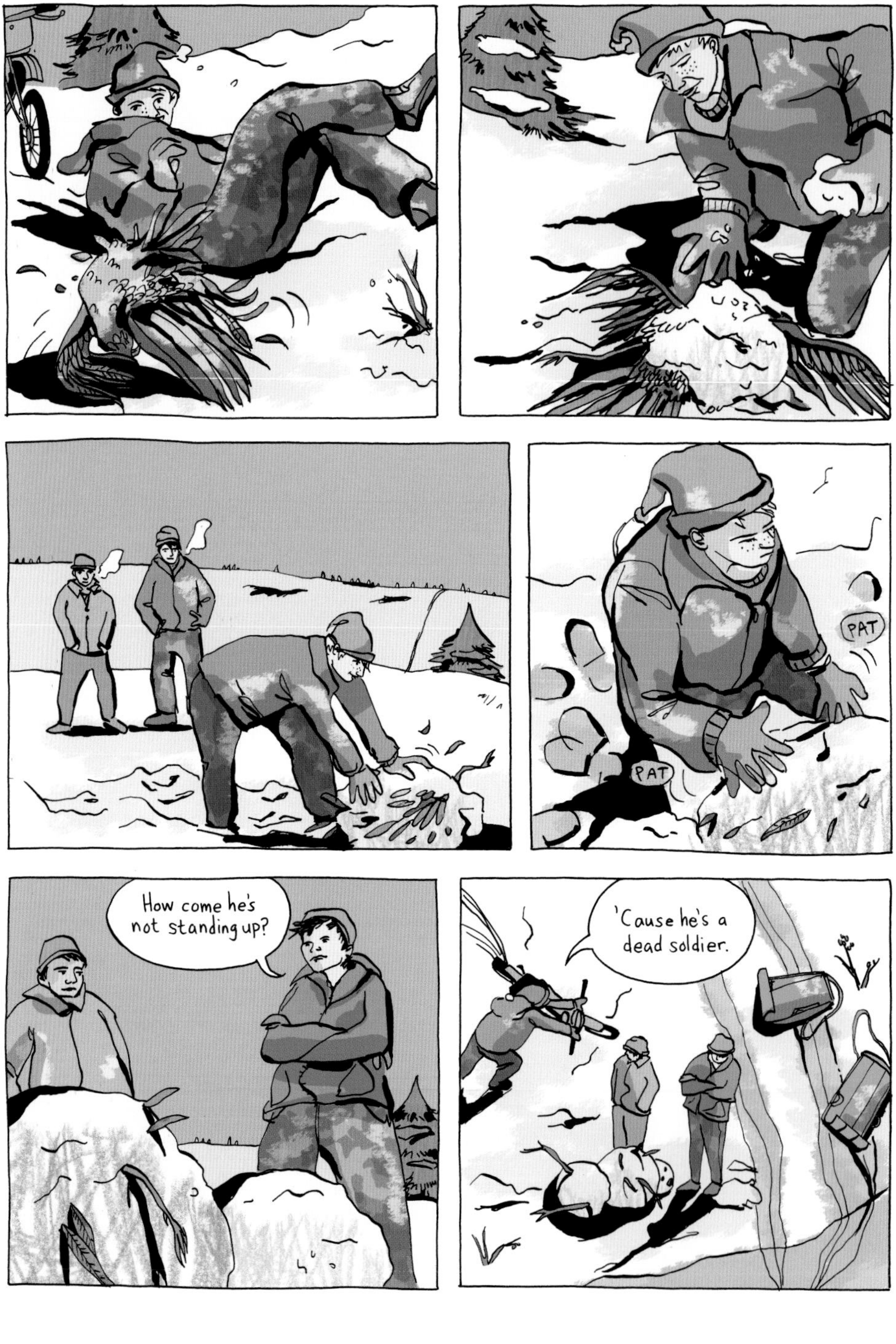
PAT
PAT
How come he's not standing up?
'Cause he's a dead soldier.

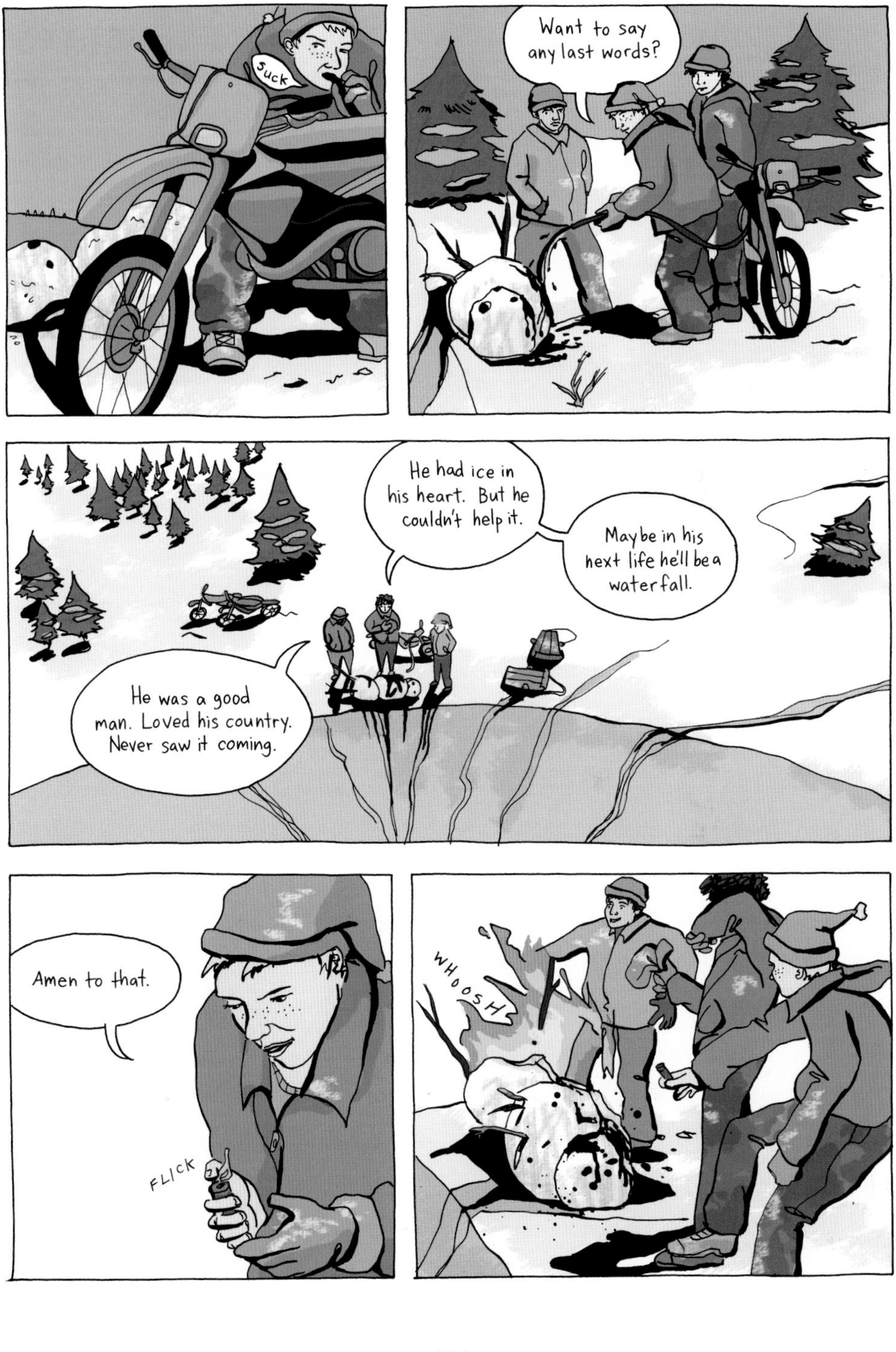
SUCK
Want to say any last words?
He had ice in his heart. But he couldn't help it.
Maybe in his next life he'll be a waterfall.
He was a good man. Loved his country. Never saw it coming.
Amen to that.
FLICK
WHOOSH

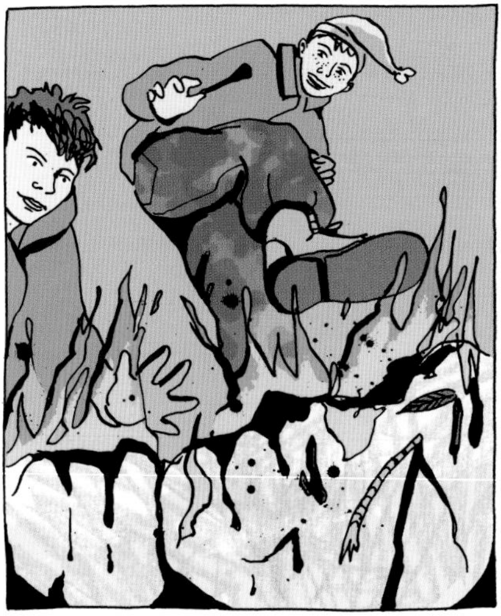

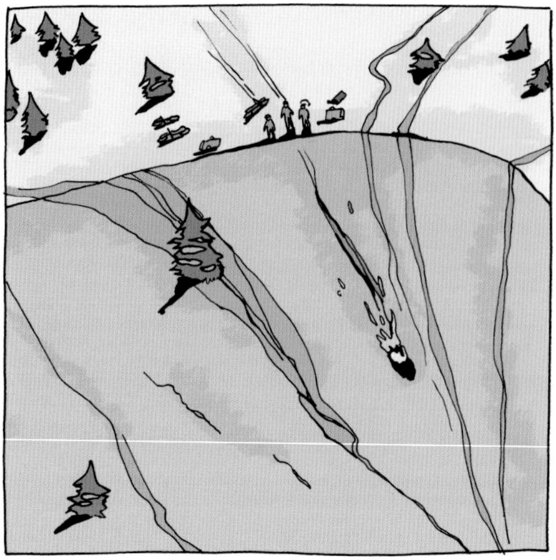

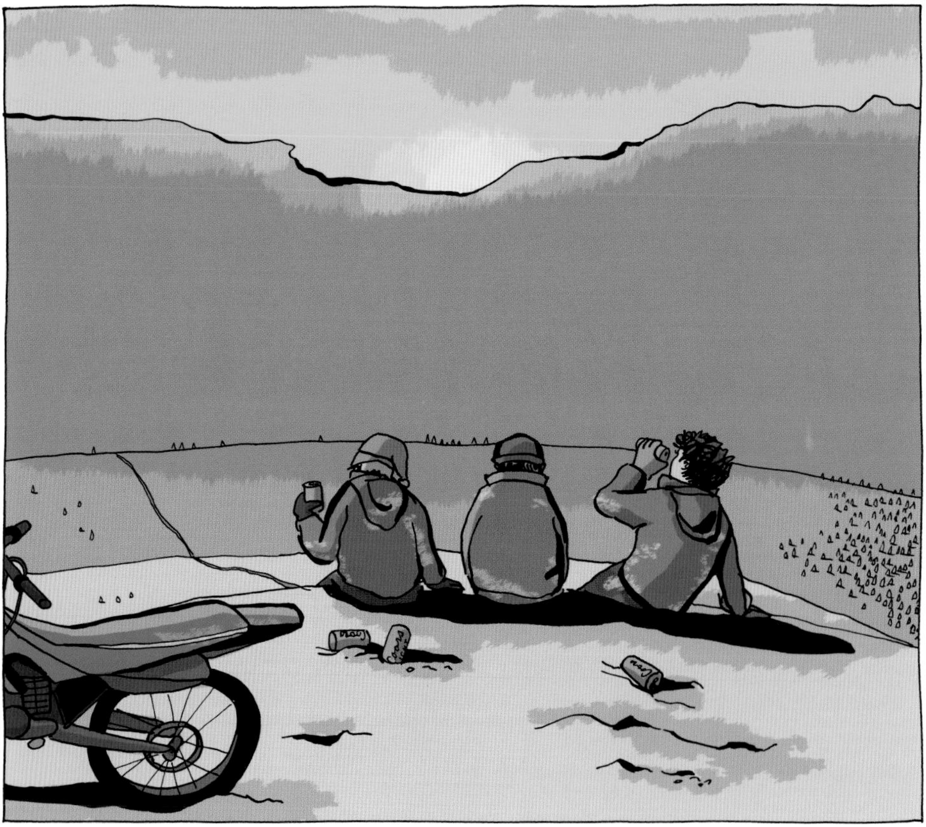

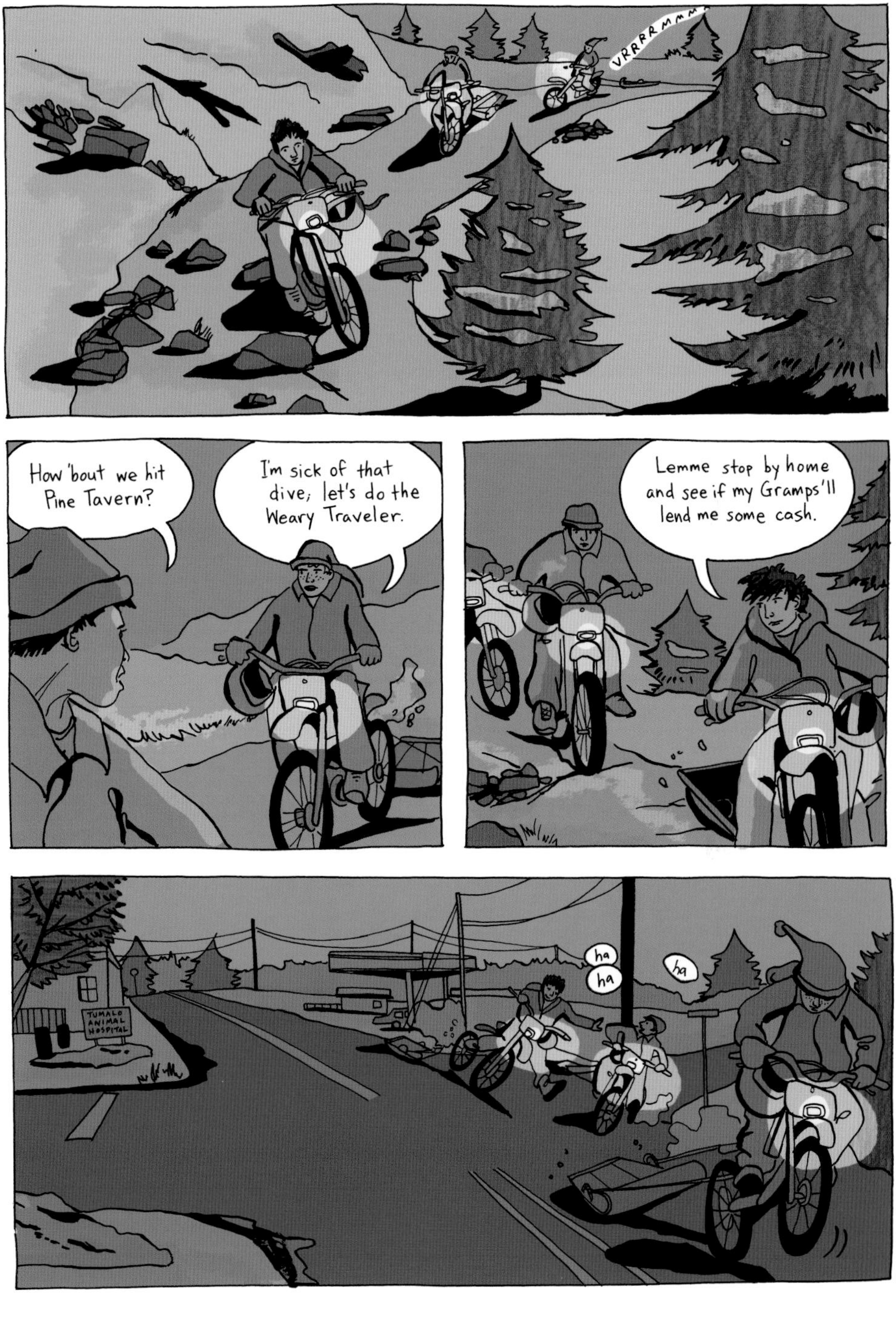
VRRRRMMMM
How 'bout we hit Pine Tavern?
I'm sick of that dive; let's do the Weary Traveler.
Lemme stop by home and see if my Gramps'll lend me some cash.
TUMALO ANIMAL HOSPITAL
ha
ha
ha

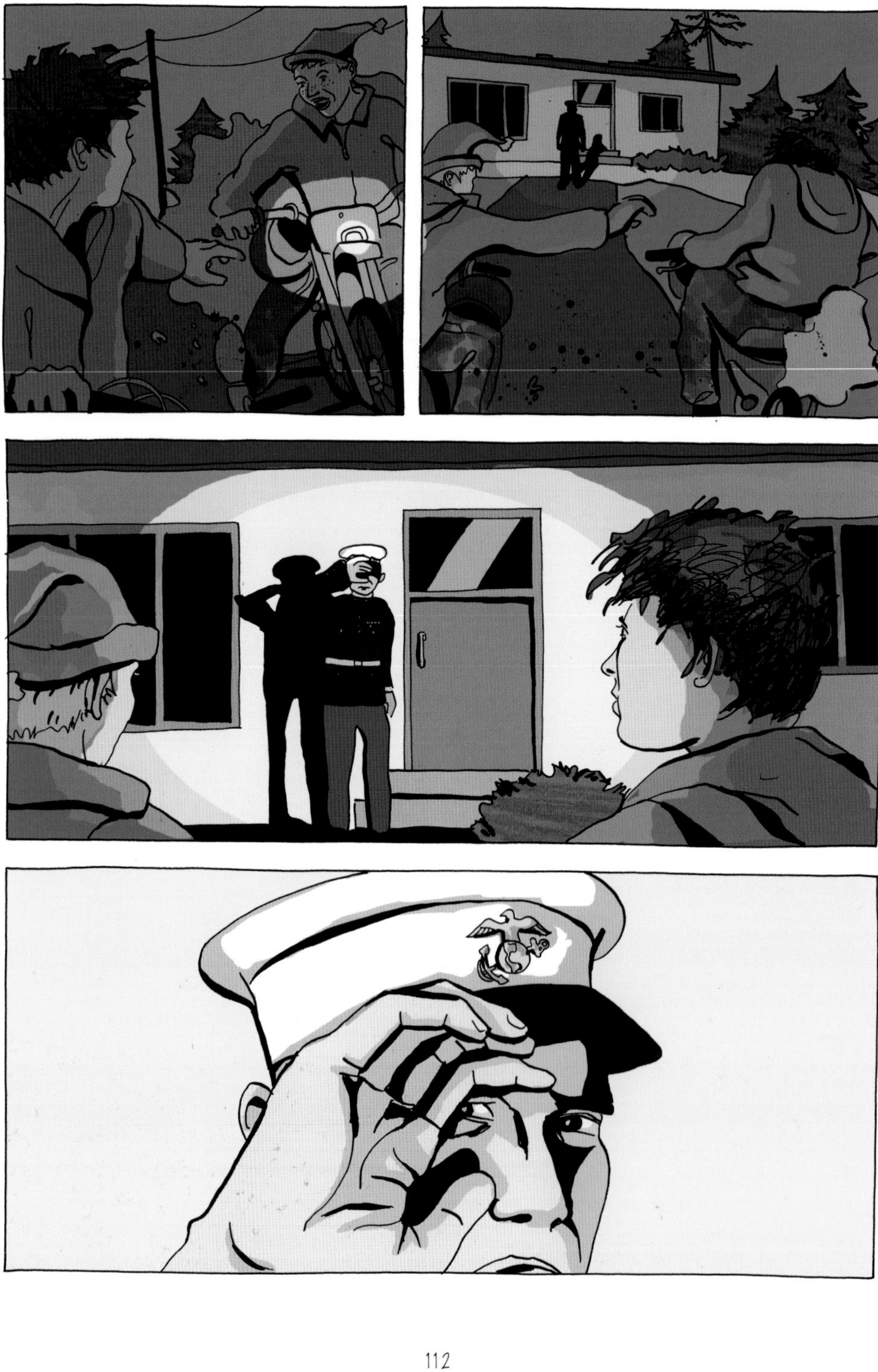

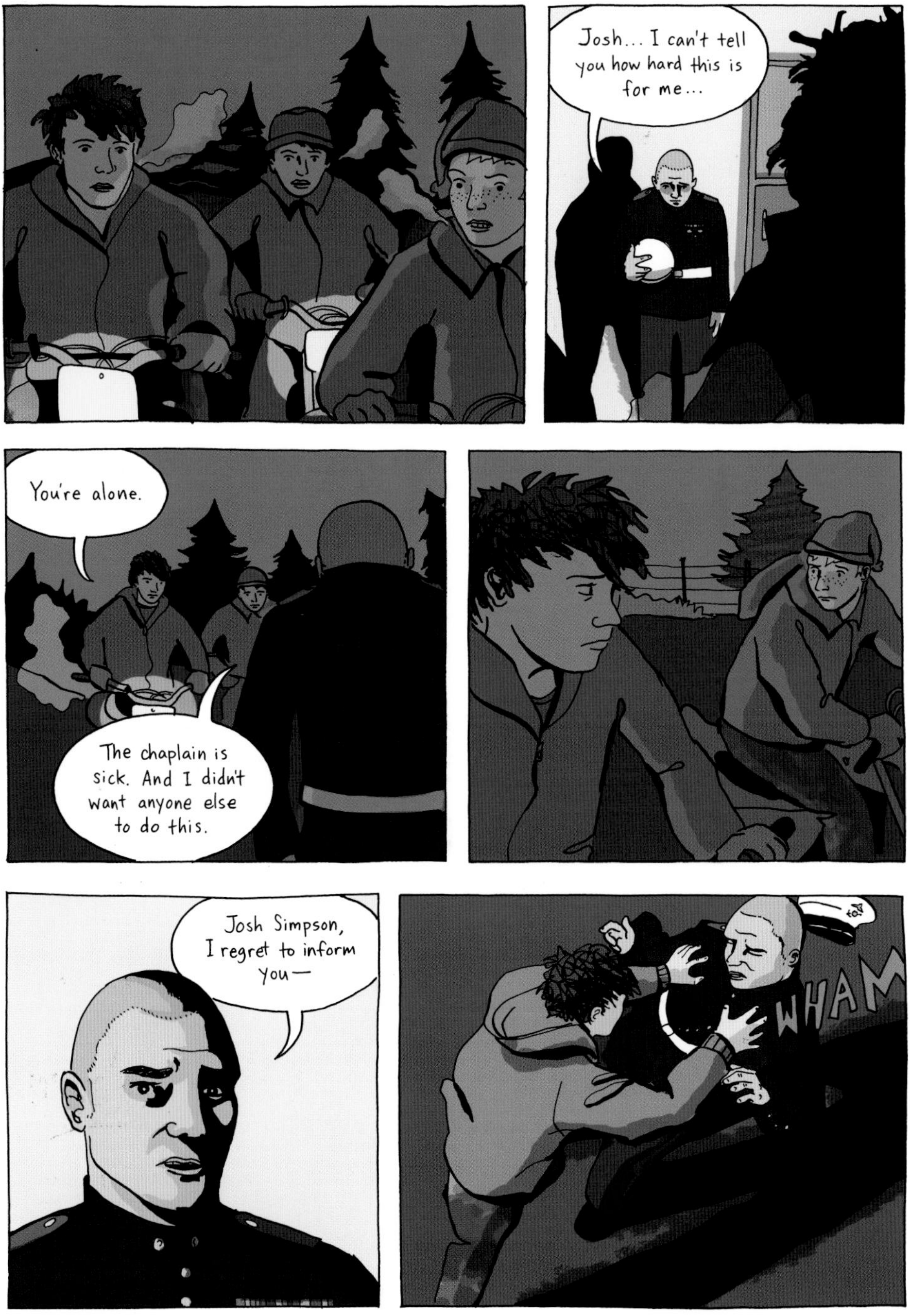
Josh... I can't tell you how hard this is for me...
You're alone.
The chaplain is sick. And I didn't want anyone else to do this.
Josh Simpson, I regret to inform you—
WHAM

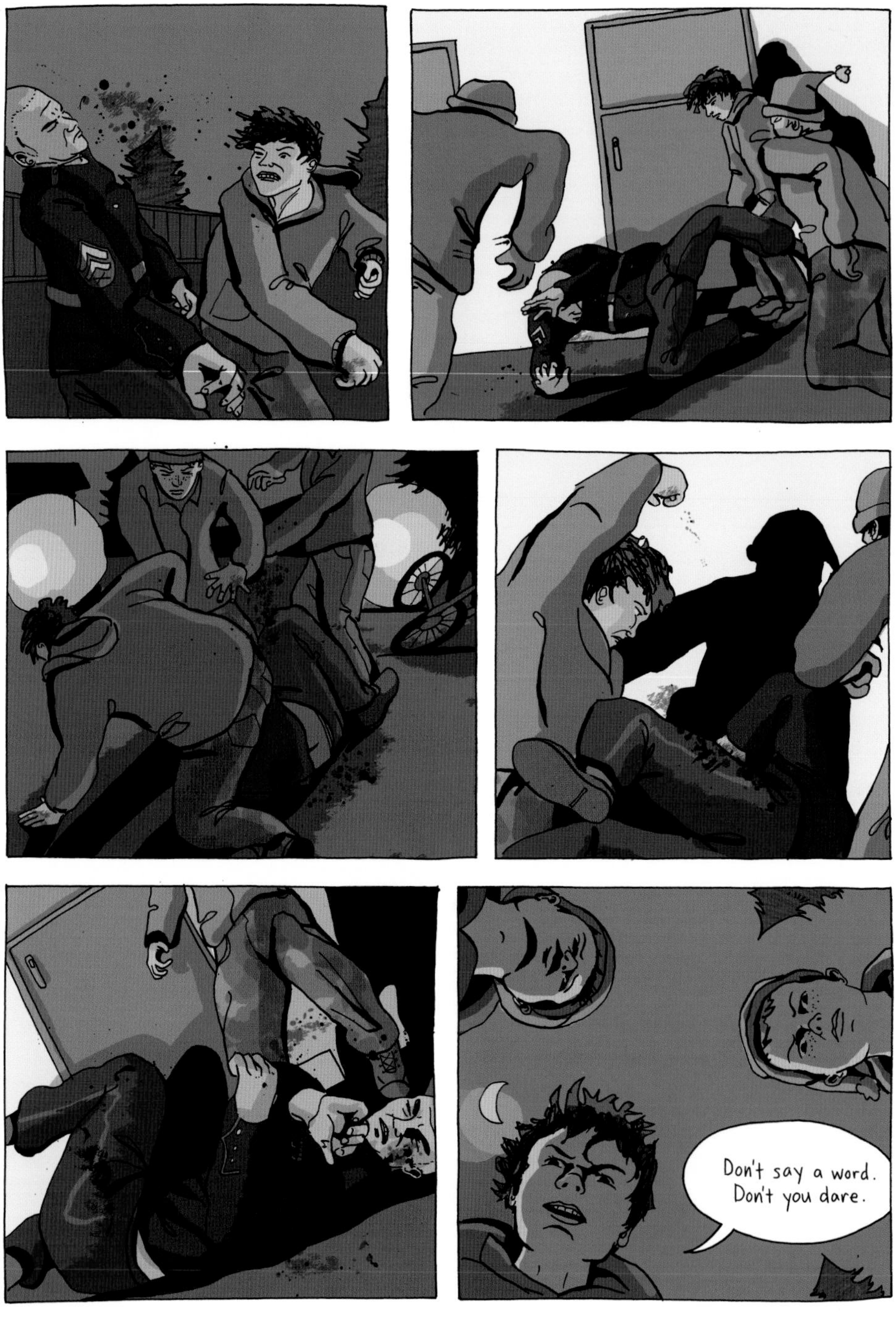
Don't say a word.
Don't you dare.

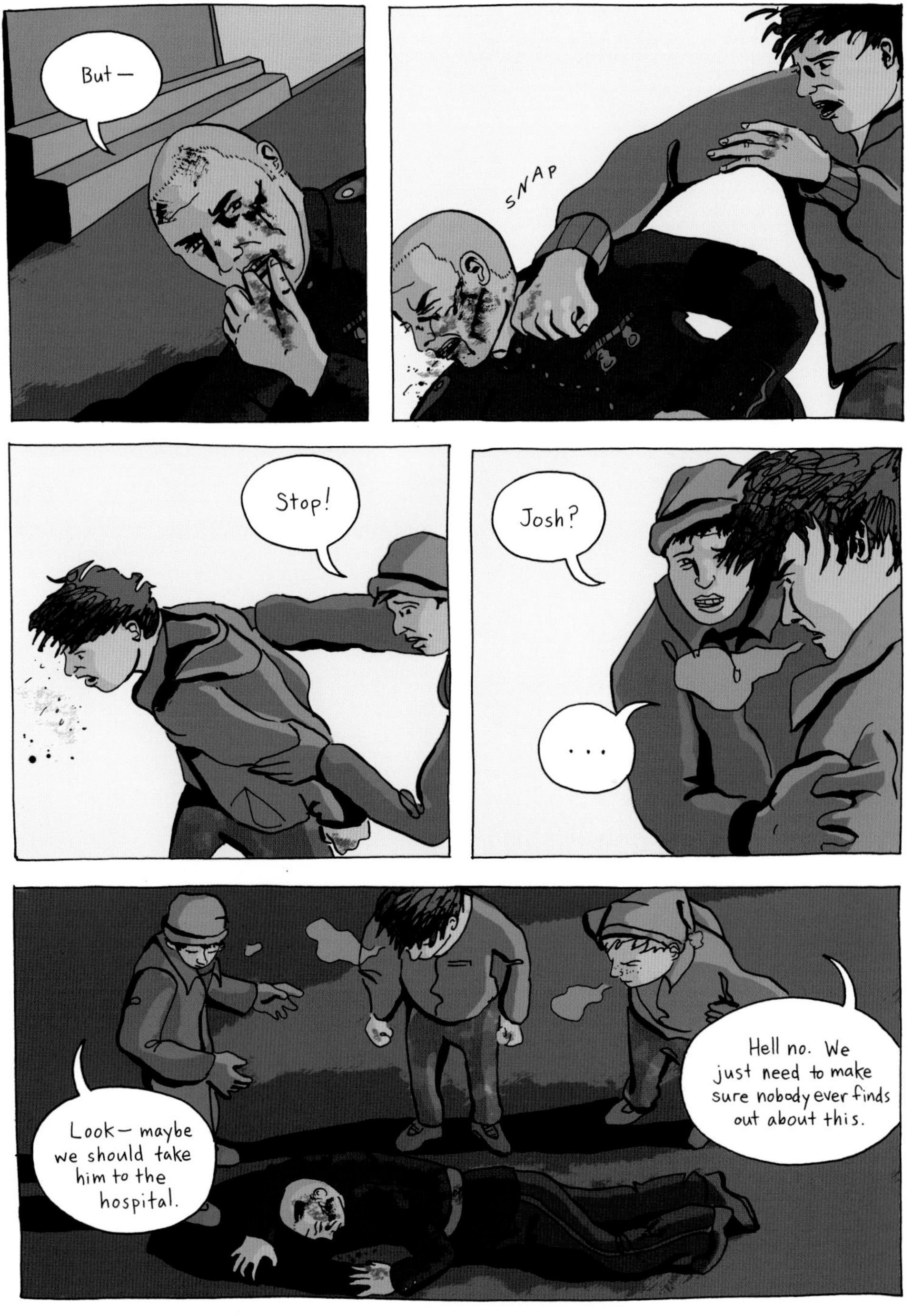
But—
SNAP
Stop!
Josh?
...
Look— maybe we should take him to the hospital.
Hell no. We just need to make sure nobody ever finds out about this.

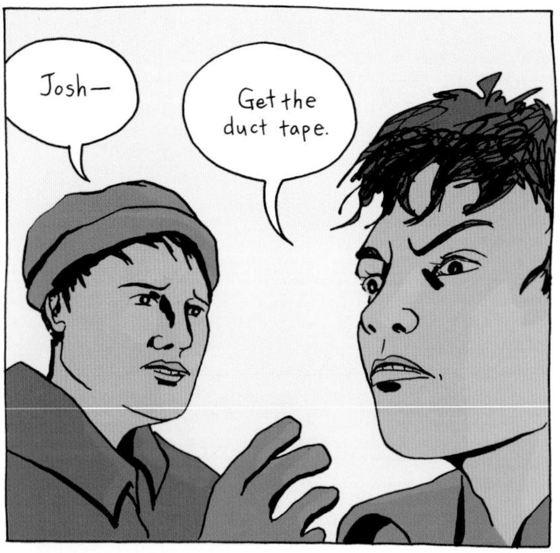
Josh—
Get the duct tape.
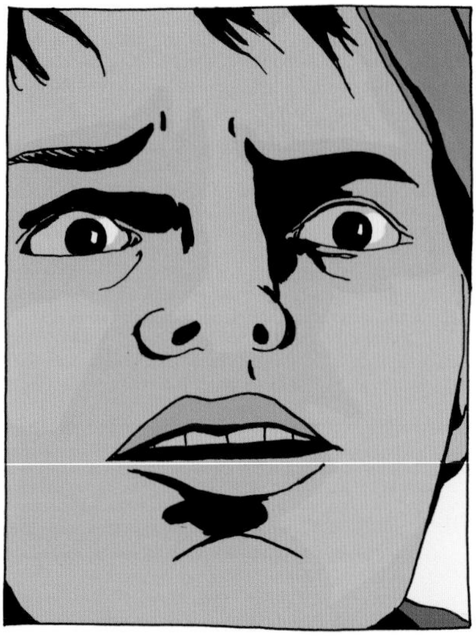
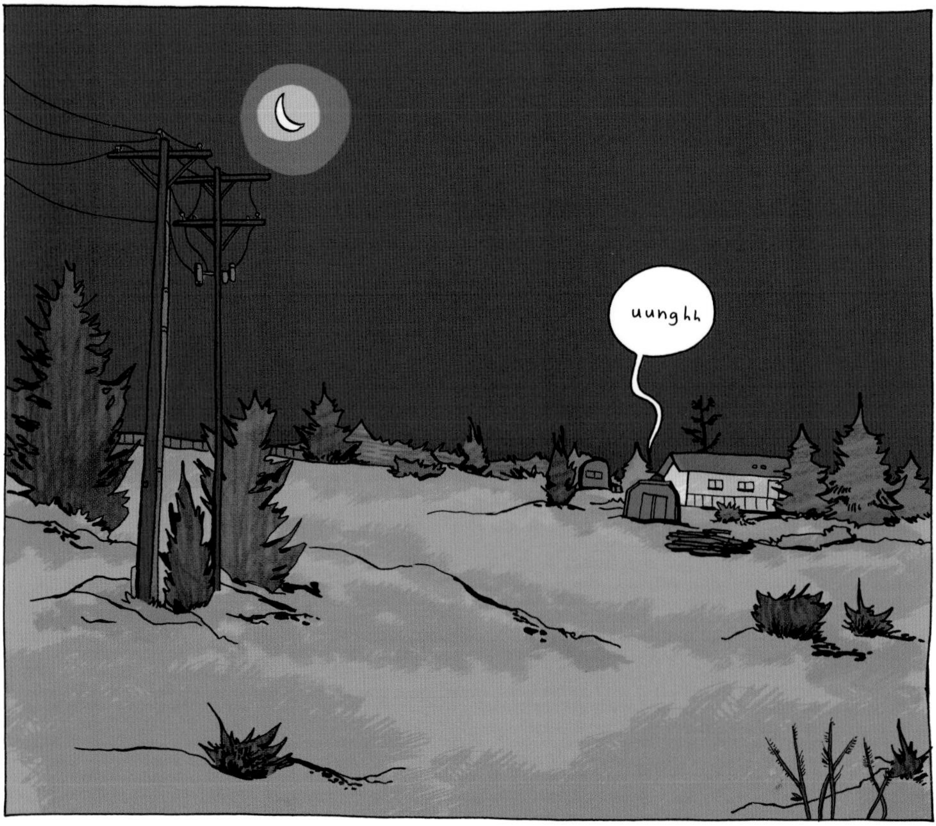
uunghh

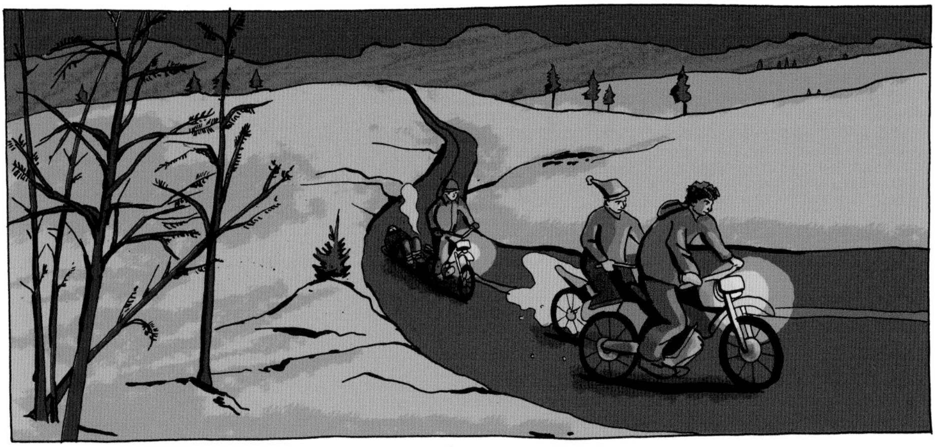

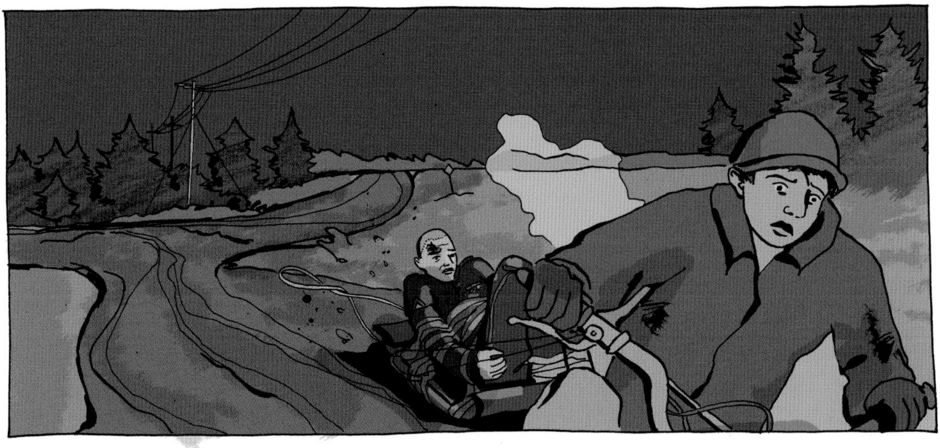

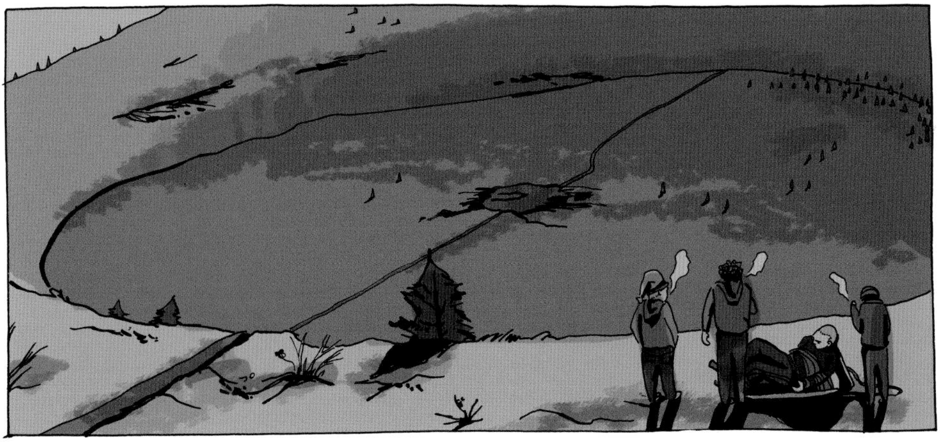

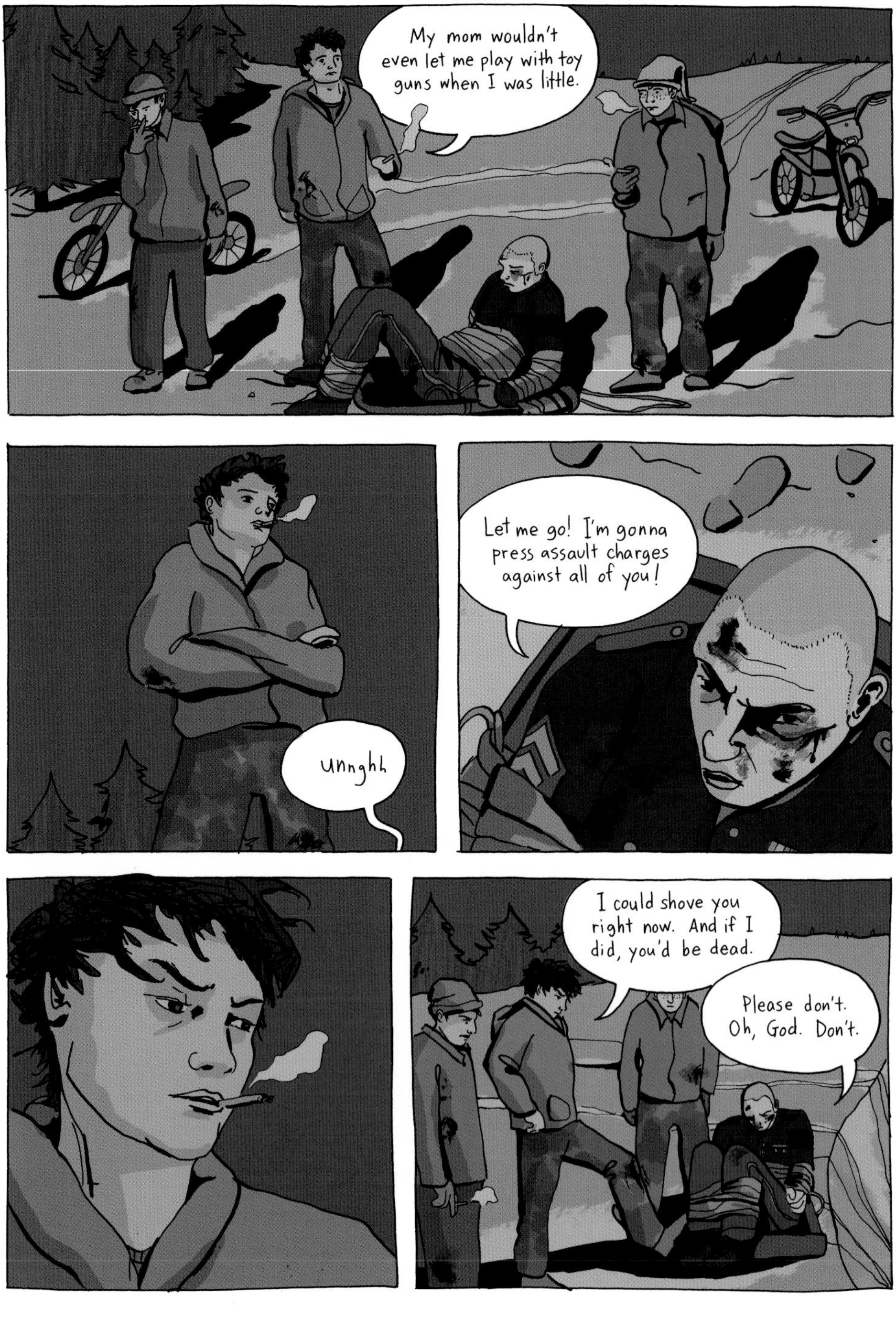
My mom wouldn't even let me play with toy guns when I was little.
unnghh
Let me go! I'm gonna press assault charges against all of you!
I could shove you right now. And if I did, you'd be dead.
Please don't. Oh, God. Don't.

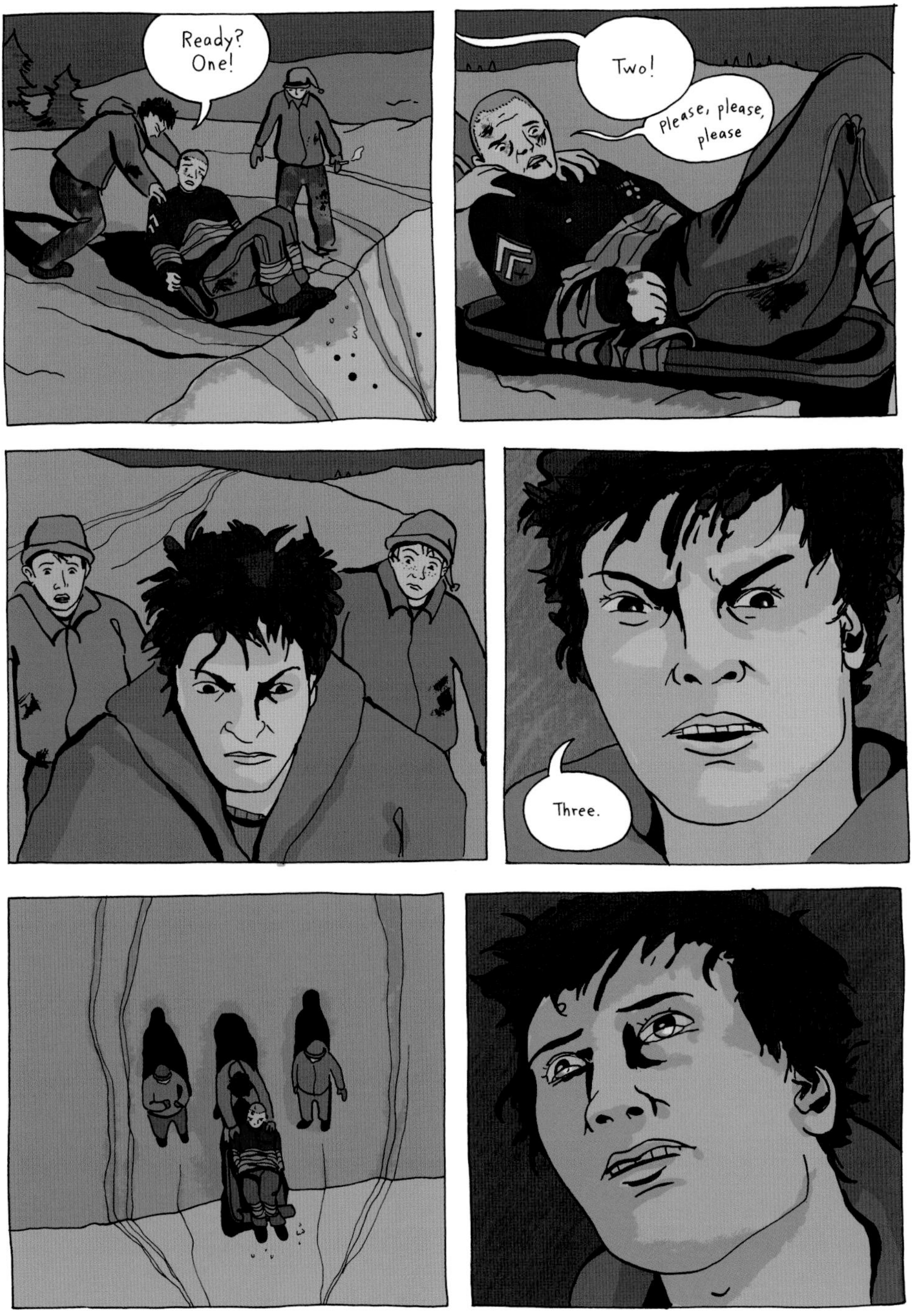
Ready? One!
Two!
Please, please, please
Three.

SSSSS
VRRRRRRM
VRRRRR

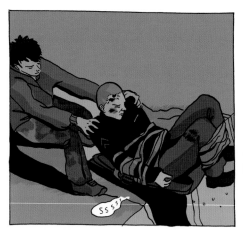

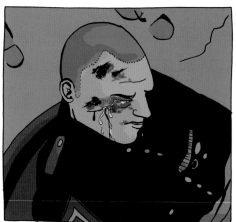

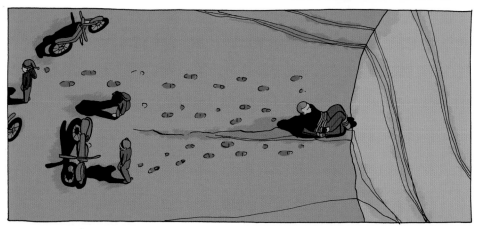

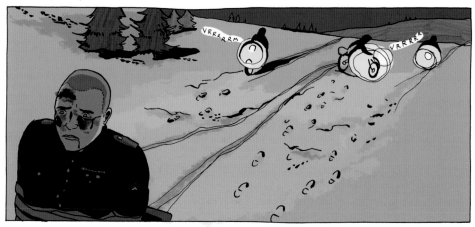

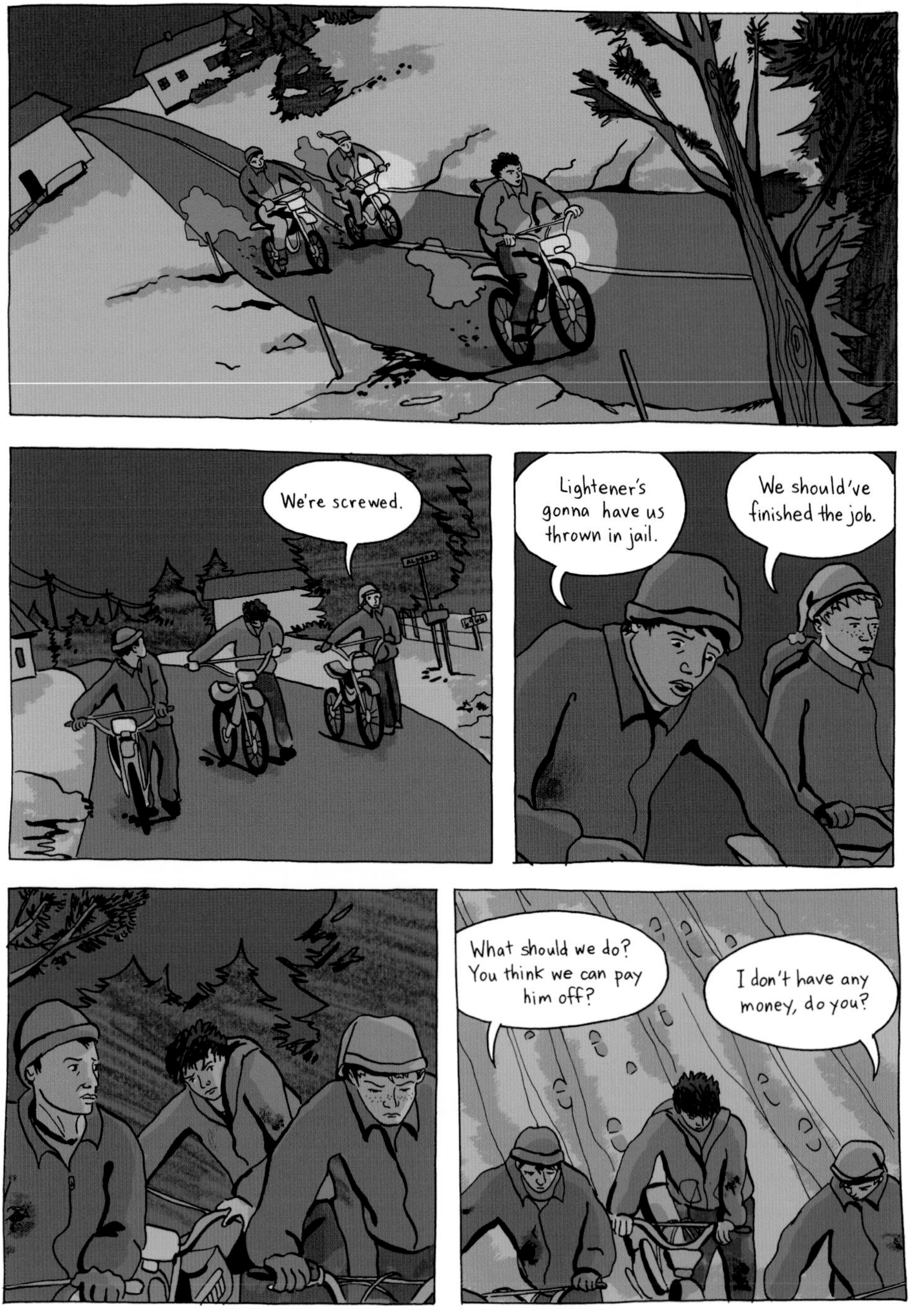
We're screwed.
Lightener's gonna have us thrown in jail.
We should've finished the job.
What should we do? You think we can pay him off?
I don't have any money, do you?

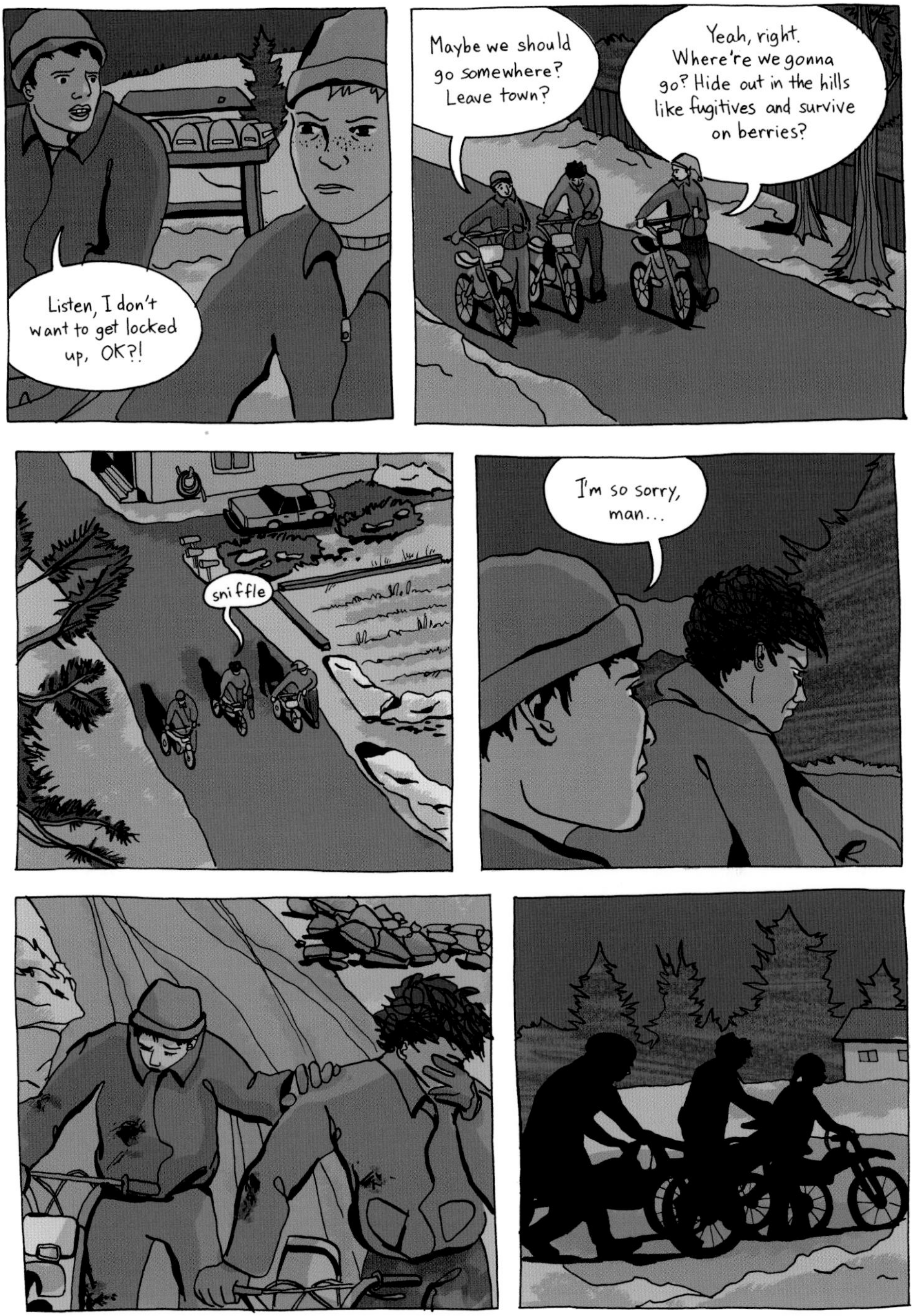
Listen, I don't want to get locked up, OK?!
Maybe we should go somewhere? Leave town?
Yeah, right. Where're we gonna go? Hide out in the hills like fugitives and survive on berries?
sniffle
I'm so sorry, man...

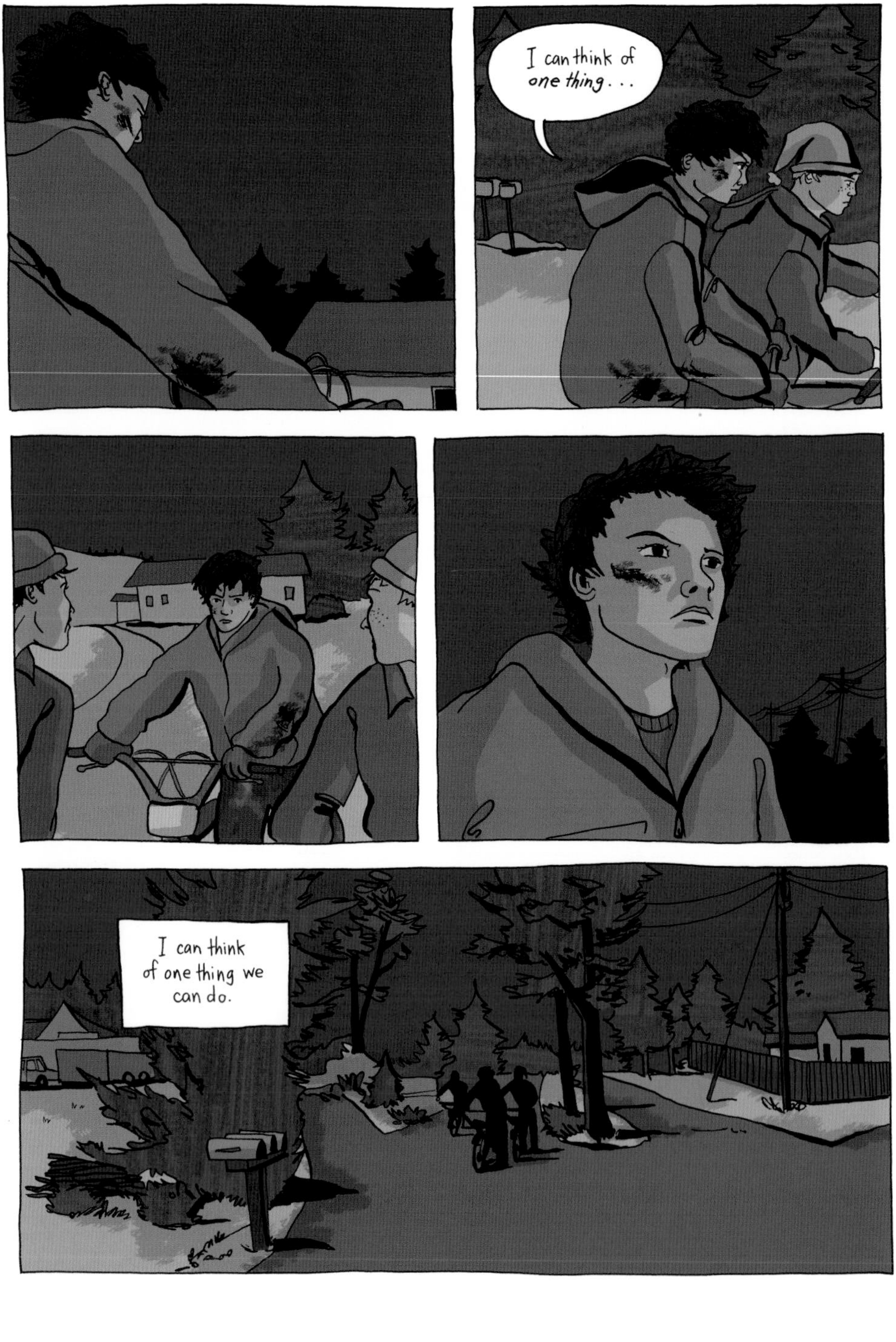
I can think of one thing...
I can think of one thing we can do.

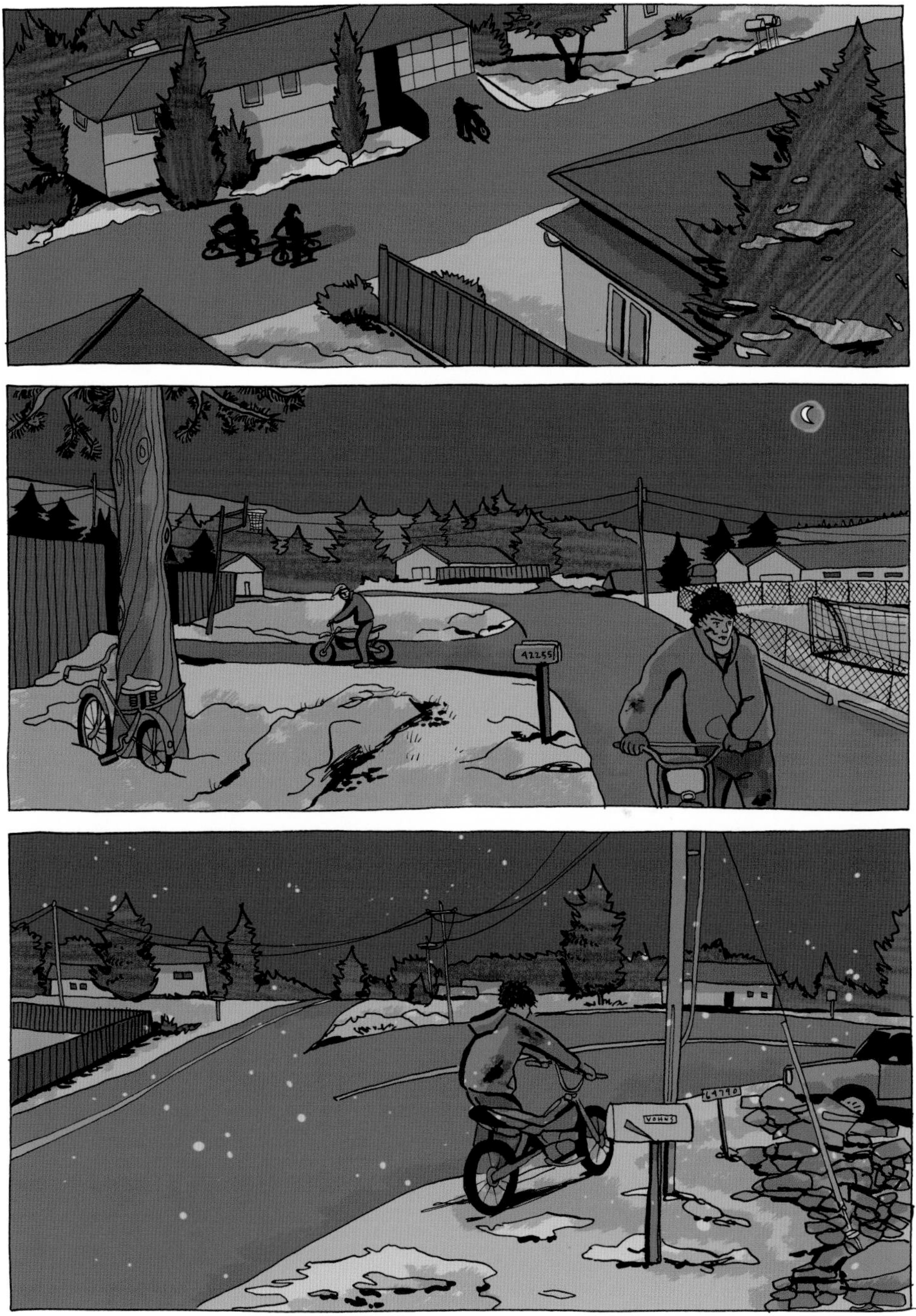
42255

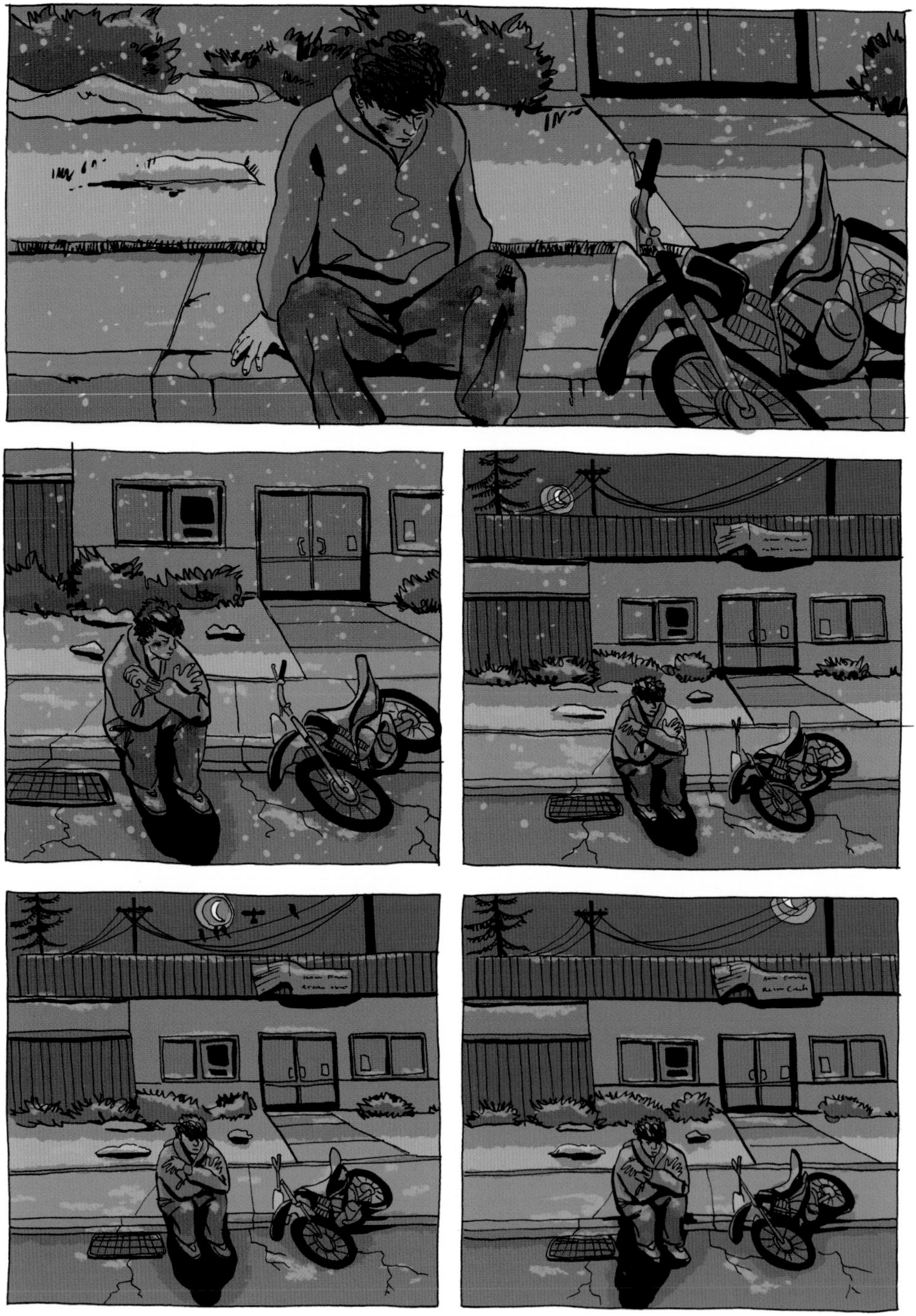

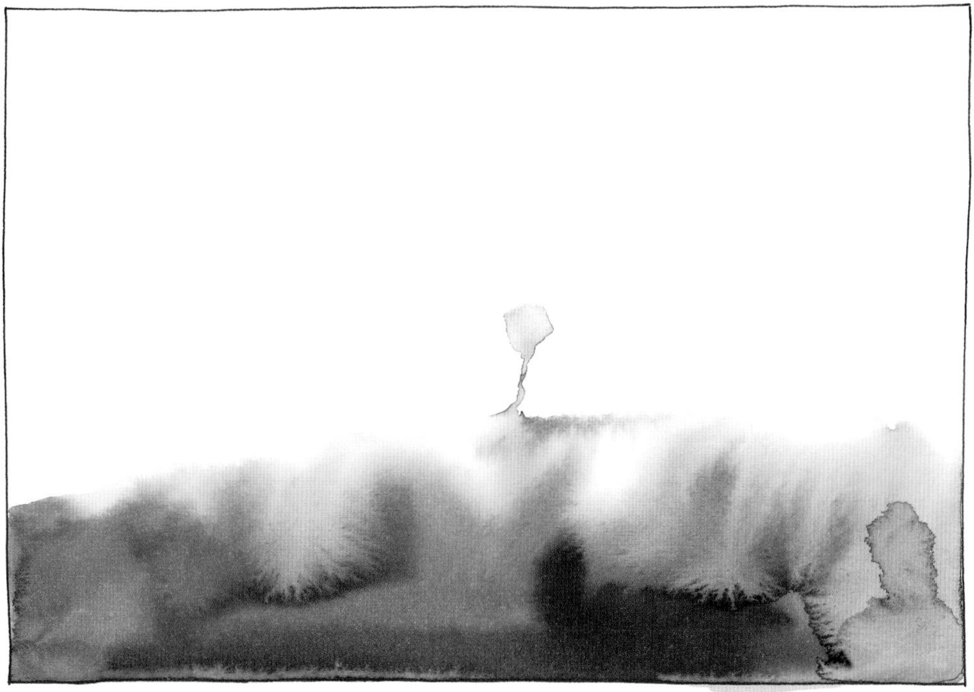
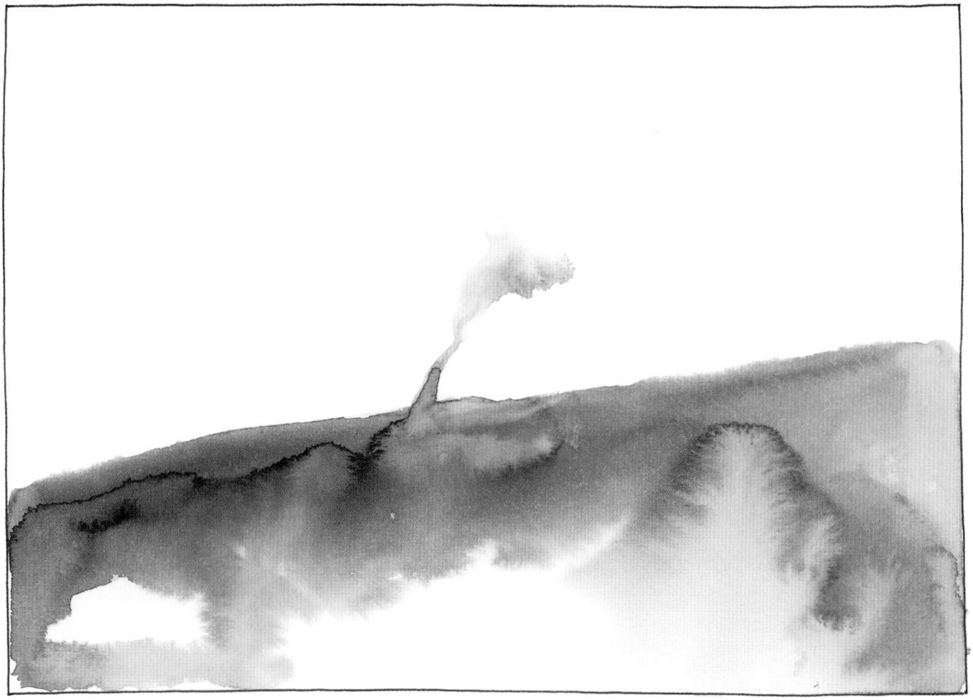

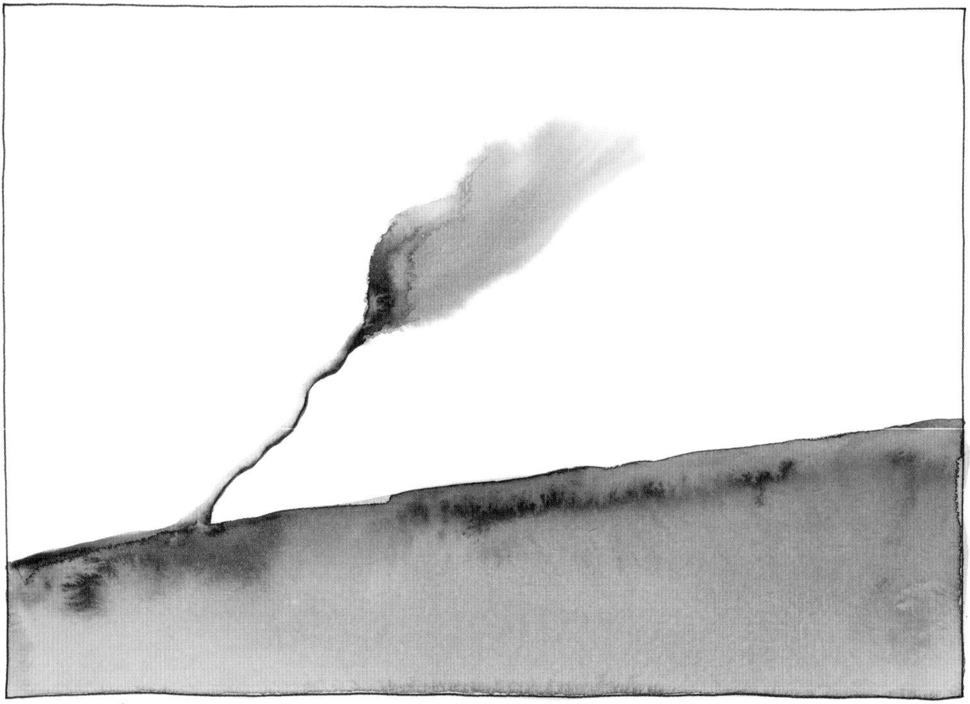

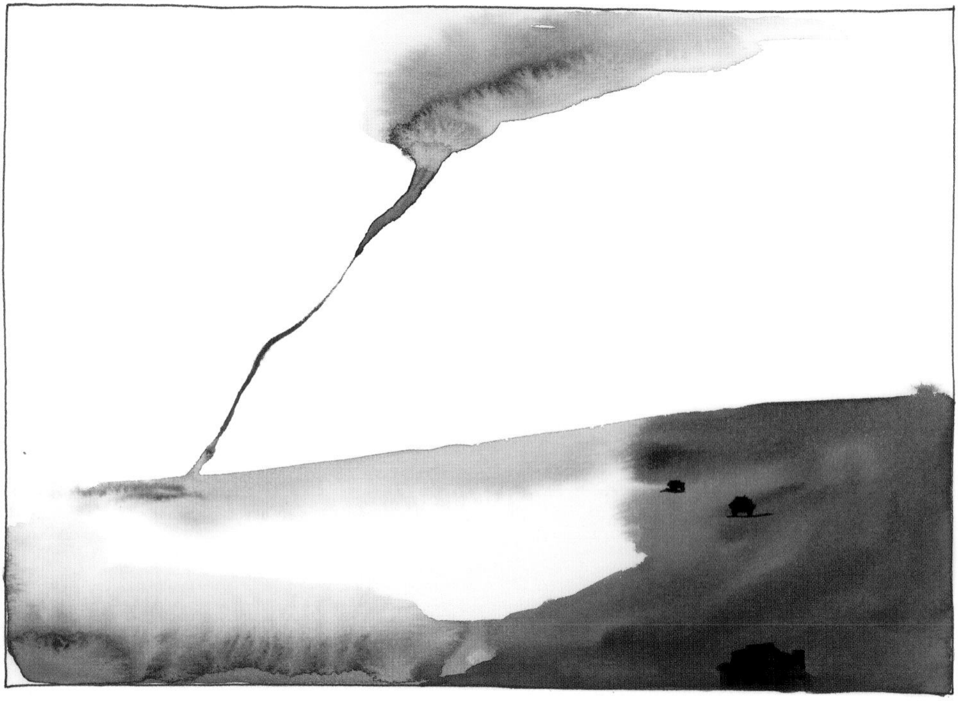

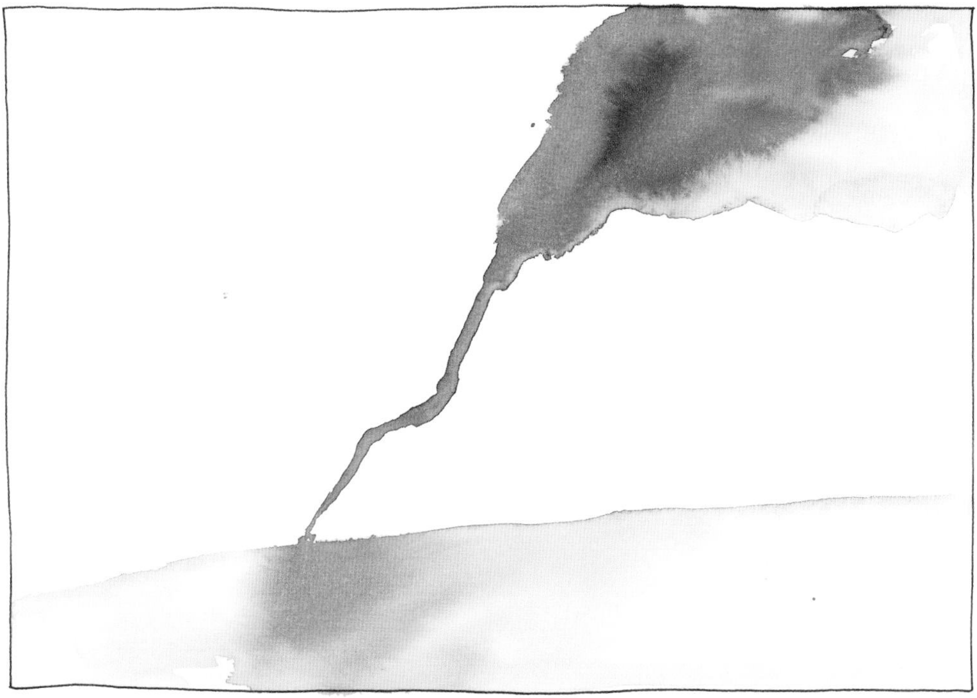
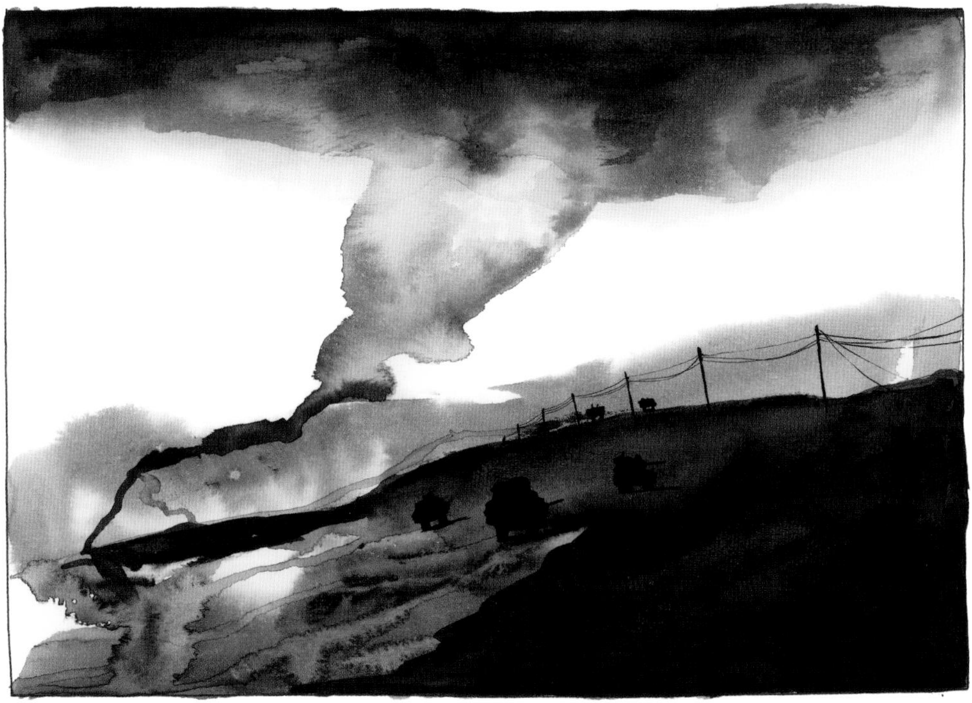

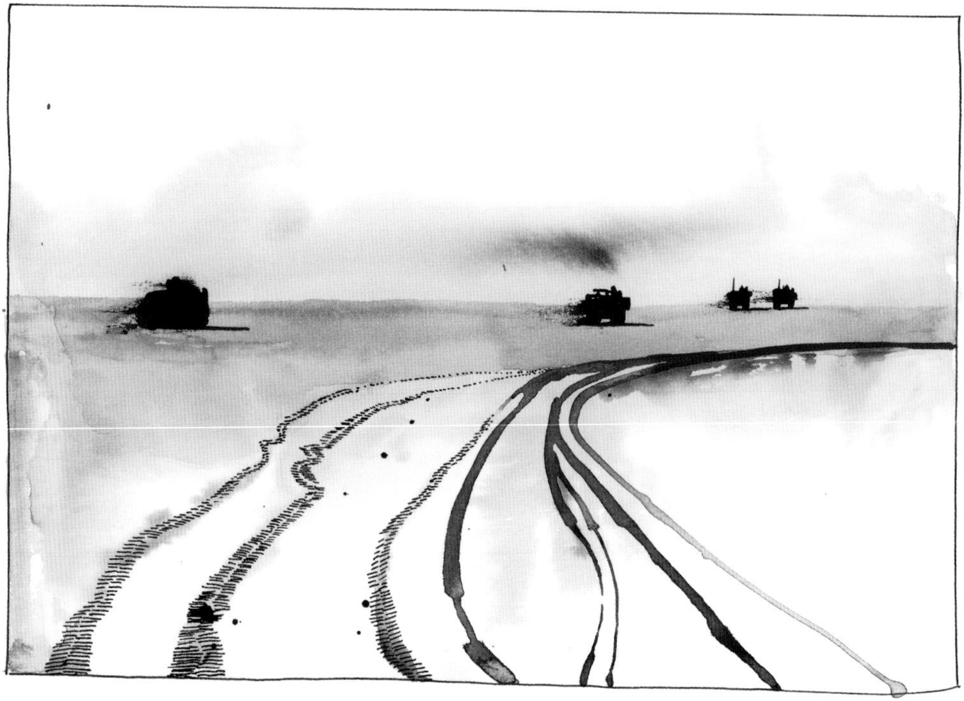

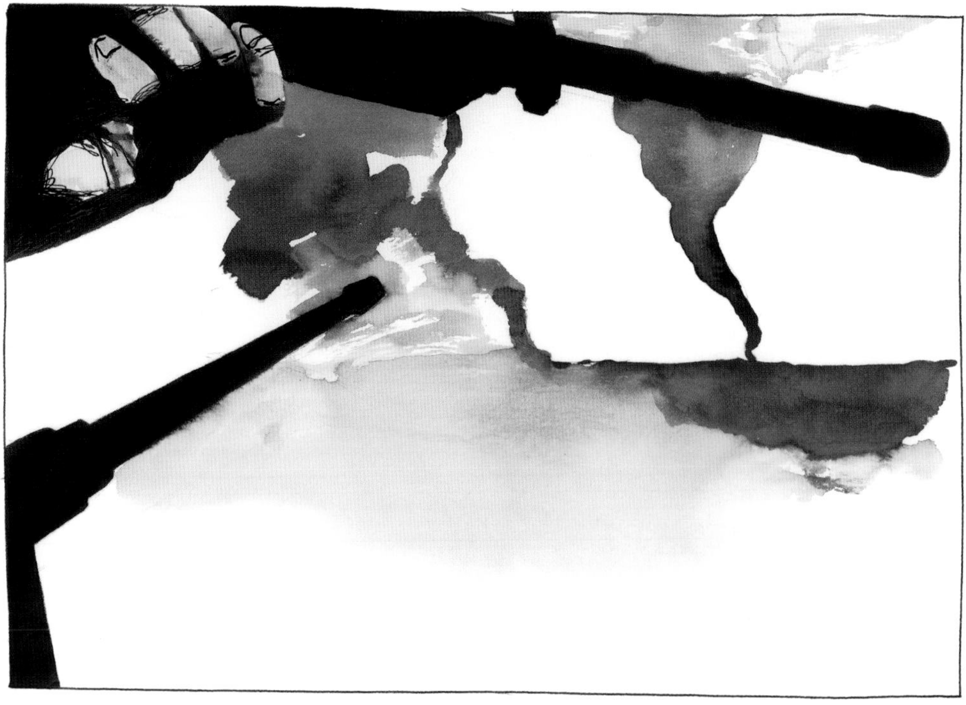

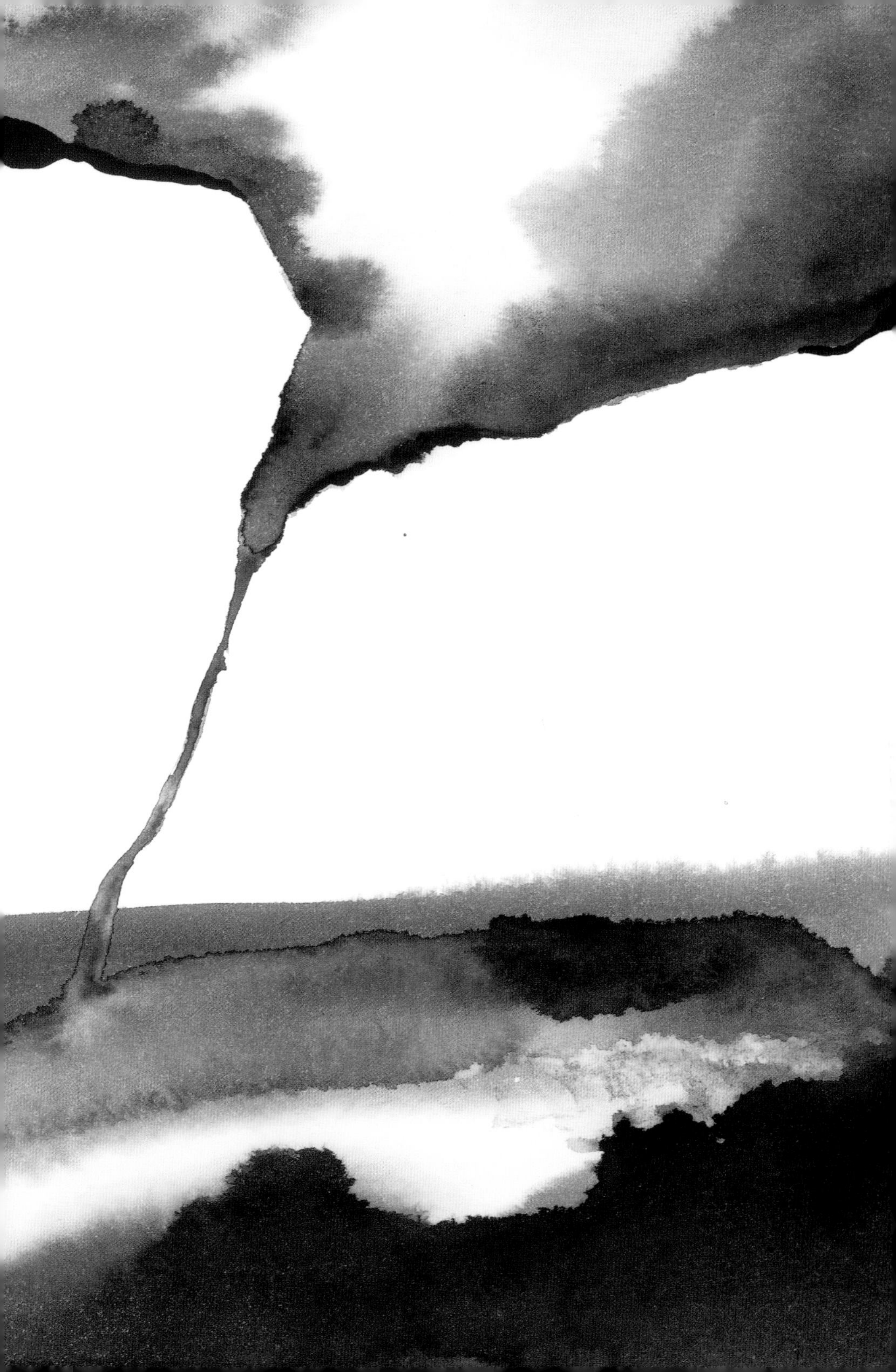

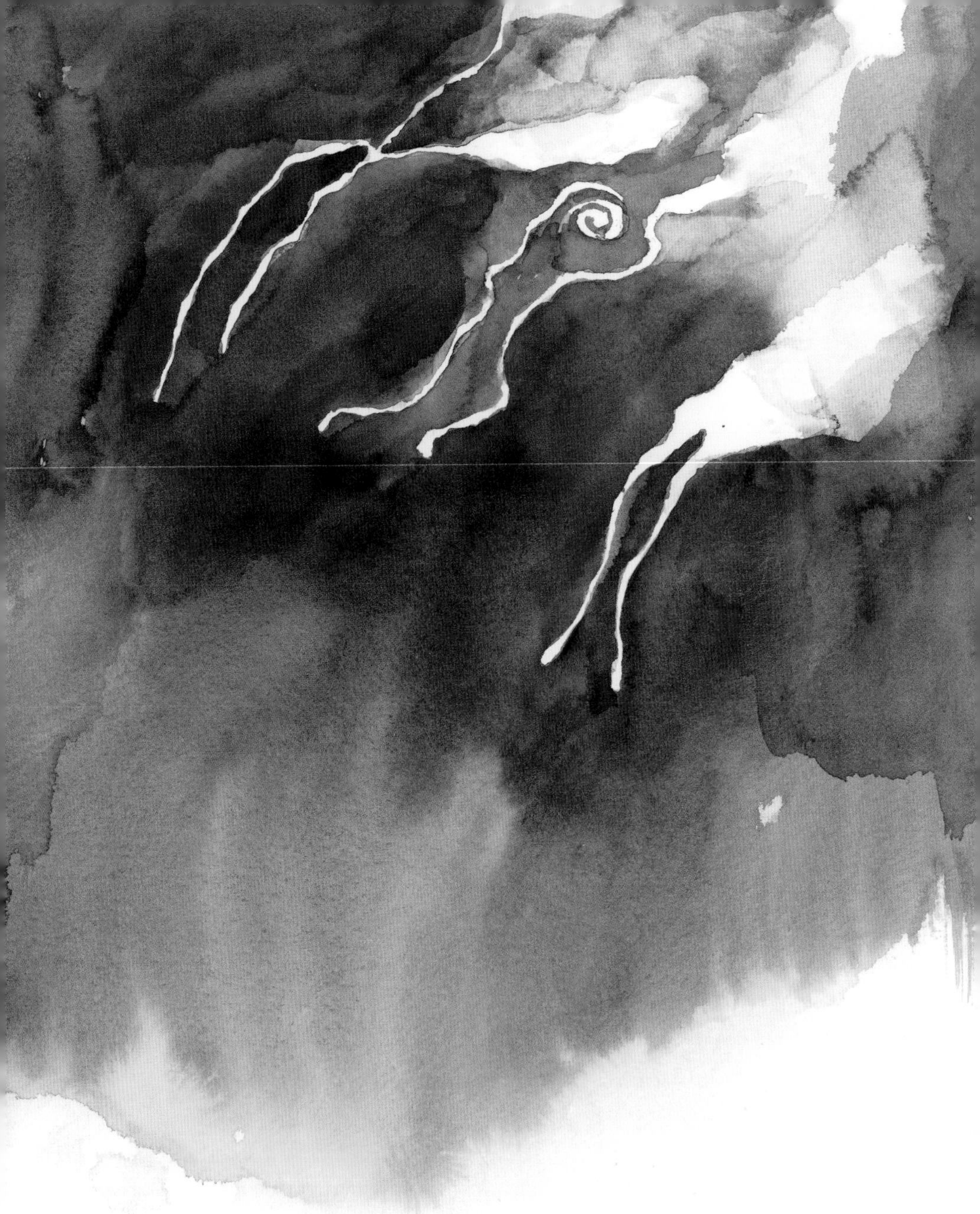

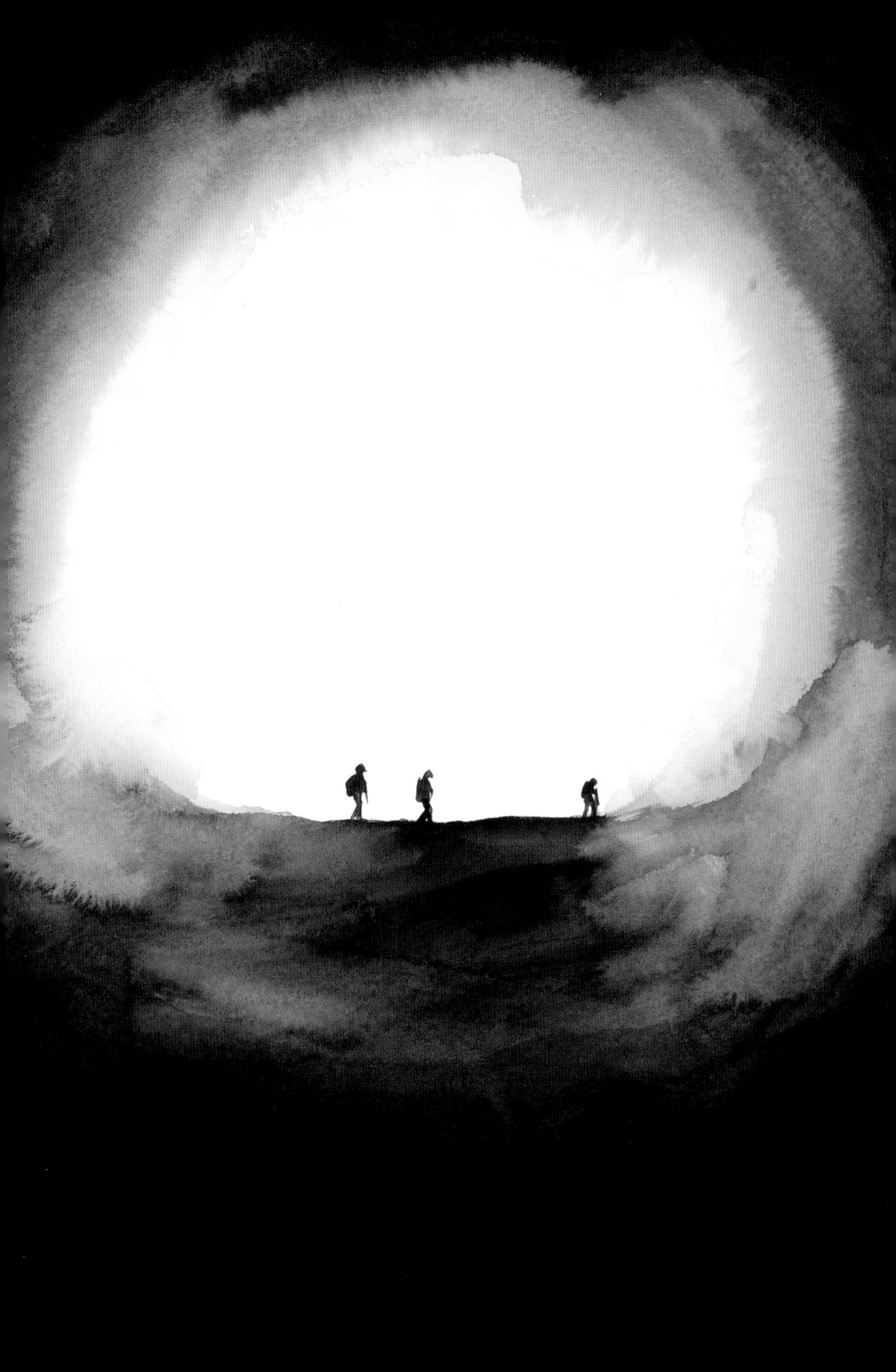

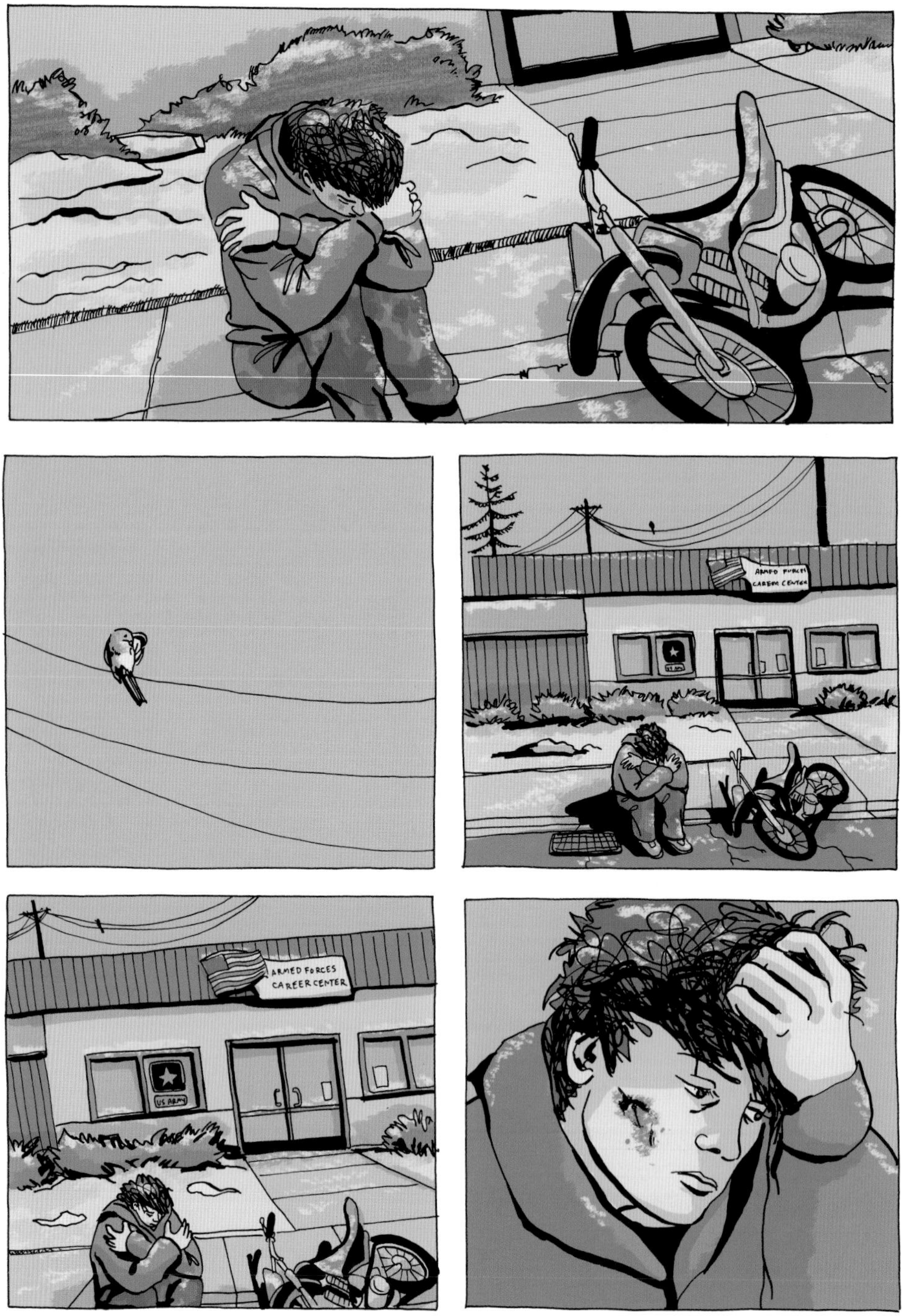
ARMED FORCES
CAREER CENTER
US ARMY

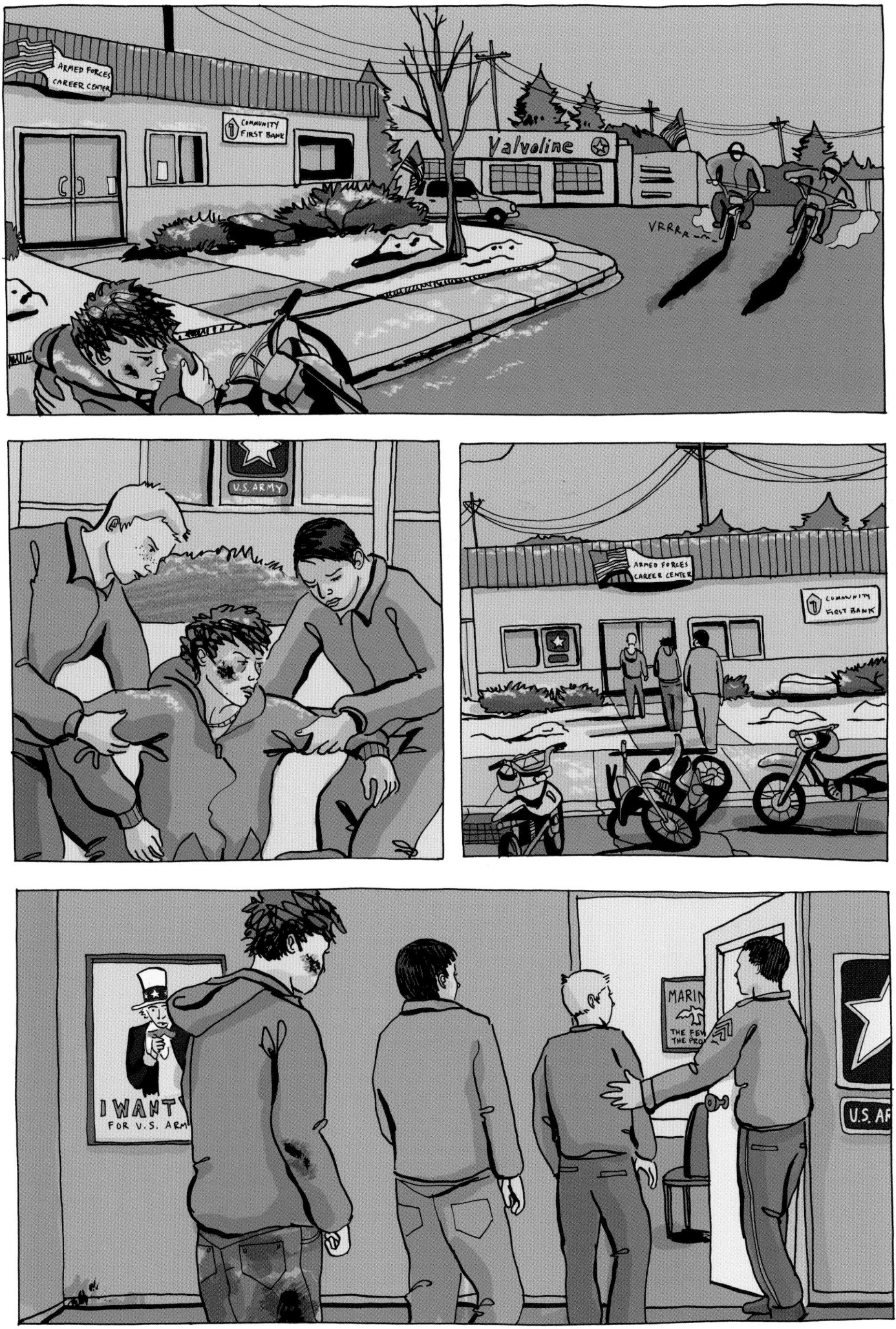
ARMED FORCES CAREER CENTER
COMMUNITY FIRST BANK
Valvoline
VRRRR
U.S. ARMY
ARMED FORCES CAREER CENTER
COMMUNITY FIRST BANK
I WANT
FOR U.S. ARM
MARIN
THE FEW
THE PRO
U.S. AR

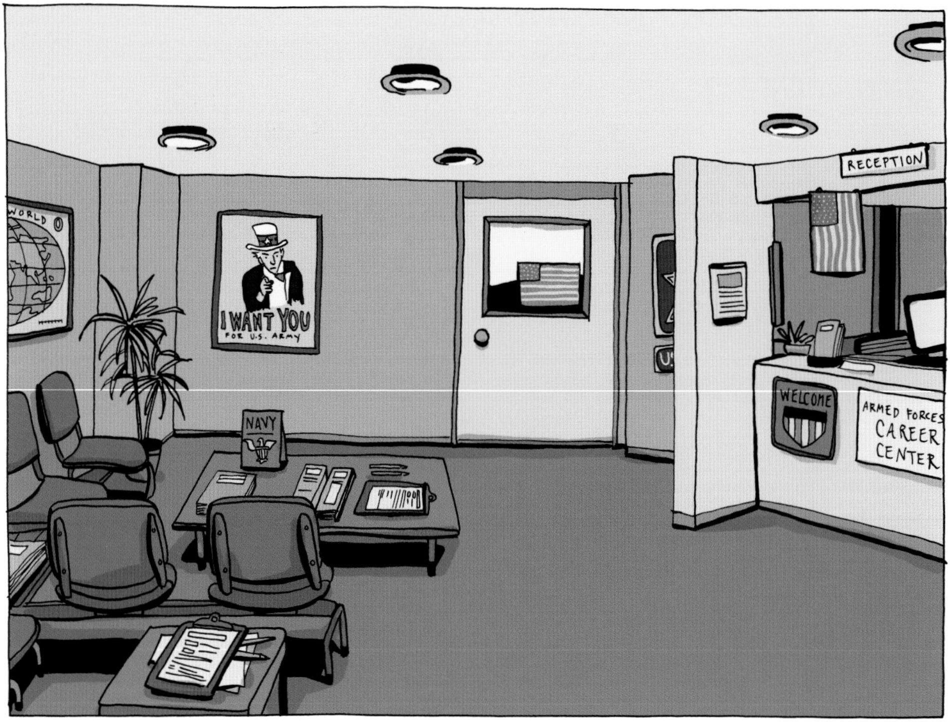
RECEPTION
WORLD
I WANT YOU
FOR U.S. ARMY
NAVY
WELCOME
ARMED FORCES
CAREER
CENTER